Madeline Leslie

Juliette

Now and forever

Madeline Leslie

Juliette
Now and forever

ISBN/EAN: 9783337414054

Printed in Europe, USA, Canada, Australia, Japan

Cover: Foto ©Andreas Hilbeck / pixelio.de

More available books at **www.hansebooks.com**

JULIETTE;

OR,

⊃W AND FOREVER.

BY

MRS. MADELINE LESLIE.

BOSTON:
LEE AND SHEPARD,
149 WASHINGTON STREET.
1869.

To

THE MEMORY OF

WASHINGTON IRVING

This Volume is Inscribed,

IN GRATEFUL REMEMBRANCE OF

THE VERY KIND ENCOURAGEMENT WHICH HE RENDERED

THE AUTHOR,

IN THE EARLIER EFFORTS OF HER PEN.

JULIETTE.

CHAPTER I.

"Of all the tyrants that the world affords,
Our own affections are the fiercest lords."

"The storm of grief bears hard upon his youth,
And bends him like a drooping flower to earth."

IN the beautiful town of H——, overlooking Long Island Sound, the traveller's attention is arrested by two large country residences just perceptible through occasional openings of the thick foliage, and only separated from each other by a swiftly-running streamlet.

One of these is an irregular stone edifice, with small bastions at the corners, capped with turrets, somewhat resembling the old castles of transatlantic countries, with large Gothic windows, and steep slated roof. It stands on a slight elevation, commanding an extended view of the sound, alive with steamboats, fishing-smacks, and whitened with the sails of a prosperous commerce.

The other building is of more modern construction; being square, with a hip-roof, a long L extending

7

back from the main house, the latter ornamented with deep bay-windows, and a spacious portico over the front entrance.

Both of these mansions are surrounded by rich grassy glades, upon which the wide-branching oaks and the stately elms throw their gnarled arms and pendant boughs over the thick carpet of the most delicious greensward.

The winding avenues by which the houses are approached are lined with beeches, intermingled with maples, horse-chestnut, mountain ash, and evergreens of various descriptions, so closely as entirely to intercept the view from the street, except through the long vistas, left open for the purpose, in which the eye delights to lose itself.

The old stone mansion, with its belongings, had descended to Horace Fearing, Esq., the present proprietor. The other house had been built by Dr. Morrison, upon the site of a more humble residence, removed to the end of the lawn, and now occupied as the farm-house.

These places being so closely connected, and the families residing in them having for many years maintained the most intimate friendship, it will not be deemed strange that Edward, oldest son of the former gentleman, being a sprightly, resolute youth of nineteen, had cultivated the acquaintance of Juliette, only daughter of the good doctor.

Indeed, to speak more accurately, neither the young man, nor the maiden, who was a year or two his junior,

could remember the commencement of their acquaintance, which dated from their cradles. If the statements of their nurses were to be credited, the first act
of Master Ned, on being introduced to his rosy (I can
scarcely say blushing companion), was to thrust his
fingers in her organs of vision; that being delighted
with the effect produced, which was the wide opening
of the tiny mouth, from whence issued a scream of
pain, he repeated the operation again and again until
he was carried forcibly from the room.

Nor, according to the same testimony, did the little
miss fail to revenge herself, but waiting a few months,
until her plump hands had learned to obey her will,
she took the occasion when her young companion was
playing at her side to give a vigorous pull at his curls.

From the time when Juliette had attained her first
year and Eddie his third, the children were seldom
long separated. If the weather was unpleasant, and
mamma anxiously suggested that the young gentleman
remain in the nursery, there would issue from thence
a series of screams, and violent thumpings upon the
door; in fact, such an outrageous rumpus, as papa
termed it, that the meek lady was forced to submit to
the powers that be, while the young heir, who had a
will of his own, early learned by experience the truth
of the homely proverb, "where there's a will there's a
way."

When baby Juliette heard his merry voice in the
hall, or his feet climbing the staircase, she expressed
her welcome by shouts of delight; and though he

often claimed all her toys, and, as they grew older, insisted upon his right as a boy to build the block houses, while she meekly contented herself with the privilege accorded her of applauding his success, yet they continued fast friends.

On Juliette's arriving at an age to attend school, it was a matter of course that Ned should conduct her there, or in cold weather draw her on his sled; his stronger will even then, as in younger years, controlling hers and forcing her to submit to his caprices.

Mr. Fearing, who was fond of the law, was anxious that his son should follow his example and choose that as his profession. Edward was undecided, but thought he should prefer a mercantile life. In the mean time, however, he was rapidly fitting for college, and, at the early age of sixteen, was entered at one of the most popular schools of the day.

Juliette remained at home, pursuing her studies in an academy in her native town, and acquiring those accomplishments considered indispensable in a young lady's education, under her mother's supervision.

For two years Edward remained contentedly in college, distinguishing himself by his aptness in acquiring knowledge, and his careless expenditure of his money. In his junior year he imparted to Juliette his determination to leave college, and go into business in connection with some large house in New York.

Possibly this information, which the young girl repeated to her mother, may have affected her future course. Dr. and Mrs. Morrison, who had long thought

Edward's influence over their daughter unfavorable to a proper development of her decision of character, rather hastily made arrangements for her to leave home, and finish her education in a distant city.

The young collegian knew nothing of this change, but having suddenly dissolved his relation to the institution, without consulting his parents, unexpectedly presented himself before them.

His father was exceedingly displeased, and vented his anger in terms such as the son had never heard from his lips; while his mild and yielding mother meekly expressed her sorrow by tearful silence.

"It is too late, sir," retorted Edward, haughtily, "for me to return to college, even if I were willing to do so, which I am not; and as you refuse me your counsel and aid in procuring a desirable situation, I shall call upon my friend, Dr. Morrison, to assist me."

Mrs. Fearing turned her meek eyes to her son's face, and thought, "his father ought to make allowance for his waywardness, he is so very handsome."

Edward walked across the room with the air of a martyr approaching the stake, and, flinging open the door, said, gruffly, "I shall take tea with Juliette, and not return till late."

"Juliette is away," cried Henry Fearing, a youth of fourteen summers; "haven't you heard about it? She has gone to T—— to attend school."

Edward hurriedly re-entered the room, astonishment, anger, and grief, by turns expressed on his countenance. Advancing to the side of his mother, he asked, hoarsely, "Is this, can this be true, and I not even informed of it?"

"Yes, my son," she responded, scarcely daring to raise her eyes to his. "It was all very sudden; and we scarcely knew of it until — certainly not in time to write you."

Edward interrupted her with a groan. Growing very pale, without another word he suddenly left the room, rushed to his own chamber, where they heard him shut the door with a crash, and fiercely turn the key.

Mr. Fearing glanced at his wife, who was weeping silently. "I had no idea of this," he exclaimed. "How long has he loved Juliette? Is there any engagement between them?"

"He has loved her longer than he can remember," faltered the mother, meekly. "I am afraid there is trouble before him. I mean, that they will not consent."

"Speak plainly for once, do, Amelia," said her husband, in a bitter tone. "Do you mean to say that Dr. and Mrs. Morrison would not consent that Juliette should marry our son?"

The lawyer drew up his figure to its full height. To one who gazed at him, it would cease to be a wonder how Edward came by his pride and inflexible will.

Mrs. Fearing wiped her eyes, though her form shrank from her husband. "Of course I know nothing about it. How can I? I only," — she hesitated and began to weep again.

"Amelia,"—the tone was stern,—"will you do me the favor to finish your sentence?"

She raised her eyes imploringly. "Sally, Mrs. Morrison's chamber-girl, overheard her mistress talking with the doctor concerning Edward. They thought he was about to return home. I think she said he told Juliette of his intention; and they resolved to remove her from him."

"Did you ascertain the reason, madam, of this manœuvre?" inquired Mr. Fearing, contemptuously.

"No, I asked no questions; but Sally heard her mistress say that Edward was so passionate—I don't think they understand him at all—and Juliette so amiable that he ruled her completely; that he always had made her yield to his whims ever since they were babies together. She didn't think Juliette would ever be happy if they were connected." Mrs. Fearing sighed heavily as she ceased, and applied her handkerchief again.

The lawyer took a few vigorous turns across the room. His thoughts were evidently not the most pleasant. At length he stood opposite his wife, and gazed at her. "Amelia," he began, in a softened tone, "though I despise the manner in which your information was gained, I am glad we have it. Dr. Morrison may be wise. Certainly if he had been present this morning, he would scarcely have chosen Edward as a husband for his only daughter."

"O Mr. Fearing!" she began, in a tone of meek reproach; "don't you turn against him. I thought — I hoped so much from your — your intervention."

"I love Juliette," rejoined the gentleman, thoughtfully, without noticing her remark. "I know no one I should so gladly take to my heart as a daughter; but I fear — yes, she is so lovely in temper, so amiable, so yielding — I fear his overbearing, haughty arrogance would kill her. Think how her parents, think how we should feel to see her drooping day by day. Oh, they are wise! they are wise!"

The poor mother wept and sobbed bitterly.

"It will be a terrible blow to Edward," added Mr. Fearing. "I had no idea of the nature and strength of his attachment. He will fume and fret like a caged lion that his will has been opposed; but he must yield. I will have no compulsion. Even if Juliette consents, there must be no marriage without the full approbation of our friends."

"But she loves him," urged the anxious mother, "I am sure she does. Only the day she went, she ran in to ask for his last letter; and she looked very sad as she said, 'Edward will be sorry I am gone. I wish I could have stayed till he came; but I'll write my goodby.' Then she threw her arms around my neck, and said, 'I love you dearly, *dearly*, almost as much as my own mother!'"

"When Dr. Morrison returns, I shall talk with him," said the lawyer, firmly. "In the mean time, they are both young, and, with such a motive before him, Edward can learn to govern his passions. Well, we shall see! we shall see!"

"And if Juliette really loves Edward, it will be a pleasure for her to give up to him," said the little lady, gazing affectionately in her husband's face.

Mr. Fearing's countenance grew tender. He stooped and kissed her cheek. "Few ladies, dear Amelia, make it the business of their lives to study their husband's pleasure as you have done. God forgive me if I have ever abused the trust!" He lightly touched her brow, and went hastily from the room.

CHAPTER II.

"Heaven oft in mercy smites, e'en when the blow
Severest is."

IT is not my purpose to detain the reader to describe
minutely the incidents which followed; but, in
order to delineate the early character of Edward Fearing, self-willed and passionate as he was, I shall glance
at events occupying more than a dozen years, before
we pass on to other characters more immediately the
subject of our story.

Dr. Morrison and his wife did disapprove of Edward
as a suitor for their daughter, and kept her away at
school for two years. When she returned, it was as
the affianced wife of Mr. Everett, a prosperous mer-
chant residing in T——.

The evening before her marriage; Edward, who had
remained in blissful ignorance of all this, rushed home
as soon as he received his cards of invitation, called at
Dr. Morrison's, and having, by a great effort, forced
himself to be calm, requested Juliette to visit with him
one of their favorite haunts.

The sun was just setting, and its red rays illuminated
the turret windows like sheets of burnished gold, and

16

lighted in brilliant patches such portions of the velvet turf as were not shaded by the gigantic trees.

Juliette, without hesitation, complied, though wondering at his ill-concealed emotion.

They wandered on by the bank of the small stream, until they were out of sight of the house, when he turned upon her with fierce reproaches for having embittered his whole life.

Trembling at his wild, haggard looks, the poor girl yet found strength to ask, "What can you mean, dear Edward? What have I done, that you should speak so cruelly?"

He pointed to a rustic seat, and then poured out the story of his love. Throwing himself upon the ground before her, he wept; he implored her, by all that was sacred, to break her engagement with Mr. Everett, and be his wife.

"He is a stranger, and you cannot love him, Juliette," he urged. "Certainly, not as you love me. Oh, speak, dear one, and say you do not! Say you will be mine, and I will brave the world for your dear sake. Think how we have played together,—how I have held you sleeping in my arms, when we sat side by side at school,—how you always ran to meet me, and called me your dearest Ned. Oh, you have loved me, Juliette! You do love me, and you will send away this stranger, who, compared with the all-absorbing passion in my breast, knows nothing about love."

Juliette rose, and would have hastened away; but he held her almost rudely.

2*

"It is too late," she said, with a quivering lip. "You ought to have told me all this before. I have loved you as a dear brother, Edward, and perhaps, had I known that you — that you wished it, I might have been your wife. But Mr. Everett is a noble man. He has sought me openly and honorably, and I will not break my word."

Edward started from the ground and stood erect before her. She laid her hand on his arm, but he threw it off as if it stung him.

"Juliette," said he, and his voice was thick and hoarse, "I have always supposed you would be mine, and only waited your return from school to demand you of your father; but forget the events of the past hour, and may God forgive us both." He turned hastily, and his form was soon lost in the fast coming twilight.

A midnight train to the city landed him in New York, and three months later he wrote to his parents to announce his marriage with a young lady in high life.

His active business habits and his unconquerable energy rendered him so important to the firm with which he was connected, that, on his attaining his majority, he was taken in as partner; and from this time wealth flowed in upon him in one continuous stream.

From the hour of Juliette's marriage, he was never heard to mention her name. When his mother announced to him the birth of her little son, whom, in memory of their old friendship, she had named Horace

Morrison, he exhibited so much emotion, that it was with a beating heart and unsteady voice three years later she bore to him the mournful intelligence of the decease of Mr. Everett.

This sad event occurred within a few weeks of the death of his only child; and while his heart was softened by this affliction, he wrote Juliette a kind letter, such as a dear brother would write, and which proved balm to her wounded heart.

Mrs. Everett, with her little Horace, returned at once to her father's; Dr. Morrison having complied with the dying husband's wish, and consented to take the care of Juliette's property, and to be a guardian to their child.

Seven years later, Mrs. Edward Fearing died, after a lingering sickness, leaving two children; a son, Henry, in his seventh year, named for Mr. Fearing's brother, recently deceased, and a daughter, Juliette Edwards, two years younger.

It is but justice to Mr. Fearing to say that he missed the tender affection of the deceased, toward whom he had ever evinced the kind consideration of a loving husband. Nor, though his thoughts often turned to Juliette, and his heart beat wildly at the possibility that she might now be his, did he visit her until his wife had been dead a year.

During this long period Mrs. Everett, whose personal charms had never been greater, and who was possessed of a handsome fortune, had received many eligible offers of marriage. Some of these her parents had urged her to accept; but the young widow replied, "In your society, and in the care of my son, I am happy. Why, then, should I change my condition?"

But when Edward presented himself before her, that beloved friend of her childhood, whom for eleven years she had not once seen, when he plead with her to be a mother to his motherless ones, when he brought his little Juliette to add her entreaties to his, her heart responded to his wish.

The bridal was a gay one, for Mr. Fearing stood high in the world's esteem; and he wished all his friends to share in his joy.

This consummation of his dearest hopes seemed to cause a favorable change in his character. He had been subject to fits of depression, — moodiness as his friends termed it, — now he exhibited a lightness of heart and a buoyancy of spirits delightful to all connected with him.

Toward Juliette's son he ever acted as a tender father, and soon won for himself the hearty affection of the amiable child. To Henry and his little Juliette, he was excessively indulgent, though he obliged them to yield strict obedience to his will. As they both appeared to partake far more of their mother's disposition than of his, this was no difficult task.

After Horace became an inmate of the family, the most lively affection grew up between him and his young playmates. Being three years older than Henry,

Horace was able to assist him in his studies, besides being ever ready for a vigorous game.

The years since her first marriage had not passed without a change also in the character of Juliette. Mr. Everett was not only an upright, honorable man in the eyes of the world, but he earnestly strove to guide his thoughts by the law of God. During the four years he lived with his wife he urged upon her the claims of religion, and on his death-bed besought her to bring up their son in the nurture and admonition of the Lord.

Thus early bereft of her loved companion, Juliette determined to follow exactly his expressed wishes, not only for her boy, but in regard to the duties of her own heart. She endeavored to cultivate firmness and self-reliance, that she might be better fitted for the right training of her child. Choosing as she did the quiet home of her youth in preference to the gayety of a city life, she had passed many hours every day in reading, and in thoughtful meditation upon what she read.

After her marriage with Mr. Fearing, she found to her sorrow that (as the result of his early training) he looked upon religion as calculated to make one gloomy and morose, — that he considered it time enough to prepare for death when certain that the hour for departure was at hand, — that if a person lived an honest, upright life, God was a merciful being, and all would be well at last.

Discussion upon this subject she found was worse than useless.

"It is of no avail, love," he would say, tapping her cheek playfully. "You never can make me believe that if you were to be taken from me, you would not go straight to heaven; and you are not, and I trust never will be, a gloomy, long-faced fanatic."

Juliette therefore prayed and sighed in secret, though she did not falter in the work of imparting religious instruction.to the dear children, nor of endeavoring earnestly to instil into their minds correct motives and principles by which they were to regulate their actions.

Horace and the little Etta were particularly susceptible to serious impressions; but Henry was of so volatile a nature that it seemed impossible to touch his heart. In fact, he feared the displeasure of his brother far more than any mere punishment; and such an influence did Horace, by his childish, but daring defence of the right, obtain over the boy, that his new mother hoped to obtain that power over him through her son which she could not bring to bear directly upon himself.

At a later period she mourned over that feebleness and timidity which had led her to yield what she knew to be right, with the hope of gradually winning her husband. Three years after her marriage to Mr. Fearing, she gave birth to a daughter, who only survived a few hours. A long and dangerous illness followed, from which she never wholly recovered. For several months she was confined to her chamber, and here her religious impressions were deepened and confirmed.

She longed for Christian companionship, for some one to whom she could unbosom all her trembling hopes, and who would strengthen and encourage her in the path of duty.

At length so earnest did these desires become, that she one day ventured to ask her husband to request their minister to call upon her; but his bitter displeasure prevented her from ever repeating the desire. Never had she seen him so angry. Could she have imagined the fierce agony he often endured at the thought of the possible result of this sickness, and his determination to drive from her mind all thought of death, which he considered a certain means of hastening that terrible event, she might not have been so shocked. As it was, he left her in displeasure, to weep hours over what she thought his want of feeling.

Since she had resided in New York she had often met a lady whose name was Osborn, the widow of a naval officer. Hearing of her long-continued sickness, Mrs. Osborn, who lived with a relative in the same street, ventured one day to call. Mrs. Fearing soon found the lady was a Christian. Their hearts warmed toward each other; and this was the beginning of a friendship which grew closer and warmer until they were separated by death.

The effect of this intercourse upon the sick lady was most happy. Her husband was rejoiced at the change, and most cordially invited Mrs. Osborn to pass as much time with his wife as her engagements would allow.

He little realized that it was the very religious sympathy which he had forbidden her, which worked such a result. Mrs. Fearing had with many tears informed her friend of her husband's bitter prejudices; and now she too dearly prized her Christian conversation to hazard its loss by imparting to him the fact that religion was the tie which bound them together.

Late in the autumn it became evident to all her friends that if her life was to be prolonged she must be taken to a warmer climate. As soon as this was hinted to him, Mr. Fearing, with his usual energy, lost not a moment in carrying the plan into execution. If he had been sure he should have lost all of which he was possessed, he would not have hesitated a moment. With him it was life or death; for he would not allow to himself that he could survive her loss. Leaving their children in the care of Mrs. Morrison, they embarked for St. Augustine, in Florida, a place highly recommended to them for invalids.

It was a dreadful struggle to Mrs. Fearing to be separated from her children. She realized that it might be forever. She endeavored to impress anew upon their tender minds the lessons she had taught them, and comforted their hearts by the assurance that though they were separated, God was near each of them, and would listen to their prayers for one another.

It was a sad trial, too, to leave her chosen friend, Mrs. Osborn; and once she hinted to her husband that in case she were worse, it might be necessary for her to have a female friend as a companion. But in his struggle to resist the convictions fast forcing themselves upon him, Mr. Fearing would not allow the necessity; and so they parted.

I need not detain the reader upon the months which followed. Late in the succeeding spring, Mr. Fearing landed in New York, by the steamer, having brought home his wife to die.

Yes, she yearned to see her children and parents once more, — to be carried to her old home, where she could gaze upon the green lawns, the broad-headed oaks, the gurgling brook, and the glorious setting sun, — before her soul took its final flight from earth. She mentioned the name of Mrs. Osborn, and her husband immediately sent for the lady, who had gone to live in the country, to come and pass at her side the hours which remained to her dying friend. Hearing that she had undertaken the care of a school as a means of support, he nobly assured her that whatever loss she might sustain by compliance with his request should be amply repaid.

For a few weeks the change of air revived the invalid, and her husband began eagerly to talk of her recovery. Indeed, nothing displeased him more than to have any one doubt that she was really convalescent.

But the fiat had gone forth, and she, about whom were clustered so many hopes, — she, who was more than all the world to her husband, and to her parents and children, — must lie down and die. None were allowed to witness the fierce conflict in Mr. Fearing's

3

breast when he was made to realize that the hour had really come for him to part with her. With a wild, protruded eye, and a pale, haggard countenance, he rushed from the room, and shut himself up, until called by an attendant to take his last farewell.

She was almost speechless; but her eye brightened as he approached, and, feebly placing her hand in his, she murmured, "Dear Edward, I am — going — to — my Saviour. My — soul — is full — of — peace. I shall — want — to — meet — you — there." She raised her eyes, as she uttered the last word, and they remained fixed. A glorious vision seemed to pass before her. She clasped her hands, while a heavenly smile played around her mouth. One slight shudder, and she was at home in the bosom of her Saviour.

> "'Calmer and calmer still,' the lady cried,
> To the friend who stood at her death-bed side,
> And asked of her how her spirit bore
> The thought of its flight to the viewless shore;
> 'Calmer and calmer still; for much doth grow
> Plain to my soul, and clear, which was not so.
> I once saw frowns upon death's pale brow,
> But it is calmer and calmer now.'"

CHAPTER III.

"She's gone! forever gone! The king of terrors
Lays his rude hands upon her lovely limbs,
And blasts her beauty with his icy breath."

WEEK after week crept wearily by, and still the bereaved husband could not tear himself from the spot where he had laid his Juliette. It was a shady knoll in a retired part of his father's estate, surrounded by sycamore and cedar trees. Here hour after hour he lingered, ever thinking of the past happy days, and brooding gloomily over the thought that she whom he so worshipped had left him forever.

Oh! could he have raised his tearless eyes to the blest regions above, and viewed her rapt spirit before the throne of the Eternal; — could he have seen her spotless robes, her crown of glory, her golden harp; — could he have heard her voice joining in the song of ceaseless adoration to the Lamb who was slain for her sins; — could he by faith have taken hold of the promise, "no chastening seemeth for the present joyous, but grievous, nevertheless afterward it yieldeth the peaceable fruits of righteousness to them that are exercised thereby," — he might have bowed humbly

27

to his heavenly Father's will, and been saved long years of the keenest anguish and self-reproach.

His father and Dr. Morrison both urged him to return to his business, and endeavor to find, in the daily cares of life, a relief from the despondency which seemed gathering like a thick veil about him. They brought his children to his arms, and bade them talk of their lamented mother, that his bitter sorrow might find vent in tears. Alas! it was all in vain; the language of his heart was ever, —

> "No future hour can rend my heart like this,
> Save that which breaks it."

He actually loathed the idea of meeting friends, who might venture to speak of the loss he had sustained. What could they know or how could they estimate what she was to him. The world contained but one Juliette. With his children, too, he was extremely fitful. If he saw them weeping and disconsolate, he would strain them to his breast, and mourn with them; but if with the buoyancy of childhood they forgot for a brief moment their sorrow, and indulged in mirth, he turned upon them with bitter reproaches, or shrank from their presence.

His friends felt that something must be done to rouse him.

One morning Horace, who was now in his fifteenth year, approached him with a satchel of books. "Father," he began, "I shall lose my place in all my classes; for I have gone on alone as far as I can. Grandfather thinks I had better go home and resume my studies."

Mr. Fearing caught the boy's hand. "My dear Horace," he exclaimed, "I fear my grief has made me selfish. Yes, you shall go. We will all go. The effort must be made. We will go to-day."

Anticipating this sudden move, the grandparents had arranged everything to forward it; and in less than four hours after the first suggestion the whole party, with the exception of the little Juliette, were on their way to New York. Mrs. Morrison, in accordance with the wishes of her dying daughter, proceeded, the next day, to place the young girl in the care of Mrs. Osborn, for her education.

Arriving in the city, Mr. Fearing at once plunged into business, and here sought forgetfulness of the past. He plainly told his friends that he wished no reference made to his affliction. He laughed and made merry over his wine, and closed his heart firmly against any merciful visitation of the Spirit. But his midnight hours were terrible. Conscience, that mysterious monitor within his breast, would not be silenced. Even in his uneasy, unrefreshing slumbers, he heard the soft, clear voice of his loved Juliette at prayer, and for him, — heard it as distinctly as he ever had heard it during the last years of her life. Bathed in moisture, he would fling himself from the couch, and stride back and forth through his chamber. But he could not shake off the terrible vision. Juliette, pale and gasping for breath, was ever before him, but with an angelic smile lisping the words, "I—am going to—my Saviour. I—shall want—to meet you there."

> "Though thy slumber may be deep,
> Yet thy spirit shall not sleep.
> There are shades which will not vanish;
> There are thoughts thou canst not banish."

Resorting, at length, to a powerful opiate, he sometimes succeeded in banishing these unwelcome visitors, while during the day he rushed madly into the whirl of speculations. Strange to say, these were always successful, and as years rolled on he came to be regarded as one of the shrewdest operators, — one of the most successful financiers in the commercial world. In the mean time, the gracious Spirit, having knocked long and loud at the door of his heart, took his departure. Was it forever?

At the age of sixteen, Horace entered college, where, by his diligence and enthusiasm in study, he soon took a high rank. Henry remained at school in the city, where, after his brother left, he became more than ever indolent and averse to application. He was a youth rather loved for his careless generosity than respected for his manly independence. He was one of those unfortunate beings who can never say "no" firmly and decisively, and therefore was often led astray, and made the tool of his far more wicked associates.

Henry wisely avoided any collision with his father, knowing that the latter had a stern, unconquerable will; and as they seldom met except at the sumptuous meals, attended by many servants, it was easy for the young man to do with himself, at other times, pretty much as he chose.

Mr. Fearing, a gay man in a gay city, knew nothing of all this. Seeing that his son was fashionably dressed, that he was gentlemanly in appearance, and respectful in deference to his own wishes, he thought that while he supplied his heir with a most liberal allowance, he discharged his whole duty toward him.

Mr. Fearing was now in the prime of life. Tall, erect, and of slight figure, his raven locks, flashing black eyes, and well-cut lips distinguished him in any company.

Henry, though often called a handsome youth, did not at all resemble his father. He had the mild blue eyes and the light auburn hair peculiar to his mother's family.

But where, all these years, is our little Juliette, the heroine of our story?

In the quiet village of D——, more than fifty miles from the city, Mrs. Osborn had established her family school. Ten young girls constituted her number; and so far she had been eminently successful in her teaching. Knowing something of her character, it will be easy to judge that, while securing to the young misses under her care all the accomplishments which would fit them to be ornaments of society, she did not neg-

lect their highest good. She endeavored, while training their bodies into natural, healthy, and therefore
graceful attitudes, to train their hearts to the love of
the virtuous, the true, and the noble; while she cultivated their intellect, to cultivate, also, their affections. While she endeavored to form in them habits
of patient, thorough investigation, she nurtured their
moral sentiments according to the standard of revealed
truth.

Juliette, who was greatly endeared to her teacher,
in consequence of the long friendship with her mother,
strongly resembled Mrs. Fearing both in disposition
and character. Like her, she was loving and generous
in the bestowment of her affections, and like her, also,
she was extremely timid and self-distrustful.

Once every year her father visited her, and took her
to his paternal home, where, in alternate visits to her
grandparents (the parents of her own mother having
long been deceased), she passed the summer vacation.

With her father she was always shy and reserved,
the gloomy abstraction of his manner, after the decease
of his wife, having fastened itself upon her memory,
to the forgetfulness of the years of fondness preceding
it. She did her best to be free with him, and talk in
the unrestrained manner she did with Mrs. Osborn;
but she was always painfully conscious of not appearing at ease in his presence, and of a sense of relief
when he was away.

Though under the fostering care of her teacher, her
health was much firmer than in her earlier years, yet

she was extremely delicate in appearance. Her complexion was pale, unless excited, and then the eloquent blood rushed into her cheeks, painting them the color of the richest rose. Her eyes and lashes were black; but there was a languid softness in them, resembling the fawn. When she was merry they lit up and beamed; but they never flashed as her father's did. Her figure, though small, was perfect in its symmetry, and her motions were grace itself.

Horace, who was a member of Yale College, was but a short distance, by the cars, from Mrs. Osborn's residence, and often passed a Sabbath in the village. He loved his sister, and found new beauties in her character in every succeeding visit. Then, she had uncommon powers of voice in singing, and accompanied herself with so much taste and feeling upon the piano that he sometimes invited his classmates to Mrs. Osborn's to hear her.

During the four years of his college course, Juliette learned to regard her brother as a kind of mentor. She kept up a close correspondence with him, relating, with girlish frankness, all the events of her school life, which particularly interested her, confessed freely her errors, and begged him to help her correct them.

One thing, and almost the only one, which annoyed him, was the hesitancy with which she expressed her own thoughts upon any subject. It was always, "Mrs. Osborn thinks so, or the girls say this or that;" but she was seldom willing to give her own independent opinion.

"Juliette," Horace said one day, "you must make up your mind upon a subject, and then be firm in adhering to your views. I do not like to have you pin your faith upon that of others. You have an undoubted right to maintain your own ground. Be more courageous and daring, my dear sister. You will not always be allowed to remain under the guiding care of Mrs. Osborn. When you are older you will often be obliged to act for yourself, and you must learn decision while you are young."

"But when I leave school," she sweetly replied, "I shall be with you, Horace; and you have promised always to tell me when I am wrong."

What could he do but lovingly tap her cheek, and press the hand so trustingly placed in his?

Of Henry, Juliette knew but little. As she had never visited New York since her mother's death, she had only seen him in a flying call at their grandfather's, during her summer vacation. He was extremely fond of city life; called the country a dreadful bore; pitied his sister for being condemned to it; longed for her to be through her education, that he might have her to make more gay his city home.

Mr. Fearing had often been urged to marry again, and one lady after another had had her charms of person or purse pressed upon his notice; but never for a moment did he consider the possibility of giving Juliette a successor in his affections.

In society, he was polished; so that he was much sought after by the fair. He was gay and gallant; but

there was something in his manner which forbade the
thought of love.

In truth, he often asked himself why he went into
company at all. Certainly it was only because his position in life demanded it; not because he enjoyed its
gayeties. He began now to be impatient for his daughter to return from school, and take her place at the head
of his household. He longed for some new attraction
to his home, and doubted not her presence would prove
the charm. Horace was nearly through the study of
law, and was, in a few months, to take his departure
for Europe, for a year's travel, before he entered upon
the practice of his profession. Henry was nominally
engaged as clerk in a large warehouse, but really seek-
ing his own pleasure in every form of dissipation.

Mr. Fearing wrote to Mrs. Osborn that he should
soon be in D——, to remove his daughter from her
care. She plead for another year; but having made
up his mind, there was no retraction; and the good
lady had nothing to do but to prepare her dear pupil to
change her quiet home for the fashion and gayety of
city life.

CHAPTER IV.

"The first sure symptom of a mind in health
Is rest of heart and pleasure felt at home."

PUNCTUAL to his appointment, Mr. Fearing presented himself at Mrs. Osborn's door, to receive his Juliette from her hands.

The young girl — for though in her seventeenth year, she looked very young — came forward, at the sound of his voice, and, with a trembling lip, bade him welcome.

"Hasten your preparations, my dear," said he, gazing with secret annoyance at her red and swollen eyes. "The cars leave in half an hour. I will see Mrs. Osborn in the mean time."

"I have endeavored, Mr. Fearing," said the lady, with ill-suppressed agitation, "in the education of your daughter, to fulfil to the letter the wishes of your lamented wife; and I am more than repaid by being able to return her to you one of the most affectionate, loving-hearts it has ever been my fortune to know. Of her accomplishments you will soon have an opportunity to judge; and even there I think you will say she excels. Her career, I can easily prophesy, will be a brilliant one. But not until you allow her the free exercise of her dearest hopes and wishes, will she be truly happy."

"What can you mean, madam?" inquired Mr. Fearing, earnestly, startled by a sudden suspicion. "I trust my daughter has been allowed to form no improper attachment?"

Mrs. Osborn smiled. "Feel no concern, sir," she answered, "on that subject. Juliette, I can assure you, is heart-whole. But she is, as I humbly hope, a Christian; and therefore —"

"Madam," said the gentleman, sternly, "do I understand that you have been imparting to my child views of religion which will prevent her enjoyment of the gayeties natural to her age? If so, I have been indeed deceived, and may live to curse the hour she was placed under your roof. How long has this system been going on? and why has it been kept secret from me? Do you know, madam, you have been interfering with all my plans for the advancement of my daughter's interest?"

"I have done nothing which will hinder the advancement of her best good," remarked the lady, with great dignity.

"Juliette shall be made to give up these absurd notions," exclaimed Mr. Fearing, angrily. "She will be a star among her fashionable friends; and amid the gayeties of city life she will soon forget all but the wish to be admired." The gentleman's lip curled contemptuously, recalling forcibly to the lady's memory painful scenes, long forgotten, in the life of his wife.

4

"Beware!" said she, hurriedly, as she heard Juliette's step approaching. "She is a tender flower, and will droop under the least unkindness."

Notwithstanding Mr. Fearing's efforts at self-control, the flashing of his eye showed that he was extremely angry. He took his daughter's hand, as she entered, and said, in a sharp tone, "Come, it is time we were off. Bid adieu to Mrs. Osborn; for, with my consent, you shall never see her again."

Startled and trembling, the young girl gave one glance into her father's face, and then threw herself into the arms of her kind friend, weeping bitterly.

With a contemptuous "Pshaw!" Mr. Fearing hastened to direct the coachman to pack on the trunks, while the sobbing girl whispered, "Oh! why is this? What have I done?"

"Nothing wrong, my darling," said the lady, controlling her own grief. "You will have sharp trials to encounter. But do right, only do right, and all will be well. I will pray for you, and write you often."

"Juliette, I am waiting," called her father.

They rode on in silence, the poor girl making no effort to restrain her grief.

"We are approaching the depot," the father said, trying to soften his voice. "Wipe your tears, or cover your face. I do not wish you to be a spectacle for others to gaze upon."

Juliette quickly pulled down her veil. Her heart was ready to burst, and in vain she tried to check her sobs. She had wept half the preceding night, at the thought of being separated from her beloved teacher and her young companions; but that grief was as nothing in comparison with the shock she had received by her father's stern manner and terrible words. In all her dreams of her city home, she had fancied Mrs. Osborn as a frequent, a loved, and honored guest; while in turn she had played the hostess to each of her young school-mates. How suddenly had these pleasant visions vanished!

During the long ride in the cars, she had only one item of comfort, and that was the thought that Horace would be living under the same roof, — that he would tell her how far she ought to conform to her father's wishes, — that he would sympathize in her distress.

As they approached the city, she put a constraint upon her feelings, drew up her veil, and tried to interest herself in the view from the window.

Mr. Fearing, who had not unwillingly resigned his seat by her side to a lady, occupied one directly back of hers; and as she lifted her veil, and, in the mirror opposite, he caught a glance of her pallid, care-worn countenance, his heart smote him. "I have made a mistake," he said to himself. "My anger has carried me too far. She is young, and may be easily moulded to my wishes. I should have aimed to influence her through her affections. Now I can see she shrinks from me. Mrs. Osborn — pshaw! I have no patience with her. It has been a long plot to deceive me. Juliette shall learn that my will must be obeyed."

When they alighted from the cars, Peter, their

coachman, was awaiting them. Giving him the checks for the trunks, Mr. Fearing tenderly lifted his daughter into the splendid vehicle.

"Come, my dear," he said; "forget the events of the last few hours, and only remember that you have a father who will endeavor to make you happy. You will have a brilliant position, Juliette. Your company will be eagerly sought for. You will be the envy and admiration of society. Indulge me with smiles when you can," he added, playfully taking her hand, "for my heart has long been desolate."

"O father!" she exclaimed, eagerly; "I will try to be all you wish;" and she raised his hand to her lips.

"Here we are!" said the gentleman, in a gay tone, as the carriage stopped before an elegant freestone mansion.

She gazed earnestly from the window at the lofty building, one story towering above another. "It looks so high and strange," she said, laughing.. "I have not seen it for six years."

A colored porter threw wide open the ponderous doors to admit his young mistress.

"Welcome home, miss!" he said, grinning till he showed all his white teeth.

Mr. Fearing laughed at her shy look and rosy blush. "Send Mrs. Cummings to me," he said to a servant. "She must throw off that girlish shyness," was his silent reflection; "and yet it is most attractive. It is absolutely reviving to see anything so fresh and pure in New York."

These were his thoughts as he led her into the parlor, and stood watching her eager, rapid glance around her.

Mrs. Cummings soon appeared and was introduced to her young lady. "Let Eliza unpack your trunks at once, my dear," said her father, "so that you can dress for dinner. It wants only an hour to the time," glancing toward a beautifully ornamented French clock.

"Dress for dinner, father?" she repeated; "dinner at six?"

"Yes, child," he answered, laughing gayly. "Where have you lived, I wonder?"

"We always have dinner at Mrs. Osborn's at half-past two, and at grandfather's at three, unless they have grand company."

"Well, we are to have grand company to-night," he responded, much amused. "No less than Miss Juliette Fearing; but run away, or you will not have time to dress, and remember your brothers will be impatient to see you."

She caught his hand, kissed it warmly, and with a most tender glance into his face, followed the staid, dignified housekeeper up the long flight of stairs to a magnificently furnished room in the third story.

Exclamations of "Oh, how beautiful! Can this be for me? What exquisite mirrors! What rich curtains!" followed one another in rapid succession.

Eliza, her own maid, as Mrs. Cummings informed her, opened the door of a room adjoining, and disclosed a beautiful apartment over the wide hall, which

4*

her father had fitted as a boudoir. In one corner stood a harp, while the choicest gems of art, both pictures and statuary, adorned the walls and niches.

The waiting-maid hurriedly pulled one article after another from the trunks, in the vain expectation of finding something more fashionable; and then, seeing her young mistress would not soon be weary of examining the bijouterie profusely scattered around her apartments, ventured to suggest that the dinner-bell would soon be heard.

"Oh, yes!" exclaimed Juliette; "and I can have time to look at all these beauties another day. Oh, how I wish Ella and Hatty and all the girls could enjoy them with me!"

Eliza smiled, and began to take down her lady's hair.

"I always do up my hair myself," cried the young lady; "and I can do it much quicker. I cannot stop to braid it to-day."

"O miss! your brother is very particular. The ladies all say Mr. Henry has such exquisite taste. You had better let me do it for you. That coil is very old-fashioned."

Juliette yielded, and her rich tresses were rapidly plaited in the latest style. Her party dress and ornaments were then brought out, and she was arrayed in them, though not without a gentle remonstrance that, after all, it "was only a family dinner."

"Your father will soon new furnish your wardrobe, miss," said the girl, who thoroughly understood her own business; "and maybe there will be a dozen guests."

"Oh, I hope not!" was the earnest response. "I want to see my brothers alone."

When the dinner-bell rang, Juliette, hastily taking from her waiting-maid a perfumed, embroidered handkerchief, ran down the stairs. Her father was waiting in the hall, and gave her his arm to the dining-room. As soon as he heard her voice, Horace came eagerly forward to welcome her, and Henry followed closely behind him.

The older brother kissed her affectionately, bringing a warm tint to her cheek. Henry stood back a moment, eyed her curiously, then raised the tips of her fingers to his lips. "Not so bad after all," he said, with a slight shrug of the shoulders.

"For shame, Henry!" said Mr. Fearing, smiling as he saw Juliette raise her head with dignity at this treatment. "For shame! Is this the way to welcome your sister?"

"Miss Fearing, excuse me," exclaimed Henry, with a tone of mock regret. "Be assured, no one rejoices more sincerely than I do at your return;" and he placed his hand in a theatrical manner on his heart.

Juliette laughed merrily. It was a clear, musical laugh, and echoed pleasantly through the spacious room. The party were evidently in the best of spirits, as Mr. Fearing led his daughter to the seat opposite his own, while the others stood waiting for her to be seated.

"O father!" she began; but, catching a glance from Horace, she quickly took the chair the servant was holding for her use.

The hour since she left him had been diligently spent by her father in forming plans for her introduction into society. He thought he saw his way clear to the fulfilment of his wishes, notwithstanding the terrible announcement of Mrs. Osborn. "I see how it 'is," he said to himself, as he wandered ruthlessly over the velvet flowers with which the parlors were strown; "I must dazzle her eyes with splendor. She will soon be in such a whirl of gayety that she will have no time for gloomy thoughts. She is very, *very* lovely; and I shall take pride in introducing her as my daughter. If I do not greatly mistake, I can govern her completely through her affections. How quickly she threw off her constraint when I treated her with tenderness. Sweet child! what a treasure my lost Juliette would have deemed her! Ah! how much I regret my mistake in wounding her gentle heart; but she seems wholly to have forgotten it. Well, henceforth her path shall be strown with roses, and in their fragrance she shall forget there is such a messenger as death."

The dinner — though for reasons easily imagined Mr. Fearing had chosen to have strictly confined to his family — was far beyond anything Juliette ever remembered to have witnessed. One course after another was brought on; many of them removed without being tasted. She was invited to drink wines, of which she knew not even the names, and when she

playfully declined, was told by Horace that a gentleman considered it an insult for a lady to refuse to
drink with him; but that, if she disliked it, she might
only raise the glass to her lips.

Before they arose from the table, the young girl became afraid she should sadly disgrace herself in the
eyes of her father's fashionable friends, and wished
for a little delay before she was introduced into
society.

In the mean time, the three gentlemen were intent
on watching her every motion. Even the pretty blush
as she took her plate from the waiter who stood behind
her chair, and the low-spoken "Thank you," when he
eagerly anticipated her wants, were irresistibly attractive.

When they returned to the parlor and drew their
chairs together, for conversation, there was a girlish
abandon, a freedom from affectation in all that she
said and did, exhibiting to her father and Horace such
a pure and lovely spirit, that they were charmed.

Henry paid her the compliment of remaining in the
parlor for an hour, and before he left declared it was
only for his peace of mind he tore himself away, as he
was more than half in love with his sister already.

"Don't be out late, my son," urged Mr. Fearing, a
shade of anxiety crossing his features.

"Father," said Juliette, when she had shyly accepted
a seat on his knee, "I'm afraid you will be ashamed
of me when you have guests. I am not at all sure I
should not in my ignorance insult them terribly, as I

did you and Horace, to-day. And they would scarcely
tell me of it as candidly as he did."

"Never fear," responded Mr. Fearing, in a gay tone.
"You have a natural quickness at adapting yourself to
the company you are in, which will do you good service. When you are in company, watch those ladies
who please you best, and imitate them."

"I would hardly advise that," added Horace, eagerly.
"I am satisfied with my sister as she is."

An hour more was passed in hearing Juliette play
and sing, her brother accompanying her in some Italian
duets; and then, as the tiny clock struck the hour of
ten, the young girl started to retire.

Mr. Fearing laughed heartily. "You are a little
rustic," he exclaimed. "Why, the New York world
are just waking up, to begin the gayeties of the night.
Henry, I'll venture to say, will attend two or three
parties more this evening. Ring your bell for Eliza,
my dear, if she is not already in your chamber. She
has nothing to do but attend upon you."

She put up her pretty mouth for a kiss, and then
tripped lightly up the stairs.

"What a girlish little thing it is, to be sure!" remarked Mr. Fearing, all a father's pride beaming in
his countenance. "She will make a great sensation, —
hey, Horace?"

The young man sighed. "What a pity it would be
for her to exchange those artless ways and pure
thoughts, for the hackneyed manners and heartless

conversation of a city belle! How long will she continue fresh and lovely as she is now, do you think?"

"True, I have thought of all this. Oh, how many times this evening I have wished your mother were here to guide her!"

"Yes, it appears to me she labors under a great disadvantage in not having a female friend on whom she can rely. Some one who —"

"I will have none of them," interrupted Mr. Fearing, sharply. "Even Mrs. Osborn has deceived me; though, after all, I owe her many thanks for returning my daughter an unsophisticated girl, instead of an affected, conceited boarding-school miss."

Horace rose.

"Are you going out to-night, my son?"

"No, sir; for once I'll imitate a worthy example, and retire to bed."

"Good-night, then. I confess I have enjoyed more this evening than I can easily tell you."

CHAPTER V.

ELIZA was awaiting her young mistress, having carefully sorted her wardrobe, and laid the clothes in the drawers.

While at school, Mr. Fearing had given his daughter a liberal allowance; but Mrs. Osborn wisely forbore the purchase of articles which, by distinguishing Juliette from the others, would cultivate an excessive fondness for dress.

Every year, however, she had received rich presents from her grandparents; generally some expensive set of jewels, or valuable addition to her wardrobe.

Eliza was quite sure that her opinion would be asked by Mr. Fearing concerning the replenishing of his daughter's attire. She was prepared to give it.

Juliette, after leaving her father and brother, hastened to her room, her heart beating warmly with gratitude and love to her heavenly Father, who had cast her lot in such pleasant places. She longed to throw herself upon her knees, and give vent to her feelings in words of praise; but the presence of her

48

maid restrained her. She allowed herself quickly to
be disrobed, therefore, though feeling all the time that
she much preferred the old way of waiting on herself;
and then, assuming a warm dressing-gown, assured
Eliza that she had no further need of her services, as
she intended to read awhile before retiring. The impressions of the evening had been so wholly pleasant,
that not until she had read her portion of Scripture and
committed herself to His hands who had hitherto ordered her path in so much mercy, did her mind revert
to the events of the earlier part of the day.

The more she reflected upon it, the more puzzled
she became to account for the excitement and displeasure exhibited by her father on parting from Mrs.
Osborn. And then those terribly earnest words, whispered with so much emotion in her ear, "You will
have sharp trials to encounter; but 'do right — only
do right' — and all will be well." What could they
mean? "What dreadful afflictions are before me?"
she asked, again and again. "I know father sometimes speaks sharply; but he is so kind and tender,
his eyes beam so fondly upon me, I am sure he loves
me; and then his words, 'Forget everything, but that
you have a father who will endeavor to make you
happy.' Certainly, I shall, as Mrs. Osborn says, try
to do right; and if I do, God will help me." And
then, with a determination to write at once to Mrs.
Osborn, in spite of the continual rumble of carriages
over the pavement, she fell into a sweet and tranquil
slumber.

In the morning she arose and partially dressed herself, that she might have time for her early devotions before she rang for her maid. Then gracefully yielding herself into the hands of her skilful attendant, she was quite startled at the image presented by her mirror; her soft, rich braids of hair being entwined with the scarlet blossoms of the fuchsia and wound around her well-shaped head.

"It is small credit to me, miss," said Eliza, smiling at the young lady's look of pleased surprise. "Such rich and abundant tresses as I have to do with. There, miss, let me hold the hand-glass for you to look behind. Your brother will be delighted, miss."

"Which brother?" asked Juliette, with a blush.

"Mr. Henry, miss. The young ladies, where I was at service last, were always talking of Mr. Henry Fearing. They thought him very handsome, and very polished, and so on."

Juliette laughed, and wondered to herself whether anybody could doubt that Horace was much handsomer and more noble-looking; but perhaps these ladies were not acquainted with him.

Being assured by Eliza that the breakfast-bell would not ring for an hour or two yet, the young girl resolved to tune her harp, and have a good practice upon it. She had scarcely touched the first note before Horace joined her.

"I must improve all the moments I have," he said, gayly; "for I prophesy you will not arise so early a month from this time."

"And why not, pray?" she asked, innocently. "I mean to take this hour for my practice in music. I cannot play well upon the harp."

The young man laughed, though he said, "I don't know but I ought to cry. Why, my dear sis, when you are out night after night at the theatre and opera, at parties and balls, you will scarcely feel like rising till noon."

"But I don't mean to do all that," she commenced, earnestly. "If I wished it, I am too young, and father would not allow it; but I do not wish it. I should not enjoy such gayeties. I like to hear a concert now and then, and go into such company as you and father approve; but I should not enjoy such a life as you mention at all. I am in earnest, brother," she added, warmly, as he continued to gaze in her animated countenance. "I could not do it; for I do not approve of such dissipation."

A quick, sharp pang shot through the young man's heart. He remembered something of the trial his mother had endured in consequence of his father's prejudice against religion. "Must this tender plant be crushed with unkindness?"

"Why do you gaze at me so, dear Horace?" she asked, quickly noticing the change in his countenance. "Have I said anything wrong?"

"Sit here by me, Juliette, and let me give you some advice," was his more serious remark. "For your sake, I do wish that your own plan could be carried out; but that is impossible. Your father expects a

great triumph for his only daughter. His heart is
fully set on it. He has impatiently waited for this
time; and nothing you could say; no influence that I
could bring to bear upon him; — and you know, dear
sister, for the sake of my mother he is very indulgent
to me; — nothing would turn him from his purpose.
He will be very loving and tender of you; he will
surround you with luxuries. You can scarce name a
wish, that money can procure, but it will be gratified;
but his word must be obeyed."

"I don't know what you mean, Horace," said the
young girl, growing a shade paler. "You look so
very sober, you terrify me. I have no intention of
disobeying my father. I love him dearly,— so much
so, that I would gladly give up all society, and pass
every evening like the last. But that, of course, I do
not expect; neither he nor you would —"

"Tut, tut!" he exclaimed, playfully patting her
cheek. "I can speak for myself when the time
comes; but now, as you don't understand me, I wish
to explain more fully. You say you don't approve of
too much gayety; you have some scruples of conscience, I suppose?"

She blushed as she slightly bowed her assent.

"Is it not a first duty to obey your father?"

"Yes, I suppose so."

"And if he were to command you to do what you
think to be wrong?"

Juliette's breath came quickly. Mrs. Osborn's words

flashed upon her mind. "This is to be my trial, then," she thought.

"I ought to obey God rather than man," was the soft and whispered response. She held her head down to conceal the large drops which stood in her eyes; and her breast heaved with emotion. Horace started from her, and walked to the window, but presently returned. "Juliette," he exclaimed, in an impressive tone, "I wish from my heart I knew how to advise you. I love and respect religion for my mother's sake; but I do not pretend to possess it. If you persist in refusing to gratify your father's wishes, I can see nothing but unhappiness before you. You are poorly fitted to encounter a will like his."

"I wish, dear brother, you knew the happiness of loving the Saviour," she responded, gently. "I have depended upon you so much to help me to be firm; but God has promised his aid." She gave him her hand, saying, "Leave me a few minutes now. I will join you soon in the breakfast-room."

Did he or her father imagine how those few minutes were passed? Yes, in that prayerless house there was one heart offering up its earnest supplications to God for help to prove herself worthy to be his child. And the answer came in peace to her own soul.

She took her place at the breakfast-table, from which Henry generally absented himself, with so bright and joyous a countenance that Horace was surprised.

When the meal was concluded, her father led her to the library, where, after an eager survey of the books

5*

and statuary, she playfully put her arms around his neck. She had already seen that he was pleased to have her demonstrative in her affection.

"Shall I sing for you, father?" she asked.

"I'm afraid you'd sing my senses all away, as you did last night. No, dear, we have important business for the morning. Eliza tells me that you have scarcely a dress fit to be seen; so I shall take you to Madame Ellstaff first. After this you must learn to supply your own wardrobe. You have only to come to me when your purse is empty. I have purchased a small phaeton for your use, my dear. When you wish to ride, Peter will drive you."

"Oh, father, you are very kind! I'm afraid your poor little girl will quite lose herself amid all this splendor."

"It is my pleasure to see you happy," he said, tenderly. "Only be obedient to my wishes, and you shall have everything your heart desires."

Why did her head so suddenly droop, and the color recede from her face?

"I love you too well to disobey you, father," she answered, in a touching tone of humility. "But you know I have a heavenly Father, too."

Mr. Fearing frowned, but immediately replied, in a tone of forced gayety: "I will order the carriage at once."

In spite of all her efforts to conceal it, the day was a weary one to Juliette. All the morning was passed in deciding upon silks, tissues, and crêpe de lisse;

then home to lunch; and afterwards out again with a lady of fashion to select hats, — dress hats, walking hats, riding hats, etc. The poor little miss began to look back with keen regret to her school-days, when one new hat at a time was deemed quite sufficient.

At dinner she saw Horace 'for the first time since the morning. Henry had sent word that an imperative engagement would prevent his dining at home. Juliette looked pale and tired, though she tried to be merry. There were one or two guests; and no private conversation was practicable. When they adjourned to the drawing-room, the young girl sang a few tunes; but it was plainly with an effort; and after an hour her father advised her to retire.

The next day brought invitations for a ball and party, and from this time callers and engagements were so numerous, there seemed not a moment left for reflection. The intelligence that Horace expected soon to leave the country saddened Juliette's heart; for though she saw comparatively little of him, and scarcely ever a moment alone; yet her heart always turned to him for sympathy and advice. Every day her father seemed more fond of her, and more gratified at the admiration she excited. To a young and ardent mind, there was indeed something intoxicating in the cup of flattery so suddenly held to her lips. Often, as she entered a party or assembly, dressed with the most exquisite taste, leaning on her father's arm, a buzz of admiration met her ears, — the words, "Oh, isn't she charming, divine?" bringing a richer

tint to her cheek, and additional brightness to her
eyes. Then her manner was so easy in its girlish
simplicity; there was such an earnest frankness and
grace in her conversation, that those who could not
be attracted by mere beauty became her most infatu-
ated worshippers. It was very flattering to Mr. Fearing, that though she responded warmly to kindness;
yet his daughter plainly preferred his attentions to any
of the eager applicants for her favor. Often, while
carrying on conversation with others, his heart would
swell with pride as he watched her graceful form float-
ing through the ballroom, or heard the full, clear
notes of her sweet, rich voice accompanying the piano.

"I knew her better than she knew herself," was his
pleased thought, as he met her eyes lighted with animation, and heard her low, musical laugh.

As one week after another glided swiftly away, one,
two, three gentlemen sought her hand in marriage;
but she answered, "I am too young."

When her father's consent was urged, she would
shudder, as she more firmly declined. There was an
unmistakable air of dissipation about these applicants
for her affection, which disgusted her pure heart. They
reminded her too strongly of her brother Henry,
whose blurred eyes, blanched, sallow complexion,
and fetid breath often caused her to loathe his
caresses.

CHAPTER VI.

" I shall the effect of this good lesson keep
As watchman to my heart."

THE conduct of Horace caused Juliette no small
anxiety. The time of his departure was postponed from one steamer to another; but though she
often saw him in company, and sometimes met his
eyes fastened upon her with a reproachful tenderness;
yet he persistently avoided her society. When they
accidentally were alone in the parlor (he never sought
her boudoir now), his manner was constrained and
cold.

This at last gave her so much pain, that one day,
meeting him on the stairs, she begged him to accompany her to the library.

"I will gladly do so," he answered, with more
warmth than he had shown for weeks, "for I have a
letter which came in an envelope to me, but which is
addressed to you. In a note accompanying it, Mrs.
Osborn complains that you have never answered one
of her letters."

"I have never received one," exclaimed Juliette,
eagerly tearing open the welcome epistle; "but I can

57

read it by and by," she added, thrusting it into her pocket, and turning to him with a deep blush. "I have wanted a long time, dear brother, to ask how I have offended you? Whatever I have done, I am sure you would forgive me if you knew how much I miss the kind care and interest you felt for me when I was at school."

Her manner was so affectionate that Horace started forward as if about to speak warmly, but, controlling himself, replied, in almost a bitter tone, "Juliette, the shy, loving sister, and Miss Fearing, the beautiful heiress, the gay belle of New York, are two totally unlike characters. Could I be guilty of the folly of supposing that among the throng of admirers my brotherly affection could be missed?"

"And do you really think me changed?" she asked, her eyelashes heavy with tears. "Ah, Horace, you have made me very unhappy!"

She turned away, and was about to leave the room; but he sprang forward and caught her hand. "Juliette," he said, earnestly, "will you answer one question?"

She trembled, but replied, "Certainly, I will."

"Are you happy? I mean, do you enjoy this life of incessant gayety; this whirlpool of excitement?"

Large, pearly drops coursed silently down her face as she answered, "You will think me very weak and foolish, I know, when I confess that sometimes I have been pleased at the attentions I have received. It was so unexpected that it flattered my pride; but the pain

has been far greater than the pleasure." She held out
her hand; and he saw that it was thin to transparency.
"This life is fast wearing me out," she said, weeping.
"This struggle between the fear of offending father
and the claims of conscience is terrible."

The young man pressed her thin fingers to his lips,
while his breast heaved with excitement. "I have had
a struggle, too," he began; "but I cannot relate it
here;" and he glanced around the spacious apartment,
as if he loathed the sight of it. "Will you come with
me to mother's grave?"

"Yes, gladly."

They were shortly on their way to the far-famed
garden, where lie the sleeping dead. Seated directly
opposite Juliette, Horace had opportunity to observe
how very pale her cheek had become, and how attenu-
ated her form. She was perusing the letter of Mrs.
Osborn, and wept bitterly over it.

"Strange!" she exclaimed. "She says she has
never received a letter from me since I left; and I
have written her often, though, since I found she did
not answer, not so frequently as before. She asks the
same question that you did, Horace, 'Are you happy?
Is your heart at rest?' Dear Mrs. Osborn! how I
wish I had never left you! Oh, you would indeed
pity, while you blamed me, for my want of firmness,
if you knew all I have suffered!"

Bidding Peter await them at the entrance, they wandered away to a retired part of the grounds, where,
for the first time, Juliette saw the monument erected

to the memory of her step-mother. Her own mother, too, lay there, and their infant brother and sister.

When she had gazed upon the low mounds in silence, Horace drew forth one of the rustic seats, and opening another beside her, he took a small Bible from his pocket. "Do you remember this?" he asked.

"Yes; I gave it to you, long ago."

She turned to the fly-leaf, and read, "To my very dear brother, Horace Everett, from his affectionate little sister Juliette."

"How well I remember writing that," she said, glancing in his face, with a smile. "Mrs. Osborn ruled it for me, and advised me to put in my whole name. I did not wish to, because it is Fearing; and I thought it would not look well that a brother's and sister's name should be unlike. She explained to me then, what I never understood before, that you were not my own brother; but I'm sure, Horace, when you are like yourself, kind and good as to-day, I love you far better than I do Henry."

"I have thanked God many times," exclaimed the young man, "that you were not my own sister; but now, dear Juliette, I must tell my tale. Ever since you gave me this little book, I have read in it occasionally. My mother loved the Bible, and died at peace with the Saviour it reveals. I knew the time when you, too, began to love Christ; and I often wondered what would be the result of your coming to live in New York. My heart ached for you the morning you so earnestly appealed to me; but when you an-

swered my question by saying so firmly, 'I must obey
God rather than man,' I was sure he would strengthen
you to do what is right. I acknowledged the power
of religion, and longed for a personal acquaintance
with it. I began to read my Bible daily; but instead
of finding peace, my soul was like 'the troubled sea,
which cannot rest.' I withdrew as much as possible
from society, and deferred from time to time my departure for Europe. There were other reasons, too,
why I could not tear myself away; but I will not
speak of them now. I read one passage after another
which condemned the life I now lead: 'Be ye not conformed to this world; but be ye transformed by the
renewing of your minds.' 'Thou shalt not follow a
multitude to do evil.' 'Come out from among them
and be separate, and I will receive you, and will be a
Father unto you, and ye shall be my sons and daughters, saith the Lord Almighty!' Shall I confess it to
you, dear Juliette, while I longed to break away from
all these gayeties, for at times I loathed them; yet I
had not strength to come out manfully and declare
myself a Christian? I dread the sneers and ridicule
I should meet, and, more than all, I dread father's
displeasure."

Juliette sat covering her face with her hands, the
tears trickling through her fingers. How clearly he
had stated the struggles of her own heart!

"Forgive me if I pain you too much, Juliette," he
added, gently touching her shoulder; "but I have
feared for you, too. I am sure the Bible is true. We

6

are either for Christ, or against him. We cannot serve two masters. By mingling in these gayeties, and pursuing them as the business of our lives, we necessarily declare that we approve of them. I met you among the eager throng after pleasure, and I feared you had forgotten your sweet hopes of heaven. I remembered that I advised to this course, and this added a keener pang to my suffering."

"Dear brother!" said the weeping girl; "I cannot tell you how I feel; but I have had more real pleasure in this short interview than in all the hours of the past winter. I see now the path of duty plain before me. I must sooner or later confess my love to Christ; and I will do it at once. Yes, I am resolved. I love father, and will yield obedience to his wishes whenever I can do so without breaking the commands of my Saviour; and you, dear Horace, will pray for me and strengthen me."

"I will do the first wherever I am; but I much regret, now, that I have engaged my passage in the next steamer, and shall sail in a few days."

"O Horace!" faltered the poor girl.

The young man remained for a moment lost in thought. "My uncle, Cyrus Everett, with his family, are going," he said, at length; "and he requested as a personal favor to himself that I would accompany them. This I was the more glad to do, as my aunt is a warm-hearted Christian. But, Juliette," he added, suddenly observing how very pale she had become, "I will withdraw my consent if I can be of service to you. My uncle will not insist when he knows. Say, Juliette, shall I stay?"

She shook her head, but did not attempt to speak.

He clasped her hand, and found it cold. "Yes, dear Juliette, on many accounts I wish to remain. Before I leave, I wish,—I have long wished to say that it is with more than a brother's love—"

He was interrupted by a party who were passing beyond them to another grave.

"No, Horace," responded the young girl, in an unsteady voice, when the persons were out of hearing, "you must not delay on my account. I have been led on from day to day, in the hope that I might,—that something might happen, which would induce father to consent that I should follow the dictates of my own conscience. I see now that I can never expect the blessing of God while I am out of the path of duty. I must give up all, even the love of my earthly father, if that is necessary, rather than displease my heavenly Father. I must remember that he has said, 'Whoso loveth father or mother more than me, is not worthy of me.' I dread it more than I can express," she added, looking in his face with a pensive smile. "I shudder at the thought of his displeasure. 'The spirit indeed is willing, but the flesh is weak.'" She sighed heavily, but after a moment looked up with a bright smile, adding, "I need not depend on my own strength. He will be with me, and he has said, 'As thy day is, so shall thy strength be.'"

"I wish Mrs. Osborn could be with you while I am

away," exclaimed Horace, warmly. "I am more than half a mind to give up travelling at all, until"—he checked himself,—"and enter on my profession at once."

His eager, impassioned glance caused the blushes to burn on Juliette's cheeks, and, rising hastily, she said, "I thank you, dear brother, more than I can express, for bringing me here, and for your faithfulness in reminding me of my duty. I shall feel strengthened, in endeavoring to do right, by knowing that you are struggling in the same path. We will pray for each other, and you will write me often."

She turned quickly away, to conceal the drops that glistened in her eyes, and stood a moment by her mother's grave. "How soon we shall all be lying here!" she said, in a trembling voice.

"Yes," he added, "and how glorious will be our rising from the tomb, if we earnestly strive after holiness! Only this morning I read the precious words, 'Blessed are they that are persecuted for righteousness' sake, for theirs is the kingdom of heaven.'"

Drawing her hand within his arm, they walked in silence to the carriage, where Peter was impatiently awaiting them. As they approached their home, Juliette said, earnestly, "I cannot attend Mrs. LeFevre's ball to-night."

"I have already declined," remarked Horace.

"I might in truth say I am too ill to go," she rejoined, pressing her hand to her head, "for indeed I am far from well; but it would not be the whole truth.

The trial must come sooner or later." She stopped suddenly, while her form shook with emotion.

It was with difficulty that the young man restrained himself from folding her to his breast, and comforting her with the assurance that he would be near to strengthen her and plead her cause. How often during the next two years did he regret that he had not done so!

"I fear you are ill, too," she said, gazing affectionately in his pale face, and trying to repress a sigh.

"No, I am perfectly well;" and at this moment the carriage stopped in Madison Square.

6*

CHAPTER VII.

"Sighs now breath'd
Unutterable, which the spirit of prayer
Inspir'd and wing'd for heaven with speedier flight
Than loudest oratory " —

JULIETTE proceeded at once to her chamber, determined to seek help of God, and then, without delay, impart to her father her new resolve. But before she reached her room, Eliza met her with a hasty note from him, stating that he had been suddenly summoned to H——, as his mother was very ill. He begged her not to follow him; he would return for her if her presence was necessary, but added, "If you wish to attend the ball this evening, Horace will doubtless go with you, in company with one of your married friends."

This short note, even though containing sad tidings, was such an inexpressible relief to the poor girl's pent-up feelings, that she burst into tears. As soon as she could compose herself, she ran down to show it to Horace. She found him in one of the parlors, gazing vacantly into the back court. "See, brother!" she exclaimed, "is it wrong to feel that the hand of God is in this?"

He glanced quickly over the note, then earnestly regarding her expectant countenance, returned it with a smile. "Grandmother is subject to these attacks," he said, after a moment. "I think there is no occasion for alarm on her account."

He presently relapsed into thought; but when Juliette returned, after having given her bonnet and shawl to Eliza, he roused himself, and drawing her toward a lounge, seated himself by her side.

"I have given orders that no callers be admitted," she began. "We will have a cosey cup of tea in the library; and then I will sing and play for you, as I did the first evening after I came home. Dear me, how simple and ignorant I was then! I have grown very old these last few months. Let us imagine ourselves back at dear Mrs. Osborn's, and that the girls have left us in the parlor, for a good long chat, as they used to do. Oh, how often the past winter I have longed for those delightful old times!"

Horace laughed, but it was plainly forced, and at last he said, "It's no use trying to conceal it, Juliette, I am half distracted between my desire to stay till this in regard to you is decided, and my promise to accompany my uncle abroad. Even the anticipation of a quiet evening with you will not turn my thoughts from this unpleasant subject."

"I will decide for you, then," she answered, speaking with animation. "You shall state all the reasons, pro and con, and then I'll decide."

"No, for I cannot; at least, I ought not to, state

all my reasons." Horace avoided her eye, and looked greatly embarrassed. "I ought not to tell you at present."

"There are two reasons in favor of your going at once," resumed Juliette, innocently, little dreaming of the tumult in his breast. "It will be so much pleasanter for you to have agreeable company; and the second is —"

"Well, what is the second?" as she hesitated and blushed.

"Why, of course, the sooner you go, the sooner you'll return. Isn't that a good reason?"

"The very best you could have named. And you will promise to welcome the wanderer back?" he added, earnestly.

"Certainly I will. Why, only think, when you are away I shall have nobody to — to take your place."

"I don't think I shall be absent but a few months, and then"—

He rose and walked to the window.

"And by that time," rejoined Juliette, "I hope I shall have convinced dear father that it is more for his interest to allow me to be a good, dutiful daughter in the way my conscience approves. I wonder sometimes, when he sees the effect of such dissipation on Henry, that he does not fear it for me."

"Poor Henry!" repeated Horace, "how changed he is! Naturally amiable, generous, and yielding, he has heretofore been more sinned against than sinning. Now I fear the worst, from the degraded company he seeks."

This was a painful thought for both of them, and they turned from it. Juliette brought her portfolio, and wrote a long letter to Mrs. Osborn, from which I make the following extract : —

"You say truly, my dear teacher, that no one can expect or claim the blessing of Heaven while engaged in the mere pursuit of pleasure. Certainly I feel this in my own case. Probably no one has ever enjoyed a more favorable opportunity to test the pleasures of fashionable life, or been more engaged in a ceaseless chase after gayety, than I, during the last few months. I do not hesitate to pronounce them unsatisfying. Yes, I have found, by my own bitter experience, that I cannot attend balls and gay assemblies, that I cannot hasten night after night from the theatre or the opera, and at the same time enjoy that sweet peace and trust in my heavenly Father which has been my portion in former times. Indeed, this round of excitement and fashion indisposes me for serious reading and prayer. I have often thought of your last words ; but little did I dream how difficult it would be for me to follow your advice. I seem only now, within a few hours, to have awaked to the dreadful dangers I have incurred, but am resolved, with the help of God, to take a stand for him. I am sure, dear teacher, I shall have your prayers that, however much tempted, I may be faithful to the end."

This letter she gave to her brother to post for her. Then the dinner-bell rang, at which meal Henry was present, and was told of his grandmother's illness.

He was greatly vexed that his father happened to be away just when he wanted a fresh supply of cash. His sister eagerly told him, she had just received a large sum from her father, which was at his service; but he only laughed. "If you have two thousand dollars, I will take it, and thank you," said he, presently. "Somehow I must get that sum to-night."

Juliette uttered an exclamation of surprise, but noticed immediately that Horace was looking very grave.

"I'll be bound," said Henry, unmindful of the presence of the servants, "I'd give all I'm worth, which, to be sure, is precious little at this minute, if I could keep out of these cursed scrapes, as you do, Horace. Why, I don't believe you spend a quarter part of your income."

"Perhaps not. I value my property too much to throw it away upon notorious blacklegs."

"Don't, Horace!" exclaimed the young man, glancing in confusion at his sister. "You shock the poor little girl. Well, I'm in for two thousand, and you know debts of honor must be paid."

"If you were really in trouble, Henry, you know I would divide my last dollar with you; but I never will give my money to sharpers. I dare not do it, for it would not be right."

The young man drank glass after glass of wine, until Horace glanced at his sister to intimate that she had better rise from the table.

They returned to the parlor, when Henry threw

himself on the sofa, and covered his face with his hands.

Juliette's heart bled for him. Oh, how earnestly her soul ascended in prayer to God that he might see the error of his ways, and turn before it was too late !

At length he started up, saying, "There is no help for it. I must go to H——," and he hastily left the house.

In the winter months there was always a bright fire in the library, and here Juliette and Horace repaired. He led her to the piano, and, turning aside the sheets containing operas, waltzes, and marches, she selected some simple melodies, which she had sung in childhood. Then they drew their chairs in front of the glowing coals, and talked long and earnestly of the subject dearest to their hearts. They spoke of his mother; and Horace called to his sister's mind the instructions she had given them. They strengthened each other in the resolution to maintain a consistent Christian character, even though persecution should follow; and then Juliette made known her strong desire to obey her Saviour's last command, and to commemorate his dying love.

"I fear," said Horace, gravely, "if you make a profession of religion at present, you will have to do it in direct opposition to your father's commands. In this case I cannot advise you; your own heart must judge."

The next morning, Mr. Fearing wrote that his mother was convalescent, but wished him to remain

another day. He added, that he would be in New
York in time to accompany his daughter to the theatre
on the following evening, when a celebrated actor was
to appear for the last time.

The color faded from Juliette's cheeks and lips.
"This will be my hour of trial," was her silent ejacu-
lation.

In the course of the day, Horace received a letter
from his uncle, begging him to execute some commis-
sions with reference to their anticipated voyage. The
Baltic was to sail the next day. The young man was,
therefore, very busy in his preparations; and his sister, though with a sad weight on her heart, determined
not to add to his cares by repeating her own. As he
had for some time been expecting to leave the country,
he had lately been to H—— to bid his friends adieu,
and now he only regretted leaving without seeing his
father once more. As the vessel was often delayed
for several hours, there was still hope that he would
arrive in time.

The last evening at home was a sad one, though,
could they have foreseen the events which would happen before they met again, it would have been far
more so. Horace promised to keep a journal of all
that would interest his sister, and copy it to send her,
while she assured him that much of her pleasure would
consist in answering his letters.

"And if anything unpleasant should occur," he exclaimed, warmly grasping her hand, — "I do not anticipate it, or I would not leave you, — but should

trouble or adversity come upon you, remember that I have an ample fortune, independent of father, and that it is my wish to share it with you."

"Thank you, dear brother," she responded, with a sad smile; "but in that case, I trust I should need nothing long."

He rose, saying, "You look weary, and I must be up with the sun, so we had better retire early."

But Juliette hesitated before she bade him good-night. There was one request she wished to make, but could scarcely gather courage to do so. "Horace," she began, "you have promised to pray for me; will you pray with me once before you go?"

The color flew to his face, and then receded, leaving him very pale. He walked across the library and back to where she stood. "I cannot refuse," he answered at length. "But, Juliette, I am just entering the narrow path, and the forms of prayer are new to me."

"We used to kneel, and say 'Our Father' together," she answered, gazing affectionately in his face.

He led her to the sofa, "Our Father pities our weakness," he said, softly. They knelt side by side, while he, in a humble, childlike manner, confessed their sins, and besought pardon and peace through a crucified Saviour. Every moment his soul warmed with increasing fervor, until his weeping companion was borne on the wings of faith to the mercy-seat, the great white throne, and the presence of the Eternal.

"O my brother!" she cried, her countenance beaming with a heavenly light, "what joys can be

7

compared to these? Oh, pray often for me, while we are separated! God has sent an answer already, in filling my soul with peace."

At an early hour the following day, the young man, having sought Henry in his room, and with difficulty aroused him sufficiently to bid him farewell, approached Juliette's boudoir for a similar purpose.

"It is necessary for me to be on board," he said; "but in all probability the vessel will not sail until afternoon, so that, in case father arrives, I hope he will drive instantly to the wharf." He then held her for one moment to his heart, and with a fervent "God bless you, my own dear Juliette, and keep you in all your ways," he hurried down the stairs to hide the emotion he could not suppress.

When he was gone, the poor girl no longer tried to keep back her tears, and wept so long and bitterly that she brought on a severe headache, and at last was obliged to return to her couch. Toward noon the voice of her father aroused her, and she tried to rise to meet him, but fell back, faint and trembling, upon the pillow. She heard Eliza telling him that she was ill, and rang her bell hastily, to say she wished to see him.

"Horace has gone!" she exclaimed, pressing her hands to her throbbing temples. "He wants you to drive directly to the wharf. If you go at once, I think you will see him. He could not endure the thought of leaving the country without bidding you farewell."

Waiting only long enough to bid her summon their family physician, unless she were soon relieved, he hastened away, saying that he should probably go out into the channel with the vessel, and return in the pilot's boat.

CHAPTER VIII.

"He withers at his heart, and looks as wan
As the pale spectre of a murdered man."

IN the mean time, Juliette lay upon her couch, endeavoring to fortify her mind for the trial before
her. She had not lived four months with her father
without learning something of his bitter prejudices
against those who professed to be governed by the law
of Christ. She had heard from Horace something of
the trial his mother had endured in consequence of it;
and she could not suppose that he would be more leni-
ent with her.

Mr. Fearing was, as we have seen, a man of generous, noble impulses, but extremely passionate, and
with an iron will. His daughter hoped that at this
time his heart would be softened by the recent illness
of his mother, and also by the parting from one whom
he loved as an own son. She prayed that he, "in
whose hands are the hearts of all men," would turn
his heart toward her, so that he would allow her to
serve God according to the dictates of her own conscience.

Hour after hour wore away, and still he did not return. The dinner-bell rang; but no one appeared in

answer to its summons. The terrible excitement was wearing upon poor Juliette. In vain she tried to still her wildly-beating heart, or by powerful opiates obtain the repose she so much needed. Her temples beat and throbbed, her lips grew dry and parched, while her eyeballs burned like fire. For some weeks she had acknowledged to herself an increasing lassitude ; but since the day she visited the cemetery it had required constant exertion to appear as usual.

At last she was compelled to allow Eliza to send for Doctor M——. She found difficulty in connecting her thoughts, and feared she were about to die, without having confessed herself to be Christ's.

At length the doctor came, and in a few moments her father followed him into her room.

The noise roused her from an unrefreshing nap, and for an instant she was confused, and did not recognize them, but soon began to talk incoherently of Horace, and "the great work I have to do."

Mr. Fearing bent over her in agony. For two days he had been suffering keenly in consequence of a stormy interview with Henry ; and now was this dear child, who had so warmly returned his affection, to be taken from him?

Juliette gazed earnestly in his face, and then suddenly clasped her arms around his neck. "O father, do let me love you! If you do not, it will break my heart. I will be a good daughter ; I will do all you wish. Father, father, I will be your nurse, your companion, and never, *never* leave you."

7*

"This is terrible!" exclaimed the poor man, starting from the bed.

"There is a high state of mental excitement," remarked the physician, in a low tone. "I shall be obliged to adopt powerful measures to prevent congestion of the brain."

"I know of no cause to produce excitement," returned Mr. Fearing, hoarsely, "unless it be that her brother has to-day sailed for Europe."

"Father! father!" again screamed Juliette, endeavoring to spring from the bed, "for my mother's sake, don't say so! Do love your poor girl!"

"My dearest child," cried Mr. Fearing, soothingly, "you are all the world to me. For your own sake, my darling child, I will love you. Oh, why do you utter such heart-rending words!"

His voice seemed to recall her to herself, for she drew his face down to hers for a kiss. "I do love you, dear father," she said, softly. "When I am gone I want you to remember that I did."

"But you shall not die!" he exclaimed, starting from her almost fiercely. "I cannot give you up."

Doctor M—— took him by the hand, and firmly led him from the room, saying, "I will not be answerable for the consequences, if you remain. She must be kept perfectly quiet, and have the most careful attention, in order to save her life. I wish it were an hour earlier, that the street might be covered with tan. I shall be obliged to apply ice to the head, and then shall leave only long enough to find an experienced nurse to remain with her."

Mr. Fearing caught his hat, and hastily left the house. An hour later, when the physician returned, bringing with him a nurse on whom he could rely to carry out his directions, he found laborers commencing their work upon the street. "Money is all-powerful," was his quiet remark to his companion.

"Except to purchase life," was her terse reply.

Within the elegant mansion, the servants were running to and fro, eager to learn what hope could be entertained for their dear young mistress; for Juliette, by her kind consideration for their comfort, her sweet, unassuming exercise of authority, had endeared herself to every one of the household.

The almost distracted father alternately locked himself in the library, struggling to resist the decree of the Almighty, which he feared had gone forth against him; and then, unable longer to endure the suspense, rushing to the door of her chamber, where his heart was torn by her incoherent cries, — "O my father! my dear father!"

Coming out of the chamber, after repeated attempts to soothe her, the physician found Mr. Fearing standing near the door, his hands pressed wildly upon his head. Dr. M—— led him, passive as a child, to the library. "What does this mean?" he asked, abruptly, "this constant, heart-rending cry for your affection? 'Father, don't turn me away. Father, do let me love you, and be a good daughter to you!'"

"They are the ravings of insanity!" cried the excited father. "From the hour she came home, more than four months since, she has never known a wish ungratified. She has repeatedly assured me that I should spoil her with indulgence."

"You said you knew no cause of excitement, unless it were the departure of Mr. Everett. Am I to understand that there is a mutual affection between them?"

Mr. Fearing started, and fixed his keen, penetrating eyes on the doctor's face. One reminiscence after another flashed through his mind, to prove that it might be so; and yet, strange to say, their intimacy from childhood, their language toward each other as brother and sister, had heretofore prevented the idea from once entering his heart.

"It may be so," he said, half aloud, in an abstracted manner; "yet the thought never occurred to me. But why did not Horace ask my consent? As there is no blood relation, I would choose him for a son before any other. Yet, if such were the fact, he would scarcely have left her. It is all dark and mysterious."

The physician sat down and leaned his head on his hand. "I ought not to conceal from you," he began, after a brief pause, "that your daughter is in imminent danger. The cause, whatever it may be, has been for some time affecting her system. As soon as the fever leaves her, she may sink from utter prostration. I see that her form is exceedingly thin and frail.

The danger is that there is not enough vitality to withstand the shock of such an attack."

Mr. Fearing stood gazing earnestly at the countenance of the speaker, the muscles of his face working convulsively to conceal the effect these words were producing; then with a deep groan he turned to the other end of the apartment.

Dr. M—— rose to return to the chamber. "As early as possible," he said, "I shall call in Dr. I—— and Dr. P——, as consulting physicians. It is not my way to deceive friends by concealing the real danger of the sufferer; but be assured, no means shall be spared to save the life of your child."

The poor father wrung his hands in silence. He followed the doctor to the door of the sick-room, where the patient, exhausted by her loud screams, and partly under the influence of narcotics, only muttered to herself at intervals; — the names of "father, dear father," and "Horace," being alternately upon her lips. As her eyes remained closed, Dr. M——, in reply to the agonizing gaze of the father, led him to the couch. Juliette's beautiful tresses had been cut within an inch or two of her head. In their stead, a bag containing pieces of ice was held in its place by Eliza, while the nurse moved here and there in accordance with the directions of the physician.

Eliza's face was very pale, and she with difficulty restrained her tears at the oft-repeated words, uttered in a low and mournfully earnest tone, "Father, I will,

only let me love you. Horace, you promised, wherever you were, to remember your poor sister."

He could endure no more, but darted from the
room, just as Henry, with a loud bang, which brought
a scream from the poor sufferer, entered the outer
door.

For two days Mr. Fearing had not seen his son, and
then, after giving him a check for two thousand dollars, parted from him in terrible anger. Now, the
youth, more than half intoxicated, was effectually
roused by seeing the house, usually at this hour so
quiet, in a blaze of light, while persons were hastening up and down the lofty flights of stairs.

Darting hastily forward, Mr. Fearing arrested his
son's steps as they were on the staircase, and led him
unresisting to the library.

"Am I awake?" exclaimed Henry, in a confused
manner, rubbing his head.

A look of contempt passed over the father's face as
he gazed upon his son.

"It is time you were awake," he began, in a hoarse,
constrained voice, "for when to-morrow's sun rises,
your only sister may be sleeping her last long sleep."

Henry started, and fell back upon the sofa, expressing his surprise by an oath.

Mr. Fearing was only restrained from a torrent of
abuse at his ill-timed words by the expression of real
distress upon his son's blanched countenance.

"Go to bed, sir," he said, sternly; "you are dead
to all sense of decency."

"Can't I see her?" faltered the young man, rising and approaching his father. "Oh, can't I see her once more?"

Mr. Fearing waved him off. This question, — oh, what a dagger to his heart! "See her once more." Alas! how little, after all, he had realized that soon he might be called to part with her forever.

Henry left the room unnoticed, and stole softly up the stairs. The chamber-girl was just carrying in a fresh supply of ice, and he, trembling in every limb, followed her. Juliette had fallen into a troubled sleep, and her attendants, scarcely daring to draw a breath, stood around her. Dr. M——, who was reclining on a lounge in the apartment, put his fingers on his lips as a caution to Henry, who arrested his steps without daring to approach the bed.

Oh, what thoughts of death and of the eternity that would follow, rushed into his mind as he stood gazing on the pallid countenance before him! How her whispered remonstrances respecting the course he was pursuing, pierced him like a dagger, as he realized that he might never again hear her voice! "Dear brother," she had said, one day, when, after a fit of intoxication, he was cursing himself and his boon companions, "Dear brother, our mother taught us there is a world beyond this."

How quickly that beautiful countenance had been changed! Those rich, brown locks, of whose beauty he had boasted over the wine-cup, where were they? Those lustrous eyes, which ever beamed upon him with sisterly affection, closed, perhaps forever! That form, graceful in its symmetrical proportions, must that be laid in the grave for worms to feast upon? Horrid thoughts! How could he endure them? All that was good and tender in the brother's heart was aroused by the sight before him. He turned silently and left the apartment. Again he sought the library; for in his distress he must have sympathy. The door was locked; but on hearing the handle turn, Mr. Fearing quickly opened it. His face was haggard, while his large, piercing eyes seemed to protrude from their sockets.

Henry burst into tears. "Is there no hope?" he asked. "Can nothing be done?"

CHAPTER IX.

"A beam of comfort, like the moon through clouds,
Gilds the black horror, and doth soothe his heart."

THE consulting physicians approved the course
pursued by Dr. M——, and recommended a
continuance of the same powerful measures. They
agreed in supposing this not to be so sudden an attack
as it at first appeared; but that the patient had for
some time been laboring under unnatural excitement.
From Eliza, Dr. M—— learned that her young mistress was often found in tears in her own apartment;
and, also, that since the morning her father left for
H——, when she visited the cemetery with Mr.
Everett, she had complained of not being well.

That some of her distress was connected with Horace, they could not doubt; but what could be the
cause of this distress, her father could not even suspect.

In his severe self-conflicts, Mr. Fearing did indeed
blame himself that he had been so. blind, and keenly
regretted that he had so often imposed his confidence
upon the young man in regard to his wishes for his
daughter.

8   85

He now recollected, what had never struck him
before, that Horace was always silent at these confidential interviews, or had merely said, he had no
doubt his sister's pure heart would guide her aright;
that nothing would pain him more than to see her
united for life to a man whose character was not above
reproach, even though his fortune and rank were
princely.

It certainly would not be true to say that Mr. Fearing's mind did not revert with the most painful solicitude to the remark of Mrs. Osborn when they were
parting, "Not until you allow your daughter the free exercise of her dearest hopes and wishes, will she be truly
happy." This, connected with the unwelcome statement that she was a humble Christian, caused a tumult
of emotion in the father's heart. He began to suspect
that after all this might be the cause of her sickness,
—that secret conflicts had undermined her constitution
and prepared the way for the awful catastrophe he
now dreaded. "And all this time," he said to himself,
"she has given up her own desires, and tried to find
pleasure in acting according to my wishes."

In the near thought of death the vanities of the
world faded before him like the morning mist. He
almost persuaded himself that could he have her restored to health and strength, he *would* allow her "the
free exercise of her dearest hopes."

Strange to say, that even at this moment the impressions of his childhood were so strong upon him
(for he had always heard his father ridicule the dis-

ciples of Christ), and so wholly ignorant was he of the claims of religion, or the joys of a true believer, that the thought of his lovely daughter, heiress of his immense fortune, desiring nothing more than meekly to follow her Saviour, was to him exceedingly bitter and humiliating. In his inmost soul he denounced Mrs. Osborn as a scheming fanatic, and his Juliette as her too credulous follower.

The excitement of the night was followed in the case of the poor sufferer by a stupor so profound that it was only by her intermittent pulse the physician could be sure she still lived. Dr. M——, hastily despatching a note to a brother physician, gave himself wholly to the work of watching his patient.

Eliza, when her services were not needed, sat weeping in the boudoir. The nurse, pale, but calm, went quietly on in the performance of her duty, with an occasional whispered remark to the waiting-woman, that the crisis must come soon. Henry, at home, in the full possession of his senses, wandered like a ghost from room to room, in the vain attempt to shake off this terrible weight at his heart; while Mr. Fearing, shutting himself into his library, endured the most terrible conflicts in his impious endeavors to fight against God.

Here, on the morning of the third day, Dr. M—— sought him to communicate the first hopeful tidings it had been in his power to convey: "The crisis has passed, and my patient still lives."

"God in heaven be praised!" burst from the father's lips.

But did he really praise God, as he cautiously followed the footsteps of the good doctor to the room above stairs? Did his heart go out in love toward Him who had been better to him than his fears? Alas, no! It was only lip-service while his heart was still far from his Maker.

As he entered the chamber, a smile lit up the weary face of the faithful Eliza. She pointed to the bed where her beloved mistress lay, pale and wan indeed, but her breast heaving softly in a natural, refreshing sleep. For the first time tears filled his eyes: he drew Dr. M—— into the boudoir, and, wringing his hands, said hoarsely, "All I have can never repay you. Your skill has saved her life."

"Not so," returned the good man, scarcely less affected. "Life and death are ordered by God; I am but a humble instrument to do his will."

He returned to the chamber to wet again the parched lips of the prostrate sufferer. It scarcely roused her; and she soon fell back into the same tranquil slumber.

"Nature's sweet restorer," he murmured, with a smile; "that balmy sleep will do more for you than any medicine." Then with minute directions to the skilful nurse, he returned home to enjoy a brief hour of repose before he entered once more upon the onerous duties of his profession.

No sooner was Juliette pronounced out of immediate danger than her brother, with a great sigh of relief,

hastened from the house in search of some excitement.
His abstinence from wine and other intoxicating
liquors had given his eyes a wild glare, and there was
a continual gnawing at his vitals which must be al-
layed. These three days and nights seemed like
weeks, so fraught had they been, not only with anxiety
for his sister, but with remorse at the course of dissipation he had been pursuing.

Mr. Fearing's heart began to swell with new hopes
from the moment Dr. M—— assured him his daughter
was convalescent. To be sure there might at any moment be a relapse, if the cause, whatever it might be,
was not removed; but hope had once more spread her
wings over him, and he trusted that all would be well.
He passed hours at a time in the sick-room, and minis-
tered to the patient sufferer with so much tenderness,
that though at first his presence seemed to excite her,
connected as he appeared to be with some painful
associations, yet she always welcomed him with a
smile, and at length became uneasy when he was
away.

With a woman's skill he smoothed her pillow,
brushed the close, short curls from her pale brow,
read to her and related the on-dits of the day. Many
times, as her strength began to return, he resolved to
ask the cause of her sickness, but he as often restrained
himself. First, because the physician had expressly
cautioned him against any subject that would excite
the invalid, and because he had a secret fear that his
present happiness would be destroyed.

8*

And what were Juliette's feelings at this precious display of her father's affection? At first she knew not how to interpret it; but presently began to hope that during the first hours of her sickness, she had revealed to him the true state of her heart, and that he thus meant to show her that he would yield his consent to her wishes. She was disappointed as day after day passed, and he made no allusion to the subject; and was restrained only from introducing it herself, by the fact of her extreme debility.

Without the knowledge the reader possesses of Mr. Fearing's character, it might seem weak and childish in Juliette to be so much in dread of his displeasure. But we have nowhere intimated that she was firm, independent, or courageous. In truth, she had never outgrown or overcome this failing of her childhood, but was constitutionally timid and distrustful of herself. She yearned for a strong arm to support her, a firm, self-reliant, God-fearing will to guide and direct her own. Now, as she lay on her couch or reclined in a luxurious easy-chair gazing at her father as he sat reading by her side, her pulse fluttered and her heart beat painfully as she realized that his fond affection might at any moment be turned to fierce displeasure. "Surely, there can be no sin in postponing the evil day as long as I may," she said to herself one night after a vain struggle to banish the subject from her thoughts. "When he commands me to do something which my conscience disapproves, that will be the time for me to confess all."

This resolve was a weak one, and wanting in child-like confidence in her heavenly Father's promise: "They that trust in the Lord shall be as Mount Zion, which cannot be removed. He will not suffer thy foot to be moved. The Lord is thy shade upon thy right hand. The sun shall not smite thee by day nor the moon by night. The Lord shall preserve thee from all evil. The Lord shall preserve thy going out and thy coming in, from this time forth, and even forever more."

From this hour Juliette abandoned herself to the delight of being loved and petted. Every day she twined herself more strongly about her father's heart. As soon as she was able to be dressed, he began to form plans for her happiness. Would she prefer to live in the country? He would purchase an estate on the banks of the beautiful Hudson. Would she like to travel? As soon as she were well, they would start for Europe, surprise Horace and his party, and accompany them to Italy.

The sick girl's eyes grew bright, and the rose-tint beautified her pale face as these, the dearest dreams of her childhood, seemed about to be realized. How earnestly she had talked with her school-mates of the delights of visiting the countries of which they then knew little more than their place upon the map! and now to wander through the streets of Rome, to sail along the shores of the Mediterranean; more than all, to visit the Holy Land in company with her brother Horace, — what on earth could she ask for more?

Mr. Fearing saw the bright blush of pleasure which suffused her checks at the thought of joining Horace, and his newly-awakened suspicions were more than ever confirmed. "My daughter," he thought, "is not one to give her affections unsought; and yet, I cannot call to mind one act of his which might not have occurred, had he been her own brother.

"Since they were children together in the nursery, Juliette has always clung to Horace, though Henry was nearer her own age, and, when separated after their mother's decease, they kept up a close correspondence.

"But so it was," he soliloquized, in my own case. "I cannot remember the time when I began to love my own Juliette; and this affection grew with my growth, and strengthened with my strength, until she seemed a part of my own being. I should be miserable, indeed, if I thought that either of my dear children, for such I must ever regard Horace, would suffer the keen pangs I endured when I found another claimed one I considered all my own. I wish I had not been so blind. Without the least sacrifice of my daughter's delicacy, I might easily have ascertained whether Horace regarded her with more than brotherly affection, and if so, after a little delay, she could have accompanied him as his wife. Yes, he is the man I should choose, above all others, as the husband of my daughter. He is manly, upright, and generous. Then he is the heir of his grandfather, which, with his own fortune and Juliette's, would render them independent. But, with such a character as his, were he not possessed of a copper, he is the son of my loved Juliette, and he should have her for the asking.

"But supposing that he only loves her with a calm, brotherly affection, such as I have always supposed to exist between them, it would be unwise to have her thrown so constantly into his society, as she would be were they travelling together."

CHAPTER X.

"Faith is the subtle chain
That binds us to the infinite: the voice
Of a deep life within, that will remain
Unsullied there forever."

THE quiet of the sick-room now began to be enliv-
ened by calls from intimate female friends, and
the constant succession of bouquets of rare exotics
from Juliette's numerous admirers. Spring was opening, and her father promised, as soon as Dr. M——
thought it safe, to take her to H—— for a visit to
her grandmother.

One day, in his absence, the invalid was reclining in
an easy-chair, opposite the bright steel bars of the
grate glowing with the blazing fire of coal. The rich
folds of her cashmere dressing-gown swept the floor,
and her tiny foot, cased in an embroidered slipper,
peeped from its hiding-place when a lady was announced
who had been a friend of her own mother. Juliette
was delighted, and eagerly asked many questions concerning her early married life. The call was prolonged,
and at last was only ended by the lady's expressing
anxiety to hear a distinguished divine from abroad who
was to preach in their church this morning.

"Oh, how I wish I could go!" exclaimed the young lady, her face beaming with excitement.

"Are you interested in such subjects, my dear?" asked the visitor, warmly.

"More than in any other," was the meek reply.

The lady gazed for a moment upon the beautiful face turned so wistfully to her own, looked at her watch, and said, "The morning is fine. I will take you there and bring you back in safety; but perhaps you are not strong enough."

"I fear father would object to my going to-day," murmured Juliette, with a disappointed air; "as I have not yet left my room; but perhaps another time you will repeat your offer."

"Certainly, I will; and not only that, but you must let me love you, and claim an early visit from you, for the sake of your mother."

The next day Dr. M—— told his patient that she had no further need of his services, as with care and prudence she would soon be well. "I suppose you have scarcely heard from Mr. Everett, as yet," he added, in an arch tone, which brought a rich color to her lips. "I wonder he did not take you out with him."

"Father intends to take me to Europe," replied Juliette, dropping her eyes before his roguish glance.

"Well, Everett is a fine fellow. I have heard his name in connection with that of Miss De Forest. Is there any truth in the rumor?"

"I don't know, indeed. I have never heard him speak of her."

"I don't believe a word of it," returned Dr. M——, satisfied by her meek, sad tone that his suspicions were correct. "With such a mother as he had, I have no idea that he will ever choose a city belle."

"I shall never forget your kindness, doctor," exclaimed the young lady, her eyes glistening with tears. "I am truly sorry to have you forsake me just as I can enjoy your visits."

"One of the trials of my profession, child, and not a small one, either." Then, warmly grasping her hand, he bade her adieu.

Juliette had rode out several times, and was beginning to count the days before she could leave for H——, when Henry was taken suddenly ill, and their departure was indefinitely postponed. She had never forgotten the promise of her mother's friend to take her to church, and was delighted to accept an invitation to pass a quiet day at her house, hoping to make some definite arrrangement for hearing Mr. D——.

Mrs. Ward Folsom stood high in society, and Mr. Fearing was much pleased with her attention to his daughter. He accompanied Juliette to her house, on their way telling her Mrs. Folsom would be a valuable friend.

The lady received her young guest warmly, and invited her to her own room, where two lovely children soon engaged all her attention. After she had amused herself with them for an hour, their mother summoned their nurse to take them to the Park; and then, turning to Juliette, said, kindly, "I have thought much of you lately, my dear; and I want you to tell me frankly all about your love for religion; for, if I do not mistake, you have begun to follow Christ."

Juliette's heart swelled with gratitude at this speech. She considered it in direct answer to her prayers, that God had given her a Christian friend to counsel her. "I shall truly be glad to do so," she exclaimed, earnestly. "You cannot tell how I have longed for such a friend."

She then unburdened her whole heart to her companion, — the trembling hopes she entertained that she was accepted of Christ, — the sorrow that she was so unworthy of him, and the struggles for courage to confess him before men.

"You attend Dr. A——'s church, I think," remarked Mrs. Folsom, much moved at this frank, artless account.

"Yes; father has always attended there; that is, he considers it his place of worship. He seldom goes himself;" and Juliette blushed deeply.

"Are you at all acquainted with the doctor?"

"I have never seen him, except in the pulpit."

"Suppose I order the carriage, and take you there. I am well acquainted with him, and will assume the whole responsibility of the call."

"I should enjoy it exceedingly; but—" and tears filled her eyes.

"Will you forgive me, my dear, if I tell you that I

think you wanting in that Christian boldness which David manifested when he said, 'The Lord is on my side. I will not fear; what can man do unto me?'"

"I will go with you at once, if you think it best," said Juliette, smiling through her tears; "but, indeed, I have a poor, trembling heart."

When they were seated in the carriage, the lady took the hand of her young friend, as she repeated the promise, "Thou shalt keep him in perfect peace whose mind is stayed on thee."

"Oh!" exclaimed Juliette; "while I was sick, I fully realized the blessedness of that precious verse; but of late it has been much easier for me to dwell upon another: 'We must through much tribulation enter the kingdom of heaven.' I don't know but it is wrong," she added, after a short pause; "but I am very much given to castle-building; and I persevere in it, though one after another of my lofty structures falls to the ground. I have often imagined that father lost all his property, and we lived in a little cottage in the country, with no other ornaments except the pretty vines I trained to run over the porch. I worked hard all day, for we kept no servant; but my heart was light, and I went singing about the house. Father at first was melancholy; but I cheered him. I had my harp, and I sang him songs that he loved; but, better than all the rest, at last he let me read the Bible to him. Oh, I was happy then!" and her face glowed with animation.

Mrs. Folsom leaned forward and kissed her tenderly.

Every moment her heart was more drawn out toward the lovely girl. "I see, my dear," she said, kindly, "that you have trials, and I more than suspect the nature of them from some rumors about your step-mother's last days. It was said she wished to unite with Christ's people, but was deterred by her husband. Some time you must tell me all you think proper. It is not from curiosity I ask it, but that I may know how to advise you."

"I don't think father would ever consent that I should make a profession of religion," faltered Juliette, with a burning cheek.

"And you think it your duty to do so. Is that it, my dear?"

"Yes, ma'am; I can't forget that it was our Saviour's last command, made just before he offered up his life for me. I know I never can expect God's blessing until I obey. But then I often tremble, I am so unworthy. You know what a terrible curse is pronounced upon those who do not approach the table of their Lord in faith and true love to him."

"If you are willing, my dear, I should like to state your case to your good pastor. He will treat you with the tenderness of a father."

Juliette hesitated a moment, and then said, "Thank you. I should like it if you think best."

"But your own heart must judge, after all. No one can decide a case of conscience for you."

"So my brother Horace said."

The coachman at this moment drew up at the door

of the pastor's house, and, after ascertaining that he
was in his study, they alighted and were shown within.
The old gentleman treated them so cordially, that Juliette soon felt acquainted, and, without at all being
conscious of it, let him into all the secrets of her
heart. ' When they left, after an hour's interview, she
was more than ever strengthened in her resolve to be
joined to the people of God, by a passage he repeated,
and which continually recurred to her mind: "Heirs
of God and joint heirs with Christ, if so be that ye
suffer with him, that ye also may be glorified together."

"What a fine thing it is thought to be," she said to
Mrs. Folsom, "to be heiress to a great fortune! I
have often heard it whispered in a ballroom, 'There
is Miss Fearing; she is a great heiress.' But how
mean compared to being an heir of God, a joint heir
with Christ to the riches of the heavenly inheritance!"

Henry Fearing's illness was caused by the excessive
use of ardent spirits. It was followed by a slight
attack of *mania a potu*. Dr. M—— assured not
only Mr. Fearing, but the patient himself, that unless
he abandoned the use of spirituous liquors, his health
would be wholly destroyed. For a few weeks the
young man remembered the warning; but after that
his gay companions gathered around him, and drew
him back into their charmed circle. They could not
afford to lose from their clubs one who spent his
money so profusely for the gratification of their de-
praved appetites.

Mr. Fearing often spoke of leaving the country, but

disliked to do so while his mother continued as feeble as she was at present. In the mean time he received a letter from Horace, enclosing one also for his daughter. This he delivered her with so marked an emphasis on the words, "A precious epistle for you, Juliette," that she quickly left the room to hide her confusion.

When in her own apartment she took herself severely to task for her emotion. "What will father think?" she asked. "I'm sure I don't at all understand why I should blush so at the mention of my brother's name. Horace is nothing more than a dear, very dear brother to me. It must have been father's manner that embarrassed me so." "But still," whispered a soft voice, "you were greatly pained at the thought of his being interested in Miss De Forest." "Certainly, because I should be sorry to see him united to any mere belle. He ought to have a Christian wife."

All these thoughts flashed through her mind while she locked the door of her chamber, drew a chair near the window, and tore open the envelope. Though it is hardly civil to read a confidential letter, yet we give it as follows :—

"I should never have had courage, my sweet sister, to have left home, had I realized what a pang it would have cost me at the last moment to tear myself away. I suppose father told you how comfortably we were situated in our cabins, and how many books my uncle

9*

had provided for the voyage ; and so I will pass on to other things. My aunt is just such a woman as you would love ; and she so won upon my confidence that before we were half the way to Havre, I had told her not only the sweet hopes that fill my heart, but related your history, too ; I mean that part of it which referred to your religious experience. She feels strongly interested in you, and said, only yesterday, 'How I wish, Horace, we had persuaded Mr. Fearing to trust his daughter with us for a tour through Europe ! '

"I need not tell you how warmly my heart responded to this wish. I was homesick all the rest of the day. Would you have come, dear Juliette ?

"Do you remember the subject of our conversation on the day we visited our mothers' graves ? You expressed a wish to unite with the church, and I feared to advise you. Mrs. Everett said you were right, and I wrong. I acknowledge this has been true many times. She says, 'It is plainly your duty as well as your privilege to take a stand with the people of God, and claim the blessing he has promised those who thus honor him.' I would I were with you to stand by your side on this most solemn occasion. I shall be with you in spirit, and shall pray that He who orders all events, may make this the means of dear father's conversion. I feel condemned that I have had so little faith that God would touch his heart. I have indeed prayed for it, but with a secret feeling that it was too much to expect. Now I mean to wrestle for him as Jacob did, and say to the angel of the covenant, 'I will not let thee go until thou bless me.' I have fully determined to unite myself with the English Church at Havre, over which one of our own countrymen is settled. Pray for me, Juliette, that I may not be deceiving myself.

"Before I close, dear sister, I must ask you to forgive me for what I said to you at the cemetery. How could I have censured you for pursuing the same course as I myself was pursuing? I confess with shame that I was in part actuated by other motives, which I did not think it best to confide to you at that time. You have ever looked with a sister's leniency upon my faults, so I will persuade myself that you will do it again, though I fancied that you were unusually grave and reserved for a day or two before I left. When I return I will lay open my whole heart before you; then perhaps you will not blame me for my many apparent inconsistencies. I shall send my journal to this date in the next vessel; and shall scarcely dare impose another long epistle upon you, unless I receive one of equal length.

"YOUR BROTHER HORACE."

Two hours after the reception of this letter, Juliette ordered her own carriage, and went to make another call upon her pastor. Dismissing Peter, she determined to delay no longer, but make known her request to be admitted to his church. It was a deeply interesting hour to her, as she stated to him the grounds of her hope that she was accepted of Christ, and answered his heart-searching questions concerning her repentance, faith, and love. It was three weeks before she would be called to make her profession of faith in public. In the mean time she must confess to her father what she was about to do.

CHAPTER XI.

"Blessed are ye when men shall separate you from their company, and shall reproach you, and cast out your name as evil, for the Son of Man's sake."

THE next evening it so happened that Mr. Fearing, who had passed many nights in the care of his son, was afflicted with a severe headache. Juliette found him reclining on the lounge in the library, and sought, with all a daughter's tenderness, to do something for his relief.

Henry, during his convalescence, was extremely irritable and difficult to please; so much so that the servants complained that they must leave. His father was the only one who could control him. He had forbidden Juliette remaining in her brother's room.

At an early hour, and just as the loving daughter was persuading her father to retire, Henry, who, contrary to his father's wishes, had left the house, returned home evidently much intoxicated.

Mr. Fearing was justly displeased; but Juliette looked so frightened, that he merely rang the bell, and ordered that Rufus be sent to assist his young master to bed, deferring his remonstrance until another time. He lay down upon the sofa again, and, with a heavy sigh, exclaimed, "That boy will ruin himself and break my heart!"

Juliette said all she could think of to soothe him; ran to her room for her vinaigrette, and was so anxious to please him, that he endeavored to throw off his forebodings of evil for his son, and show her that he appreciated her affection. They talked a long time of Horace, of his love for his beautiful mother, of the length of time before he would return, until Juliette thought he had never been so tender before. "Why," she thought, "shall I not improve this opportunity, and unburden my heart of this secret, which weighs so heavily upon it?" With a silent prayer for strength and wisdom to guide her, she took advantage of a brief pause to say, "Father, are you well enough for me to tell you something?"

He started up, fixed his penetrating eyes on her face, as he signified his assent.

"I have wanted to tell you for a long, *long* time," she went on, lifting his hand to her lips, "but I have delayed because — because I feared that you would be displeased." She trembled a little at his searching look, but added, softly, "Shall I tell you now, father?"

Again he answered only by a bow.

She stood up, and wound her arm around his neck, as she murmured, "I love my Saviour, and have promised to confess him before the world."

"Never, with my consent," he shouted, throwing her from him.

"O father, father!" she cried, falling at his feet, "don't say that. I have prayed and longed for you to be willing. I will be a good daughter to you, I love you so dearly; but I cannot disobey my God."

"Who has dared to counsel you in this? Speak, child! I know you would never have gone into such mad folly if you had been left to yourself."

"It was the Bible and my own conscience, father. I dare not act contrary to the word of God. My Saviour says, 'Do this in remembrance of me.'"

"Juliette!" cried Mr. Fearing, and his voice shook with anger, "I have cursed Mrs. Osborn for daring to impose her mad fanaticism upon you. Do not let me curse you. But no," he added, with a mighty effort controlling his passion; "my daughter will not thus return my lavish affection. Give up these foolish notions, and I will forgive all."

"O father!" exclaimed Juliette, with a burst of tears, "ask me anything but that. I cannot, I ought not to sacrifice my own soul. I can die, father, but I cannot live as I have done, denying my Saviour."

With a terrible oath, the infuriated father began to curse his daughter; but, interrupting himself, cried out, "Leave me; but remember I will hear no more of this! You must and shall obey me! Oh, what a curse is an ungrateful child! And to think till within an hour I had been deceiving myself with the idea that my daughter, my only daughter, loved me, and was obedient to my wishes."

Poor Juliette sobbed as if her heart would break.

She approached her father, and would have kissed
him, but he haughtily waved her away. "No," he
exclaimed, "not until you promise to give up forever
your absurd, insane idea of obtaining notoriety by the
course you mention, will I accept your caresses. Go,
child, before I shower curses on your head; and remember that you have caused your father a sleepless
night." He groaned aloud, but, at a fierce gesture,
his weeping daughter desisted from urging him, and
turned in sorrow from the room.

Hurrying through her toilet, she evaded Eliza's anxious inquiries, and, dismissing her from the chamber,
sought relief in prayer. Notwithstanding her deep
distress at her father's conduct, her heart was more at
rest than it had been for months. "I have done my
duty," she exclaimed, with streaming eyes. "I have
sacrificed my father's affection to my love for my Saviour, and still I can say, 'Though he slay me, yet
will I trust him.'"

It would be difficult to describe the tumult that
raged in Mr. Fearing's breast after his daughter left
him. As I said in the commencement of this chapter,
the conduct of his son had given him great anxiety.
He could not understand why Henry, situated similarly
to himself at the same age, could not resist the temptations by which he was surrounded, — why the gam-
bling-saloons, and all the haunts of iniquity, from which
he had shrunk with contempt and loathing, should lead
another captive at their will. Within a few weeks he
had paid large sums to redeem Henry's debts of honor,

as he falsely termed them, and his headache on the
present occasion arose mainly in consequence of a
stormy interview with his son, in which he positively
refused to advance another dollar for such a purpose.
He tried, as we have seen, to shake off the thought
of his son, and enjoy the affectionate care of his
daughter. If she had only then been aware of it,
she could scarcely have chosen a more unfavorable
opportunity for her confession. After she left him,
he strode fiercely across the spacious apartment, almost
ready to curse the day he was born. "Who can it
be," he asked himself again and again, "that has
dared to influence my child to an act like this? A
profession of religion, indeed! As if I would allow a
daughter of mine to go before a public assembly to
proclaim herself a sinner, and all that sort of foolery!
Pshaw! Religion is only a sham. In all my experience, there are no greater cheats, none who are so
ready to take advantage of their fellows, as these same
fanatics in religion. As I have often heard my father
say, they will pray in the corners of the streets if men
will be fools enough to listen; they will talk long and
loud of their piety, their benevolence, their purity; and
yet no greater scamps can be found on the face of the
earth. Religion is a cloak to hide their enormities. I
see it all now. Mrs. Osborn (how I have been deceived
in her!) persuaded my poor, timid Juliette into embracing her views, thinking that she would thus induce me to
leave her longer under her care. I am sure, if she had
been left alone, she would have been a child after my

10

own heart. I don't know that I should object to the lady trying her power with Henry. A little sobering of his senses would not hurt him at present. But Juliette!"—

Mr. Fearing, like many others, considered a certain degree of religion as adding to his respectability, but greatly deprecated the idea of being considered righteous overmuch.

Here the father's feelings began to soften, as he recalled all his daughter's acts of dutiful affection. The agony he had experienced during her recent sickness flashed upon his memory, and he sighed heavily as he said, half-aloud, "If I violently oppose her wishes in this respect, she may be taken from me. Poor little thing! I wonder what she would say if I were to give my consent after all. I can conceive just how her eyes would beam with pleasure, and how earnestly she would say, 'Dear father, I will be such a loving daughter to you that you will never regret this kindness.' Foolish and absurd as I consider her, I have no doubt she attaches the utmost consequence to this public profession, as she calls it. 'Ask me to do anything but that,' she said; 'I can die; but I can't deny my Saviour.' Well, I really did not believe she had so much spunk; but let women alone where their will is concerned. Some are just as strenuous about a new set of jewelry, a fashionable hat, or new style of cloak, whatever it may be; if you oppose them, the cry is, 'Anything but that.' "

At a late hour he retired to his couch, which, as he

had anticipated, was a sleepless one. The great question
to be decided was this: "Shall I yield my wishes, or
require her to do so?" Many times her amiable temper, her sweet, winning manners, her frank, artless affection for him, almost determined him to offer no obstacle, if she still persisted in thinking it a duty to profess Christ. But that iron will which had seldom been
successfully opposed, how could it yield now, and to a
mere child? When the morning dawned he had determined upon his course, which we shall learn from the
events that followed.

CHAPTER XII.

"Walk
Boldly and wisely in the light thou hast:
There is a hand above will help thee on."

JULIETTE, whose pillow had been wet with her tears, arose early, and passed more than her usual time in private devotion. She truly felt the need of an Almighty arm to support her in this hour of distress. Eliza begged her to return to bed, and allow her to bring a cup of chocolate to the chamber; but she declined, though she actually started when she caught a glimpse of her pale, haggard face in the mirror.

When she entered the breakfast-room she found her father there, engaged in reading a hasty note from H——, informing him of his mother's relapse, and requesting him to come to her without delay.

He started up when his daughter entered, and gave her the note to read; then led her to the table, evidently pained by the marks her countenance bore of her late excitement.

"I should like to go with you," she said, raising her eyes timidly to his.

"It will depend wholly on yourself whether you do so," he answered, impressively, with a glance at the

112

attendants. "I will talk with you on the subject after breakfast."

After this, she could scarcely do more than to raise the cup to her lip. With all her soul she shrank from another encounter like that of the preceding night. When the mere form of eating was concluded, Mr. Fearing said, "Will you come to the library for a few minutes?" She followed him in silence, her heart sending up a prayer to God for help to be faithful to him.

He drew a chair for her near the table, and, avoiding her eye, said, "As you may well suppose, my daughter, your sudden and unexpected avowal last night caused me the keenest regret and displeasure. Probably I was too harsh in my expression of it, and I have asked you here that we may have a calm and dispassionate conversation on the subject."

Juliette's countenance brightened, and, looking at him affectionately, she said, "Thank you, sir; that is what I should like." She then, at his request, gave him a brief account of her wishes, the length of time she had entertained them, and the means she had adopted for their accomplishment, carefully avoiding any mention of Mrs. Folsom's influence.

He was moved by her frank avowal, though he endeavored to appear indifferent, and then said, "I wish to make two propositions to you, but the answer to them may be deferred till my return from H——, unless you at once decide upon acceding to the first, in which case I should like to have you accompany me

10*

there and remain with your grandmother as long as you choose. It is this. That you give up these foolish notions you imbibed from Mrs. Osborn, and accompany me to Europe in the next steamer, where we shall at once join Horace, and travel in connection with his party."

"And what is the other?" she faltered, as he paused, pressing her hand upon her heart.

"It is this. Go forward as you expressed your determination to do, and make yourself a byword and reproach. Let the finger of scorn be pointed at you as the ungrateful, disobedient child; and my house can no longer be your home. I shall disinherit you at once, and you must no longer look to me for protection."

While he was speaking, Juliette was obliged to clutch the chair for support. The color faded from her cheeks and lips, and her father feared she would fall. She raised her eyes to heaven, and with a quivering voice feebly articulated: "Even so, Father, for so it seemeth good in thy sight."

Mr. Fearing, not understanding the import of her words, but, fearing from her manner that she refused to obey him, exclaimed in a sharp, impatient tone, "You cannot realize what it will be to be thrown upon the world for protection; you, who have been brought up in the lap of luxury, to earn your daily bread. Think well before you decide. Obey your father, which is a duty enforced in your Bible, and share my fortune equally with your brother, have every wish of your heart gratified, and my unbounded gratitude and affection. Disobey me, and be an outcast from your home and from society, a disgrace to all connected with you. I leave for H——in an hour; when I return, I shall expect your final answer."

"Father!" the tone was heart-rending; "I need no delay. The trial you force upon me may, indeed, prove my death; but I cannot give up my Saviour. No! even if I leave home, kindred, and friends, to follow him. This is my answer;" and, with a flood of tears, she attempted to rise and leave the apartment.

"Rash, mad, unthinking girl!" he cried, seizing her hand to detain her; "but I will not waste words with you. Reflect well before you decide. I will not accept your answer until my return."

He walked hastily from the room, leaving the poor girl so faint and trembling that she could scarcely gain her own apartment.

Nearly an hour later, she heard her father's voice in the hall, and with a sudden resolve went out to meet him. He stopped and gazed eagerly at her, hoping she had come to retract her decision. Her face was pale, and fixed as marble, though her eyes were brilliant as if lighted by fever. "Good-by, dear father," she murmured, softly. "Will you kiss me once more?"

"Never!" he exclaimed, angrily, "until you can learn to obey me."

With a sharp cry of pain, as if he had struck her, she turned wearily away, and entered her boudoir.

Before he reached the foot of the staircase, he turned back with a mighty longing to hold her once to his heart, but pride forbade, and he hastened on.

During the long hours of that terrible day, Juliette lay upon her bed, stunned with the awful blow that had fallen upon her. She tried to rouse herself, and endeavor to form some plan for the future, but was totally unable to connect her thoughts. Eliza was fully convinced that her young mistress was about to have another attack of brain fever, and was strenuous in her plea that Dr. M—— ought at once to be summoned. Toward night the young girl fell into a light slumber, from which she awoke more composed. Sometimes she resolved to send for Mrs. Folsom, or her pastor, to come to her aid; but always unaccustomed to act for herself, she dared not take such a step. Then she determined to visit Mrs. Osborn, and obtain her assistance in some plan for self-support. But this she knew would incense her father, and was given up. She at length arose from her bed, and having taken some slight refreshment, sat down to read a portion of Scripture. She opened the book, and her eyes fell upon these words: "Though I walk in the midst of trouble thou wilt revive me; thou shalt stretch forth thine hand against the wrath of mine enemies, and thy right hand shall save me." "Cast thy burden upon the Lord, and he shall sustain thee."

"Yes," she repeated, "I will trust thy gracious word. I have no earthly arm to lean upon; but my Father in heaven will never leave me nor forsake me." Once more she bowed the knee and committed herself to his care, and then returning to her couch, her exhausted nature found refreshment in sleep.

The stars were still shining when she awoke, confused with the vague remembrance of some painful event; but presently the incidents of the previous day rushed into her mind. In imagination she once more beheld her father placing before her the temptations of the world to allure her from her Saviour: a beautiful country home, and a journey through foreign lands. She knew she had done right; but oh! what might Horace think when told she had refused to join him? She buried her face in her hands, and wept bitter, *bitter* tears as she realized that she might never see him more.

"Oh, why, why must I give up all my friends? My trial is greater than I can bear!" For a few moments, the thought of all she was about to resign,—a luxurious home, a high position in society,—which, though she had never valued it much, seemed alluring now that she was about to exchange it for poverty and contempt,—her dear friends, her pastor, and the church of which she was about to become a member,—all this overwhelmed her with anguish. She wept convulsively, bathing her pillow with her tears. But in the midst of her distress, she seemed to hear a sweet voice saying, "Blessed are ye when men shall hate you, and when they shall separate you from their company, and shall reproach you, and cast out your name as evil, for the Son of man's sake. Rejoice

ye in that day and leap for joy; for behold, your
reward is great in heaven."

Poor, afflicted, yet happy girl! what blessed peace
and joy filled thy soul! She lay for some time, her
hands folded on her breast, musing on these precious
words, as the gracious Spirit unfolded their true import: "These afflictions are but for a day, and thy
quiet submission to them shall be rewarded with an
eternity of bliss." Her tears ceased to flow, and she
was able to collect her thoughts for the formation of
some plan of action. Her father might return at any
hour, when a repetition of the scenes of yesterday
could only result in his increased displeasure. Juliette felt it to be her duty to place herself out of the
way of temptation. She had already chosen her path;
and she would write him that it was her final decision
to follow her Saviour, even though it led her far away
from the protecting care of one who was bound to
cherish and support her.

Having resolved to leave home, it was wonderful
how easy everything appeared. She rang her bell,
and directed Eliza to pack into a trunk what would be
necessary for an absence of a few months, selecting
the simplest articles from her wardrobe; and in the
mean time was pleased to find that her last allowance
from her father remained untouched. A few tears
were shed as she recalled the words of Horace: "If
anything should occur, dear sister, remember that I
have an ample fortune, and I expect to share it with
you." When the trunk was ready, she ordered break-

fast in her boudoir; and when the waiting-maid had gone to hers, she passed the time in selecting some valuable jewelry, given her by her grandparents and brother Horace, which she locked in her dressing-case, and crowded into the bottom of her trunk.

Eliza, who was extremely fond of her mistress, looked exceedingly grave as she found her already arrayed in her travelling dress, and ventured to ask whether she might not accompany her.

This question quite unnerved poor Juliette, who had been fortifying her mind against the dreadful thought of going alone, she knew not whither. For one instant she determined to take her, but then rejected the plan as unwise. "You have been a good girl, Eliza," she said; "I shall never forget your kindness to me while I was sick." She selected the largest ring from her finger and added, "Wear this for my sake."

After ascertaining that Henry was sleeping off the effects of his night's dissipation, she gave up the idea of seeing him, but determined to write her farewell. Then, sending word to Peter that she should wish the carriage in an hour, she sat down and wrote her father as follows, —

"MY DEARLY BELOVED FATHER, — Never have you seemed so dear as now, when with streaming eyes I take my pen to bid you a long farewell. The memory of all your love, your tender care during my recent illness, your constant acts of affection rush over me with almost overpowering force;

but I am about to leave you. Yes, you have placed this alternative before me, and, in compliance with my Saviour's commands, I must leave all and follow him. I had vainly fancied that by my dutiful affection I might win from you the privilege of acting as my conscience dictates, and yet remain under your roof. Oh, how ardently have I longed and prayed for this! But that hope has gone forever, and nothing remains but for me to submit. I go forth ignorant of the ways of the world, and not knowing whither to direct my steps; but my trust is in God, who has promised to sustain, strengthen me, and comfort my poor, trembling heart. Could I believe that my daily and nightly prayers for you would be answered, and that the love and peace of God would fill your soul, even as amidst the keen anguish of parting from all I hold dear, they do my own, I could praise him through all eternity.

"When you write Horace, will you give him the best wishes of his sister's heart?

"Dear, dear father, farewell.

"Your loving, weeping

"JULIETTE."

"When my father returns give him this," she said to Eliza, who stood tearfully obeying her last orders. The servants collected at the door, tears glistening in their eyes, and uttering remonstrances against her sudden departure. She caught Mrs. Cummings by the hand and tried to speak, but could not command her voice. They all felt that something was amiss;

but no one dared utter the suspicion; and, with a hasty glance around the loved home of her childhood, she hastened down the steps, and was almost lifted by Peter into the carriage.

"Where shall I drive, miss?" he asked, putting his head in at the window.

"Take me to the Harlem cars," she faltered in an almost inarticulate tone.

Throwing herself back in the carriage in all the abandonment of grief, one line in a favorite song, in connection with this terrible parting, continually recurred to her mind, —

"It may be for years, and it may be forever."

After this she seemed like one walking in a dream. She had a vague remembrance that Peter asked her if he should buy a ticket for New Haven, that he placed one in her hand and also a check for her trunk; but she was stupefied with grief, and rode on mile after mile, unable sufficiently to compose herself to decide upon her future course.

11

CHAPTER XIII.

"My conscience hath a thousand several tongues,
And every tongue brings in a several tale,
And every tale condemns me for a villain."

ON the morning of the third day after his daughter's departure, a note came from Mr. Fearing, addressed to her. Mrs. Cummings was half distracted at this confirmation of her fears that he was not aware of her absence. At last, trembling with dread of his displeasure, she tore open the envelope, and read the enclosed note, in order to decide whether it was her duty to inform him of the sad event.

The hasty lines were evidently written while his heart was subdued by grief, and were as follows, —

"My beloved Daughter, — I write from your grandmother's room, which I have scarcely left for a moment. The physician has now informed us that she cannot survive many hours. She has just expressed a wish to see you once more. If you take the next boat you may possibly find her alive. Dear child, I long to see you and fold you in my arms. Try to banish every hard thought, and remember that I love you, and *under all circumstances*, will endeavor to make you happy.

"Edward Fearing."

122

"What shall I do?" exclaimed the anxious house-keeper to Eliza, who stood pale and trembling at her side. "He thinks her safe at home. I wish Mr. Horace were here, or even Mr. Henry, to relieve me of the responsibility of acting by myself. I must either go or write, and have only an hour to decide which." Presently she rang the bell and directed Peter to have the carriage at the door as quickly as possible, when, hastily arraying herself in a riding-dress, she told him to carry her to Mrs. Folsom's.

The lady was engaged in writing, but came at once when she learned who wished to see her.

"Excuse me for calling, madam," began the visitor, in a strange, hurried manner; "but Miss Juliette suddenly left home two days ago. We all thought there was something wrong about it, and to-day this letter comes to her from her father."

Mrs. Folsom read the letter in silence. She alone possessed the knowledge which might explain the young girl's conduct. Her cheek flushed with indignation as the possible meaning of the underscored words flashed through her mind; but this was no time to give it vent. "You must go to him at once," she said, firmly.

"I dare not be the one to tell him," cried the house-keeper in alarm. "At such a time, too, it would kill him."

"Write then, write immediately, or it will be too late; stay, I will write in your name; what shall I say?"

"Oh, whatever you please. Eliza says her mistress directed her to pack clothes enough to last several months."

Mrs. Folsom pressed her hand to her head uncertain whether to inform Mr. Fearing of the absence of Juliette, or to request him to return without delay. Putting her pen to paper she rapidly traced the following words, —

"MR. FEARING, — I opened your letter, as your daughter is away from home. Please return as soon as possible.

"SARAH CUMMINGS."

Contrary to the expectation of the physician, Mrs. Fearing lingered until toward morning, and then sank away into the sleep that knows no waking. Several times, in the course of the day and night, she inquired whether her grand-daughter had arrived, and expressed disappointment in not seeing her.

Calling her son to the bed, she motioned for him to put his ear to her mouth, and then with difficulty uttered these words: "Tell Juliette that I loved her and left her my blessing. She is to have all my wardrobe and jewels; but all I have can never repay her for her earnest prayers for me. Tell her I died resting on Christ."

She paused and seemed greatly exhausted, but presently added : "Dear Edward, there is nothing can reconcile me to death, but Christ. He —" A fit of coughing interrupted her, and she never resumed her sentence.

When it was announced that all was over, her son rushed from the chamber and locked himself in his own apartment. "This, then," he exclaimed to himself, "is the source from whence my mother derived that peace and resignment which has filled me with wonder. There must be a reality and power in religion that I never imagined. Ah, my poor Juliette!"

The ensuing hour was one he never forgot. Remorse for the course he had pursued toward his children, — for in that dreadful heart-scrutiny he feared he had sinned as much in not restraining his son, as in his cruel taunts to his daughter, — and terror at the idea that the grim messenger might even now be on the wing to summon him to his dread account, struggled for mastery in his breast. Then his thoughts turned to Juliette. He wondered that she had not obeyed his summons. How disappointed she would be in finding herself too late!

In the midst of all these thoughts the haughty man was pleased that the sad affliction which had befallen him would give him the opportunity, he now really desired, to retract what he had last said to her. He could even anticipate the grateful affection that she would lavish upon him, as he consented to her living the life of a Christian.

A low knock at his door startled him. He approached it, expecting to see Juliette, but it was only a servant, who put a note in his hands with the addi-

11*

tional information that it ought to have been delivered the day before.

It was not even in Juliette's well-known writing. He tore it open, vexed at himself for a feeling of anxiety; but had scarcely glanced at its contents, when he cried aloud, "Juliette away from home! What can it mean?"

He crushes the note in his hand, and begins to walk the room. Of course she is only absent, making a call perhaps on her friend, Mrs. Folsom. He looks at his watch. "It is not too late for her to come by the morning boat. But why does Mrs. Cummings wish me to return? At such an hour she must be aware that I cannot leave this place. I fear there is something more than meets the eye."

In accordance with a hasty resolve, he goes below stairs, where he finds Dr. Morrison endeavoring to comfort his father. Calling him aside, he inquires whether any arrangements have been made for the funeral, saying he would send an undertaker from the city.

"But surely you will not leave your father until after the funeral," urged the doctor.

"I expected Juliette. I have received this," faltered the distressed man.

Dr. Morrison glanced at the crumpled note. "Probably Henry has had another attack of delirium, which has frightened the good woman," he remarked. "That boy will kill himself, unless you put him under restraint."

"Yes, that must be the case," exclaimed Mr. Fearing, with a sigh of relief. "I forbade Juliette to enter his room on a former occasion, and, like a dutiful child, she has now absented herself. Her mind and heart are too pure for such a scene."

By the time he reached New York, he had succeeded in convincing himself that it was wholly on Henry's account he was summoned home. Mrs. Cummings recognized his hasty ring, and, before Rufus, the porter, could answer any question, presented herself tremblingly before him.

"Where is my daughter?" was his first eager inquiry.

With her handkerchief at her eyes, the woman answered, "She has not yet returned."

"Returned! From what place? Where has she gone?"

"Ah, sir! that is what we do not know. She left the morning after you did. Now I think of it, Eliza has a note for you, which, no doubt, will explain."

"Tell her to bring it to me."

Struggling for calmness, he entered the parlor, and languidly threw himself into a seat. The letter, addressed to "My dearly beloved father," was in his hands, but he could not summon courage to open it. "Bring me a glass of wine," said he to Eliza who lingered, longing to hear something concerning her young mistress. When he had drank it, he added, "Tell Mrs. Cummings that my mother died this morning, and that no one is to be admitted."

The note has been already given to the reader, and
it may well be imagined, in the softened state of Mr.
Fearing's heart, what its effect would be upon him.
Sorrow and bitter remorse had begun their work. For
three days and nights he had watched beside his mother's couch, snatching a few moments of sleep in a lol-
ling-chair at her side; but he had scarcely thought of
fatigue. Now, when he needed all his strength and
clearness of thought, he found himself weak and helpless as a child. His brain whirled; he clung to the
side of the chair for support, and presently, with a
loud crash, he fell forward upon the floor.

The porter was the first one who reached him, and,
with a sharp scream for help, tried to raise his master
to a sitting posture. Other servants rushing in, he was
laid gently upon the lounge, Mrs. Cummings ordering
Peter to go at once for Dr. M——.

At this command, Mr. Fearing opened his eyes and
made a gesture of dissent. "I was faint," he spoke
with difficulty. "I shall be well, shortly. Mrs. Cummings, will you order a cup of coffee to the library?
I have eaten no breakfast." Feebly raising himself,
he endeavored to walk across the room, but was obliged
to lean upon the arm of Rufus. "Leave me," said he,
as the servant brought him a plate of hot rolls with
his second cup of coffee. "I can eat nothing more."
He arose and locked the door, feeling as if the weight
of years had fallen upon him. "O Juliette! Juliette!" he groaned aloud; "child of my heart, come
back to me. My beloved daughter, I will never thwart

you more." He extended his arms, while his protruded eyeballs seemed fastened upon the door; but no light step was heard approaching; no graceful form timidly sought his embrace; nothing could be heard but the wild beating of his own desolate heart, echoing to the thought, "She has gone from me! gone forever!"

Once more he opened and perused her letter, every word of which was like a dagger piercing his inmost soul. Not one expression of anger, not one sigh of complaint. "Father, you have placed this alternative before me; you bid me choose between my luxuriant home, blessed by your affection, and my crucified Saviour. I love you, father; but I dare not sacrifice my soul, which Christ shed his precious blood to save." Oh! those soft, pleading, earnest eyes, which were upturned to his face, when she uttered similar words, how clearly they were daguerreotyped on his memory! how had he resisted their eloquent entreaties!

At length, with a mighty effort at self-control, he rang the bell, and directed Eliza to be sent to him. From her he learned all that has been narrated to the reader connected with his daughter's departure from home, and the fact stated by Peter, that he had seen her on board the Harlem cars.

At this last intelligence, Mr. Fearing started to his feet, exclaiming, in an eager tone of delight, "Without doubt, she is with Mrs. Osborn. What a fool I have been, not to surmise this before! I will follow her at once, and see her before I sleep."

He was hastening to the door; but, before he reached it, staggered, and would have fallen, but for Eliza's assistance.

"My long watching has unnerved me," he said, apologizing for his weakness, as she led him to the sofa. "I cannot go myself. Tell Peter to go to the store, and ask the head-clerk to come here directly, prepared to go out of town for the night."

The afternoon car for New Haven left at five. There would be abundant time to reach it, and also to attend to preparations for his mother's funeral. While Peter was gone, he bade Eliza bring him his writing-desk, and with a trembling hand penned the following words, —

"Come back, my daughter, to your father's arms. Come back; and there shall be no more dissension between us."

Ah, how many months and years of anguish might have been spared, could she have received that short epistle! But I must not anticipate.

In less than two hours, the clerk, whose name was Hooper, reached D——, and lost no time in proceeding to Mrs. Osborn's school. Upon sending his name as a clerk of Mr. Fearing, the lady instantly appeared.

"Is Miss Fearing with you?" he asked.

"I am somewhat surprised at your question," replied the lady, drawing herself up with some dignity, as she recalled her last interview with Mr. Fearing. "I have never seen my former pupil since her father took her away, last autumn."

"Nevertheless, madam, my employer sent me here with a note to his daughter, whom he believed to be in your family."

Mrs. Osborn's countenance began to express anxiety as well as surprise. "How long has she been absent from home?" was her eager, hurried inquiry.

"I did not ascertain. Mr. Fearing has just returned from the country. His mother died early this morning, and, upon his return to the city to make preparations for the funeral, he found her absent. It is to inform her of this sad event, I was sent to find her. At least, this is what I inferred, though I acknowledge there is a mystery about her absence, and her father's ill-concealed anxiety in consequence of it."

The lady sat gazing thoughtfully at the speaker, the shadow deepening on her face. "Was the young lady in good health?" at length she inquired.

"She has never looked strong since her severe and dangerous illness early in the season. It occurred just after Mr. Everett sailed for Europe, and rumor connected the events together."

"Strange, that I never heard of it," faltered Mrs. Osborn, half aloud; "but where can my poor Juliette be?"

Mr. Hooper then gave the lady an account of the brilliant success of the young heiress during the past winter, — the parties and balls made for her benefit, — the grace and dignity with which she presided over her father's elegant mansion, and the excitement her beauty and artlessness had occasioned among the bon ton.

The lady was more pained than she cared to express to a stranger. That her beloved pupil should create a sensation was what she had easily prophesied; but had she passed this ordeal without endangering her own soul? Suppressing her emotion, she inquired, "When shall you leave for New York?"

"As early as possible. It seems important that Mr. Fearing should know I have failed in meeting his daughter here."

"Certainly. Why not take the midnight train?"

"I was not aware that there was a train till morning; but I shall do so, without fail."

"Mr. Hooper, you are a stranger to me; but I am about to ask of you a favor. Miss Fearing was committed to my care by her dying mother, who was my dear friend. She was with me for years; but since she left, I have received but one letter from her, in answer to a score that I have sent. Your errand causes me the greatest anxiety, and I must beg of you to write me, or suggest to her to do so, that I may be relieved of my solicitude on her behalf."

"With pleasure, madam. You may expect to hear from me within a week;" and, taking leave of her, he returned to the hotel to wait the arrival of the cars.

The agony of Mr. Fearing may be better imagined than described, when, at the earliest hour he could gain admission, Mr. Hooper called to announce the entire want of success in his mission.

He sat upright in bed, gazing in the face of his clerk, as if he could scarcely comprehend his words;

but presently rousing himself, called out, in a loud voice, "Quick, let no time be lost. Send for the chief of police!"

Sooner than could have been expected, the gentleman made his appearance, and was immediately put in possession of the facts, as far as concerned the young lady's departure.

His cool, self-possessed air, and the confident tone in which he said, "We'll find trace of her before night," went far to tranquillize the almost distracted parent. One after another, the servants were called, and underwent a close examination as to the minutest circumstances, the officer carefully noting in a small book whatever he deemed of importance. Then, after a full description of her personal appearance and dress, accompanied by a miniature of Juliette, he turned to Mr. Fearing, with the remark, "Probably you are aware of some cause your daughter may have had in leaving your protection. Without any desire to be impertinent, I ought to inform you that were I acquainted with the facts, it would aid me much in my search; for instance, had she an unfortunate attachment?"

"Nothing of the kind," returned Mr. Fearing, with an indignant flush, as he realized that his cruelty had subjected her to such a suspicion. His voice changed, and his countenance grew pale, as he added, "There was a reason, as you suppose. I was unwilling she should make a profession of religion, and in order to force a compliance with my wishes, threatened, if she

disobeyed me, to withdraw my support and protection.
I need not tell you," faltered the distressed man, "that
this was but a threat, and that I regret it most
keenly."

No one could doubt this who witnessed his ghastly
countenance, from which cold drops were constantly
exuding; certainly the chief of police did not. Without a word of comment he reiterated his expectation
of finding the lost one, and left the house.

With him departed all the father's new-born hopes.
Imagination was rife with the most dreadful visions,
while the tooth of remorse gnawed painfully at his
heart. He scarcely thought of his mother's decease;
or, if for a moment it flashed through his mind, it was
succeeded by a feeling of relief that she could not
share in this terrible anxiety. He called loudly for
Horace, cursing himself that his illness prevented his
personal participation in the search; but turned
fiercely upon Henry when he offered his services.
Toward night his excitement became so alarming that
Mrs. Cummings assumed the responsibility of sending
for Dr. M——, who immediately insisted that his
patient should take a powerful anodyne.

Though it was scarcely possible that anything could
be learned of the poor wanderer until the arrival of
the evening cars, yet the slightest noise, — the ring
of the door-bell, the stopping of a carriage, — caused
Mr. Fearing to tremble with emotion. Fixing his
keen eyes upon every one who entered his chamber,

he yet feared to ask a question lest the awful ap-
prehensions of his mind should be realized.

> " O conscience ! into what abyss of fears
> And horrors hast thou driven me ; out of which
> I find no way, from deep to deeper plunged."

CHAPTER XIV.

"None have accused thee; 'tis thy conscience cries,
The witness in the soul that never dies;
Its accusation, like the moaning wind
Of wintry midnight, moves thy startled mind;
Oh, may it melt thy hardened soul, and pour
From out thy frozen heart life evermore!"

HENRY FEARING, who needed the most power-ful motives to induce him to leave his boon com-panions, was now completely sobered by this accumula-tion of trials. His grandmother deceased, his sister a homeless wanderer, his father distracted with horrible forebodings, it became him to act his part like a man. The servants, who had hitherto regarded him with ill-concealed contempt, now looked with wonder upon him as he stood consulting with their kind physician, and attending to the business necessary to be done. As-certaining from Mr. Hooper that an undertaker was to be sent from the city, he also despatched one of his father's clerks to H—— to inform his grandfather there of his illness, and afford what aid might be needful.

It was nearly six o'clock when a loud, decided ring at the door-bell seemed to announce tidings either of good or of evil. An officer was admitted, sent by the chief of police, whom Henry, according to directions, accompanied at once to his father's chamber.

Mr. Fearing was dressed, and reclining on a lounge. On seeing the gentleman he started to his feet, but immediately sank back trembling with fear.

"Speak," he exclaimed hoarsely; "have you found her?"

"We think we have got upon the right track," answered the man. "But if you will allow me, I will give you the particulars."

Henry drew a chair for the officer opposite his father's lounge, when he proceeded,—

"With your daughter's miniature and a full description of her dress in my hand, I took the Harlem cars for New Haven. A young miss travelling alone, her eyes red with weeping, was observed by the conductor, who remembered the day in consequence of some questions about her trunk. She told him she was unused to the care of baggage, and begged his assistance in having it sent to the place where she intended to stop."

Mr. Fearing breathed a deep sigh of relief, while Eliza's tears flowed freely, as she exclaimed, "Oh, I'm sure that is my dear mistress!"

With a gesture of impatience from the excited father, the officer went on. "I had no doubt I was on the right track, and having noted in my pocket-book the name and number of the street where the young miss wished to go, I showed the picture to the conductor. But he had only caught a glimpse of her face, dis-

12*

figured by excessive weeping, and failed to recognize
it. The dress, as nearly as he could recollect, answered to the description.

"On reaching New Haven I went directly to E——
street, and inquired whether a young lady by the
name of Fearing was staying there. 'No,' was the
prompt reply. At this answer I stepped inside the
door, and informed the servant that I had business of
importance with her mistress. I was well aware that
a lady might, for reasons of her own, take a feigned
name, and I determined not to rest satisfied until I had
seen her. The lady of the house presently made her
appearance, when I arose and introduced myself. 'A
young miss,' I said, 'left New York on Tuesday of
this week. I have traced her to this house, and shall
be greatly obliged if you will allow me to see her.'

"Without a word of comment (a woman of sense
she was), she stepped to the door and called 'Alice;'
when a pretty girl tripped down the stairs and entered
the door."

Mr. Fearing caught his handkerchief and held it to
his eyes, while tears, the first he had shed, trickled
through his fingers.

"Well, sir!" cried Henry, impatiently.

"I was informed Miss Fearing wore her hair short
and curling; this Alice, as they called her, had
abundant tresses, twisted into a large knot at the back
of her head."

"Then it was not our Juliette, after all." Henry

spoke indignantly, while his father groaned and sobbed aloud.

"They were very curious to know why I wished to see her; and I told them sufficient for my purpose.

"Miss Alice started up, her face aglow with excitement! 'I think I can help you,' she said. 'A beautiful girl occupied the same seat with me, and, while I wept, she kindly took my hand. I noticed she sighed often. I told her I was hastening to a friend who was very ill. The tears came to her eyes as she replied, — ".I, too, have bitter trials; but our heavenly Father sends them to us in love to draw us to him."'"

Mr. Fearing's sobs ceased; he gazed in the face of the officer as for his life.

"That sounds like my dear mistress," muttered Eliza.

The officer continued.

"'Did she look like this?' I asked, presenting the picture. 'Her countenance was much more sad,' she answered, in a tone of disappointment, 'but not really unlike it after all. She sat at my side, so I could not look her in the face; but I think she must have been the one. When the cars reached New Haven, I asked where she was going; and I remember now that I thought her somewhat embarrassed, as she answered, "I am not sure, but I think I shall go as far as Boston."'

"All this time she held the picture in her hands, and said, 'I see more likeness the longer I look at it; but her eyes were not so bright, and her face was thinner.'

'Miss Fearing has been sick,' I said, 'which might account for that. Did you notice her dress?' 'Not particularly, I was so much absorbed in my own grief; but I think she wore a genteel travelling dress; and I remember she had a very small foot, neatly cased in a boot of the same color as her dress. She tried to make it stay on the foot-rest, but it kept slipping off.'

"I thanked the young miss, and, having gained all the information in my power, I joined my associate at the depot, repeated to him what I had learned, and despatched him to Boston, while I returned to prosecute more particular inquiries between New Haven and New York. I authorized him to employ as many of the Boston police as were necessary to effect his purpose, and promised to join him to-morrow, unless he telegraphs me that he has succeeded in his search. There is only one fact which prevents me from fully concurring in the opinion of Miss Alice, and that is this, — her trunk was checked to New Haven, and would, of course, be taken out there unless the check was changed, and this I thought the lady would not think of except at the suggestion of the conductor. I determined to sift this before I advanced a step further.

"First I went to the baggage-master; but he remembered no such exchange, so I had nothing to do but to wait for the conductor. He eagerly inquired about my success, when I told him all that had occurred. He rubbed his head, and tried to recall any such circumstance; said if I had inquired the next day he might possibly have remembered it; but young ladies unused to travelling were so much in the habit of asking his advice, he could not fix upon one individual with certainty."

As the officer paused, Mr. Fearing sank back, the color receding from his face and lips, leaving his countenance of a ghastly pallor.

Henry started forward and offered him a glass of water; but he waved him away, and pressed his hands tightly upon his heart.

The officer rose to take leave, but waited a moment, as if wishing to add a word to what he had already said. Mr. Fearing's distress, however, prevented, and, motioning Henry to the door, he said, "I have thought it barely possible that your sister may have regretted her hasty step, and returned in the next train to New York. Have you no friends with whom she would be likely to seek protection?"

"A capital idea!" exclaimed the young man. "What steps would you advise?"

"To send at once to each and every house where her more intimate friends reside."

"But this would give publicity to her flight."

"Which cannot possibly be avoided," returned the officer, emphatically. "If this does not bring her to light, advertising must be resorted to."

Late in the evening Dr. M—— called, and found Mr. Fearing in a dangerous condition. He ordered powerful draughts to the feet, and quieting powders repeated until sleep was induced. It was really painful to see this strong man submitting so passively to

the will of others. At first he seemed surprised that
his son should assume so much authority; but after a
while was uneasy when the young man left the room.

The next day the funeral of Mrs. Fearing was to be
attended, and Henry much wished to hear the result
of the search in Boston before starting for H——.
There was no telegram, however, and the officer left
in the early train for that city, having ascertained that
Miss Fearing was not visiting any of her friends in
New York. The next day he and his associate returned, wholly without success; when, after consulta-
tion with Dr. Morrison, who had come to the city with
Henry immediately after the funeral, the latter proceeded to advertise in all the public journals.

The poor distressed father was by this time sunk so
low that fears began to be entertained for his life. His
bereaved father left the new-made grave of his deceased wife and came to weep by the couch of his son.

Once when they were alone, the distracted man
gazed earnestly in his father's face, and with a cry of
horror, exclaimed, "I have killed her! I have killed
her!" And, indeed, terrible suspicions, too vague and
dreadful to be put into words, began to assume an
awful reality, as messengers were despatched to the
dead-house by the chief of police. This gentleman
pursued the search with praiseworthy shrewdness and
zeal, until convinced that it was wholly useless. As it
was now a week since Juliette's departure, her body, in
case it had been recovered, must have been buried-long
ago; and it was by this time beyond recognition.

Dr. M——, who greatly feared the result of this announcement, was gratified, though astonished, to observe that from this hour his patient began slowly to recover strength. Juliette deceased, which he had at last convinced himself must be the case, was not half so terrible to his imagination as Juliette living in poverty or want.

At the end of a month he announced his intention of sailing at once for Europe. The house and furniture were let for two years, the servants dismissed; and, with the impatience which was natural to him, after his plans were formed, Mr. Fearing gave himself no rest until he and his son were ready for embarkation. It is not to be supposed that such events transpiring in the very midst of the aristocracy of New York society, should pass without creating excitement and comment. From time to time certain articles, cautiously worded, appeared in the daily press, hinting at the probable causes of the young lady's sudden absence; but these were carefully kept from the knowledge of the distressed father, by the watchful care of Dr. and Mrs. Morrison, who never left the bereaved husband of their Juliette until he and his son were safely on board the Astracan, bound for Liverpool.

At this time it was nearly two months since the decease of Mrs. Horace Fearing, and the sad events so closely following it; but these months had not passed without effecting a great change both in her son and grandson. Mr. Edward Fearing looked at least ten years older, and there was an appearance of subdued grief upon his countenance never observed there before. His words were few, but they were kind, and often showed that they came from an aching heart. He clung to his son, and seemed to depend so much upon his affection for all the comfort that remained to him, that Henry found it far easier than he had supposed to give up the life of dissipation, the pleasures of which stimulated but never satisfied his unhallowed desires and appetites. In his eye, formerly so bloodshot and blurred, now shone the commencement of manly purpose. There was, to be sure, at times, an almost irresistible craving for strong drink; but his kind friend, Dr. Morrison, assured him that this thirst would become less frequent the longer he abstained from gratifying it, and pointed to present experience to prove that he was already happier, as well as in better health, than when involved in the whirl of sensual indulgence.

During this period several letters had been received from Horace, some of them directed to Juliette. He was unceasingly earnest in his demands for intelligence from his sister, as not one word respecting her had transpired in their correspondence. But no one had the heart to inform him that henceforth she was to be considered as much lost to her friends as the lady whom he styled grandmother, though the place of her sepulchre no one knew.

In that vast city there were two hearts that ached bitterly at this most sad result of their counsels. These were the Reverend Dr. A—— and Mrs. Ward

Folsom. Though neither of them doubted that, whether living or dead, the persecuted girl would never cease to be grateful that she had been enabled by divine grace to forsake father and mother, houses and lands, for the Son of man's sake, knowing that her reward would be great in heaven; yet they wept tears of sorrow at her untimely fate.

13

CHAPTER XV

"The grief that on my spirit preys,
   That rends my heart, that checks my tongue,
I fear will last me all my days,
   But feel it will not last me long."

BUT was the lovely girl really deceased? Had she been called to offer up her young life a sacrifice to her ungodly father's bitter prejudices? Let us go back to the hour when she fled from further temptation, fearing lest in her weakness she might be overcome, and thus virtually deny her Saviour.

She had chosen the Harlem cars simply because it was the route she had last travelled with her father, and led through D——, where Mrs. Osborn's school was located.

Glancing timidly around among the passengers, her attention was arrested by two modest-looking girls who occupied the seat before her. From their conversation she learned that they had been away at school for six months, and were returning home for the first time. Their cheerful anticipations of the cordial welcome they should receive from father, mother, brother, and a certain young man by the name of Dudley Houghton, smote upon the heart of the sorrowing

146

Juliette, with a keen pang. Tears gushed to her eyes, at the bitter thought, "I have no friends to welcome me." She pressed her hands to her breast to stop its wild beating. "Where am I going?" she asked herself, in an agony of emotion. "Alas! alas! I am a poor, homeless wanderer, an outcast for my Saviour's sake."

A low groan caused the young girls to turn around just in time to see that their fellow-passenger was fainting.

In one moment all was confusion and excitement. One gentleman rushed to the next car to summon the conductor, while the ladies searched their pockets for salts or cologne.

It was some minutes before Juliette revived, notwithstanding the vigorous fanning and chafing of her hands by her attentive friends; and then she found herself leaning against the shoulder of an elderly lady, while the young girls who had attracted her attention were sitting opposite, and tenderly holding her hands.

As soon as she could talk, they were very earnest to know the cause of her sudden illness. "Was it the close air of the cars?" They would open the windows; though the lady at her side had objected until she were better.

Poor Juliette, unused to equivocation, could only sigh and shake her head; but as they thoughtlessly urged their inquiries, and volunteered everything in their power for her relief, she said, at length, "I have been very ill, and I suppose I am not so strong as I hoped."

"How far are you going?" inquired the one called Maria.

Juliette had heard them mention Stamford as their native place, and with a sudden impulse named it as her destination.

Maria glanced at her sister, and then said, "How lucky! We are going there, too. Have you friends in Stamford?"

"No," said the young girl, in a sad tone; "I am an entire stranger there. Perhaps you can tell me of some quiet place where I can board until I can arrange my plans."

"Why can't she come with us?" eagerly inquired Susan, the younger girl. "I'm sure she is not well enough to go among strangers. Mother wont object, I know."

Maria hesitated a moment, but meeting Juliette's eyes fixed upon hers with such a wistful expression of entreaty, she answered, "Yes, so she shall."

How little these artless school-girls could realize the relief these words brought to their new companion. With an impulsive motion she caught Susan's hand, and pressed it to her lips, while she inwardly acknowl-. edged the watchful care of her heavenly Father in thus ordering her steps.

"Have you much baggage?" inquired the practical Maria.

"Only one trunk," said Juliette.

"Some one will come for us in the wagon," she continued, in an apologizing tone; "I was only thinking how we could get all our trunks home."

"Oh, we'll manage somehow!" exclaimed Susan. "And if we can't get it all in, there's my largest trunk I sha'n't need for a week. Father or one of the men come to the depot every day or two."

"Only two stations more," responded her sister, gazing eagerly from the window.

"Do you feel better, dear?" inquired the old lady, turning to face her young companion. "I am a little deaf," she added, as Juliette thanked her, and said she was quite well.

"Yes, the color has come back to your lips;" and she patted the pale cheek affectionately.

"Stamford!" shouted the conductor, putting his head within the door.

The girls started to their feet and hastily took down their carpet-bags from the rack. "Here, let me carry yours, too," cried Susan, catching the more stylish one from Juliette's hands. "You run and see to the baggage, Maria, and I'll find father. Have you a check for your trunk, Miss —— "

"My name is Juliette Edwards," responded the young girl, her cheeks burning as she put her check into Susan's hands.

An honest-looking farmer stood near a large covered wagon, his eyes fixed eagerly upon the few passengers who alighted from the cars.

13*

"There's father!" exclaimed Susan, running toward him, followed by Juliette at a short distance.

"How do do, child?" said he, giving her a loud kiss. "Where's Maria?"

"She's seeing to the trunks." The young girl approached nearer, and said a few earnest words in a low tone.

"That's right," he answered heartily.

Susan then led Juliette forward and introduced her.

"Sorry to hear you've been sick, miss," said he, with his honest, friendly voice. "We'll cure you up, though, and put a little color into your cheeks. Here Susan, you stand by the horse, and I'll go and see what's got into Maria."

At this moment the young girl came in sight, walking leisurely by the side of a young man. They were so earnest in conversation that they did not notice the others. Susan laughingly approached them. "How do you do, Dudley?" she asked. She then introduced Miss Edwards, and presently inquired, "Are you going by the farm?"

"Yes," he answered, coloring a little. "I was down this way with our store wagon, and I told your sister if she would ride with me I'd be happy to take her home."

The merry girl glanced at her sister, whose face was suffused with blushes. "Dudley will take my trunks," she said. "The one belonging to Miss Edwards was checked for New Haven, and had to go on; but Dudley found a friend in the cars, who promised to see it taken out and sent back by the next train; so there will be room for all."

The young man insisted, however, upon taking all the baggage, which he could well stow into the back part of his express wagon, and soon drove gayly off with his Maria by his side. In the covered wagon Juliette occupied the back seat, numerous packages from the store being piled up by her side, while Susan sat in front with her father, and asked twenty questions about mother, James, and home, without giving him time to answer.

It was more than two miles from the depot to Mr. Smith's farm; but the country looked beautifully; the peach-trees were full of blossoms, and in front of every house was a neat bed of flowers.

> " The fields did laugh; the flowers did freshly spring;
> The trees did bud, and early blossoms bore,
> And all the choir of birds did sweetly sing."

Juliette's heart echoed Susan's earnest, " Oh, how glad I am to be in the country again ! " She liked all she had seen of her new friends, and thought, if the mother proved as cordial in her welcome as her good husband had been, she should be content to remain with them as long as her funds would permit.

At last the wagon turned up in front of a comfortable farm-house, the sound of the wheels bringing mother and brother to the door. Shading her eyes from the sun, the woman gazed earnestly into the carriage. "That's our Susie," she said to her son; "but who's the other?"

"There's Maria with Dudley," shouted James Smith, just as the first-comers stopped at the door. His hearty, rather boisterous laugh ceased instantly as he caught sight of the pale face on the back seat. With a deep blush he returned Susan's sisterly kiss, and then as she said, turning toward Juliette, "This is my, brother, Miss Edwards," he made an awkward bow, and retreated behind his mother.

Throwing the reins over the back of the horse, Mr. Smith took Juliette's hand and led her toward his wife. "Here is a poor, delicate little flower," he said, "which I have brought for you to tend. I'll warrant, under your care, the lily will shortly turn into a rose."

A keen, searching glance on one side, and an appealing, wistful earnestness on the other, and the homeless wanderer was folded tenderly in the mother's embrace.

Oh, what a rush of grateful joy swelled her breast almost to bursting! "How safe it is to trust in God!" was the language of her heart. "I went out, not knowing whither I went; but He has led me to this place."

While the trunks were being taken from the wagon, Susan began to joke Maria about her ride. Dudley, though with a heightened color, stopped her by saying, "I tried to persuade the conductor to allow Miss Edwards' trunk to be taken out. It was put in with the New Haven baggage. I insisted that we could not be answerable for his mistakes; but it will be back this evening, and I'll see that it's brought here safely."

"It was marked for New Haven, I suppose," exclaimed Juliette, "and my ticket was for that place. I am sorry to give so much trouble, but I have never travelled alone before, and I didn't understand about the stations."

Her manner was slightly embarrassed as she realized that though this was truth, it was not the whole truth.

"Come upstairs," called Susan, gayly. "I'll show you where to put your things. Mother! she'll go in the blue room, I suppose."

"Yes, dear, I'll come presently, and see that all is in order."

When they were alone in their room, the impulsive girl threw her bonnet and mantilla on the bed, and, putting her arm around Juliette's neck, kissed her affectionately. "Oh, dear!" she exclaimed, as the young girl took off her bonnet, disclosing her soft, dark curls; "how funny you do look! just like a little boy!"

"My hair was cut short when I was sick," returned the other. "I had a brain fever. I hardly know what to do with my tresses now."

"I'd give the world if mine curled so!" exclaimed Susan, decidedly. "Why, I'd have it cut off in a minute, if I thought 'twould look so sweetly."

Mrs. Smith, who had entered while they were talking, laid her hand softly on the silky locks, and was much surprised when the grateful girl caught it and pressed it warmly between her own. The good woman had waited below to ascertain something more of the young stranger, and Maria eagerly communicated what had passed in the cars.

"That's all I know," she added, "and I shouldn't have ventured to bring her home if Susan hadn't been so earnest about it."

Mrs. Smith turned an anxious glance upon her husband, but her face brightened again, as he replied, "Take my word for it, wife, she may have been imprudent, but she isn't wicked; not while she can look you straight in the face with those truth-telling eyes. When she clung so lovingly to you, I couldn't help thinking of the good verse, 'Be not forgetful to entertain strangers, for thereby some have entertained angels unawares.'"

"If you would like to take off your riding-dress, Miss Edwards," exclaimed Susan, beginning to disrobe herself, "I can lend you a wrapper till your trunk comes. You're such a tiny thing nothing else of mine will fit you. For my part, I'm so warm I mean to take a good bath."

"Thank you," replied Juliette, warmly; "but I think I shall not be uncomfortable. I shall grow cooler while I wash and arrange my hair."

"Not a very serious job, that," returned Susan, gayly, twining her finger through one of the short curls. "But I must run to my own room, to be ready for dinner. I hope, mother, you've got something real good; I'm dreadfully hungry. Miss Edwards, I shall be right in here; if you want anything, please sing out."

"Call me Juliette, please," responded the young girl, smiling at the gay, easy tone of her companion. To her mind, depressed by her heavy trials, there was something inexpressibly charming in Susan's cordial gayety. Carefully closing and bolting the door to her room, it occupied but a few moments to bathe her face, neck, and arms; and then resuming her travelling habit, she bowed her knee in humble gratitude to her Almighty Friend, who thus far had fulfilled his promise to her, and ordered all things well. With a heart swelling with emotion, she implored blessings on the kind friends who had so cordially received a stranger to their home, and prayed that her residence among them might be productive of great good.

In the mean time, Maria and Dudley had parted for a few hours, and the young lady had joined her mother and sister in the room next to Juliette's. While the latter was arranging her toilet, she could distinctly hear the sound of their voices, as they chattered merrily together.

"Has Dudley gone?" inquired Susan. "It was real good of him to meet us at the depot."

"I thought it likely he would go," rejoined Mrs. Smith, "he asked James so particularly about the time you were expected." She smiled as she glanced at Maria's blushing face, but immediately added, "I wish we knew something more of Miss Edwards, though I think that she looks honest and truthful."

The good woman felt a praiseworthy anxiety that her daughters should not be brought into intimate acquaintance with one whose society might prove injurious, especially with one whose prepossessing appearance and manners might give her an undue influence over them.

Susan began to talk of their school and the teachers, gayly humming a line of her favorite song, —

"There's no place like home."

But Maria, who was hanging her travelling dress in the closet, silenced her sister by placing her finger on her lips, and beckoning her mother to the closet door.

From this place, separated from the next room only by a thin partition, they could hear the low voice of Juliette, uttering her prayer in the ear of her kind Father in heaven. Standing motionless for a moment, the mother's eye glistened through a tear, while Susan's cheek was suffused with a heightened glow, and then each, with a heart subdued by the influence of this pious act, returned to her own duties.

The dinner-bell called Juliette from the window, where she had been feasting her eyes upon the lovely, quiet scene before her. The house stood only a few feet back from the road, but directly beyond was a beautiful orchard of trees, thickly covered with their variously hued blossoms, while still further on a low range of hills skirted the horizon.

" 'Twas a goodly scene.
Yon river, like a silvery snake, lays out
His coil l' th' sunshine lovingly, — it breathes
Of freshness in this lap of flowery meadows."

" Come, Juliette ! " cried Susan, after a low tap at the door. " Father is one of the punctual sort. We must hurry downstairs. Come, a penny for your thoughts."

" I was scarcely thinking at all," returned the young lady, with a smile. " I was enjoying your beautiful home."

The family were gathered about the table as they entered, and while all stood behind their chairs, Mr. Smith solemnly invoked a blessing on their food.

This was a novel mode to the young stranger, whose heart warmed more fondly toward her new friends, when she found them loving her Saviour. Since her illness she had had little appetite ; but now the simple country fare, so deliciously cooked by the matron's own hand, relished so agreeably that it would have been easy for her to echo Susan's hearty exclamation, "O mother, how good your food does taste !" Maria, though a pleasant girl, free from affectation, did not impress our heroine so favorably as the free, outspoken Susan. There was a cordiality and sincerity about the latter which caused a warm glow in the heart. "Perhaps, though, it may be," thought Juliette, "that Maria's mind is absorbed with her friend Dudley."

14

CHAPTER XVI.

"Here too dwelt simple truth; plain innocence;
Unsullied beauty; sound, unbroken youth,
Patient of labor, with a little pleas'd;
Health ever blooming; unambitious toil;
Calm contemplation, and poetic ease."[1]

AFTER dinner the three girls accompanied by their brother wandered all over the farm, visited the bossies in their pen, the hens in their neat rows of coops, where Juliette was delighted with the soft, downy chickens, and even the litter of young pigs in the sty.

James, with many blushes, answered all the questions which the city girl in her ignorance asked, and did not laugh at them as his sisters did. Indeed, he watched every graceful motion of their young visitor with such evident pleasure that Susan could not restrain her love of fun, and playfully pinching his arm whispered, "Isn't she lovely? You must thank me for bringing her home."

"Do you like bread and milk?" inquired the merry girl, as after a few hours they sat around the tea-table.

"I have never eaten any," was Juliette's smiling reply.

"I thought so by the looks of your pale cheeks," remarked the farmer, playfully. "Wife, pour out some

158

milk in a bowl, and don't be sparing of the cream, either. I want to see her looking rosy, like our country girls. Now break into it some of that sweet brown bread, and you'll find it delicious."

"How soon will the honeycombs be ripe, father?" asked Maria. "I always want baked sweet apples in my milk."

"By the last of August, child. The tree hangs full of blossoms."

Juliette made her entire supper of bread and milk, and thought she should enjoy such fare for a month; though the kind mother pressed upon her at least a taste of the preserved cherries, and the light home-made cake.

"I shouldn't think you'd eaten anything for a week," muttered James in his sister's ear, as she allowed her father to heap tarts and cake on her plate.

"Well," she exclaimed, "I should like to have you away at boarding-school for six months, where they only have dry bread and bad butter, with little thin slices of cake. I guess you'd be thankful to come home to mother's fare."

"I'm thankful without going, Susy; but I don't believe you had so bad a time as that."

"No," said Maria, laughing; "we lived well enough; but mother's butter is sweeter than anybody's else."

When the meal was finished, Susy brought her father the Bible, who read without rising from the table, and then all knelt at the family altar. Mr. Smith prayed like one who was accustomed to pour out his soul before God. His petitions were simple, but fervent, and touched the hearts of the whole circle with a conviction of their sincerity.

Juliette sobbed like a child, but her tears were not caused by sorrow; no, they welled up from a heart overflowing with gratitude and praise. She could scarcely refrain from uttering the sacred words which so aptly expressed her own emotions. "I will bless the Lord, who hath given me counsel; because he is at my right hand, I shall not be moved. The lines are fallen unto me in pleasant places; yea, I have a goodly heritage."

Soon after tea, Dudley came driving to the door, bringing Juliette's trunk. Having tied his horse to the post, James assisted him in carrying it upstairs, and then the whole family adjourned to the porch, running the whole length of the spacious L. Presently, however, Susan exclaimed, "Father, I'm going to the pasture for the cows!" and invited Juliette to accompany her. "I suppose I must have a broad-rimmed hat, if I'm to live in the country," returned the young girl, playfully accepting the offer of Maria's school one.

The pasture was a quarter of a mile from the house; but the air was balmy, and Susan delightfully merry. The setting sun threw long shadows across the fields, and over the winding path. Juliette was really surprised at herself for her keen enjoyment of the beauties of nature. Everything around her, even the society of the good farmer and his kind-hearted wife, the awkward earnestness of James, the warm, though unexpressed, attachment between Maria and Dudley, and the frank, naïve manners of the light-hearted Susan served to divert her thoughts from her own peculiar trials. As she retired to bed that night she said to herself, "If I only knew how my dear father bears my absence, I should be happy to remain here forever. How little I expected last night to be so delightfully situated. Surely I have reason to say 'The Lord is on my side, what can I fear?'"

Early the next morning Susan entered her room on tiptoe and waked her with a kiss. "I'm going out to the barn-yard to see father and James milk," said she; "don't you want to go, too? It's a splendid day;" and she looped back the curtain, letting a flood of golden light into the chamber.

The young stranger opened her eyes and gazed wildly around the room. Her sleep had been long and profound, and she could not at first comprehend where she was. The small, neat chamber, with its white muslin curtains, and sprigs of blue flowers dotting the walls, was so unlike her spacious apartment, with its draperies of rose-colored damask and embroidered lace, the lofty walls hung with gilded paper, that she seemed to herself to be still dreaming. Susan's merry laugh soon recalled her thoughts, though she rubbed her eyes sleepily as she said, "I thought I was at home, and Eliza had come to dress me. Yes, I should admire to go, and I'll be ready directly, nearly as soon as you are."

"I'm sure," exclaimed Susan, "I can't think what

14*

people do who don't live on a farm. I should die to be shut up between brick walls, and never see the green fields, nor the new-mown hay."

"Perhaps they have never seen how beautiful the country is," answered Juliette, pleasantly. "I was at school in the country many years; but I never was on a farm before."

"Good-morning, sis," exclaimed James, coming with a couple of large tin pails from the house. "Good-morning, Miss Edwards. You are an early riser, I see."

"She deserves no credit for that," laughed Susan; "she would have slept till noon if I had not had compassion on her. But I've taken her under my protection, and I mean to have her breathe our fresh morning air. Do you want to see me milk, Juliette?"

Our heroine stared. "I don't believe you can," said she.

Susan advanced to her brother, but he waved her back. "Not this one, sis, she's apt to kick; you may milk Daisy, and welcome." But before he was ready, she ran to the house for some dough which she scattered plentifully about in front of the small coops for the chickens.

"Are you going to raise this calf?" she presently shouted from the barn. "It's too pretty to kill. Oh, how I used to cry," she said, turning to her companion, "when the butcher came for the calf, or for a darling lamb! I would not speak to him for weeks afterward, except to call him an ugly, cruel man. Wait here a minute, Juliette, I'm going up that ladder

to the hay-mow, for I believe there is a nest of eggs
there. I saw a hen fly down last night;" and, laughing
at Juliette's earnest remonstrance, she quickly began to
ascend.

"Ha, Susy, up to your old tricks, hey!" and the
farmer came into the barn, followed by Maria.

The young girl was trying to steady the ladder with
her tiny hands; but Mr. Smith, with a laugh, took her
place.

"Oh! oh! dear me!" came a smothered voice
through the hay; "here's fourteen, fifteen, sixteen,
new-laid eggs. I'm afraid I shall break them coming
down,—I want to ask mother to cook some for
breakfast." Holding them carefully in her apron she
slowly descended from her lofty height. "There,
father, see what you would have lost if I hadn't come
home."

She looked so fresh and rosy that Juliette could not
resist the temptation to give her a kiss, and then they
walked into the house together to help mother about
the breakfast.

"I'm right glad you're home, girls, for one thing,"
remarked Mrs. Smith, about the middle of the fore-
noon. "My caps all need doing up. You know I
never had any taste at millinery."

"If you'll starch them," whispered Juliette, "I'll
help you trim them; I should like to."

"No, don't you go to troubling yourself," said Mrs.
Smith, as Susy gayly repeated the remark.

"Perhaps if I do them to suit you, Susan will let me

help her about her other work," added Juliette, with a rosy blush.

"You may do anything you please, child, while you're here," returned the good woman, tenderly.

On the Sabbath, Juliette accompanied the family to church, Susan riding with her brother in the farm-wagon. The services were solemn and impressive. During the short intermission, as the young girl sat with Mrs. Smith in the pew, the thought occurred to her that here she might join the people of God, and commemorate his dying love. She determined to take an opportunity that very evening and consult her kind friends upon the subject, though she knew that it would involve a necessity of relating to them, in brief, the trials through which she had passed.

In the mean time Maria and Susan had joined their old class in the Sabbath school, from which they adjourned to the singing seats, Dudley Houghton being leader of the choir.

"How inquisitive people are!" exclaimed Susan, as they took their places at their late dinner on their return from church. "Ever so many people asked me who you were, Juliette. You seem to have attracted a great deal of attention."

"What did you answer?" inquired the young girl, her face growing very pale.

"I told the truth, that you were a friend of mine, who returned with me when I came from school."

"I said the same," repeated James, with a heightened color. "Mr. Pond, the depot-master, asked me, and two or three others."

After dinner, which, on the Sabbath, was after the second service, and which was concluded before four o'clock, Juliette, finding Mrs. Smith reading in the parlor, frankly said, "I want to ask your advice about myself."

Until this time she had never referred to her own situation, and her friends had too much delicacy to intrude upon her confidence. The good woman, in truth, was much pleased at the thought that the mystery evidently attaching itself to her young visitor might be solved. On the day after her arrival, Juliette had expressed her wish to remain through the summer, which Mr. Smith had agreed to at merely a nominal price. Now she drew a low ottoman to the good woman's feet, and, in as few words as possible, related her sad story. When she came to describe the meeting with her father at the time he placed the alternatives before her, — a luxurious home, his love and support on one side, and her Saviour on the other, her sobs choked her utterance.

Nor did she weep alone. Mrs. Smith folded her arms about her, as if she would protect her from all coming danger, and with streaming eyes assured her of their increased affection.

"Poor lamb!" she exclaimed, tenderly passing her fingers over the silky curls; "you shall share with us as long as we have a home. But, my dear, your father may relent. Perhaps your firmness in doing your duty may be the very means God is taking to lead him to the knowledge of himself."

" Oh," sighed Juliette, "do pray that it may be so."
She then went on to state her wishes with regard to
professing Christ, and Mrs. Smith promised to consult
her husband on the subject. She received Juliette's
ready assent that he should be informed of her real
condition, but begged that this knowledge might, for
the present, be confined to their own breasts.

Mr. Allen, the clergyman of the parish, was absent
for a few weeks, and it was thought best to defer the
application to the church until his return. In the mean
time the young girl was treated with increased cordiality by the family at the farm. Maria and Susan were
aware that their parents had been informed of Juliette's earlier history, and saw that the knowledge added
to their respect and affection for her. In a few weeks
she had so won upon them that it would have been
considered a great affliction to part with her. She followed Mrs. Smith from her dairy to the kitchen, became initiated into the mysteries of butter-making,
and the more difficult kinds of cooking; wandered at
pleasure over the farm, feeding the chickens, who soon
learned to come at her call; accompanied the sisters
in their visits to their neighbors, and assisted them in
whatever they were engaged.

Mr. Smith taught a class in the Sabbath school, and
on more than one occasion our heroine had heard him
regret that he had not a commentary, which would assist him in preparing for the lesson. She tried to
devise a plan to procure one for him, and at last resolved to make a confidant of Dudley, and engage him

to purchase the books when he went to New York.
Knowing that it might be weeks before she should see
him alone, she frankly told Maria that it would greatly
oblige her if Dudley would do a little business for her,
and that she would write on paper what she wanted.
She did so; and though the other wondered not a little
at this sudden friendship for her lover, who made the
most of the mystery, and insisted upon a private interview with Miss Edwards, the frankness of her young
friend prevented any misunderstanding.

Two days later, a large bundle, containing "Henry's
Commentary," in five volumes, was brought to the
house, directed to Miss Edwards, and thus the mystery
was explained.

The good farmer wiped his glasses repeatedly, before
he could see to read the little note which she put into
his hands, —

"Mr. SMITH: Dear Sir, — Please accept the
books accompanying this, as a token of the gratitude
of one toward whom you and your dear family so cordially exercised your hospitality. 'I was a stranger,
and ye took me in.'"

"She is a blessed child," he said to his wife, when
they were alone, "and shall always be welcome to a
home as long as we have one."

Nor was Dudley the confidant of Juliette alone. On
one of his trips to the city he received a secret com-
mission from James, and presently brought to the farm

a dainty straw hat, tied with broad blue ribbons, which
the young farmer blushingly declared would "fit no
head but Juliette's."

The young girl acce ted the pretty gift with so much
pleasure, alleging that it was exactly what she had
been wanting, that poor James was obliged to leave the
room to give vent to his delight. He was a most worthy young man, an earnest, working Christian, acting
well his part in the sphere which Providence had assigned him. He had a clear head, and an honest, affectionate heart. Independent in his views and opinions, he was awkward and confused only in the presence
of her he loved. Yes, it was no use to try to deceive
himself longer. Keenly susceptible in his nature, he
had found it absolutely impossible to remain two
months in constant intercourse with one so lovely as
Juliette, without lavishing upon her the best affections
of his strong heart.

True, this intimacy was not unmingled with pain,
for he had sense enough to perceive that he was totally
unfitted by education and rank to become the husband
of one so delicate and refined. But what reasoning
or argument will ever induce an ardent lover to give
up hope? Thus far he had treated her with the tenderness, but not with the frankness, of a brother, and
she had never once suspected the nature or extent of
his attachment.

CHAPTER XVII.

"But doth the exile's heart serenely there
In sunshine dwell ? Ah ! when was exile blest ?
When did bright scenes, clear heavens, or summer air,
Chase from her soul the fever of unrest ? "

BUT was Juliette really as happy as she seemed? Did not her heart yearn for her kindred? Would she not have rejoiced to exchange her present condition for the luxuries of her city home, the gayeties of fashionable life?

It would have been strange indeed if thoughts of the dear ones she had left behind had not often caused her eyes to overflow, and her heart to beat painfully with anxious care. She found it an absolute necessity to be busily employed, or this excitement would have preyed upon her spirits to the injury of her health. But could she have been assured that the step she had taken, though the very furnace of affliction it had proved, could be instrumental of good to her father and brother, she would have been more than content to remain months or years in her present situation, trusting that He in whose hands our life and breath are, would turn the heart of her father to herself.

It was strange, but true, that the idea of his regretting and wishing to retract the cruel words he had spoken, had not once occurred to her mind. Could she have been aware of his hours of agony, and his nights of remorse, — the incessant longing of his heart to fold her once more to his breast, and hear her pronounce words of forgiveness, — how quickly, how joyfully, would she have flown to his side and lavished the wealth of her affections upon him!

But, alas, she knew nothing of all this! The inmates of the farm-house were quiet, orderly persons, who stayed at home, attending to their own business; knowing little of the world at large, except what was communicated through the columns of the "New York Observer," which came regularly to them the last of every week. Whatever attention might have been directed to herself by the advertisements extensively circulated throughout the country (and we know that her first appearance at church did excite the remarks of many persons) was satisfactorily explained by the statements of the family that she was a friend who accompanied the young ladies home on their return from school.

In addition to her anxiety for her father, the thought of Horace was scarce ever absent from her mind. His form mingled in her cares by day and her dreams by night.

> " There's not an hour,
> Of day or dreaming night, but I am with thee;
> There's not a wind but whispers of thy name,
> And not a flower that sleeps beneath the moon,
> But in its hues and fragrance tells a tale
> Of thee."

Sometimes she had such an irresistible longing to hear from him once more, — to have his approval of the course she had pursued, — that she resolved to write Mrs. Folsom and beg her to obtain information of him, and the place where he might be addressed abroad. But there was a secret feeling of delicacy which forbade this. "If he were my own brother, I would do so," she repeated, again and again. "What could he mean by saying he thanked God that he was not my brother?"

Yes, poor Juliette had many causes of secret sorrow, among which the approbation of Mrs. Folsom, the approval of her kind pastor, Dr. A——, even the opinions of her fashionable friends, were not the least. She knew that the former would at once suspect the reason why she had so suddenly fled from her home and friends; and they had both of them represented it as a test of her love for her Saviour that she should forsake all for him. But among the latter she was equally aware that her absence would cause excitement and suspicion, — that her motives would be wholly misrepresented and misjudged. Had it not been for her childlike trust in the allotments of Providence, her increasing interest in her devotions, she might have sunk under these trials, which she kept so closely locked in her own breast. Often, on retiring to rest, she felt the breathings of the divine Comforter, and with her whole heart could repeat the beautiful words, —

> " ' Thy will be done!' In devious way
> The hurrying stream of life may run;

Yet still our grateful hearts shall say,
'Thy will be done!'

"'Thy will be done!' Though shrouded o'er
Our path with gloom, one comfort, one,
Is ours; to breathe, while we adore,
'Thy will be done.'"

Then, as I said before, every hour of the day was filled with useful employment or recreation. For weeks she dared not trust herself to sew except in the presence of some of the family, lest her thoughts should take wings and fly away, sometimes to the splendid mansion in Madison Square, and often over the deep, blue sea.

It was a great relief to the young girl when Mrs. Smith consented to confer with Mr. Allen in her behalf. She knew it would be necessary to inform him of some parts of her former history, and she shrank from relating it to one so much a stranger. After this, it was easy for her to answer questions as to her personal experience of the power of religion, and her readiness to accept Christ as her Saviour.

The good pastor treated her like a child, and while he assured her they should gladly admit her to the church, he advised her to make one more dutiful appeal to her father, informing him of her intention and begging his blessing. "True," he added, "his conduct has been harsh and unfeeling, as a parent, to say nothing of his hatred of religion; but the Spirit of God may have made use of this very event to subdue his proud heart. At any rate, you will show him that the religion you wish to profess, teaches you to honor him in all things, except where his commands are opposed to the will of God."

Juliette burst into tears. "You do not know my father," she faltered, trying to control her voice. "He is the most indulgent parent that a child ever had. I could scarce name a desire, but he would find means to gratify it; but upon this one subject his prejudices cannot be shaken."

"Do not disparage the grace and mercy of God, my child," said the clergyman, laying his hand softly on her head; "his compassion is infinite."

"Thank you! thank you, sir! you have given me fresh courage to pray for him. I will write immediately."

"That is best, and, as our communion service does not occur for three weeks, you will have abundant time to receive an answer from him."

That evening she retired to her own room, and, after an earnest prayer for divine guidance, seated herself to commence her epistle. But even after she had taken her pen in hand she sat for a long time lost in reverie. "How will my letter be received?" she asked herself. "When by my own act I have cut loose from the tie of nature, will he wish any further communication with me? Oh, that my dear mother were alive! I feel sure in that case I should never have been forced to this step; but how do I know that he is well, — that he is living?" At this terrible thought her tears began to flow. "I will not write," she exclaimed, "I will go to him. He may be ill and need my care." She sank

back again with the terrible recollection, " He has cast
me off. Oh! how could I forget his dreadful words,
'I shall disinherit you at once; you can no longer
have my support and protection'? "   Deep sobs for a
time convulsed her whole frame. " He may relent,"
she said, half unconsciously. " Yes, God's power is
infinite."   Once more she lifted her heart to him who
loves to listen to the prayers of his children, and then,
with a mind more composed, seated herself and wrote
as follows, —

"DEARLY BELOVED FATHER, — It is now ten weeks
since, in obedience to your command, I made my choice
whom I would serve. I need not tell you that for a
few hours there was a dreadful struggle in my mind
before I could decide to forsake you, my too indulgent parent, my dear brothers, the home your love
had rendered so attractive, and follow alone, and by a
path beset with trials, the footsteps of my meek and
lowly Saviour. I knew, indeed, my duty, but oh ! my
flesh was weak. All night I bathed my pillow with
my tears, and cried unto God for help; and he did
graciously appear for me. He poured the balm of
consolation into my bleeding heart; he gave me
strength to do his will.   The morning you left, I went
out of my chamber, at the sound of your voice, resolved
if you showed the least relenting, to throw myself at
your feet, and once more plead, that, while I obeyed my
Saviour, I might also be permitted to perform the sweet
offices prompted by a daughter's love. But, as you

will no doubt remember, you still considered me disobedient, undutiful; and you would not encourage me
even by a parting kiss. I returned to my room heart-
broken. I threw myself on my knees, but for a long
time I could not pray, — I could only think of you. 'I
poured out my soul like water;' I earnestly besought
God for you, that you might retract those dreadful
words. Through the day I kept my couch, starting at
every sound, longing, oh, so eagerly ! for your return.

"Then there came a change in my feelings, and the
thought flashed into my mind that I ought to leave home
instantly; that by remaining I should only expose
myself, unnecessarily, to temptation. God had once
delivered me; but would he if I threw myself into
trouble? No, my duty was plain, and, however great
the trials I might have to encounter, I must endure.
them for Christ's sake, if I would win my reward.

"Not until my simple preparations were made, had I
the heart to write my farewell. Oh, you can never
know the agony of that hour ! I loved you more than
ever. All your tenderness and affection rushed over
me, so that more than once I was obliged to throw
down my pen and cry aloud. The thought of my keen
anguish even now so unnerves me that I can scarcely
write.

"Perhaps you will wonder, dear, *dear* father, why I
now address you; perhaps you will be displeased; but
my heart urges me to the act. Even if you never
answer me, if you only read this, you will better understand my motives for acting contrary to your com-

mands. Oh, if you would forgive me and receive me again ; if you would allow me to be where I could look upon your face and listen to your voice addressing me as you did the past winter in tones of fond endearment, I should be happy indeed ! You would, I am sure you would, if you realized how much I suffer. Often I wake up from my troubled sleep fancying that my hand is in yours ; that I feel its soft pressure while your voice echoes the blessed words, ' Juliette, I forgive you.' Dear father, at such times my trial is greater than I can bear.

"I have not yet taken any decided stand as a Christian. I am a stranger in this place, and could not feel courage ; but unless I hear from you, — oh, my heart beats wildly at the very thought ! — I shall be received as a member of the Stamford church at the next communion.

"Father, for one moment imagine me as of old, seated on a taboret at your feet, your kind eyes resting on mine, and ask yourself whether you would not be happier now, and more at peace with yourself when you lie down to die, if you give your consent to this, and allow me to return to you. I cannot love you more than I do now, for as I write my heart swells almost to bursting ; but if my whole life devoted to your comfort will prove my gratitude, how gladly would I dedicate it thus !

"Hoping and praying for an early answer, I subscribe myself your loving daughter,

"JULIETTE.

" P. S. — As you will see, by my address, I am within a few miles of Mrs. Osborn; but as you forbade me to see her, I have found pleasure in the thought that in this I could obey your commands. If you write, please direct to Juliette Edwards, care of Mr. Samuel Smith, Stamford."

The excitement consequent upon writing this letter was so great that poor Juliette did not shut her eyes in sleep till morning, and then awoke, after an hour of unrefreshing slumber, with so severe a headache that she was unable to rise from her bed.

Mrs. Smith, who quickly followed Susan to her room, advised a cup of sage tea, which she soon made and brought to the couch; then, closing the blinds, she promised that the house should be kept quiet if the poor sufferer would try to sleep.

It was near noon when she at length awoke, wholly relieved from pain, but with a sense of lassitude through her whole system. She had no idea of the time, but quickly consulted her watch, hoping she had not over-slept so as to be too late for the post. Her letter, when sealed and directed to her father, she had the night before enclosed in another envelope to Mrs. Folsom, with a request that she would forward it at the most favorable opportunity. But now, upon further reflection, she thought it would be better re-ceived if sent according to the first address, and there-fore she tore off the outside envelope and destroyed it.

This she wished herself to carry to the post, feeling sure that if her simple-hearted friends should become aware that their guest was the daughter of Edward Fearing, the rich banker, they might be somewhat embarrassed in their treatment of her. Juliette knew that she had only to ask, in order to have some method contrived for her to go where she wished, even if. Mr. Smith or James left their farming to accompany her.

At the dinner-table she was welcomed as warmly as if she had been absent for several days. She was still very pale, which Mrs. Smith thought was owing to her working too steadily.

Juliette smiled as she replied, "If you think so, I'll play this afternoon." She then ventured to express her wish to ride as far as the village, when James declared himself ready to accompany her at any hour she might name. This he said with so much earnestness that Susan laughed aloud.

It was hard to tell, then, who appeared the most confused, Juliette or her friend the young farmer.

It was in vain that Mrs. Smith looked grave and shook her head at the lively girl. She had got on one of her high keys, as her father called it, and she might just as well have it out; and her merriment proved so contagious that at last they all joined in, though James insisted that he didn't know what on earth they were laughing at.

At three o'clock the covered wagon drove to the door, and the young girls, for Juliette had begged Susan to accompany her, took their seats, while James, dressed in his Sunday suit, and presenting a fine specimen of an American yeoman, gathered up the reins and drove gayly off.

Little did Juliette's companions imagine the anxiety with which she went to deposit her epistle. She tried to smile in answer to Susan's lively sallies; but it was with a heavy pain at her heart.

"Where will you go first, Miss Edwards?" was James' inquiry, as they were approaching the village.

"To the post-office, if you please," she answered, with a blush.

There was quite a crowd of men standing about, and the modest girl shrank from entering alone.

"Don't get out," cried Susan; "I'll hold the reins, and let James go in for you. Run in, James, and inquire for Miss Edwards."

"No, please help me out," urged Juliette; "I had rather go in myself."

The young man saw she was in earnest, and, though he rather wondered, he did not oppose her. Scarcely touching his hands, she jumped lightly to the ground, and made her way to the door.

James at first hesitated whether to follow her, but, at a word from his sister, stepped forward and escorted her toward the part of the building where she might inquire for a letter. Just outside the little room, a small frame, on which the words, "Letter-box," were printed, arrested Juliette's attention; and saying in a low tone, "You inquire, please," she stepped back, and unnoticed by any one dropped her letter within it.

His endeavors to procure one for her were of course unsuccessful; but she did not seem at all disappointed. On the contrary, she went back to the carriage in much better spirits than before.

"Now we will go to Mr. Allen's," exclaimed Susan, "and then call for mother's things at the store as we return."

Here Juliette had two errands. The ostensible one was to ask the pastor's acceptance of half a dozen white cravats she had been hemming for him; the other will be learned in its place.

"How long are you going to stop?" asked Susan. "Shall we all go in?"

"Just as you please," was the answer; "my business will occupy me but a moment."

"Do you want to go in, James?" inquired his sister.

"Yes, I always like to call here."

"Well, then, we'll get out; and you can tie the horse."

As they stood at the door, waiting for the young man to join them, Juliette whispered, "I wish you would contrive for me to see Mr. Allen alone a moment; I can't give him these if his family are present."

The good clergyman and his wife received them very cordially. Mrs. Allen presently engaged the young man, who was a favorite with her, in conversation, while her husband talked with the ladies.

Presently Susan, who had not forgotten Juliette's charge, arose from her seat saying, as she pointed to the open door, "That is Mr. Allen's study. May I show Miss Edwards the view from the window?"

The pastor, of course, gave his consent, and followed them as in duty bound.

The prospect was extensive, and the young lady expressed her admiration of it. Then, approaching the good man, she gracefully placed her small offering in his hands. When she looked around, after receiving his thanks, she saw her companion had joined the party in the other room, and in rather a hurried, embarrassed manner said, "There is one thing I ought to say to you, sir, — I forgot it yesterday, or rather I did not feel it to be so necessary as I now do. My name is Juliette Edwards; but that is not my whole name. I am the daughter of Edward Fearing, of New York city; but, if possible to avoid it, I should prefer not to be known as such, for reasons you can easily imagine."

"Indeed!" exclaimed Mr. Allen, with a start of surprise. "Well, I will try to manage it for you. Do your friends, glancing toward the parlor, know of this?"

"No, sir, they only know me as Miss Edwards. Perhaps you will be pleased to learn that I have just posted my letter."

On their return to the parlor the conversation became general; and Juliette was quite delighted and rather astonished to see with what manliness and ease James expressed his opinion on the various topics introduced. There was nothing at all of the shyness

16

with which he generally addressed her. They conversed of the state of religion in the parish, of some
new arrangements in the Sabbath school, and the
young farmer exhibited a soundness of judgment, and
good common-sense she had not known him to possess.

During their ride from the parsonage to the store,
she exclaimed, frankly, "James, I am glad you went
in. I never heard you talk so much before." And
she looked in his face with such an expression of interest that his manly heart glowed for the rest of the
day.

"Did you hear what Mrs. Allen asked me?" inquired Susan.

"No."

"I told her we were going to Mr. Houghton's store,
and she whispered, 'Are we to have a wedding
soon?'"

"You must ask Maria," said I, laughing heartily.
"How do you suppose, James, she heard of their engagement?"

"Perhaps from Dudley," he remarked; "he makes
no secret of it; and I wouldn't, if I were he." The
young farmer glanced shyly at Juliette as he said
this.

CHAPTER XVIII.

"Upon her face there was the tint of grief,
  The settled shadow of an inward strife,
  And an unquiet drooping of the eye,
  As if its lid were charged with unshed tears."

BEFORE the close of the third day, our young heroine began to feel impatient for an answer to her letter; but she was destined to be disappointed. As the reader is well aware, her father and brother were long ere this on their way to Liverpool; and the clerk, to whose care all correspondence was consigned to be forwarded to them abroad, being absent for a day, the precious epistle, freighted with love, and followed by prayers, was carelessly dropped into a drawer with other papers, and was not again brought to view until nearly a year later. Then it was enclosed in another envelope and mailed for Vienna, where Mr. Fearing was supposed to be staying.

As one week tardily followed in the footsteps of another, and no tidings from home; no word even to tell the poor disinherited daughter that she was forgiven, — she grew pale and wan, her appetite left her, and she was oppressed with such a sense of lassitude that it required constant exertion to perform the daily tasks she had assigned herself. She was often obliged

183

to retire suddenly to her own room, to give vent to the grief which she could not suppress.

> "O remembrance!
> Why dost thou open all my wounds again?"

In vain Mrs. Smith prepared little dainties to tempt her appetite; in vain Susan invited her to the berry parties so frequent at this season; in vain Mr. Smith and Maria proposed rides, walks, or more nourishing food; while James, with a sad pain gnawing at his manly heart, regarded her with eloquent silence. Her sorrow had sunk into her soul, and no arm but an Almighty one could remove it; no sympathy but that of her Saviour could soothe and comfort her.

One day, having passed the morning in tears, she invited Mrs. Smith to her chamber, and, throwing her arms about the kind woman, exclaimed, "Oh, I am miserable indeed! I have deceived myself in thinking I am a Christian. I am impatient under trials. I did not calculate aright my own strength, and I am unsubmissive to the will of God. I bow my knees before him, but I can find no comfort in prayer; I can only cry aloud, O my father! my father! would to God that I had never left you! O Mrs. Smith! sometimes I wake up, bathed in perspiration, dreaming of him calling for me, sick, and longing for my presence. It is dreadful. I feel sure I cannot endure it long. Perhaps I was too hasty; perhaps he would have revoked his terrible threat. I cannot believe he would have thrust me out. But, then, why does he not write me?"

"Don't, dear child! don't cry so! you will kill yourself! Don't, Juliette! You did what you thought was best. Your motive was a right one, to avoid temptation. Suppose, dear, you had waited till his return, and then your courage had failed? Suppose you had consented to give up your Saviour, would you have been happier now? No, indeed! You forsook all for him, and he will surely fulfil his promise to you. No wonder you feel your father's displeasure. I've been afraid you were brooding over your sorrows, for you have faded like a broken lily. Come, dear;" and the kind woman, choking back her own tears, drew the weeping child closer and closer to her bosom.

"Our hearts have ached for you," she added, softly stroking Juliette's head, "and many's the earnest prayer we've put up that you might hold out in the good cause. As Mr. Smith said last night, 'tisn't many in these days are called to go through such fiery trials; and to our short-sighted vision it seems strange that such a little, weak, delicate creature as you are, should be called to them; but God knows best, dear, and we must trust him. You remember the saints about the throne, clothed in white robes, are those 'which came out of great tribulation.'"

The sobs grew less frequent, and at length Juliette murmured, "I should like to see Mr. Allen. If he knew how rebellious my heart is, perhaps he would not admit me to the church."

"You shall go, dear. I'll contrive it some way;" and, leading the young girl to a chair, Mrs. Smith hastened below.

Juliette little realized how inconvenient it would be for her to be carried to the village, or she would on no account have expressed the wish. It was in the midst of haying, and Mr. Smith, his son, and several extra hands were hurrying to get the hay under cover while the dry weather continued.

When the good woman went below, she found James hastily eating his luncheon in the kitchen, her husband having finished his and returned to his work.

"I suppose the horses are all in use," said she, hesitatingly.

"Yes, mother, all in the hay-carts. It looks showery, and we have three or four loads well dried." He held the bowl of milk to his lips, drained it, and then set back his chair with a heavy sigh.

As he took his straw hat from the hook, he caught a glimpse of her face as she was thinking, "Perhaps this evening will do." He saw she had been weeping, and coming directly to her he asked, in a hoarse voice, "What is it, mother? Is Juliette —"

"She is miserable this afternoon," she began, interrupting him, "and wants to see Mr. Allen."

James turned from his mother to the window, not liking to have even her eye witness his distress. Presently, with his back turned toward her, he said, "I'll have the carriage at the door in fifteen minutes."

He spoke indistinctly, and then, with a heavy sigh, passed into the shed.

His mother followed him, and put her hand softly on his shoulder. "It troubles me," said she, "to have you take this so to heart. I wish your love could be returned, my son, but I'm afraid for you. If she lives, which to me is doubtful, she will be in a different society from ours."

"Don't! don't, mother!" he cried, his face growing very red, and then suddenly becoming pale; "you don't know how you pain me;" and he put his hand to his heart as if he could quiet its wild beating. "If it is as you imagine I must pray for strength to bear it; but I can't stop to think of myself when she's suffering."

By this time he had removed his overalls, and said, "I'll take one of the horses out of the cart and slip on the harness, and then I'll dress me. Don't tell her it's inconvenient, 'cause I can go as well as not."

With a silent petition for her poor boy, whose unrequited love for their suffering guest she had long suspected, Mrs. Smith returned to the chamber to assist Juliette in preparing for the ride.

"The air will do you good, at any rate," she said, tenderly, as she stood watching the young girl bathing her eyes, "and Mr. Allen is a kind man."

"Yes, he is; but not so kind as you are;" and the tears began to flow again. "Sometimes I'm afraid your patience will wear out."

"When it does, I'll let you know," returned Mrs. Smith, trying not to appear moved.

At this moment Maria's voice was heard out of doors, —

"Are you going to the store, James?"

"I'm going to the village," was his grave reply.

"Why! father said he couldn't possibly spare the horse to go."

No answer.

"Well, I'll run and get my bonnet, for I'm going with you. I want some thread."

The reply was in a low tone, but, in the stillness about the farm-house, was plainly heard.

"I'll get some thread for you, or carry you this evening, but you can't go now."

By this time he had tied the horse to the post, and ran to the sink to wash.

"I want four spools of number fifty," responded Maria, seeing from his grave look it was no use to urge him; "but I may as well write it to Dudley, you'll be sure to forget it."

"I ought not to go," sighed Juliette. "I'll wait till another time."

"No, no; he'll be ready in a minute. It'll be a pleasure to him to do anything for your comfort;" and with a sigh for her son, Mrs. Smith kissed Juliette's cheek.

The young farmer brought the carriage to the door a few seconds after the expiration of the fifteen minutes. He glanced anxiously in the young girl's face as he tenderly lifted her into the vehicle, but did not speak.

She smiled feebly. "I'm afraid I'm giving you a great deal of trouble," said she.

"I'd go to the ends of the earth if 'twould give back your health and peace." He checked himself, his face as red as fire, while he added, "I mean, we all feel for you, Miss Edwards, though we don't rightly understand your troubles."

She was silent and embarrassed for a moment; then, turning her moistened eyes to his with a look of sorrow that penetrated his soul, she said softly, "Mine is a sad story. I will ask your mother to tell it to you some time."

"I'm afraid I'm a dreadful bungler," exclaimed the young man with an air of self-reproach. "I didn't mean to pry into your secrets. I was only trying to say how much we all sympathize with you. Why, the first look I had into your eyes, I saw sorrow there. But after a while you seemed happier, and I thought maybe you'd get used to us, and mother's nursing would do you good. It seemed hard to think such a one as you should be in want of friends to care for you."

James stopped. His feelings were carrying him too far. Not for the world would he intrude his own sorrows upon her; and so he ended his sentence rather awkwardly, by saying, "I hope Mr. Allen will be able to comfort you."

"Thank you," she answered, with more warmth. "I am grateful for your kindness, though I may not appear so. I have thanked my heavenly Father, every day since I came to Stamford, that he has given me such kind friends. I tremble to think what I should have done without your mother and all of you."

Oh, how earnestly the young farmer longed to clasp that little hand lying so passively on her lap, and pledge his life to the work of making her happy! His athletic frame shook with the fierce struggle to control himself. Fortunately, as she sat by his side, she did not notice his emotion, and in silence they rode on until they reached Mr. Allen's gate.

The pastor happened to be sitting near the window, and came forward eagerly to meet them. "I am glad to see you, my child," he said, in an impressive tone. "I was only waiting for the sun to go down a little before I started to walk to the farm; but I'm glad you came. Come in, come in. Two miles is something of a walk for me. Walk into the parlor, Mr. Smith."

"No, I thank you, sir; I've an errand at the store, and I'll call again in a few minutes."

Mr. Allen went to his study, after giving his young friend a chair, and presently returned with a newspaper. "I can imagine," he began, "that you have come to tell me your disappointment at not receiving a letter;" and he gazed in her face in a manner she did not exactly understand.

"Partly that, sir," she replied, in some confusion.

"Yes, I supposed so. Well, after dinner, I took up this 'New York Journal of Commerce,' supposing it the last number, and read on some time before I noticed my mistake. I was just about to throw it aside when my eye caught the following paragraph."

"Stop a minute! Oh, stop!" cried Juliette, every particle of color leaving her face and lips, as the horrible fear that her father was dead, rushed into her mind.

"No, let me tell you, now. It is not so bad as you imagine, my poor child. It will relieve you to hear it." And as she faintly bowed her assent, he read,—

"We regret to say that Edward Fearing, Esq., having recovered from his late illness, has sailed for Liverpool in the Astracan, Capt. Spooner, with the intention of remaining abroad for some years. His son, Mr. Henry Fearing, accompanied him. Mr. Fearing, Senior, is one of our most successful merchants, and his well-known benevolence toward the public charities of our city, as well as his high integrity and shrewdness in business, render his departure a serious calamity."

"Thank God!" exclaimed the excited girl fervently, clasping her hands; "I feared he was not living."

"I ought to have been more cautious in telling you. This is dated some weeks back, so that your letter did not reach him, but will doubtless be forwarded to him abroad."

"Yes, sir; he has a confidential clerk that attends to all such business. Oh, you can scarcely imagine what a relief it is to me! I feel almost sure he will forgive me and arrange some way for me to join him."

A bright, beautiful blush mantled her cheek at the thought of meeting Horace, also, and with an animation he had never seen in her before, she said, playfully, " I should like to keep this paper if you have done with it. It does my father no more than justice."

" Certainly, take it and welcome. Happy days are in store for you, I do not doubt." He then, in a fatherly way, inquired the state of her heart in regard to the vows she was soon to take upon herself.

She humbly related the experience of the last few days, received his sympathy and encouragement to persevere in aiming after a high degree of holiness, and then, perceiving James driving up to the gate, hastened to meet him, bidding the pastor adieu in quite a cheerful voice.

CHAPTER XIX.

"Not rural sights alone, but rural sounds
Exhilarate the spirits, and restore
The tone of languid nature."

ONE glance into Juliette's beaming face served to show her companion that whatever her cause of anxiety might have been, it was removed, and his honest countenance at once expressed his pleasure.

"How quiet and beautiful the country is!" she exclaimed. "See how regularly those men work, cutting hay!"

"They are cradling oats," answered James, laughing. "Did you never see any such work before? We have a fine piece of oats to get in when our haying is done. You must come out and see us."

"I should like to," she answered, leaning from the carriage to watch them; "it looks so prettily."

"Farming is a first-rate business to my mind," remarked the young man, enthusiastically. "You know Adam was a farmer; and I've sometimes thought, if Eve hadn't eaten the apple there wouldn't have been any other business done."

Juliette laughed. "I don't know how that would have been," she replied. "I'm no theologian."

17　　　　　　　193

Mrs. Smith was watching for them, and could scarcely believe her eyes when she saw James, a broad smile brightening his face, jump from the carriage and lift Juliette carefully down the step, while she was speaking in a tone of cheerfulness they had not heard from her for weeks.

"You are better, I'm sure," she said, warmly.

"Yes, indeed!" cried the grateful girl, cordially returning the woman's kiss. "If you will come to my room I will tell you about it."

"Mother!" called James from the back door, "will you step this way a minute?"

She ran to answer the summons, saying, as she went, "I'll be up there presently."

"I've got something here," said the young man, giving her a small parcel enclosed in a paper bag, "that I want to get you to cook for supper. A man came along with pigeons while I was at the store, and I thought maybe a bit of the breast would relish a little."

"Oh, I understand now!" she exclaimed, her look of wonder changing to one of merriment; "I understand, and I'll cook part of one to tempt her; she never eats much more than a bird, and I've sometimes been afraid our great dishes of meat take away her appetite."

"Well, mother, do what you please with them, only don't let her know ——"

His words were suddenly brought to an end by seeing Juliette standing close behind his mother. The color flew to his face, and he hastily retreated, just as she was about to thank him for her ride, which, on alighting from the carriage, she had forgotten to do.

Though she had heard his words, she seemed not to have comprehended his meaning, and waiting while Mrs. Smith laid the paper parcel in the ice-chest, she followed her to the chamber. Here she related what the reader is already acquainted with, and read the paragraph before alluded to, omitting only the name of her father.

Mrs. Smith was sanguine that her letter would be answered, and that all would come out right in the end. "I shall try not to be selfish;" she said, "but it would be hard for all of us to part with you." Then kissing the bright cheek, on which the tear of filial love still glistened, she exclaimed, "God will order all for your good, my dear child; and who knows but your consistent adherence to your religion may win him to Christ?"

"Oh, how happy I should be!" was the delighted response.

They were interrupted by voices in the entry, and presently Maria came in. "Why, have you returned?" she inquired, in surprise. "Where is James?"

"In the field, by this time, I'll warrant," replied his mother, with a laugh. "He'll do a day's work between this and dark. He's a smart lad to work, if he is my son."

"He's got a large heart and a warm one," earnestly responded Juliette. "I shall never forget his kindness to me."

"Susan," called out Maria, "they've come home. Juliette's in here."

"How much better you do look!" cried Susan, embracing her affectionately. "What have you been doing to yourself? You're so changed I can scarcely believe it's our pale, sad girl. I move James carry you to ride every day;" and she glanced archly in her companion's face.

"I must wait till haying is over," replied Juliette, innocently.

"Do you like thimbleberries?" inquired Maria.

"Yes, very much. We used to have them at Mrs. Osborn's school."

"Did you go there?" eagerly asked Susan. "Why it's close by Stamford, and father thought some of sending us, but he found it was too expensive."

"I was with Mrs. Osborn several years," remarked Juliette, with a slight blush. "There was a thick hedge of thimbleberry bushes about the house, and the girls used to pick them when they pleased."

"They are very thick back of our barn," rejoined Maria. "We've gathered two or three quarts this afternoon. I wonder whether James brought me anything from Dudley."

"He laid a small bundle on the kitchen table," suggested Mrs. Smith; "perhaps that is for you."

"Susan, you run down and get it; that's a good girl," said her sister, throwing herself lazily into a large chair.

"I don't know about that," muttered the other.

"When one has a beau she ought to pay the penalty. I shall expect to do my own running when I have one."

"Is this the bundle?" asked Juliette, who, unperceived, had slipped from the room and brought it from the table.

"I'm sorry you went," said Maria. "Yes, it's my thread."

A tiny note dropped to the floor, which Juliette restored with an arch glance.

"I wonder how it feels to be in love," exclaimed Susan, laughing.

"Ask James, and perhaps he will tell you," remarked Maria, gravely.

Susan shook her head with an earnest glance toward Juliette. "Perhaps he wont," she retorted, quickly.

"Girls, don't you want to go out and rake after the cart?" called Mrs. Smith, from the foot of the stairs. "There's a shower coming up."

"Yes, ma'am, we'll come;" and they were soon on the way to the meadow, as the large field was called, and which was but a short distance in front of the house.

It was a novel and interesting scene for Juliette. Large cocks of fragrant hay were scattered over the field, which men were hastily loading on the large racks. They approached one where James was at work, standing in the middle of the cart, and packing the hay in place as fast as two men could pitch on. He called out merrily to his sisters to take the rakes from some

17 *

men who were following after, gathering up the small locks left behind.

They did so, and entered into the sport with so much enthusiasm, trying to see who could gather the most, that Juliette began to long for a rake to imitate them.

The men immediately left for another part of the field, to assist Mr. Smith in loading his cart.

The sun was now clouded, so that it was delightful to be out; and our young friend, relieved from the dreadful burden which had oppressed her, gayly followed from one cock to another, until the cart was filled to its utmost capacity.

"I hope James wont ride on that high load to the barn," she exclaimed, as one of the men took hold of the bridle to lead the horse away.

"Oh, he's used to it!" responded Susan. "See how straight he stands, scarcely touching his pitchfork."

"It don't seem safe to me, and I don't want to see him do it;" and Juliette turned away, and followed the girls to their father's cart.

The men were working with all their might, casting frequent and anxious glances toward the western sky, where a black cloud was gradually spreading along the horizon.

"If it'll hold off half an hour more, I think we shall be safe," said Mr. Smith. "James is wonderfully quick at unloading."

"He works this afternoon as if he was possessed," answered one of the men. "It c'enamost takes away my breath to see him fly from one end of the cart to the other, calling out 'more here,' and 'more there;' and then his load looks like a picter when it's done; no great gouches sticking out; all even and smooth."

"He takes to farm work as natural as a mother takes to her own child," rejoined the farmer. "There, Susan, is a bunch behind you."

"I wish I'd worn my gloves," exclaimed the young girl; "I've a great blister already."

"Take mine," cried Juliette, pulling them from her hands. Susan laughed as the delicate articles were held up before her.

"They wouldn't last a minute," she said, gayly.

"Well, then, I'll run and get yours." And she went hastily toward the house.

On her way she met James returning for his last load.

He bowed and smiled, but passed without speaking.

"Are they almost done?" inquired Mrs. Smith, who was putting a large glass dish full of thimbleberries on the supper-table.

"Only ten cocks more," answered Juliette. "They are hurrying as fast as they can. I want Susan's gloves."

Mr. Smith drove hastily to the barn, hoping to be able to unload by the time James came with the remainder, which, if necessary, could be left inside the barn on the cart till morning.

"Oh, I do hope they'll get it all in!" cried Juliette,

as she gave Susan the gloves; "I'm afraid my going to the village detained them."

"Don't trouble yourself about that," answered James, from the top of the cart. "Ten minutes more and we're all right."

"I wish I could help, too."

He only laughed. "Here, Tom; throw a fork full to the middle. That's right! Now in front, Mr. Hanson! Drive on for the last cock. Whew! there's a drop of rain. Hurry up, my good fellows. We'll have time to cool off afterward. Here goes!" And the sweet-scented hay flew through the air, while Maria and Susan ran here and ran there; Juliette, in her enthusiasm, catching a bunch in her arms and holding it up for the man to take on his fork.

"I guess miss was made for a farmer's wife," said Tom, with a cunning wink at his young master.

"Drive on," shouted James, sternly, his color growing some shades deeper.

Five minutes more, and the horses, all in a foam, drove into the barn, just as the windows of heaven were opened and the rain began to descend in torrents.

The men threw themselves on the hay, perfectly exhausted, and began to wipe the perspiration from their foreheads.

"I call that lucky, Mr. Smith," said the man named Hanson. "'Twould have been a terrible pity to have had that well-dried hay get wet."

CHAPTER XX.

" A pure heart,
That burns to ashes, yet conceals its pain,
For fear it mar its hopeless source of love,
Is not to be despised, or lightly held."

WITHIN the house the table was set for supper, and a most inviting meal it was, too. Fried fish, crisp and brown, early potatoes, smoking-hot fritters, thimbleberries and cream, while directly in front of Juliette's plate was a tiny, covered dish, an object of curiosity to all present.

But I am too fast for my story, for I would not have the reader suppose that the good matron would run the risk of her tempting viands growing cold, while her family were making ready for the meal. Please imagine, then, the fish sizzling and crackling in the frying-pan, the mealy potatoes bursting open in the oven, while Maria, taking an old-fashioned horn from a high shelf, exclaimed, "Juliette, come and hear me call the people from the barn."

The well-known signal was instantly responded to by James, who appeared at the barn-door, and shouted back, "Well done, Miss Smith."

201

"Come right in," screamed his sister, at the top of her voice. "Supper is ready, and for the men, too."

She had scarcely finished speaking when an open wagon whirled around the corner of the house. Dudley, who was wet to the skin, making all haste for one of the large horse-sheds near the barn.

The rain still descended in torrents, while small extempore rivulets were running swiftly by the sides of the road, and standing in huge puddles near the doors. Looking from the window, the girls laughed merrily as one of the men after another, starting from the barn-door, rushed toward the house, where they stood in the woodshed shaking the rain from their wet garments.

James, unwilling to expose himself in such an awkward plight, made a dive for the back stairs, to his chamber, from which in an incredibly short time he reappeared in company with Dudley, arrayed in a clean suit, and ready for a good laugh over their adventures.

They were greeted, as they probably expected to be, with a shout of mirth, at the ill-fitting dress of Dudley, who had donned a pair of James's thin pantaloons, a thick, winter vest, and Mr. Smith's long-tailed go-to-meeting coat. His collar, which he generally wore turned loosely over his cravat, now stood up, shining and erect, to the imminent peril of his ears.

Marching along in a stiff, dignified manner, he endeavored to take Maria's hand; but she snatched it away, and sank back on the sofa nearly convulsed with laughter.

Susan and Juliette, too, joined in the mirth; the latter especially entering into the joke more heartily than they had ever seen her before.

"I never saw you look so handsome, Dudley," cried Susan, archly; "I advise you to borrow that suit to wear on a certain grand occasion, it becomes you so well."

The mother's voice was now heard proclaiming that supper was on the table, and an additional plate being laid for Dudley, Mr. Smith invoked a blessing, and they all took their seats.

"What's in this little dish, mother?" inquired Susan, pointing to the one by Juliette's plate.

"Open it, and see, child. There, Juliette, is the breast of a pigeon, which was sent to you with a request that I would cook it nicely."

"For me, Mrs. Smith!" cried the young girl, opening wide her eyes, and glancing from one to another around the table. "Not for me alone?"

"Yes, no one is to taste but you."

James's eyes were fixed intently on his plate, his cheeks and even his forehead intensely flushed; but that, of course, was the result of his violent exercise.

Susan, wicked girl, pinched his arm under the table, and at length burst into a merry laugh.

"I can guess who sent it," said Juliette. "It's perfectly delicious. 'Twas good Mr. Allen. He was coming to see me this afternoon if I had not gone there. But anything would taste good to-night, I'm so hungry."

Mrs. Smith drew down her mouth, while the face of her son preserved, as it had from the beginning, the most imperturbable gravity.

The family now addressed themselves with praiseworthy diligence to the discussion of the meal; and then Susan as usual passed her father the family Bible, for their devotions.

At the close of the evening, Juliette, after reading once more the scrap of paper which she had cut from the " Journal of Commerce," sang in a low voice her favorite hymn, —

> " How sweet to be allowed to pray
>   To God the Holy One;
>   With filial love and trust to say,
>   O God, thy will be done !
>
> " We in these sacred words can find
>   A cure for every ill;
>   They calm and soothe the troubled mind,
>   And bid all care be still.
>
> " Oh, let that will which gave me breath,
>   And an immortal soul,
>   In joy or grief, in life or death,
>   My every wish control !
>
> " Oh, could my soul thus ever pray,
>   Thus imitate thy Son !
>   Teach me, O God, with truth to say,
>   ' Thy will, not mine, be done.' "

For a long time our heroine had not enjoyed so refreshing a slumber, as followed this, to her, eventful day. She awoke feeling more calm and trustful in regard to the future; but with an evident quickening of the pulse, when the possible result of her joining her brother Horace flashed through her mind. She lay in the early morning light, her eyes fixed on one of the blue flowers on the wall; but her memory far away in the past, gathering up all the precious assurances of his affection. Stamford, and the scenes of the past months were swept away at a breath; and she was once more sitting by his side as on the last evening before he left the country. Again she heard him say with a flushed face, "No, Juliette, I cannot tell you all my reasons for wishing to postpone my departure." And again she asked herself what he could mean by this want of frankness.

"I wonder where he is now," she said half aloud, sighing as she recalled her truant thoughts, "and whether he thinks of me? I suppose long ere this he has made a profession of religion. Let me see, — what did he say about it?" She sat up in bed and reached from the table at her side a small box containing all the letters she had ever received from him. Smiling, as she opened one and another, she came at last to the epistle she sought. "How much he thinks of his aunt! I wish I knew her. Oh, how delightful it would be to travel with such a party! Dear Horace, what a kind brother you have always been to me!"

Mrs. Smith's voice at the foot of the stairs calling, "Maria! Susan!" interrupted her pleasant reveries. Hastily putting the precious epistles in their place, she locked the box and returned it to the drawer, wonder-

18

ing, while she took her bath, what was the cause of
her father's illness, and whether it had been severe.

The girls were talking earnestly in their own room,
and Juliette, quickly dressing herself, invoked God's
blessing on all the labors of the day, and then went
below to lay the table, — a light task she had insisted
on performing.

Mrs. Smith, who was busy in preparing breakfast,
greeted her with a cordial smile, and asked whether
she had seen or heard the girls.

"I think they'll be down soon," answered Juliette;
"I have heard their voices for some time."

"Mr. Smith and James have been mowing since four
o'clock," added the good woman. "It's going to be a
beautiful hay-day, and they expect to get along finely
with their work. Breakfast wasn't quite ready when
they came in, because I didn't expect them so soon, so
James went to pitching off the hay left on the cart. I
suppose 'twill sound kind of proud for me to say it,
but there isn't another in the whole town will come up
to him for driving work, or for planning it either. But
I do wonder where those lazy girls are?"

Before Juliette had time to reply, a dreadful shriek
of distress, followed by loud, confused voices, was heard
from the barn, and presently Mr. Smith and one of
the men were seen bringing poor James toward the
house.

"What is it? Oh, what has happened?" inquired
the mother, her heart sinking with fear, as she beheld
the deadly pallor of her beloved son.

"Not much, mother, I hope," answered the young man, speaking with great difficulty.

"Have the bed ready in the room below," cried the farmer, sharply; "we must lay him there till the doctor comes. Oh, dear!"

"Where is he hurt?" asked Juliette, timidly speaking to the man.

"Can't tell, miss; he's smashed up generally. He fell backwards off the load on to the barn floor."

The young girl felt sick and faint; but struggling for composure, she ran to assist Mrs. Smith in relieving the poor sufferer.

Before they had crossed the parlor, poor James groaned as if in great pain, and they were obliged to lift him quickly upon the bed, when, with a hoarse rattle in his throat, his eyes became fixed. He had fainted.

"Jump on to the horse, Tom, and ride for the doctor!" called out Mr. Smith, in a loud, sharp voice; "ride for your life. Mother, have you got the camphor! Oh, dear, he looks like death! Where are the girls? They might be bathing his hands."

Maria and Susan, hearing the unusual noise, hastened below. "What's the matter? Is anybody hurt? I smell medicine." They advanced to the bedroom where Mrs. Smith was holding a bottle of hartshorn to her son's nostrils; while Juliette, tears streaming unconsciously down her cheeks, was timidly chafing James' hard, bronzed hand.

Mr. Smith, overcome with grief, had retired to the

parlor, where he was weeping aloud, "O James! James! I'm afraid you've got your death-blow! Oh, dear! Never father had such a son, so smart to work, and with such a tender heart. Spare him, O God! Take him not away in his youth! Oh! oh! what shall I do? what shall I do?"

Trembling with anxiety, Mrs. Smith bent earnestly over her boy, when, with a slight contraction of the brow, and a long-drawn sigh, he feebly opened his eyes.

"He's reviving," cried Juliette, tears gushing from her eyes. "He knows us!"

Even at such a moment a thrill of joy ran through the young man's frame as he met her glance of tender interest, and became conscious that she held his hand in hers. A groan of distress, forced from him by his terrible pain, followed. The pallor about his mouth increased, and he seemed about to faint again. "Is the doctor — coming?" he asked feebly, gasping at every breath, and, in spite of all his efforts to repress them, his groans filled the room.

Susan, crying aloud, ran to the door to watch for the doctor, while Maria, hastening to the parlor to beg her father to be more composed, found Juliette sitting on the stairs almost ready to faint with terror.

Lifting up her heart to God for strength to meet this terrible calamity, Mrs. Smith, pale, but outwardly calm, continued vigorously to chafe the cold limbs from which life seemed almost departed.

Susan ran like one distracted from the bedroom to

the door, and back again, in the vain expectation of seeing the doctor's buggy approach.

Mr. Smith at last grew so impatient for his arrival, that, after one glance at his suffering boy, he set out with rapid strides for the village.

It was nearly an hour after the sad accident that the anxious watcher perceived a carriage dashing furiously down the hill, and, as it drew nearer, recognized it as the doctor's well-known vehicle.

"Come quickly! I'll tie the horse," she cried, earnestly; "James is dreadfully hurt."

"Not so badly, perhaps, as you imagine," he answered, taking his box of medicines and making his way quickly to the side of the bed.

"We're glad enough to see you," said Mrs. Smith. "He seems terrible faint. I've had as much as I could do to keep life in him."

"Have you any brandy in the house?"

"I think there is a little left in the phial."

James, in the midst of his distress, heard his question and what was passing, and made a dissenting motion with his hand.

"He means to say he has promised not to taste it," explained his mother. "He belongs to the Sons of Temperance."

"Nonsense!" cried the doctor, "I'll absolve him now. A few drops may be necessary to save his life."

Maria, who had run to get the phial, now presented it to the doctor, who gave him a teaspoonful, clear.

"Now," said he, in an encouraging tone, "some of

18*

you must go out of the room; I must make an examination. Where's your pain, James?"

Susan and her sister ran away just as their father, accompanied by Dudley, drove into the yard.

Tom, after going for the doctor, had called at the store to tell the sad news, and the young man, leaving his business with his clerk, made all haste to go to the farm and offer his services. On the way he overtook Mr. Smith, who related the particulars of the accident.

"After mowing an hour or two," he began, "we thought 'twas breakfast-time and went up to the house. Mother said 'twasn't quite ready; so I went out to see to the cattle, and James, hating to lose a minute, said he'd be pitching off the load we got in before the shower yesterday. He ran up the ladder to the mow, jumped on the cart, and had not thrown off but three or four forks full, when I heard a terrible noise, as if the barn was coming down. Tom screamed for help. I ran in to the barn floor, and there was my poor boy lying just as he fell, backwards off the cart, his fork across his feet. He lay perfectly still, and my heart stopped beating, for I thought he was dead. I guess my scream of terror brought him to a little, for he opened his eyes and gazed about kind of wild." The father covered his face with his hands and groaned aloud, while his companion, feeling there was little comfort he could offer, rode silently by his side.

It seemed a long, weary time to the excited, anxious group outside the bedroom, before Mrs. Smith, who had insisted on remaining near her son, appeared among them to say the doctor thought a broken shoulder and two broken ribs was the extent of the injury. The setting of the shoulder was very painful for the time; but now the poor fellow was greatly relieved, and would be glad to see them.

The grateful father hastened to the sick room, his heart overflowing with love and praise to his heavenly Father, who had so graciously spared his son's life, while the mother made a slice of toast, which, with a cup of coffee, the physician had ordered for his patient.

Susan, after running to Juliette's room to convey the joyful tidings, set the long delayed breakfast on the table.

"Where is Miss Edwards?" inquired James, as an hour or two later his mother entered his room.

"Poor child! she looks terribly pale and drooping. She ran off while the doctor was here, 'cause she couldn't bear to hear you groan. She's in the kitchen now, helping the girls. They thought I could do better in here."

"Would you mind, mother, asking her in here a minute?"

She glanced anxiously at his pale face, tinged with the faintest flush, and then went out to do as he requested. She sighed, however, as she said to herself, "He's building hopes on her feeling so much for him; but it's no use. I wish I might tell him what I know of her history."

When she entered the kitchen Juliette was shelling some peas. The mother herself was embarrassed, in

making the request, but after a minute said, "I must
be working over my butter, girls, or I can't do it to-
day. Perhaps you will sit with James a little while,"
she added, turning to Juliette.

The young girl looked frightened. "What if he
should faint again?" she asked, quickly.

"Oh, there's no danger of that, my dear child!
When he lies still, he says he don't suffer much. 'Twas
his broken shoulder that distressed him so; and the
doctor said the way he was laid on the bed made it ten
times worse. You may take your peas in there, if
you'd rather."

Juliette rose, though rather reluctantly. The vision
of his pallid, ghastly countenance was still before her.
Mrs. Smith accompanied her, carrying the pan, which
she set down just inside the bedroom door.

"If he wants anything, speak to me," she said, and
then, smoothing back his damp hair from his forehead,
returned to her work.

The young girl timidly approached the bed. "How
do you feel?" she asked, speaking scarcely above her
breath.

"Very comfortable and very grateful," was his
gentle reply.

She stood a moment looking at his shoulder, which
was tightly bandaged. "Doesn't it pain you?" she
inquired.

"Not much. The doctor relieved me very quickly."
He colored, and tried to say something, but had not
the courage.

"I'll shell the peas here, if it wont disturb you," she added, in a more cheerful tone.

"No, let me shell them; I can do them easily with my right hand."

She laughed. "No, indeed! Your mother put me here to watch you, and I shall be a very strict nurse. You must not stir, nor scarcely breathe, while I stay. You see, I mean to do all I can to help you get well."

"Juliette!"

He had never called her so before, and she smiled as she looked up from her work.

"You can't imagine what a comfort it was to me, this morning, to have you here. I couldn't speak then, but I've been wanting ever since to tell you so."

She cast down her eyes, and blushed deeply; not so much at the words, but at the look which accompanied them.

"It was terrible to see you suffer so," she answered, softly.

Her heart beat quickly, and she began to be impatient for Mrs. Smith or one of the girls to take her place. She went on steadily with her work, however, not venturing to raise her eyes.

He seemed more than content to watch her varying color, and built airy castles upon her seeming confusion, which, alas! were destined to fall to the ground.

"How do you get on with your patient?" queried Susan, coming softly behind her young friend.

"You must ask him. I'm afraid I am not a very good nurse."

"I should be content to be sick all my life, with such care, if that was the will of God," returned James, warmly.

Juliette was really distressed, and blamed herself for the answer she had given. She took up her pan and quietly went out of the room, leaving Susan in charge of her brother.

From this time, though she frequently visited him for a moment, it was always in company with one of the family, and her manner, without being reserved, was such that he had not courage to tell her one word of that love of which his heart was so full.

On Sabbath morning, Mr. Smith, in his prayer, supplicated special grace for her who was on that day to take upon herself the vows of God, and to partake of the Saviour's body broken for sin, in commemoration of his dying love.

Since James's accident prayer had been offered in the room adjoining his. Juliette was much affected, and, as they arose, was about to retire, when he called her by name.

She hesitated a moment, and then, seeing his mother was with him, approached the bed.

"It's the greatest trial I've had yet," he said, deeply moved, "not to go to church to-day. But though I'm obliged to lie in bed at home, my heart will be there, and I shall pray that it may be a day of peace to your soul."

His countenance was lighted with heavenly fervor,

as if the spirit of that peace which passeth all under-standing was dwelling in him.

Her own face reflected the light from his, as she earnestly uttered her thanks. She retired to her own apartment, feeling that such prayers would prove indeed a blessing.

The day was one never to be forgotten. As she re-ceived the elements of her Saviour's love, and realized that His blood had been shed for her salvation, her heart overflowed with gratitude. She fervently re-newed her vows to him and to his service, and con-sidered no sacrifice too great, to be counted among his disciples.

The distance was so great, and the intermission so short, that the family from the farm usually remained until after the second service; but Mrs. Smith, being anxious concerning her son, returned after the admin-istration of the sacrament, her husband coming back in season for the afternoon sermon.

After tea, as they were sitting together in the parlor, James requested his sisters to sing.

Susan had a very sweet treble voice, and Maria sung a good alto. They brought out the books, and, with Dudley as a leader, passed an hour pleasantly in sing-ing from Mason's Choir; Juliette, though pressed to join them, declaring she would much prefer to be a listener.

At last Susan, in answer to her brother's call, went to his bed, when she received a message from him to her young friend.

"James wants to have you sing the hymn he has heard from your room. Do please gratify him, and all of us, if you can."

Juliette consented, though she blushed deeply as she said, "I have seldom sung it without my harp; but I will do my best." Then, with a voice rarely equalled in richness and pathos, she commenced the hymn I have already given to the reader.

Her little audience held their breath to listen; and when she had finished, begged so warmly for another and yet another hymn, that she could not refuse to gratify them.

Poor James was glad that she could not witness the emotion her singing produced on him. His whole soul was entranced, his breast heaved, while big tears coursed down his manly cheeks. "Tell her," said he, to his sister, "that she has done me good; that I have no words to thank her."

CHAPTER XXI

"On you, most loved, with anxious fear I wait,
And from your judgment must expect my fate."

AFTER the lapse of a week, James began to be impatient of his confinement to the bed, and, with much urging, persuaded the physician to allow him to sit up in an easy-chair, his arm supported in a sling and propped by pillows. For greater convenience the chair was placed in the common sitting-room, where he could be pushed to the table during their meals, which was considered a great improvement by the young man upon the mode of eating by himself.

One day Susan, who had been to the village on an errand, ran into the room, exclaiming, "Only guess, James, who I saw this morning! But I don't believe you'll guess right in a month of Sundays. Somebody who inquired for you and blushed rosy-red when I told her you were sick."

"How can I tell?" asked her brother, his own color deepening as he saw Juliette's eyes fixed with a peculiar expression upon him.

"You're real stupid not to know, when I've told you so much. Why, it's Josey Attwood. She's coming

19   217

here to pass the afternoon, and her cousin with her, who has been in the Lowell factory. Josey as much as told me she'd come before I had time to ask her."

James glanced anxiously at his mother, and seemed really annoyed, while Juliette's eyes danced with merriment. She was conscious of great relief, and secretly called herself a fool for being miserable at his fancied affection for her.

"I shall be right glad to see Josey," remarked Mrs. Smith. "She was always a favorite of mine; but who is this cousin?"

"I don't know, I'm sure. Josey introduced her as Miss Darley. She is quite a dashing, showy girl."

"You don't look half as pleased as I expected," rejoined Susan, archly gazing into her brother's face. "You used to say she was the prettiest girl in the town."

"How foolish you do talk!" exclaimed the young man, trying to conceal his flushed face. "That was years ago, when we were only children."

"I have always heard those were the strongest attachments which commenced in childhood," persisted the merry girl, unmoved by her brother's frowns. "Don't you think so, Juliette?"

"Certainly, I do," was the blushing reply, as the young girl recollected that she had loved Horace ever since she could remember.

"I have a great mind to get father to roll my chair into the bedroom, and stay there until your company has gone," muttered James, impatiently.

"That would scarcely be civil to your old playmate, my son," urged Mrs. Smith, who had her own reasons for wishing that his early affection for Josey might be revived.

"Little boys must try to be good when they are sick, and obey their ma's," added Susan, with a tone of mock gravity.

"And not be rude to their sisters' company," rejoined Juliette, archly.

"I'll do my best," urged James, with an attempt at a laugh; "I'm always thankful for good advice."

In the afternoon the young misses arrived early. Josey Attwood was in her eighteenth year, just Juliette's age, — a petite figure, but full of sprightliness and grace. In complexion she was a blonde, with a profusion of light waving hair, combed low over her forehead, in the prevailing mode. Her mouth was wide, but well formed, and, as she was scarcely ever silent, displayed continually two rows of beautiful teeth.

In the few minutes occupied in removing her bonnet and mantilla, Juliette had formed a very favorable opinion of the young lady, who blushingly inquired in a low voice of Susan, "what James said when he found she was coming?"

"Oh, it would never do to tell!" exclaimed her companion, coloring a little at a roguish glance from Juliette. "But come in and see him."

Our young heroine had a natural desire to witness James's reception of his early friend, and followed her and Miss Darley directly to the sitting-room.

It was really curious to witness the embarrassment
in the manner of the invalid, occasioned by the sudden
rush of old memories her lively presence called forth,
commingled with the newer and far more intense emotions inspired by his intercourse with Juliette. She
burst upon him like a sunbeam, her eyes dancing and
her rosy cheeks rosier with pleasure.

James cordially grasped her hand in his, and held it
a moment while he gazed into her loving eyes; but
presently, catching a glance of Juliette's mirthful countenance, he suddenly realized what her conclusions
must be, and, with a flush that mounted to his brow, he
let fall her hand, and turned almost rudely to the other
lady, whom his sister Maria was introducing to him.

Miss Darley was a tall, well-formed girl, with a sensi-
ble countenance, but with no claims to beauty. As
was learned from her conversation in the course of the
afternoon, she was early left an orphan; but was taken
as a dependent into the family of an uncle. Feeling
unhappy in this situation, she determined to make
every effort to fit herself for a teacher, and succeeded
so well that she was advanced to be mistress of a town
school when she was in her seventeenth year. After
teaching for two terms, she accidentally met a young
friend who had been working in one of the Lowell factories, and who represented the life there as so superior
to that of a village school-mistress that she gave up
her school and obtained a situation in the same factory
with her friend. She had now been an operative for
three years, and was so well pleased with the employ-

ment that she would on no account exchange it for that of a teacher.

Miss Darley spoke with great enthusiasm of the privileges the factory girls enjoyed. The moment the bell rang for them to be dismissed they were free to employ their time as they pleased. Many of them formed societies for mutual benefit, when they read, worked, and conversed together. On the Sabbath great attention was paid to their improvement in the several churches of the city, as they formed no unimportant part of the whole community. Bible classes with the best of teachers were gathered, and all who wished invited to join.

"But," suggested Mrs. Smith, after listening with great interest to the animated account, "I always supposed the labor was severe, and that it was unhealthy."

"Not at all, ma'am; certainly not in the weaving rooms, where I work. They are well ventilated and kept with great neatness. I dare say it may be the case in some of the dye-houses, and, perhaps, in the woollen factories, where there is a bad odor from the wool. Then a good hand can earn four, five, or even six dollars a week beside her board."

After an early tea, Maria proposed a walk around the farm, to which all consented with readiness, except Josey, who evidently preferred remaining with James. While her cousin had been talking, she had sat busily engaged with her work, her eyes every now and then stealing a glance at him. Several times the blood was

19*

sent swiftly coursing through her veins as she saw that,
instead of returning these glances, his gaze was fixed
on the fair girl on the other side of the room, whose
downcast eyes, shielded by her thick, curling lashes,
afforded him a most favorable opportunity to contem-
plate her exquisitely cut features.

Even Josey, beginning to be moved to jealousy of
one whom she feared might be a rival, could not help
acknowledging to herself that Miss Edwards was very
lovely. There was a purity in that low, broad brow,
an expression of truthfulness in those soft, beaming
eyes, a winning sweetness in the tiny mouth, an air
of high breeding in the carriage of the small head, set
so daintily upon her shoulders, that, though she did not
thus define each charm, made a strong impression on
the beholder.

From being indignant at his indifference toward herself, — a state of things wholly new in her former experience, — she began to wonder how she should compare with this beautiful stranger, and ended by humbly
underrating her own attractions.

When the walk was first proposed she was pleased,
as she thought she might easily find an excuse for remaining within, and have an opportunity to come to a
better understanding with James. But when he so
strenuously urged her to accompany his sisters, she
went, carrying a heavy weight at her heart.

Juliette, in passing out, gave him a reproachful
glance, and, taking advantage of a momentary delay
of the party in the hall, said, in a low voice, " You are

not keeping your promise to do your best. She is a very lovely girl."

How little either of the party imagined what an important bearing the events of this short afternoon would have upon the future destiny of one of their number! But I forbear.

Weeks flew by until the early sweetings, Maria called honeycombs, were ripe. The hay, oats, rye, and barley were gathered in the barns, though Mr. Smith would not consent that James should "lift a hand" toward the work, for fear his shoulder was not yet strong. Maria and her sister were commencing their preparations for returning to school, and Juliette began to count the days before she could reasonably expect an answer to her letter.

Her kind pastor, Mr. Allen, had informed her that a vessel ordinarily sailed from New York to Liverpool in four weeks; but, as she supposed her father and brother had gone directly to the continent, some time longer must elapse before it could reach him. Then the weeks necessary for a return would carry it quite into the autumn.

She tried to be patient and submissive to the will of God, whatever it might be. But of late she had had some trials, which were more severe because she was obliged to keep them locked in her own breast, and could not find sympathy from the motherly heart of Mrs. Smith, as she had heretofore done.

Ever since the visit of Josey Attwood, James had been at times moody and fitful, wholly unlike his former easy good temper. His father insisted that his fall had produced some injury not yet wholly revealed. But his mother, with a keener insight into human nature in general, and her son's nature in particular, knew that the injury was in his heart, and feared it would be difficult to heal. With Juliette's conduct she was entirely satisfied. No sooner did she suspect the nature of his affection than she withdrew herself as much as possible from his society, never allowing him an opportunity to see her alone.

This excitement, like every other, constantly weighing upon her mind, affected her spirits, and within a few days she had determined to relate to him her former history; and even, if necessary, to show him that he had no hope from delay; to acknowledge that her heart was not in her own keeping. Once assured of this, she was convinced he had too much good sense to cherish an attachment which never could be reciprocated.

Having once made up her mind to this course, she became impatient for an opportunity for its accomplishment. In company with Maria and Susan, she was often invited to parties of young persons in the town. A few times she had accepted the invitations, but generally preferred remaining quietly at the farm with Mrs. Smith. It happened, just at this period, fortunately as she thought, that an excursion was planned to a neighboring village, and James earnestly invited her to accompany him.

She hesitated a moment, wishing first to consult his

mother; but the good woman, not understanding her
reason, called her from the room and said, "You had
better go this once, my dear. He will never be satisfied until he has told you his feelings. I'm afraid you
will think him a very foolish, aspiring boy."

"Oh, no, indeed! He has a noble heart any one
would be proud to win; but there are many reasons
why I cannot return his affection. My father away,
and—"

"I understand you, my dear; but James is waiting.
May I tell him you will go?"

"If you think it proper and best. If I go, I shall
relate to him what I have already told you of my life
before I came to Stamford."

"That is right." Mrs. Smith warmly kissed her
cheek, and then went to announce to her son the acceptance of his invitation.

The young farmer had taken the precaution to hire
a handsome buggy,—indeed, the handsomest in the
village,—before he spoke to Juliette, and on the day
appointed drove gayly to the door, dressed in his new
suit of black broadcloth.

As he stood waiting a moment for his companion,
his countenance radiant with happiness, for the poor
fellow was building bright hopes on her consenting to
accompany him alone, his mother could scarcely refrain
from hinting the probable result of the excursion.

Susan, who, with Maria and Dudley and a young
gentleman of her acquaintance, were to go in Mr.
Smith's carriage, gazed earnestly at her brother, and

at last exclaimed, in her own impressive way, "James, I never saw you look so well. If I wasn't your sister I'd marry you right off."

At this moment Juliette appeared, dressed in a rich silk she had never worn in Stamford, and with an expensive bracelet of gold and pearls clasped on her polished arm, but with a pale, troubled countenance.

Mrs. Smith, at once comprehending her reason for this change in her hitherto strictly plain attire, smiled her approval; and, with many charges to her son to bring the young girl home in safety, bowed her adieu as they drove away.

Poor James! He had passed half the night before in composing a suitable speech for this occasion; but now, as he was seated by the side of this richly dressed lady, her round, slender arm, encircled with an ornament costing more than all he was worth in the world, lying so daintily across her lap, just within his line of vision, it seemed preposterous, absurd, and he discarded it in disgust.

"But how shall I tell her?" he soliloquized, as they swiftly made their way toward the rendezvous of the party. "I can't, and wont bear this any longer, while I have a tongue to speak, or ears to hear her reply. Somehow or other I must end my suspense this afternoon; but it's a terrible job. I'd rather cradle the biggest piece of oats I ever saw;" and, taking his white handkerchief from his pocket, he wiped the perspiration, which seemed oozing from every pore of his face.

Juliette—I am sorry to be obliged to say it—

smiled, — yes, *smiled*, when she ought to have shed tears over the downfall of his dearest hopes. She suspected the cause of his confusion, and determined to forestall the declaration she saw he was gathering courage to make. All at once she began to talk in her gayest tone, pointing out the beauties of the landscape, and asking who lived in this house, and who in the cottage back in the fields.

"How far is it from Stamford to A——?" she inquired.

"About ten miles; but there is an early moon, and at any rate I don't mean to be late."

Standing near the village school-house were carriages of every description, awaiting the arrival of the remainder of the party. James drove up to the door, snapping his whip in style; but Juliette preferred not to alight.

"Our young farmer seems to be in high clover," muttered a man in an open carriage near them. "'Tisn't every one can have a chance to ride in 'Squire Lyman's new buggy, with a girl as handsome as a picter a-sitting by the side of him."

Juliette's face was crimson. She snatched down her veil, and tried to turn her head away.

James colored, too, but it was with pleasure. "No," said he, in a tone meant only for her ear, "I wouldn't change my place this afternoon for that of a king on his throne."

One company after another arrived, and soon the signal was given for starting away. Dudley Houghton, as the projector of the excursion, led the procession, and James Smith followed him.

"Now is my time," thought Juliette. "I am determined to save him the mortification of being refused;" but, before she could choose words to commence, her companion, summoning all his courage, said, —

"Miss Edwards, perhaps you can imagine why I invited you to come with me alone this afternoon. From the time you alighted from the carriage the day you came home with our girls, looking so pale and sad, I've loved you. When you gazed so wistfully in mother's eyes, and flew to her arms like a poor bird scared from its nest, I made a vow to myself that while I had arms strong enough to earn you a home, you should have one. I loved you then, a stranger as you was to all of us. I saw truth and purity in every action; but, O Juliette! words can't express how much L love you now. I know I'm an ignorant country farmer, earning my living by the sweat of my brow; I know I am unsuited to you in many things, refined, delicate, and accomplished as you are; but, if you will only say you'll try to return my love, I'll pledge myself, before the God we both try to serve, to devote my life to making you happy."

CHAPTER XXII.

" Father of spirits, hear !
Look on the inmost heart to thee revealed ;
Look on the fountain of the burning tear."

POOR Juliette ! Several times she had endeavored
to interrupt him, but her fast-flowing tears and
the eagerness with which he was borne on by his feelings prevented her. As soon as she could speak she
said, "Don't, James ! Don't say any more ! You
make me very unhappy."

The young farmer gasped for breath. He knew by
the sad tone of her voice that his suit was a hopeless
one.

"I do love you, James," she added, softly laying
her hand on his arm ; "love you as a dear, warm-
hearted Christian brother. I will not pretend that I
have misunderstood your many acts of kindness ; but I
hoped to spare you this avowal by telling you some
things about myself."

"Nothing you can tell me of that kind will alter my
feelings," said the young man, in such a tone of utter
despondence that her tears flowed afresh.

"I knew you had suffered," he added, sighing ;
"but I loved you the more on that account. Oh ! I

have longed so to make you happy, to try to have you forget the past."

"James, James, you will break my heart! You are too good, too noble, not to have a wife who can, with her whole soul, return your affection. James, I love one I knew long before I met you, and I am very unhappy, too."

He started, and gazed at her in silence for a moment. "Whew!" he exclaimed; "I wonder I never thought of that. I can scarcely credit it that any one you loved could treat you ill."

"He has not. He is good and kind. We were brought up like brother and sister, our parents having married. But he is gone away for years, and I am a poor wanderer, turned from my father's house because I would not deny my Saviour."

James's eyes flashed fire. "Wicked wretch!" he exclaimed.

"Oh, don't say so!" she cried in agony. "He is my father, my beloved, indulgent father; indulgent in everything but this. Yet he was brought up with bitter prejudices against religion, and he really believes that he is saving me from great unhappiness. Of late, I have often thought of going to my grandfather's; but I fear he would oppose me even more than my father has done."

The young man did not seem to hear her last remark. There was a terrible struggle going on in his breast. His hopes of happiness with her he loved with the whole strength of his manly heart were suddenly

blasted; and at first he could not be resigned to his
fate. "It is worse than death," he said to himself.
"I cannot endure it." But James was a Christian, and
believed that for such all things were ordered for good.
His heart went up to the throne of grace in an earnest
petition for strength and submission to the will of his
heavenly Father; and while he asked, God answered.

Turning his glistening eyes full upon hers, he said in
a subdued voice, "Juliette, it is over now. At first I
was stunned. I had hoped you could learn to love
me; but that is past forever. You say you were turned
from home because you loved your Saviour. I hope
he is my Saviour, too, and for his sake I offer you a
home as long as you can be happy with us. You say
you love me as a brother, and here I pledge you a
brother's love and support." His lips quivered with
ill-concealed emotion, while he held out his ungloved
hand, which she caught in both of hers and pressed
to her lips. "Now let me say one thing more," he rejoined, when he could command his voice, "I want
you to promise that if ever you need my services, you
will call upon me. You can't imagine how much good
it would do me to be of use to you. Don't be afraid I
shall misinterpret your feelings; for after what has
passed between us I shall never hope, as I have done.
No, I want you to forget all that; or just to remember
it when it wont give you pain; only let me feel, after
this, that I am your out-and-out friend. Maybe I
shall be dull at times;" and he heaved a dreadful sigh
as he began to realize what a terrible void had been

made in his heart. "But God will give me strength to
endure it. I think I might even be happy if I could
see you so.

"There, don't cry so, Juliette. I may call my sister, Juliette?" She could only nod her assent. "Do
let me comfort you;" and he choked down a sob that
threatened to suffocate him.

"You have comforted me," sobbed the weeping
girl; "you do not know how thankful I am. I think
God turned your heart to me in answer to my prayers.
I shall always thank him for giving me so good, so
kind, so noble a brother. I came to Stamford so desolate, and now I have a father, mother, brother and
two sisters. Yes," she added, after a momentary
pause, and becoming more composed, "my Father in
heaven has fulfilled his promise to me. He has
raised me up friends who have comforted me in my
sorrow."

They rode on for some time in silence; and then she
began to talk of her step-mother, of her early death,
the agony of her father, her removal to the school, her
happiness when she began to love her Saviour, her
return to New York, her sin in entering into the dissi-
pations of the gay city, her determination to break
away from them, and the sad result which followed.

These she dwelt upon at length, James listening
with rapt attention and expressing his sympathy in his
own peculiar manner. When she stopped, he said
softly, "Tell me of him."

The name of Horace she had purposely omitted,

fearing it would give him pain. At his request, however, though with a heightened color, she spoke of his
early life, how kind he was to her, how considerate of
her wishes; then when they were separated, how often
he had written her, and when he was in college how
frequent were his visits to Mrs. Osborn's school.
She told him of their residence under her father's roof;
how a remark she made turned his thoughts to the subject of religion, and then, when he saw her becoming
more and more conformed to the world and passing
her life in the vain pursuit after pleasure, how he had
feared for her and warned her; and last, she spoke of
his departure for Europe, and, with a choking voice,
of the tenderness of his farewell.

"I always thought my brother Horace superior to
any man I knew, except my father," she exclaimed,
with a deep blush; "but I never knew how much I
loved him till he was gone."

All this James heard, smothering the pain her
frank avowal gave him, and then, in his honest,
hearty way, said, "I wish you all the happiness with
him that you deserve. He must be worthy, or you
could not love him as you do."

"Thank you!" cried Juliette, fervently. "I may
never see him again, though I hope to; but if I do
not, I never shall be married."

"No, you ought not;" he answered manfully. "I
have often thought that no life could be so miserable
as to be married to one person and love another."

"That would be one reason, if there were no other,

James," said Juliette, looking archly in his face, "why I could not have married you. Only think how wretched we should both have felt, if, too late, you should have discovered that, after all, you loved that sweet girl you have known all your life."

"Poor Josey!" murmured James. ".I'm afraid she thought me very unkind. Well, I shall know how to sympathize with her, now;" and he resolutely repressed a sigh.

"But here we are. I shall never forget this ride. How short it has been!"

On alighting from the carriage Juliette found Maria and Susan waiting to conduct her to the anteroom adjoining the hall, where supper was to be served. Just before they were leaving it for a promenade around the tables, our heroine perceived Josey Attwood standing near a middle-aged man, gazing sorrowfully at their group.

"I do pity Josey," whispered Susan. "There she is with her sister and brother-in-law. She refused ever so many invitations from the young men. . She's a great favorite with all of them."

"I suppose she has accompanied your brother on similar occasions," answered her companion, calmly.

"Yes."

"Let's go and invite her now. I see a number of the gentleman have a lady on each arm. I'm sure James will enjoy having his old friend in our company."

Susan gave a piercing glance into Juliette's ani-

mated countenance; then, unmindful of the presence of
others, suddenly leaned forward and kissed her warmly, whispering, "You're the dearest girl that ever
was!"

"Come!" exclaimed Juliette, putting her hand
within James's arm, "we're going over to talk with
Josey."

As they made their way through the crowd, who
were talking and laughing gayly, she added in a low
tone, "I'm going to use one of my privileges as a sister and offer your disengaged arm to a friend."

"Just as you say," he answered, coloring; "but I'm
afraid it will only make matters worse."

The young girl saw them approaching, and turned
quickly away to hide her tears. But Susan, hastily
disengaging her arm from that of the gentleman who
accompanied her, sprang forward and caught her hand.
"We all want you with us," she said eagerly.

Josey turned a wistful glance toward James and his
companion, when the former, urged by a slight pressure of his arm, added, "Yes, come with us. It seems
odd not to have you in our party." And offering her
his arm, she blushingly accepted it, and they at once
joined the procession which had begun to form around
the room.

Juliette talked and laughed, and gave them no time
to feel awkward. And in her disinterested effort to pro-
mote kind feeling between her two companions, she
entered into the excitement of the occasion until she
became the life of the whole company.

When they returned to the anteroom to don their outer garments, Juliette, who had planned a little project of her own, drew Josey aside and said, "You know James and I have adopted one another for brother and sister; so for his sake you must love me a little. We came in a buggy; but as you and I are both small, there will be plenty of room, and you shall return with us."

Poor Josey's lips quivered; she choked, then burst into tears. At last she answered, speaking with difficulty, "Thank you, I'm sure; but I'm afraid James wont like it. He don't treat me at all as he used to."

Juliette was really distressed. She was too truthful to assert that he would probably wish her company; but presently, with a bright thought, she exclaimed, "I have noticed a difference in James since he was sick. He has had some things to trouble him; so we must do all we can for his comfort."

Josey's countenance beamed with sympathy. "I'll do anything in the world I can for him; and, if he don't object, I will ride in your carriage with pleasure.

Mrs. Smith was somewhat surprised to see James and Juliette riding up to the door in such good spirits, and, while her son went home with the buggy, still more so to hear Susan's lively account of the excursion.

"I do believe our Juliette is a witch, mother; and we ought to be thankful that she didn't live in the old times, or she would have been hung. In the first place, the eyes of all the gentlemen, present company always excepted," making a low bow to Dudley, "were fixed upon her, to the utter neglect of their own lady-loves, while nothing could be talked of but Miss Edwards,— Miss Edwards's bright eyes, Miss Edwards's brilliant color, her silky curls, her ease, dignity, and grace in company."

Susy stopped to recover her breath, but presently resumed. "Then, in the second place, she so bewitched our James that he didn't know whether he was on his head or feet. And there he strutted about, with her on one arm and Josey on the other, the envy of half the beaux and the detestation of the other half."

"It's all true, mother," added Maria, when the shout of merriment had subsided. "I wont even except Dudley; for I caught his eyes playing truant more than once."

Mrs. Smith noticed that, though Juliette laughed with the others, her thoughts were not with them; and, with a mother's anxiety to know what had passed, she advised the young lady to retire to rest, and presently followed to the chamber.

"James is a noble man!" cried the tired girl, throwing her arms around Mrs. Smith's neck. "He knows all now; and has promised to be a friend and brother still. Josey came home with us, and I can see he will turn to her for comfort."

"God will bless you, my dear," answered the good

woman, straining the young girl to her heart. "You have done just right."

She had scarcely reached the bottom of the stairs before James entered the kitchen. He did not perceive her, and, throwing himself listlessly into a chair, covered his face with his hands.

She softly approached him and put her hand on his head.

"O mother!" he cried in agony, "I have lost her. My heart seems crushed, but she is too good and too beautiful for me." And covering his face again, his stout form swayed to and fro with the fierce emotions that agitated his breast.

A shout of laughter from the parlor reached him, and, starting up, he was about to rush to his own room, when he suddenly turned back and said, hoarsely, "Mother, will you pray for me? Oh, I did hope I could make her happy! But she must never know this. No one but God shall know what I suffer." He wrung the hand she held out to him, and left the room.

As he passed Juliette's door, he heard her voice softly uttering her evening prayer. Unconsciously he stopped and listened. She was thanking her heavenly Father for giving her such kind friends to be a support to her in her hours of trial, separated as she was from her own kindred.

"Yes, and I will be a friend!" he exclaimed, hastening to his own chamber. "I must and will school my heart; and, God helping me, she shall never suspect how miserable she has made me."

CHAPTER XXIII.

" Her heart sunk in her,
And every slackened fibre dropt its hold,
Like Nature letting down the springs of life."

IT was nearly a month later than the events related in the preceding chapter that the horse and buggy of the village doctor were seen driving up to the farm.

Within the house Mrs. Smith was anxiously bending over Juliette's couch, the young girl having at last fallen into a light slumber.

"How is my patient to-day?" inquired the physician entering from the side door into the kitchen, where Maria and her sister were at work.

"I don't know, exactly," answered Susan, coming forward. "Mother took care of her last night and said the poor girl did not get any sleep. Do you think she will have a fever?"

"She has a fever already; a slow, nervous attack, not severe, nor immediately dangerous; but there is nothing like it to prostrate the system." And so saying, he went softly up the stairs.

Mrs. Smith came quickly from the chamber to meet him with her finger on her lip.

"She's just fallen off," she remarked in a whisper. "The first sleep she's had for twenty-four hours."

"How's her appetite?" he inquired in the same tone.

"She has none at all. I don't think she's taken a teaspoonful of nourishment since you were here yesterday morning."

"Much fever?"

"By spells. She was hot and restless all night." She pushed open the door behind her and entered on tiptoe, the doctor following closely.

As she lay there, the dark, thick lashes shadowing her white cheek, she looked so much like one resting in her last, long slumber, that the physician started forward and put down his ear to listen whether she breathed. Then he laid his fingers gently on the frail wrist lying outside the counterpane, shook his head impressively, and motioned Mrs. Smith from the room.

"Where are this child's friends?" he inquired, when the door was again shut.

"Her father is abroad. I do not know whether she has other relatives." She was evidently embarrassed both at the question and the searching look which accompanied it.

"They ought to know her situation."

"Then you consider her very ill?"

"Not so much that, but the delicacy of her constitution excites alarm. Did you observe that white ring about the mouth and the pinched look of the nostrils? They denote extreme prostration."

"She always has that when the fever is off. Her cheeks were bright-red all night."

He stood a moment gazing abstractedly upon the floor. "I think I must venture to try a tonic," he muttered, half-aloud; and, opening the door of the adjoining room, he went to the table, and prepared a number of little· powders, which he ordered to be given once in three hours.

"I'll look in again before' bedtime, if possible," he added, turning to go downstairs. "In the mean time, get her to take as much arrow-root, toast-water, or rice-water, as you can."

The kind-hearted woman returned softly to the chamber, and, finding her patient still asleep, went to a closet in the entry for some sewing.

Presently a door opened at the end of the hall, and James beckoned her toward him.

"What does the doctor say?" he asked in a hurried voice.

"He thinks her very ill."

"Dangerously so?"

"He said her friends ought to be informed of her condition."

A low, quick gasp, and without another word he entered his room again.

Oh, the agony of the hour that followed! With clasped hands and streaming eyes, he besieged the mercy-seat in her behalf. "Gracious Father, spare her; take her not away in the midst of her days.

21

Restore her to life, strength, and happiness; and do
unto thy servant according to thy will."

Then, comforted by the assurance that God was a
hearer and answerer of prayer, he· stole unperceived
down the back stairs, and returned to his work again.

About the same hour Juliette awoke. At first, she
gazed in the face of her devoted nurse, as if she did
not recognize her, — but almost instantly recovered
herself, and smiled. "I have had a beautiful dream,"
she said, softly. "I thought James went to the office,.
and found a letter there for me from father, — and he
wants me to come to him at once."

" Perhaps it may come true, dear. We will send to
the office and see. But you will need a good deal
more strength before you can start on so long a journey; and here is a powder the doctor left for you."

Juliette took· it, as she did everything else, without
a word of remonstrance, and then swallowed a spoon-
full of arrow-root after it. Her heart was full of her
dream; and she could not refrain talking about it.
"How much better I feel!" she said again and again.
"I believe, if I should hear from father, I should be
well very quick."

Mrs. Smith brushed back her hair and kissed her.
"You mustn't talk too much, dear, for fear it will
bring on your fever. If you'll promise to be a good
girl, and not be too much disappointed if the dream
doesn't prove true this time, I'll slip down and get Mr.
Smith or James to ride to the village. How should
you like to have Mr. Allen call and see you?"

"Very much. He's a good man."

Mrs. Smith knew how much pleasure it would give her son to go; and therefore telling Susan to go up to Juliette, but not to let her talk, she put on her sun-bonnet, and went out to the field where he was at work, harvesting his vegetables.

The young man dropped his spade at once, and, without waiting to change his dress, harnessed the horse into the wagon and rode quickly away.

He drove first to Mr. Allen's and gave his mother's message, and then, with a palpitating heart, made his way across the common to the office.

"Any letters for us to-day, Mr. Jones?"

"I'll see. No," he added presently, "there are none."

"Wont you look particularly, and see whether there is one for Miss Edwards? She's expecting one."

The man fumbled over some papers, and then answered "No," again; little suspecting how that one short syllable caused the young man's heart to sink within him. He dreaded to go home the bearer of ill tidings; and, finally, concluded to call at Mr. Allen's again, and get him to go to the farm at once.

Mrs. Smith found that her young patient was eagerly listening for the carriage, and feared she was too confident of receiving a letter. She tried to divert her mind from the subject, and even hinted that James might be unsuccessful; but Juliette only smiled. Her dream had seemed so real. The "My dearly loved daughter" at the commencement, and the "Ever your

loving father" at the close, with the tenderest little
postscript from Horace, were as clearly before her
mind's eye, as the face of her faithful, untiring nurse
was before her physical one.

Still, when the sound of wheels was heard approaching, her quick, sharp "Hark! isn't that James?"
betrayed so much of nervous excitement, — the very
thing the doctor had condemned, — that, in order to
allay it the sooner, she hastened down the stairs.

James had already jumped to the ground, and was
holding the reins for Mr. Allen to alight. One glance
at his troubled face told her he had not succeeded.
Inviting Mr. Allen into the parlor, she returned for a
minute to the door.

"There was nothing for her, mother," he said,
avoiding her eye. "I'd have given half I'm worth to
have brought her a letter.

"I don't know how she'll take it," murmured the
good woman, speaking to herself. "She seemed very
sure you'd bring her one."

"And more than that," he exclaimed in a low, angry
tone, and with a flash of his deep blue eye, "I don't
believe they ever mean to write her. The man's a
rascal, to my thinking."

"Hush! James, hush! You don't know what
you're saying." She was really alarmed to hear him
talk so fiercely ; and, with a glance of mingled reproach
and tenderness, she hastened to relieve Juliette's
anxiety, and announce Mr. Allen's arrival.

When Mrs. Smith first caught sight of her patient,

she was looking toward the door, with a face of such eager, pleased anticipation, her eyes so brimful of hope, her cheeks so brilliant with triumph, that the heart of the woman sank within her.

"Give it to me, quick," she said, earnestly; "I can bear it. Oh, don't make me wait! please, dear Mrs. Smith."

The sympathizing nurse, though not given to crying, could not restrain her tears. "You must wait a little longer, my poor child. There was no letter to-day."

The bright color faded suddenly, all hope died out of the beaming eye, and the poor girl, sinking back into her pillows, covered her face with her hands, and wept bitter, bitter tears of disappointment.

For a time, Mrs. Smith did not try to check her grief; she only laid her hand tenderly on the throbbing temples, and uttered soothing sounds, as one would to a frightened child. "There, dear, don't now! Maybe there'll be one to-morrow."

Juliette shook her head; and, after weeping for some time without restraint, while her anxious companion was wondering what she should do with her, said abruptly, "Don't think me ungrateful. If you only knew how sure, how very sure, I was. I knew every word of it by heart; but now I feel I am unforgiven. I shall never hear from him again;" and she uttered such a cry of distress, as the truth of this seemed to burst upon her, that Mr. Smith, who was with their pastor, came hastily up the stairs to inquire the cause.

21*

"Memories on memories! to my soul again
    There come such dreams of banished love and bliss,
  That my wrung heart, though long inured to pain,
    Sinks with the fulness of its wretchedness."

Mrs. Smith did not speak, but only pointed to the
bed, where Juliette, in a violent fit of hysterics, was
sobbing, until her frail form was shaken from head to
foot.

The good farmer, wholly unused to such scenes,
descended more hastily than he came up, and begged
the clergyman to go to the relief of the poor girl.

Mr. Allen, fortunately, was more conversant with
sickness both of the body and mind. He asked Mrs.
Smith for her bottle of ammonia, and administered a
few drops with his own hands. Then, addressing the
sick girl in a firm, but mild tone, he said, "You must
try to control yourself; it will kill you to give way to
your feelings, and God has more work for you before
he calls you home."

Perhaps it was his words of authority; perhaps
because her grief had spent itself, and exhausted
nature could weep no more; but her sobs came at
longer intervals, and at last ceased altogether.

She was, however, in such a state of utter exhaus-
tion, without the least particle of color in her face and
lips, that he did not deem it expedient to address her
again. He took her hand in his, and, caressing it as
he would one of his own children, he knelt by her
side, and in a few well-chosen words, commended the
poor, stricken lamb to the care of the good Shepherd,
then passed silently from the room.

James was waiting below to carry him home. His heart was too much oppressed for conversation, and they rode more than half the distance to the village in silence, when Mr. Allen said, abruptly, as if it were but the continuation of his thoughts, "She may never hear from her earthly father; but I think her heavenly Father will soon summon her home. Thank God, she seems prepared."

He had no suspicion what a dagger he was driving into the heart of his mute companion, who turned very pale, while a groan of agony forced itself from his lips.

But I must not delay on this part of my story. Juliette, after lying in about the same state for a fortnight, began slowly to convalesce. Nothing could exceed the devotion of good Mrs. Smith and her daughters during this period. And, as she became able to sit up for a part of the day, the farmer and his son often dropped in to cheer and amuse her. With her quick, sensitive nature the invalid soon perceived that the latter grew paler and paler at every interview. She questioned Mrs. Smith upon the subject; but her inquiries were either evaded or wholly unanswered. What could it be? To her he seemed as kind as ever, but somewhat constrained.

It was not till a week later that her gradually formed suspicions were increased to a certainty, thus bringing clearly before her the necessity of a change in her residence.

In consequence of her sickness, the fall work in the

farm-house was greatly retarded; the girls had postponed returning to school, and now were every moment engaged with their mother in making pickles, preserves, drying apples, peaches, and plums, for winter use. The young girl insisted that now she was fully able to take care of herself.

Since her convalescence, it had been her frequent habit to lie down in the bedroom adjoining the parlor, where James had been sick, and one day she was awakened from a short nap by the sound of Mrs. Smith's voice in the parlor. She seemed urging some point with great feeling. "I would go, James. Change of scene will do more than anything else to wean you from her. While you see her every day,—see her feeble and dependent,— your sympathies are constantly called forth."

"You don't know what you ask, mother," he replied, his voice so thick she could scarcely recognize it. " I can't go away and deprive myself of the only comfort that is left me. I haven't strength nor courage to do it. No; I'll take the school here for the winter. I can help father morning and night, to pay my board, and then all my earnings will go to pay you and the doctor for her sickness."

Juliette gave a quick gasp and clenched her hands.

"But I have told you before," remonstrated the kind woman, "that she is entirely welcome to all I've done, and the girls say so, too. The doctor's bill, I suppose, will be considerable, but he wont be in a hurry for it. I wish you could be persuaded to take the school that

has been offered you in T——.   Your father wishes
it, too."

Maria's voice at the door ended the conversation, and
Juliette, arising from her couch, stole unobserved to
her chamber.   There was a new resolve in her bright
eye as she hurriedly pulled from the bottom of her trunk
a well-filled purse, and poured part of the contents upon
the bed.

"She said it would be considerable.   I wonder how
much that is.   Here are two hundred dollars in gold,
my father's last allowance.   How little time that would
have defrayed my expenses in New York!   Oh, what
a noble heart James has!   I shall never see Horace
again.   Couldn't I teach myself to love him as he
wishes?"

She stood still and caught her breath, as a rush of
precious memories swept over her.   "No, it would be
sin.   I couldn't do it; but, James, as long as I live I
never shall cease to be grateful to you."

Gathering up five eagles, she wrapped them in a
paper, and, enclosing them in an envelope, directed
them to Dr. —— , hoping to be able to give them to
him in the course of the day.

Then she locked the door, and sitting on her trunk
with her eyes fixed abstractedly on the floor, she took
counsel of her own heart.   Many, *many* times since the
visit of Miss Darley, especially since she had renounced
all hope of being reconciled to her father, she had
turned her thoughts toward the Lowell factories as a
feasible means of support.   The graphic account given

by that young lady of the pleasantness and healthiness
of the employment, the taste and order which prevailed,
and especially the measures taken for the improvement
of the operatives, had made a strong impression upon
her mind. Now that she was firmly resolved to leave
Stamford, and to leave it at the first moment her health
would permit, this seemed to her a direct intimation
of Providence as to her path of duty.

She knew her friends would object, and oppose every
obstacle in her way; but she was sure that, after she
had gone, they would consider her conduct both wise
and honorable. One hundred dollars, which was the
sum she determined to leave for Mrs. Smith, was, she
knew, a small compensation for all her motherly kindness and care; but even this she was sure they would
refuse if possible.

With a sudden, pleasant thought, she unlocked her
jewel-case, and, taking from it one article after another,
pronounced her judgment upon them as suitable presents for the girls. They were each of them too costly
and rich to correspond with their most elaborate toilet;
but at last she selected a valuable bandeau of pearls,
and, enclosing it carefully in a separate box, resolved to
find a way to exchange it for some tasteful, but less
costly articles for each of them. To James she had
long wished to present a Bible, and laid aside another
eagle to be devoted to that purpose.

Having made these concise arrangements, her mind
was intensely relieved. She replaced the articles in

her trunk, dropped the envelope for the doctor into her pocket, and went downstairs.

The resolutions she had just formed effected a change in her whole appearance. She felt stronger and more self-reliant. Even her carriage was more erect, as, with a flushed cheek and kindling eye, she approached the table where Mrs. Smith was ironing, and playfully asked for some work.

CHAPTER XXIV.

"There is a kind of mournful eloquence
In thy dumb grief, which shames all clam'rous sorrow."

THE morning was pleasantly and usefully employed.
First she pulled out some lace her good friend had
been starching for caps, and wound it smoothly around
a bottle; then she assisted Susan in picking over some
dried beans for the next day's baking, the young girl
whispering meantime, "See how glum Maria looks;
she and Dudley have had a spat. Oh, how glad I am
that I am not engaged!"

It was only when the men (as Mr. Smith and his
son were called) came in to dinner, and she stole a
glance at James's pale, grave face, with the recollection
of what she had overheard, that her lip quivered, and her
eyes grew moist.

The conversation at table turned upon the school,
and she learned, with a thrill of pleasure, that the young
man had decided to carry his acceptance to the com-
mittee that very evening. She had been so fearful
that he would yield to the solicitations of his mother,
and leave home! Then her self-sacrifice in quitting
these generous friends, and throwing herself once more
upon the cold world would fall short of its intentions.

Toward night, the doctor, in passing, drove up to the door, and Juliette hurried to meet him. Detaining him a moment in the small entry, she said, "Here is some money, doctor, to pay your bill. There are fifty dollars; and if that is not enough, I'll run and get more, only don't say anything about it."

"Whew! whew!" he cried out with a laugh, "quite a windfall. But, child, half of fifty dollars is more than enough to pay for my poor services. I should never have charged more than ten."

"I have never paid a bill before," she remarked with a deep blush. "I had no idea how much it would be. You have been very kind and attentive. No, sir, no, indeed!" she exclaimed, as he put back four of the eagles into her hand; "you must certainly take half of them; take three; well then, take two," as he firmly refused. "I wont consent to your taking less than two."

"Well, I'll take twenty dollars, and thank you into the bargain. Now, let me give you a receipt;" and, smoothing out the paper in which the money had been folded, wrote, "Received from Miss Juliette Edwards, two gold eagles in full of all demands for medical attendance."

This he gave to her with a laughing remark, "That's the way to do business, child."

"I wonder how old everybody considers me?" queried the young girl, thrusting the remaining gold pieces into her pocket. "You, and Mr. Allen, and ever so many call me 'child.'"

"About fourteen, I imagine."

22

"I'm almost eighteen, sir," she answered, drawing up her form. "I suppose my hair being short, makes me look younger, though."

During the evening, though she occasionally joined in the conversation, her mind was busy revolving her plan for leaving Stamford. At one time, she thought of making a confidant of Dudley, who was now in the parlor trying to reconcile his ladylove; but finally, she concluded to confide the whole to Susan, and ask her advice and assistance. To Dudley, however, she was obliged to commit the bandeau of pearls, with full directions in writing for its exchange.

She had scarcely retired to her room when Susan ran up, out of breath, exclaiming, "Here, miss, what have you been doing? How can you account for this?" and she held up the crumpled receipt of the doctor, which, in her haste, Juliette had dropped on the floor.

"You can't imagine," cried Susan, "how they are abusing you downstairs; mother, and James, and all of them, but father. He didn't have a chance to speak a word."

Here the wicked girl, being wholly exhausted, sank into a chair, laughing heartily.

"Never mind," answered Juliette, taking the paper in some confusion; "I know they wont say more than I deserve; and I want to talk with you about something." She then, with a heightened color, and not without tears, made a full expose of her situation, and the determination to which she had arrived.

Susan, impulsive, warm-hearted girl that she was, scolded, and exclaimed, and threw her arms tightly around her friend, and declared she should never leave Stamford. She go into a factory? No, indeed! Juliette might stay quietly at the farm, and she herself would go, if necessary; but finally, as Juliette knew would be the case, she was prevailed upon to be her confidential adviser and friend in this sad emergency.

"James will kill me; and so they all will," she cried out; "but, if you say I must do it, why, I will."

Entering her friend's room two days later, "I'll tell you what," she cried, "I've got a splendid plan. We, that is, you and I, will go to Aunt Sukey's, — that's father's sister, you know, that I was named for, — to make a visit. I'll make an excuse to take your trunk, and then, — why, if you will carry out your mad idea of going into a factory, you can go from her house. It is five miles nearer New Haven than this is. Now give me credit for being more wise than you thought.'

"You are, indeed, my good angel, as you have always been since I first met you in the cars," exclaimed Juliette, warmly. "Oh, you did not imagine what a lonely, desolate, chilled heart was behind you the day I saw you there! You can scarcely imagine, even, how eagerly I watched your bright, expectant face, and drank in the rich tones of your merry voice. I knew at once you were a saucy girl, Susy," — giving her an eager kiss; "but I knew as well, that you were a warm-hearted one. I shall never forget you when I'm away."

The tears came in her eyes, and Susan, seeing them, began to cry aloud, and declared that it was no use trying any longer to convince her; she knew it was wicked for her to help Juliette off. If anything ever happened to her, she should feel guilty to the last hour of her life. "So now," she ended, "I give you fair warning,' and, before her companion, alarmed by this fresh outburst, could speak to prevent her, she rushed down the stairs, where the whole family were assembled, and bursting open the door, exclaimed, in a loud, excited tone, "Mother, Juliette's going off to Lowell, to work in the factory!"

"Susan Smith, are you crazy?" cried her father.

"What *do* you mean, Susan?" asked her mother, starting to her feet.

"It's one of her foolish jokes," muttered Maria; "you forget it's the first of October instead of the first of April."

James said not a word, but he grew very pale; and there was an expression of suffering on his features, which his mother too well understood.

"I know I've broken my word," continued the young girl, beginning to cry again; "but I've known it two days, and I should burst if I had to keep it any longer. She's going away from here, because — because — "

"Never mind the reasons now, Susan," interrupted Mrs. Smith, with an anxious, sympathizing glance at her son, "I'll talk to her: she'll take my advice, I know she will."

A loud knock at the door startled the company; and Susan, holding her apron to her face, darted out into the shed.

It was a gentleman and his wife to see the young ladies; and Maria waited upon them to the parlor, and then called James.

He did not seem to hear her; but as soon as the door was shut, began,—

"Mother,"—he spoke in a voice which he vainly endeavored to render firm,—"to-morrow, I shall give up my school in the West District, and go to T——. It is not too late. It is on my account, I am sure, that Juliette is going away."

"But what is to hinder your staying at home? and her staying, too?" inquired Mr. Smith, not being enlightened on all points.

"I'll ask her," said the good wife, and immediately sought the young girl in her own room.

After an hour she came back, with evident marks of deep emotion.

"She is decided to leave Stamford," she said, in answer to an entreating glance from her son; "whether you go or stay, it will make no difference. She has had it in mind ever since Miss Darley passed the afternoon here, in case she did not hear from her father; and now the poor thing has given up all hope of that."

James's lips moved, but no sound came forth.

"I said all I could to persuade her to give up her wild plan," continued Mrs. Smith; "but she thinks it

22*

her duty, and that she may as well begin her struggle with the world now as any time."

"If she was strong and tough, like our gals," urged the farmer, bringing down his fist upon the table, "I wouldn't say a word against it; but to have that little, delicate creature, that has no more courage than a kitten, set out alone, and try to battle her way through them city factories, or anywhere else, it's what I can't give my consent to."

James caught his father's hard hand, and gave it a very demonstrative squeeze.

But, notwithstanding all her friends felt for her, Juliette knew she ought to go, and go she did; though not without many tears, and a sickening fear and trembling at what might be before her. Whenever she stopped to question herself whether this sacrifice was required of her, the conversation she had involuntarily been a listener to, between Mrs. Smith and James, rushed to her mind. "No," she said to herself, "my money will soon be gone; and I will never be a burden to friends who have already done so much for me." She promised, however, to write them often; and, if possible, to return for a visit during the next summer.

It was a great relief to Juliette, at last, that she was not obliged to leave Stamford in a clandestine manner. It was an unspeakable comfort to impart her intentions to her good pastor; and, after playfully reasoning down his remonstrances, to receive his benediction and a letter commendatory to any church she might wish to attend. But after all, it was a hard, bitter parting;

and, as she stood awaiting the carriage that was to convey her to the depot, and suddenly began to realize the trials before her, and all that these friends had been to her in her hours of sorrow, it would have been an easy matter to have persuaded her, at least, to delay this rude encounter with the world.

In an envelope left upon her table was enclosed the ten eagles directed to Mrs. Smith, with a letter, expressing the gratitude she could not trust herself to utter. The presents for the girls, to her disappointment, had not come to hand; and she therefore could only hint that they might expect a trifling remembrance from her to be worn at Maria's wedding.

The Bible, a handsome English edition, bound in maroon velvet, and fastened with gold clasps, she determined, with her own hands, to present to James; and did so, calling him into the parlor at the moment of their starting.

"When you read this, dear friend," she said, tearfully, "remember God hears the prayers of the pure in heart; and sometimes offer up a petition for your absent sister."

James took the book, pressed his quivering lips upon the hand that offered it, bowed his assent, and hastened to the carriage. On their way to the village he scarcely spoke. He knew his only safety lay in silence. She had enough to do to bear her own trials, and he would not intrude his grief upon her. He lifted her from the carriage and showed her into the ladies' room, procured her a ticket for Boston, gave her the check for her trunk, then, taking her hand in both of his, he thrust a small paper parcel within it, and with the whispered words, "May God bless you and keep you!" he turned away. But looking from the cars as they were dashing out beyond the depot, Juliette saw his pale, wistful face still watching her. With a burst of grief, she suddenly covered her face, and that was the last she saw of Stamford.

CHAPTER XXV.

"When, overwhelmed with grief,
My heart within me dies,
Helpless, and far from all relief,
To heaven I lift mine eyes."

THOUGH the early morning had been fair, as the day advanced, heavy clouds overspread the sky, and by eight o'clock, the time our weary, heart-sick heroine reached her destination, the rain was falling fast.

For the last hour the poor girl had been trembling at the thought of her utterly forlorn condition. A stranger in a strange land, what should she do when the cars stopped? She supposed there were boarding-houses for the factory-girls; but who would direct her to a suitable one?

Her lips grew pale, and her hands numb, as with throbbing nerves she ejaculated, "Oh! what will become of me? What if I should be carried to some dreadful house? I have heard of such things."

Suddenly a still, small voice seemed whispering to her soul, "Trust in the Lord with all thy heart, and lean not unto thine own understanding. In all thy ways acknowledge him and he shall direct thy paths."

261

A gush of grateful tears relieved her over-excited feelings, and presently, with a wild whoop and a tearing shriek, the cars, ringing their bells, dashed through the streets and drew up at the long depot.

The passengers poured out into the darkness, and Juliette followed them. By the light from the street-lamps she saw rows of carriages; and she had scarcely touched the platform before half a dozen voices screamed out, "Have a hack, miss? Have a carriage, lady?"

Perfectly bewildered at finding herself in such a new, unprotected position, Juliette stood still until a gentleman, who had sat near her in the cars, stepped toward her, and said in a kind, manly voice, "Can I help you to a carriage, miss? I see you are alone. Have you baggage?"

"Oh! I thank you, sir. I am a stranger here. I have but one trunk, and here is my check."

"Where do you wish to go?"

"To a good boarding-house. I have come to work in the factory."

He noticed the unsteadiness of her voice. "Ah!" he exclaimed, with a little start of surprise; but added, instantly, "I am glad that I can direct you to a good place. Here, Morris (to a hack-driver), take this check, and find the trunk answering to it, and take us to Lawrence Corporation. Walk into the ladies' room, miss, if you please, out of the damp air. Morris will call us when he is ready."

He glanced with his keen eyes into her face as they

went into the lighted room, and then, appearing satisfied, he said, cordially, " I am an agent for the Lawrence Mills. As you are a stranger, perhaps I had
better take you home to my wife, and let you become
acquainted with the Lowell boarding-houses under
more favorable auspices. How would that do?"

"Thank you, sir," replied Juliette; "b t I have
travelled all day, and am very tired. Perhaps I had
better go at once to the boarding-place, if you will be
so kind as to recommend one."

"All ready, sir," called Morris, at the door.

After a ride of about five minutes, they drew up
before a house very unlike her home in New York.
The gentleman, meanwhile, had carried on a brisk
conversation with his young companion, who interested
him more and more. When the carriage stopped, bidding the driver wait, he ran hastily up the steps, rung
the bell with a quick jerk, and Juliette could see him
in earnest conversation with a woman in the entry.

"How wonderfully my heavenly Father works for
me!" was the language of her heart. "How safe to
trust him!"

"Let down the steps, Morris," called out the gentleman, turning again to the woman.

Juliette alighted, and quickly ran into the house,
as the rain was still falling heavily, gave her name to
the landlady, thanked the agent warmly for his kind
attention, received his directions where to apply for
work, and saying to the woman that she wished for
nothing but to be shown to her bed, was lighted up-

stairs to an apartment about twelve feet by fifteen, in which there were two wide beds, and one narrow cot.

The latter place was assigned to her, and then the woman, a bustling person with a sharp face and thin lips, bade her good-night, and returned to her busy cares below.

Shutting the door, which was guiltless of a lock, the wearied girl cast a glance of dismay around this crowded, meagre apartment, her thoughts flying back to her spacious, richly-furnished rooms in New York; and then, with a sinking heart, to the neat little chamber she had more recently occupied at the farm. It had never once occurred to her that it would be necessary to share her room with another; but here were five, four of them strangers to her, to occupy this.

To say she was homesick and heart-sick would but feebly express the utter desolation of her spirits. Pushing a chair against the door, she threw herself on her knees. "O God!" she cried, "save me! save me from myself! Help me to be resigned to my lot. Teach my wayward, complaining heart to say, 'Thy will be done.'"

The rattling of the door-latch made the blood rush to her very temples.

"Yes; that's the room!" shouted the landlady from below; "carry it right in."

It was a man with her trunk; but Juliette glanced around in vain for an empty space to put it. He, however, soon relieved her; for, throwing up the valance of the bed, he thrust it quickly out of sight.

Taking a night-dress from her travelling-bag, she hastily disrobed, putting her clothes together in the most compact form, and crept into bed, trembling with nervous fear lest her room-mates should enter before she were ready.

Resolutely turning her thoughts from her present most unpleasant situation when she found her tears beginning to flow, she repeated hymn after hymn that she had learned in childhood, and presently, fatigued with her ride, she sank into a heavy sleep. In her dreams she was a merry child again; and with Horace, firmly holding her hand, seemed to be marching through a vast open space, the end of which was beyond their vision. They went on, on, on, until she was oh, so weary! But whenever her companion, yielding to her pleadings, began to slacken their pace, a bright, shining form appeared before them. Pointing onward, ever onward, his presence at once inspired new courage and vigor, until at last they arrived at a mansion such as their most lofty imagination had never reached.

"Sarah!" cried a sharp voice close at her ear, "do put out your lamp. It smokes, and I can't get to sleep."

Juliette started up in bed, exclaiming in terror, "Where am I?"

"You're in Lawrence Corporation, number five," an-

23

swered another voice from a bed at her side; which reply elicited a coarse laugh from the other girls.

Sarah, as she was called, suddenly extinguished the lamp, the odor of which proved almost insufferable.

"I can't endure this," said our poor heroine to herself, after waiting till she hoped her companions were asleep. "I must open a crack in the window."

This was closed, however, with a spring, and she could not succeed in raising it an inch. Then she crept softly to the door, and, having unlatched it, went quietly to bed again.

But slumber this time was out of the question. In vain she closed her burning eyes and courted the advances of the fickle god. The loud, heavy breathing of the four sleepers combined to form a sound sufficient to frighten him away. She pressed her fingers in her ears; she pulled the bedclothes around her head until she was almost suffocated. But all to no purpose. The dawning day found her weak, dispirited, and nervous; in a poor frame to encounter new trials.

Arising early, before her companions were awake, she went downstairs to find the landlady, fully resolved upon having a room by herself. But this the woman said was impossible; every place where a bed could stand was packed full already. She ought to be thankful to have a whole cot to herself.

For several days it rained incessantly; and the homesick girl, regarding the advice of a fellow-boarder, did not venture from the house except to provide herself with a dress more suitable for her new employment, a pair of thick boots, and a bonnet that would not be injured by the rain. These were absolutely essential to the wardrobe of a factory girl.

During this period, the delicate beauty of the newcomer, her evident superiority in education and refinement, subjected her to many low taunts and jeers of ridicule. But this was nothing compared to the scoffing laugh of her room-mates when they found she was a praying Christian. Her assuming the attitude of devotion was a signal for the commencement of loud-whispered jokes upon subjects too low to be given to the reader, and at last she was obliged to postpone her supplications until they were asleep.

"O Horace! O father!" she would often cry out in the anguish of her heart, "why do you leave me thus exposed to insult and abuse?"

To one of a keenly sensitive nature like hers, accustomed to the most refined society, the daily and hourly intercourse with such an incongruous set was perfect torture. If she bravely endeavored to meet their taunts unmoved, and to give exercise to the stock of patience and resignation she had been prayerfully striving to gain, they met her meek endurance with ridicule. If, suddenly overcome by their unkind, cutting suspicions, she gave way to a passion of tears, they made a mock of her grief.

She yearned for one word of sympathy, one look of affectionate interest; but, alas! as she glanced up and down the long table, from the busy operatives to their more busy landlady, she realized more than ever that

she was alone in a strange land. Often she retired
from her meals having merely gone through the form
of eating, to throw herself upon her bed and cry,
"Would God it were evening!" Then at night, when
weak and exhausted by excessive weeping, "Would
God it were morning!"

In after years she always considered these the most
dreadful trials she had undergone, because her God
seemed to have forsaken her, and darkness, like a thick
curtain, shrouded her soul. It was a time, too, of
dreadful temptation. Finding her weak and unresisting, the arch-fiend suggested, "See what reward you
have gained by throwing off allegiance to me and
choosing God as your portion;" while her own heart,
torn with anguish, feebly echoed, "Was this sacrifice
really required?"

Alas! alas! where was her trust in Him who had so
often appeared for her relief, — who had promised to
make her peace as a river, and her righteousness as
the waves of the sea? Her cry was with the psalmist,
"All thy waves and thy billows have gone over me;"
but not like him could she sing, "Thou wilt show me
the path of life; in thy presence is fulness of joy; at
thy right hand there are pleasures for evermore."

It was on a clear, bracing morning, near the middle
of October, that, in company with one of her fellow-
boarders, she made her entrée into the new life she had
chosen. It was a novel and exciting scene. Hundreds
of girls hurrying in one direction in answer to the
eager ringing of the bells, which, to the throbbing

heart of the stranger, seemed to say, "Be quick! be quick!" approached the ponderous doors, and one after another were lost to view.

Keeping close to her companion, she mounted one flight of stairs after another, until they reached the weaving-rooms; the immense looms being arranged in tiers, like seats in a school-house. Here she had only time to cast a quick glance around and notice some pots of flowers in a window near her, before her companion introduced her to the overseer.

A few brief questions served to convince him that Miss Edwards, though a stranger to this business, would soon make a profitable operative. Asking her to follow him, he went the entire length of the building, to a tier of looms near the window, where, in turn, he introduced her to a tall, dignified young lady, with a request that she would give the new-comer such assistance as might be necessary; then, assigning her one loom, which was as much as she would be able to tend at first, he returned to his desk.

"Take off your bonnet and hang it there," said the young lady, smiling at the evident bewilderment of her new charge.

Juliette stared and shook her head. The thundering sound of the machinery prevented a syllable from reaching her ears.

"You'll become accustomed to it soon," added the miss, whose name was Agnes Barnard, in a louder tone. "I was stunned at first."

The sun was shining cheerfully through the many

windows, its rays falling upon numerous pots of ver-
benas, geraniums, and monthly roses with which the
girls had liberty to adorn the part of the building peculiarly their own.

It was quite amusing to Juliette to see, hanging at
short distances on the walls, tiny mirrors (private
property), of the use of which she did not long remain
in doubt; for, as soon as the looms were well in motion,
the operatives began to unloose their long tresses, and
while they went on with their work, proceeded to plait
and curl, and beautify generally.

Then from the pocket of one and another, a clean
collar, a breast-knot, a brooch, or a dress-apron came
forth, were arranged by a glance into the tiny mirror,
and their toilets were made for the day.

In the excitement of her new employment, our heroine had almost forgotten the discomforts and vexations
of her boarding-house home; but as she hurried downstairs with Agnes, at the ringing of the loud bell for
dinner, she longed to ask her whether all these houses
were under the same regulations; or whether it might
not be possible to improve her condition.

There was no time for it now, however; for the
young girl, parting from her with a smile, ran gayly
into another building, saying, "You've done finely for
a beginner."

Though only about half the period was allowed for
a whole dinner, consumed in a single course at her
father's table, and then the earnest, quick, ringing call
was heard again, Juliette found time to run hastily to

her room for a brief offering of gratitude to God for the brightening prospects before her.

The more she saw of her young instructor, the better she was pleased with her. One incident which occurred at night impressed her still more favorably.

After the bell had rung for work to cease, a number of the operatives stood outside the door, talking earnestly about a lecture they wished to attend in the evening. Agnes was among them; indeed, she seemed to be the guiding spirit, and in an earnest tone was pressing her opinions on her companions, when a man, connected with their factory, came up and began to talk in a most familiar manner.

Juliette shrank behind her friend, as she caught his eye fixed boldly upon herself, her whole soul revolting from his gaze, and rude, coarse speeches. One and another of the girls laughed as she was addressed, but to Juliette's great delight, Agnes, with an appearance of dignity which cowered him, drew herself up, and, without condescending to reply, swept away from the group, pulling Juliette's hand within her arm.

"Why! what are you trembling at?" she asked, with a laugh, as she witnessed her little pupil's pallid cheeks.

"I'm afraid I shall not do for a factory girl," was the faltering reply; "that man's dreadful eyes and coarse talk frightened me so; but here is my home," she added, with a sigh; "I wish I could go with you."

"Well, come with me to the end of the street, and I'll talk with you about it. There's five minutes yet," glancing at the clock on a neighboring church. "I know by experience how dreadfully homesick one feels, turned into a room with a dozen, more or less, of operatives, some of them, all the time they are asleep, keeping up a lively tune with their nasal organs. I bore it a good while; but I've got away now. I get my dinner at one of the corporation-houses, because there is no time to go further; but I take the other meals and sleep in a private family."

"Oh, that would be delightful!" cried Juliette, warmly.

"There are only two girls there beside myself; and I'm sleeping alone, now; so if you wouldn't mind occupying a room with a stranger, I think I can arrange it."

Juliette's beaming face showed her pleasure as she answered, "Thank you, it would be paradise compared to the place I'm in now."

"Run back then, for to-night, as fast as you can, and have your trunk all ready, if it's sent for in the morning."

The thought that this might be her last night with her present landlady rendered her trials much more endurable; and, being exceedingly tired in consequence of standing all day, she found it easier than before to imitate the example of her room-mates, and soon was beyond the reach of any annoyance.

CHAPTER XXVI.

" The wise and active conquer difficulties
By daring to attempt them."

AS Miss Agnes Barnard has been introduced to the reader and will act a somewhat prominent part in our story, it is but fair to give her history a little more at length.

In the northern part of New Hampshire, near the dividing line between that State and Vermont, overlooking the beautiful valley of the Connecticut River, was the old homestead of the Barnards, now in the hands of Josiah Barnard, father of Agnes.

With a large family dependent upon him for support, including his aged parents and orphan nephew, the wherewithal to carry on the farm was not always forthcoming; and, as a necessary consequence, debts were incurred, crops grew less and less, until at length a crisis was reached such as had long been feared.

To avoid a greater calamity, that of being obliged to sell land, every foot of which was endeared by memories of boyhood, youth, and riper years, Mr. Barnard, with a groan, consented to raise a few hundred dollars for the present emergency, by giving a note secured by mortgage, to the 'Squire of the village.

273

The next year both his parents died ; a small legacy left them, barely serving to pay the doctor's bill, while all other necessary expenses incurred in their sickness rendered it impossible to pay off any part of this debt as they had intended. The year following the interest was added to the principal, until at last despondence succeeded melancholy, and the farmer, scarcely beyond middle life, declared, with a burst of manly grief, that he could not meet his expenses ; that he did no know which way to turn ; that, in fact, they must leave the dear old spot and begin life anew.

All this time, Agnes and one older brother had been attending the Academy in the next village, walking eight miles a day for the sake of acquiring an education, that inheritance of every New England child.

Caleb Barnard was well fitted for a teacher of a district school. His secret hopes had carried him much beyond this ; and, though well aware that he could not incur the expense of a college education, he had thought it possible to acquire what would be equivalent to it under the care of a private tutor, and thus qualify himself for what he considered the highest office of earth, that of a Christian minister.

Agnes, fourteen months his junior, had been for the last six months an assistant pupil in the school. Tall and erect, with a tinge of hauteur in her manner, her countenance one that would attract attention by its ever-varying expression, she had won both among teachers and pupils many stanch friends.

Gifted with a quick discernment and a vast amount

of that desirable element called common-sense, she had become more thoroughly acquainted with her father's affairs than any one supposed. Well aware that her parents had exercised great self-denial, and strained every nerve to give their children a thorough education, she was now ready to take her share of the burden,— to bring some of her young strength and hopefulness to the rescue.

Walking home one night the four miles from school, she had abundant opportunity to perfect the plan, which not now for the first time was suggested to her mind. Caleb, absorbed in reverie (unlike his wide-awake sister, his reveries were not practical ones), did not notice her unusual abstraction, nor, as they approached the farm, did he observe the flashing of her fine gray eye, the dilation of her well-shaped nostrils, accompanied by a firmer tread of her foot as she saw the wagon of 'Squire Owen standing at the door.

Trip, the old family dog, came out growling his welcome, quickly followed by the 'Squire himself, prinked, primmed, and pomatumed for conquest.

Agnes, more than suspecting his errand, confronted him with a defiant glance from her clear, unshrinking eyes, made a haughty bow, and passed on.

She found her father crouching over the fire in the very attitude of despair. Naturally hopeful, energetic, and somewhat imperious, his accumulation of difficulties had bowed him to the earth. He had just received a visit from his mortgagee, hinting at a way their differences might be satisfactorily adjusted.

Now, in order to realize the state of mingled wrath and consternation into which the father was thrown, it is necessary to state that the name of 'Squire Owen had for years been associated in his native village with all that was mean, low, vile, and licentious. To settle his bill with the 'Squire in the way he wished, by giving him his daughter Agnes in marriage, only seemed to the despairing father in other words like selling her to the devil.

"What did he want?" asked the young girl, suddenly appearing in the room, like a bright rainbow on a dark thunder-cloud.

Her voice was full and clear, but neither father nor mother had the heart to answer her.

"I can guess," she rejoined with a hearty laugh. "He came courting. He is willing to take me soul and body in lieu of any claim he has upon this dear old farm.

"Now, father, I want you to cheer up, and go to driving the oxen with a will, as you used to before you got into the 'Squire's clutches; for I promise you that to-morrow morning you shall be out of that man's power, and I wont be in it either."

Mr. Barnard opened wide his eyes, groaned terribly, while his wife murmured with a shaking voice, "O Agnes! you don't know what you say."

"Yes, I do, mother. I've seen what it was coming to, and I've got my plans all ready. Come, father; instead of sitting there brooding over your troubles, I want you to harness old Duke for me. I'm going to test one of my ancient copies, 'Where there's a will there's a way.'"

Agnes spoke in such a self-reliant, hopeful tone, that, though her father did not at all believe that the work he had labored and toiled for years to accomplish could be effected by the hands of a young school-girl, be she ever so sharp-witted, yet he looked up with a tinge of his old impatience, as he cried out, "I say, Agnes, what do you mean?"

"I mean that unless old Duke is ready soon, I shall have to walk back as far as the centre. I've business to do there; and you used to tell me when I had, not to let the grass grow under my feet."

Without another word, Mr. Barnard rose from his old-fashioned, flag-bottomed kitchen chair, went to the stable; and, when his daughter, having effected a slight change in her dress, and abstracted from his old carved desk all documents pertaining to her father's business with the 'Squire, made her appearance at the door, he was ready for her; not very brisk or hopeful, certainly, but still a vast improvement of his appearance when he sat over the fire.

"Wont you tell mother," she said, gathering up the reins, "that I shall want some of her best fritters to-night, as a kind of celebration of our freedom from, you know whom; and don't take tea till I come. I may be late, but the children wont mind waiting for once."

"Well, good luck to you, child," he answered, as

24

she gave him a parting bow; "but I haven't the most distant idea what you're up to."

To confess the truth, the girl herself had not the most lucid ideas on the subject. But money was wanting, and money she must have, to take up the mortgage of the 'Squire. Her own common-sense taught her, that if there was no other way, it might be possible to effect a transfer of the mortgage to some less unscrupulous person; but she had a vague plan in mind worth two of that.

It was nearly eight o'clock; Clara and the younger boys, tired and hungry, had eaten their bread and milk and gone to bed, when the sound of wheels turning into the yard brought the whole wakeful family to the door.

"Well, Caleb," she said in a cheerful voice, "I've got home again. Put the horse up as quick as you can, and come in. I'm hungry for my fritters."

Mr. Barnard was, by this time, pretty thoroughly "worked up," as he termed any state of unusual excitement. He gazed searchingly in his daughter's face, as, with the most provoking air of indifference, she hung her shawl on its appropriate nail, and took her seat at the tea-table.

Catching a glimpse, however, of his pale, worn countenance, on which care, of late, had been ploughing deep furrows, she pushed back her plate, piled with her favorite cakes, and leisurely taking a soiled document from her pocket, held it out to him, so that he could catch a glimpse of the name, and then tearing the paper in two, threw the pieces scornfully upon the floor.

"Agnes! child! you're mad! you've ruined me!" shouted the old man, gasping for breath. "That's the 'Squire's mortgage, and he'll make us smart for destroying it."

To the surprise of all present, she looked coolly in his face, and laughed; a short, self-complacent chuckle, that mystified them more than ever.

"I'll be even better with you than my bargain, father," she cried, turning to her plate again. "That document is useless; the 'Squire will never ask for it, because the money's paid; and, more than that, I've given him my answer, too! Can you guess what it was? Why, mother! you needn't shake, and look so frightened. It was the most terrible blessing he ever asked for yet, — with a snap on the end of it, as father says; and Major Maltby standing by to hear it all. Oh, it was rich!" and Agnes ha'-ha'd to her heart's content.

But Mr. Barnard did not even smile. The relief from his dreadful burden of care came almost too suddenly. Covering his face with both his hands, his form shook like a child. No one, not even his wife had realized what he had suffered, at the idea of giving up his home, and going among strangers; for he could never live in sight of that cherished spot, and see others cultivating his fields, or gathering around his hearthstone.

What a wild tumult swept over him in the few

moments following his daughter's declaration! Life itself seemed hanging on her words. How she had effected this, he knew not; and at first scarcely cared; but she had ventured to destroy that paper, which, ever since he had given it, had been a source of constant anxiety and terror,—a kind of sword hanging over his head, ready at any moment to destroy him; now, for the present, he was safe.

Agnes gazed at her father with a peculiar expression, as he sat thus; but as soon as he uncovered his face, she drew her plate toward her again, and began to butter her fritters, her mother and Caleb regarding her with a kind of awe.

"But, Agnes," began Mr. Barnard, as soon as he could command his voice, "I can't imagine where you got the money to pay it with. You're sure you ar'n't mistaken, nor nothing of that kind."

"I'm sure the 'Squire thought I'd mistaken my calling, when I undertook to settle up his business with him," added the young girl, with a perfect shout of merriment, at the recollection of his mingled astonishment and rage. "I expected every minute to see the blood spirt out of his face. Major Maltby said he would have sworn terribly, if he hadn't been so frightened, and so drunk he couldn't."

The father sighed; "I'm afraid you've made an enemy of him, child. He never forgives an insult. But you can't tell how glad I am you got that paper back."

"Now, I suppose, you want to hear my story;" and

Agnes pushed her chair from the table, and drew up nearer to the group in the old-fashioned chimney-corner.

"Yes! yes!"

"Well, let me see, where shall I begin? But first, I want to ask you something, mother." Agnes tossed her head, and put up her hand as if to smoothe her hair, but in reality, to conceal a blush.

"You know our parlor chamber?"

"Yes, child."

Mrs. Barnard looked, however, as if she didn't know what a room that was opened but a few times in the course of the year had to do with the subject.

"Well, as we don't need it for ourselves, I've let it."

"Let it! how?"

"Why, Mr. Ashley has been trying a week to find a boarding-place; and I told him you'd take him."

This time the heightened color was so evident that it could not be turned off.

"Why! how could you, child? He never will be contented to live as we do."

"It's in the bargain that he's to have farmer's fare. The good room was the great thing for him, and a quiet place to study; but we'll talk about that to-morrow.

"I don't suppose father ever thought such a wild girl as I am, could have any serious hours; but for a long time I've seen that our affairs were growing worse and worse; and that you and he were looking more

24*

and more careworn and downhearted. I knew
something would have to be done pretty soon, and
a talk the 'Squire tried to have with me last week led
me to understand his wishes. Now, aside from his
character, I know the 'Squire will never see his fiftieth
year again; and, as I'm only nineteen, I am of the
same mind as the girl who, when a gentleman of fifty
proposed to her father for her hand, answered promptly,
'If it makes no difference to you, sir, I should prefer
to have two husbands of twenty-five.'

"No, sir," said I to myself, "I must contrive some
better plan to relieve father than that. All the way
to school this morning, and all the way home to night,
I was thinking, and thinking; and the result of it is,
that, now it's coming spring, Caleb must give up his
studies, and work like a man with you, sir, in trying
to bring the farm to. I've often heard you say that it
would pay well, and yield a good income, if you had
only money to enrich it; so, to obtain that, I'm going
to Lowell next month to work in the factory."

Mrs. Barnard sank back in her chair with a feeble
cry, while Caleb, now fairly roused, exclaimed:
"Agnes, you're a noble girl, and I'm proud of you;
but I'll never consent to such a plan. I'm the one to
leave home, if anybody does."

Agnes glanced in his face archly, and then rising,
said, "Now I am going to bed!"

"But you haven't told us, child, how you got the
money to pay the 'Squire. I can't sleep till I know
that. It seems terribly like a dream, any way. He

said — you know, wife — he'd come here to-morrow
to know the answer to — "

"He wont come for that, you may depend," said the
young girl, with a haughty toss of her head. "But,
if you must know where I found the means to pay
him, I borrowed the money, and gave my note for
it."

"Yours! Your note!" was the excited exclamation from father, mother, and son.

"It was considered satisfactory security against all
loss," she added, archly. "In justice I ought to say
that, as I assumed the debt, no security was required;
but I insisted."   •

The three faces, eagerly turned toward the speaker,
showed that they were more and more mystified.

"It was Mr. Ashley," she added, with a deeper
blush. "I met him on my way to Major Maltby's, and
he offered the accommodation. If he continues to board
here, it will be paid in that way; if not, I'll earn
money to take up my note."

This time Agnes made such a decided move toward
the door, that no one stopped her, though the others
remained by the smouldering embers talking and
wondering till midnight.

CHAPTER XXVII

"She was the pride
Of her familiar sphere; the daily joy
Of all who on her gracefulness might gaze,
And in the light and music of her way
Have a companion's portion."

THE events related in the last chapter had occurred nearly two years earlier. Agnes left home for Lowell three days after Mr. Ashley. had become settled in his new quarters, and had remained in the factories ever since, except two visits, of a fortnight each, to the old homestead. The note for money received had been returned and destroyed long ere this; and affairs at the farm had assumed a more prosperous appearance. The timely relief afforded him gave Mr. Barnard new courage; and he went to work, driving his oxen and all other business "with a will," as his daughter had urged.

A most favorable arrangement had been made for Caleb to continue his studies under the direction of his pastor, in pay for which, Cæsar, Mr. Ashley's black horse, received a cordial welcome to the hospitalities of the stable.

Much of this Juliette did not learn until a later period; but as the arrangement to remove her from

284

the Corporation boarding-house proved successful, she soon both loved and respected her new friend.

The widow Palmer, in whose family she had now a much more congenial home, had one daughter, who worked in the factory, and had the charge of four looms near the place where Agnes stood. In this way they had become acquainted; and, finding that her mother would receive a few select boarders, a pleasant company was soon made up.

Mrs. Palmer had formerly been in affluent circumstances, as many articles of rich furniture about the house bore witness.

Juliette's heart beat with pleasure, as, on the first evening after her removal here, she heard the full, rich tones of a piano.

" That's Annie Palmer ! " exclaimed Agnes. " Let's go down and ask her to sing."

Juliette gladly consented, though she had assigned this evening to writing her friends in Stamford.

One piece of music followed another in quick succession; sometimes a march or favorite waltz, but oftentimes a song, in which the others could join their voices.

At last Annie sprang from her seat, exclaiming, " Perhaps you play, Miss Edwards."

Juliette blushed, as she answered, "I used to; but I have not touched the piano for some months."

Her companions were all eager to hear her; and, taking her seat, she gave them some simple melodies, as an accompaniment to her sweet but powerful voice.

They, listening with almost breathless delight, would not release her until she had gone on from Handel to Mozart, and from Mozart to Beethoven.

It was at a late hour that she rose resolutely from the instrument, and, receiving their cordial thanks for the pleasure she had given them, retired to her room to fulfil the task she had assigned herself. She knew her friends at the farm would become painfully anxious to hear from her; but, while situated as she was at the Corporation boarding-house, she had not the heart to write them; and was well aware that, if she told them the whole truth about herself, they would insist upon her returning to Stamford.

Now, however, that she was so pleasantly situated, and had been two days in the factory, — long enough to be able to say that she thought she should like the employment, — she resolved to delay no longer. Perhaps an extract from the letter may be of interest to the reader.

"DEAR FRIENDS, — As I may now consider myself established in my new business, I hasten to write you, as I promised. After the last glimpse I had of James, you may well believe I had not much interest in what was passing around me. Indeed, I could not for a long time read a word of his kind, brotherly note, my eyes were so blurred with tears at the thought of the friends I was leaving behind me. Please, dear brother, accept my thanks for the little parcel accompanying your note, which I shall keep,

knowing, should I refuse to do so, I should give you
pain; but which no circumstance I can now appre-
hend would induce me to make use of. Oh, how
often since I left you have I longed for one hour,
or moment even, to run in to the pleasant sitting-room
to throw myself into your motherly embrace, dear
Mrs. Smith; to hear your husband say, in his old
friendly way, 'Our lily is brightening up, wife;' to
feel the warm grasp of James's hand; to receive
Maria's kiss, and Susan's cheerful welcome! I hardly
dare tell you how my heart ached when I remembered
that it must be months before such a visit could be
made. . . . . . I did not go out of the house
last Sabbath, as it was very rainy; but from what I
hear of Mr. B——, and his kind interest in the
operatives, I think I shall attend his church; and, if
so, I shall carry him my letter from Mr. Allen.
When you write, I want to hear all the news; whether
James continues to like his school; how Dudley succeeded in doing my business; how far Mr. Smith has
proceeded with his fall ploughing; and how soon you,
girls, return to school.

"It is nearly eleven o'clock, and I must stop writing
and go to bed; if not on my own account, for the
sake of my room-mate, who has been trying to sleep
for an hour.

"Your grateful friend,

"JULIETTE.

"P. S. — I fairly long for a bowl of your good bread
and milk!"

This epistle was received with great joy at the farm; and Susan lost scarcely a moment in commencing her reply, which she sent off by return of mail.

"O Juliette! What a naughty, *naughty* girl you are! I wouldn't have believed such wickedness of you. No wonder you cried in the cars. I have no doubt your left ear tingled dreadfully, for we all abused you, calling you all manner of hard names. I shall throw up all faith in signs if your ear didn't burn then. Father said, by way of excuse for you, that you were a poor, innocent thing, not knowing the ways of the wicked world, or you wouldn't have gone and left such a host of money behind you. Then, when I said, 'I'll bet anything it was every cent she had,' mother sat down and began to cry, while James grew red and white, and all manner of colors, and flew round like one distracted; and then volunteered to go right after you and bring you back.

"Maria was the only reasonable one among us; and she brought us to our senses by saying, 'James, how like a fool you act! Just as if you couldn't change the eagles into bills, and send them to Lowell any day.'

"So, Miss Edwards, that is what we intend to do, as soon as we find that this letter reaches you safely.

"Father, mother, and all of us want me to say that it was a great comfort to have you here. (Mother misses you dreadfully about her caps, and can't be persuaded to put on a decent one. She's saving all that boxful you did up for her for Maria's wedding, because, she says, with a terrible sigh, 'I've no Juliette to do any more.') So they don't want one cent of pay. Please excuse my long parenthesis; but when I write letters I must put down just what comes into my head, Miss Cook, my composition teacher, notwithstanding.

"Now I have scolded you enough for that, I hope, to make you feel the enormity of your guilt, so I will go on to something else.

"Two days after you left, Dudley came walking in one evening, with a kind of mysterious, pompous air, which I was sure betokened no good. After we had teased him a while, he produced from somewhere two boxes, and gave them to Maria and me. They contained the most exquisite pearl brooches and bracelets that ever were made. Maria fairly danced with delight, and I really believe wanted to be married the next day in order to wear hers.

"I, being one of the calm kind, you know, and, having no lover in prospect even, you can easily imagine, sat down and folded my hands demurely across my lap, moralizing upon the vanities of this awful world.

"But you ought to have seen James when Dudley told him the two sets cost seventy-five dollars. He covered his face and fairly groaned; and, until your good letter came, continued to torture himself and us with visions of you lying in the gutters, or by the wayside starving to death, with no good Samaritan at hand to take you up and minister to your necessities. I believe he is doing well in school; at any rate, the scholars like him.

"Now, my dear little Juliette, if you will listen to the advice of one much wiser, if not older, than yourself, you will be less extravagant in your presents (the doctor told us that you tried to force fifty dollars upon him), and lay up your money for more useful purposes.

" With love and best wishes of all, including Dudley, your friend, Susy.

"P. S.—Father's all done ploughing, except the place for the summer garden, and we're going to school two weeks after Thanksgiving."

This letter, so characteristic of her friend, Juliette had many a laugh over, and, at last, as she grew more intimate with Agnes, read it to her.

The close intimacy which soon existed between these young girls was a benefit to both of them. Agnes, older by only two years than her friend, was ten years in advance of her in maturity and practical knowledge. Circumstances had wonderfully developed her powers, and, being naturally confident and self-reliant, she had made her way into her present position with far less to wound and shock her sensibilities than Juliette could have done.

All that she had learned by experience was now freely imparted to the young girl, who so trustingly confided in her for protection.

Agnes had been from infancy an ardent lover of music: From the solemn notes of the church-organ to the merry whistle of the boys in the street, every sound of melody inspirited her. But she had never enjoyed an opportunity to gratify this fondness by learning the science of music.

Night after night she pleaded with Juliette for one more, and then one more song, her whole soul entranced, as

> "At last a soft and solemn breathing sound
> Rose like a stream of rich distilled perfumes,
> And stole upon the air."

"Why don't you learn to play?" asked our heroine one night, as, after they retired to their room, Agnes continued to sing snatches of the last piece she had performed.

A loud, though rather heartless, laugh was the only reply.

"I'll teach you, if Mrs. Palmer will allow her piano to be used," added Juliette, more earnestly.

Agnes caught her breath with delight. "Are you in earnest?" she inquired, eagerly.

"Certainly I am. You have such a taste for music, and have learned so readily to read it, I have no doubt you would make a good performer. The time for practice is all you would need."

"Don't, don't raise any objection now! You have put the cup to my lip, — do let me drink it. Why, I would get up an hour or two sooner and go without my meals in order to learn. O Juliette! you've worked me all up, as father says. When will you begin?"

"To-morrow night."

"Why not now? It isn't late."

"Well, I'm willing. With such a zealous scholar I shall get a good reputation."

"Who lives in this house?" inquired a gentleman of the agent of the L—— Mills, as they were walking past Mrs. Palmer's, early one evening.

"A widow lady by the name of Palmer. She has a daughter who is one of the operatives in our factory. Possibly she plays."

"Possibly, but not probably," returned the other. "Just hear that, and the voice, too! I declare it's equal to Jenny Lind! Do you know this Miss Palmer?"

"By sight, merely."

"But she probably knows you, and I want you to introduce me. Come!"

The agent with some reluctance consented, and, greatly to the surprise of the young ladies, the gentlemen were presently ushered into the parlor.

Juliette rose hurriedly from the piano in the midst of a song, and instantly recognized in one of them the person who had been so kind to her on the night of her arrival.

"My friend, Mr. McIntire," began Mr. Proctor, "found it impossible to get by, and pressed me into the service of introducing him."

The young lady was then importuned to go on, and

complied with an ease and gracefulness which made it apparent to them that she had been in polished society.

Following her own fancy in the selection, she played and sung some inspiriting pieces, and then closed by a plaintive air which melted her listeners to tears.

One of them, at least, could but apply to her the words of the poet,

"Ah me! what hand can touch the string so fine?
Who up the lofty diapason roll
Such sweet, such sad, such solemn airs divine,
Then let them down again into the soul?
As when seraphic hands a hymn impart,
Wild warbling nature all, above the reach of art."

In the course of the week following, Mrs. Palmer received a note from Mr. and Mrs. Proctor, inviting herself and family of young ladies to an evening party at his house.

"Now, Juliette," said Agnes, with a look of mock gravity, after she had been gazing with admiration at her young friend, attired for the occasion, "your dress is simple and graceful, but by no means indicating contempt of worldly splendor. I think it necessary to caution you against pride, or rather vanity. Pride I have too much of myself to speak a word unfavorably of it. Your mirror, though small, tells you that you look irresistibly charming, and then your whole appearance is so *recherche;* but, my dear, don't forget that you are only an operative, and don't lose your heart to that Mr. McIntire, who was so bewitched with your music the other night."

" Thank you," said Juliette, blushing deeply ; " but
25*

there is very little danger of my losing my heart at present." She sighed as she uttered the last words in a plaintive tone, and her friend, not understanding or encouraging these sad reminiscences, quickly dispelled them by leading her below.

Juliette was dressed as on the occasion of her ride with James, but, as she found it was to be a large gathering, in addition, had ventured to wear her least expensive ornament for the head, as her hair, though growing fast, still hung in natural curls. But her brilliant appearance excited so much attention, even among their own family circle, that, had not Agnes firmly protested against it, she would have left her jewels hidden in their casket at home.

The party was of such a select nature, that Mrs. Palmer was sure her young boarder's music was the sole occasion of their being invited, though, from whatever cause, she was pleased to have her daughter introduced into such company as before the sad change in their circumstances she had always been accustomed to.

Mr. McIntire for an hour before their arrival was on the *qui vive* in order to introduce Miss Edwards to friends in whose presence he had been expatiating on her wonderful musical powers.

Agnes, who carried herself with the dignity of a queen, glanced archly at her friend as he politely offered her his arm, and led her the entire length of the rooms to a group near the bay-window. Here she was delighted to meet Mr. B——, to whose pastoral care she had been committed by Mr. Allen. She had already called and given him the letter, and been assured of his interest in her spiritual welfare. He looked so good and kind that she longed to sit down by his side and talk on those subjects, which, into whatever company she was thrown, interested her most deeply. But after a few words with him, Mr. McIntire hurried her on to other friends, and at length led her to the piano.

She firmly declined, however, to be the first to play, but obligingly consented to follow others better known to the company.

At a late hour the party broke up, Mr. McIntire still assiduously polite in his attentions, and scarcely willing to leave when he had escorted the party to their own door.

CHAPTER XXVIII.

" Dost thou deem
It such an easy task, from this fond breast
To root affection out ? "

THE excitement of this new life, the busy cares occupying thirteen hours out of the twenty-four, and the increasingly numerous engagements for the evening, Juliette found prevented much of the calm religious enjoyment she had known in Stamford.

Though she considered herself extremely fortunate in finding such a home, and daily acknowledged it among the blessings sent by her heavenly Father in answer to prayer, it was a sore trial to her that she was not among Christian people. True, Mrs. Palmer and her daughter were constant attendants at church, openly avowed that they respected religion, and firmly believed by these outward observances they would secure the favor of Heaven.

For a time our heroine hoped that they were experimental Christians; that they knew what it was to have the love of Christ shed abroad in their own souls; to feel the power of religion shaping their characters and ruling their lives. But she was at length obliged to acknowledge to herself that she had been mistaken.

296

She was often deeply pained by remarks, made at table and elsewhere, ridiculing those who believe in converting grace, and the offices of the Holy Spirit in renewing and sanctifying the heart.

Then the Sabbath, instead of being welcomed with delight, was deemed insufferably dull and tedious, unless there was some exciting novel at hand to beguile the weary hours. There was no recognition in this family of the Bible, nor of the God of the Bible.

With the exception of Juliette, all the boarders shared the feelings of their landlady on this most important subject. On the first evening of her arrival, when at a late hour she finished writing to her Stamford friends, and took her Bible to read a short portion, she could see that nothing but politeness prevented Agnes from joking her upon her piety. As she arose from her knees, after a hurried effort to commend herself to God, there was the least approach to a sneer in her companion's voice as she asked, " Have you any more performances before you come to bed?"

But when Juliette earnestly apologized for keeping her awake so long, saying that "She feared, after all, she would regret having taken her for a room-mate," the young girl responded at once, "It was all my fault, for teasing you to sing so long; so now, say you forgive me for my rudeness, and let us go to sleep."

On Sabbath morning, which occurred after Juliette had been in the family four days, the bell, which

usually called them up to prepare for breakfast, was
delayed until eight, and the meal was not finished by
nine. The hour and a half before morning service
was passed in dressing for church, or in chatting
merrily over the events of the past week.

Juliette, having arisen at the usual hour, silently
dressed, and, throwing a shawl over her shoulders,
began to read her portion of Scripture for the day.
But, after a while, finding it very cool, softly descended to the parlor, the coal fire in the grate being
kept over night, and here enjoyed a delightful season
by herself. Here, too, she made many resolutions of
living in such a way that, by her example, she might
win those about her to the love of her dear Saviour.
She determined, also, to seek an opportunity of con-
versing with Agnes upon the subject of personal
religion, and to press upon her the claims of her
crucified Lord.

When the first bell rang, she went to her room to
prepare for church, so as to be in readiness to attend
the Sabbath school, which was held before the first
service.

It was in vain, however, that she urged Agnes to
accompany her. A significant shrug of the shoulders,
together with the remark, "If I attend church twice,
it will be as much as can be expected of me," proved
to her friend, that as yet, she had no realizing sense
of her guilt as a sinner before God, and therefore no
desire to appropriate to herself the rich offers of me-
diation by his Son.

Though disappointed in being obliged to make her way alone among strangers, yet she was comforted by the thought that all those who thus met together assembled for the same purpose which drew her there ; and that here she might find that delightful Christian companionship which was denied her at home.

She had scarcely entered the large vestry, before she perceived Mr. McIntire eagerly approaching her.

"Will you take a class, Miss Edwards?" he inquired, after showing her to a seat; "or would you prefer to join one of the Bible classes?"

Juliette blushingly replied that she should much prefer the latter, unless her services as teacher were really needed.

"Excuse me for asking, Miss Edwards. Are you a professor of religion? Some of our church are strenuous that none others should be placed in that responsible office."

"I belong to Mr. Allen's church, in Stamford, was the modest reply; and brought a letter from him to Mr. B——."

"Oh, I am very glad!" and he gave her a searching look. "There are a number of small classes in need of teachers ; but as they are mostly foreigners, perhaps you would object."

"Oh, no, indeed! not on that account. If they will consent to try me, I shall be most happy to render myself useful."

"There is every opportunity to do them good," he added. "There, yonder, is a class of bright-eyed

Germans. I will introduce you to them, now if you please, as I see the superintendent is almost ready to call the school to order for prayer."

Our young teacher was so delighted with her new employment that she could scarcely believe an hour had passed, when the ringing of the bell for public service warned the superintendent that it was time to close the school. With all her heart she joined in the closing hymn,—

> " Blest be the tie that binds
> Our hearts in Christian love;
> The fellowship of kindred minds
> Is like to that above.

> " We share our mutual woes,
> Our mutual burdens bear;
> And often for each other flows
> The sympathizing tear."

The instant the singing was ended, Mr. McIntire was by her side, to ask whether he might have the pleasure of waiting upon her to a pew. So she had only time to smile and bow her farewell to her class, and express a hope she should find them all in their places on the next Sabbath, before she found herself walking up the steps into the church. She was a little disappointed at this attention, for she preferred to hire a regular seat of the sexton, to which she could go unattended. But even this slight trouble was dispelled, when, as they passed through the porch, he whispered, "This is a good seat; and, as it is vacant, I can secure it for you permanently, if you wish it."

Mr. B—— was already in the desk, and she speedily forgot everything else in her interest in the services. As she stood up with the assembled congregation to receive the benediction, her heart fervently responded to the words of the Psalmist, "I had rather be a door-keeper in the house of my God, than to dwell in the tents of wickedness."

After tea the question was asked whether any one was going out to the evening service? Mrs. Palmer replied, with a suppressed yawn, "that she was too tired." The daughter echoed this sentiment, while Agnes laughingly declared, " she thought two meetings quite enough for one day."

Juliette, looking brighter and fresher than any of them, had just confessed that she should enjoy going out again, when a quick ring was heard at the door, and Mr. McIntire's voice directing the servant to ask her whether she purposed to attend the evening service.

She went herself to thank him for calling; but declined to accompany him, and returned to the par-lor to find herself the object at which all their jokes were to be aimed. She was glad, therefore, to take her seat at the piano to put a stop to them, though she refused to take a part in any but sacred music.

From this time, her position as an uncompromising disciple of Christ was well understood, and as she became more known and appreciated, the love and respect which she won for herself prevented the ex-

26

pression, in her presence, of opinions such as had heretofore been a source of much pain to her.

She soon became so much attached to her class of German girls, that no weather, however severe, detained her from meeting them. When Agnes or her other friends remonstrated, she reminded them that the wintry storms did not prevent her going to her regular employment through the week, and, therefore, ought not to detain her from doing what good was in her power on the Sabbath.

But there was another reason, and an increasingly urgent one, why she feared she must, for a time, resign her class. By some means or other, Mr. Mc-Intire always contrived to meet her soon after she left the house, and walk by her side to the vestry. If, in order to avoid this, she started earlier, still he joined her, carried her books, held the umbrella when it was storming, or insisted upon giving her the aid of his arm when the ice or snow rendered the walking insecure.

To be sure there was nothing in his manners unpleasant, nor in his conversation unsuited to the day. On other occasions (for he took frequent opportunities to call through the week), he was lively and full of wit; but, on the Sabbath, humble and devout. She often heard him spoken of, as an earnest, working Christian; and, from his position as assistant superintendent, she supposed he was generally respected. She would have liked him as a friend; but shuddered at the bare idea of receiving his attentions in any other light.

For the last week or two, when he called, he had inquired for her by name; and, if she had not insisted upon the family remaining, would have been obliged to receive him alone in the parlor. As his manner became more tender and *empressé*, she was conscious of becoming reserved; and most ardently hoped he would understand this as a check upon his attentions. Twice she remained writing in the dining-room when he asked for her, sending word she was particularly engaged. But this, instead of damping his ardor, only inspired the young man to fresh vigor in the pursuit; and Juliette, deeply pained at the situation in which he had placed her, was meditating what course she ought to pursue, in order to save him the mortification at length of finding himself baffled in his wishes, when a letter from Stamford convinced her her conjectures were only too true.

It was from Susan, and ran as follows, —

"DEAR JULIETTE, — As you may suppose, we were all thrown into the utmost consternation, by hearing from Mr. Allen, that a young gentleman, by the name of McIntire, had written him, as the only friend he had heard you mention, for liberty to address you. Mr. Allen did not know what to say, but brought the letter to mother for advice.

"Mr. McIntire, certainly, as our good pastor says, has acted in the most honorable manner; has given Mr. B—— his pastor, and many other gentlemen of high standing, as references, to whom your friends may apply in regard to his character and position in society. Mother said, after she read the letter, that his heart seemed fully set on winning you.

"Poor James, who has never recovered his cheerfulness since you left, looked like a ghost when I told him about it; but, on his return to the room, which he suddenly left, bade me tell you, when I wrote, that he most sincerely wished your happiness and welfare in this connection, if it should take place.

"Now, Juliette, what would I give to run in and talk with you a minute. I could tell, by one glance into your truthful eye, after I had asked the question, whether you loved this ardent fellow. I should be willing to bet my beautiful pearls, though I admire them so much, that there is a feeling in your heart which forbids you to accept him. I have a reason for this, too, that I will tell you, though mother and Maria have tried in vain to screw it out of me, when I declare, as I am always doing, that you'll never be Mrs. McIntire.

"Soon after you left, I was sweeping your room, when a small bit of crumpled paper fell down behind the table. I picked it up, smoothed it carefully out, and read these words, written by your well-known hand, —

"'O Horace! Dear, *dear* friend! Where are you now? Have you forgotten your promises to your poor Juliette?'

"Now, don't set your little heart to beating, and don't blush so terribly, for no eye but mine has seen the paper; and, to prove that they never shall see it, I will enclose it to you.

"I have no idea what Horace this is, as I never heard you mention a friend of this name; but I guess (I have a right to guess, being a full-blooded Yankee, you know), that he is, or has been, in a relation to you which will keep this young McIntire from being any more to you than he is at present. Do write as soon as you receive this, and tell me whether my pearls are safe.

"If your friend should hereafter be in want of a wife, please recommend me. From what I hear of him, as active, zealous, and, withal, ardent, I have no doubt I should suit exactly. Gentlemen always choose their opposites, you know; and here I am ready and waiting, a quiet, demure damsel, who never ventures to have an opinion of her own, nor to speak above her breath.

"Mother wishes me to say that father consents to keep the money, but only in trust for you; and that he has put it where it will be earning interest.

"O Juliette! how I hate to bid you good-by! I love you more than ever, which shows that I am of a lovely, amiable disposition; for if you were anybody else, I should be sick of your name even. If I ever do anything, no matter what, the cry is, 'Why can't you be more refined, or more careful of what you say, like Juliette?' James never does this; and, by the way, he and I are getting dreadfully intimate. He does everything he can think of for my improvement,

26*

and, in return, I talk of the virtues of my absent friend.

"But no more at present from your own

"SUSY."

This letter, which she was reading for the second time, having withdrawn from the parlor to her room for the purpose, she had scarcely closed, when she was summoned below to meet the gentleman in question.

"Oh, dear!" she cried, half vexed with herself for becoming so excited, and sitting down again to attain some composure. "Why can he not see that I do not return his affection? How trying it will be to tell him so!" She sighed heavily as she murmured, "There is but one person living from whom I could hear such a question without pain; and he is where I shall probably never see him more."

It is enough to say that Mr. McIntire was very much in earnest in his suit; that he endeavored to overrule all objections; and that at last Juliette was obliged, with burning cheeks, to confess that she had no heart to give.

He walked the room in agitation for some minutes before he could be at all resigned to this sudden termination of his dearest hopes; while the poor girl wept in silence.

At last he gave her his hand, as he said, "Though you have occasioned me some of the bitterest moments I have ever known, yet, I do you the justice to believe that it was your wish, as you say, to have saved me this mortification. I see, now, that I have been too much carried away by the ardor of my affection to see or understand any action designed to show that my attentions were not desired. For my own peace, I shall, for a time certainly, withdraw from your too pleasing society; but I shall always be glad to remember that you have called me a valued friend."

.He held her hand in both his, raised it respectfully to his lips, and quickly withdrew; while the poor girl, who inwardly blamed herself that she was obliged to give pain to all her friends, retired to her own chamber to weep, and to long for one word of love from her dear, absent Horace.

CHAPTER XXIX.

"I delivered thee when bound,
And, when bleeding, healed thy wound,
Sought thee wandering, set thee right,
Turned thy darkness into light."

DAYS multiplied into weeks, and weeks into months, until the warm breath of spring began to expand the buds, and clothe all nature with fresh verdure.

The class of four little emigrants, with which Juliette commenced her labors as a Sabbath-school teacher, had increased to nine, and was one of the most regular in its attendance in the whole school.

Contrary to the ordinary plan of the teachers, she required them to commit a few verses of Scripture each Sabbath, encouraging them to great accurateness in the recitation by a reward to the one who was most perfect; and then gave them oral instruction upon the duties of every-day life, often illustrating her meaning by a simple narrative.

The row of brightly beaming eyes fixed so earnestly upon their teacher was in itself a proof of her aptness at imparting instruction. Mr. Howes, the superin-tendent, frequently found himself drawn to the immediate vicinity of her class, and, man of fifty years as he was, shed tears at her simple, earnest appeals to their hearts.

Even if she had done these ignorant, uncultivated girls no good, the effect of this teaching kept alive the devotion of her own heart. She could not meet them one week after another without praying for them, until, at last, her whole soul was engaged in their conversion. This one hour was to her, perhaps, the happiest in the week; and any unusual tenderness on their part, any signs of an awakened conscience, encouraged her to more earnestness in prayer on their behalf. In her own experience she proved the truth of the remark, "No Christians are so happy as *working* Christians."

But the zeal for her class did not at all diminish her interest in the family where she dwelt, especially in Agnes, whose warm, noble heart and untiring energy she earnestly desired to see consecrated to the service of her Saviour. For many weeks she had avoided any personal conversation on the subject, contenting herself with pleading for her at the throne of grace.

Contrary to her habit for many weeks after Juliette began to room with her, Agnes now remained undressed while her companion read her evening portion of Scripture; and once, when the young disciple returned from the closet where she had retired for prayer, she found her in tears.

"Juliette," exclaimed Agnes, one Sabbath morning,

as the former, according to her custom, rose early in order to have a season by herself before the hour for Sabbath school, "you needn't move around so softly; I'm wide awake, and want to ask you a question."

Her companion smiled, and went on dressing.

"I want you to tell me honestly whether you go Sabbath after Sabbath to teach those little dirty-faced children, because you love to do it, or because you think it is your duty?"

"Don't call my dear scholars names, Agnes, and I'll tell you all about it. The first Sabbath I went I was a stranger, you know (I never told you how disappointed I was that you refused to accompany me), and I confess I went from a sense of duty, hoping to be admitted to a class where I might be gaining instruction; but now it would be almost the severest disappointment you could name to be compelled to give up my scholars. I wish you could see how eagerly they watch the door for me, and how their eyes brighten with pleasure as I take my seat in front of them, and shake hands with each one in turn."

Agnes sighed. "My Sabbath-school teacher never shook hands with her class, or even smiled upon them. She came in, took her seat, heard one after another recite the lesson, said coolly, 'Very well learned,' and then looked over the Sabbath-school books until the time had expired."

"I pity both you and her with all my heart," answered Juliette, with moistened eyes. Then being dressed, she turned to go below, as the parlor was always empty at this hour; but Agnes, sitting upright in bed, said quickly, —

"I've a good mind to go with you to-day. I suppose there are Bible classes for the older scholars, and then I could go to Mr. B——'s church."

"Oh, I should be delighted!" was the glad reply.

Mrs. Palmer was much surprised to see Agnes come to the table ready dressed for church; and still more when she found her intent on accompanying her friend to the Sabbath school.

Mr. McIntire, who still filled the office of assistant superintendent, came forward at a glance from Juliette; and, at her request, introduced her companion to Mr. Monson, teacher of one of the Bible classes. The lesson was an interesting one, and, under other circumstances, would have roused the inquiring mind of Agnes; but she was studying a deeper problem. She was, and had been for weeks, comparing her own useless, self-devoted life to that of Juliette's useful, disinterested one, and asking herself what motive-power caused the difference. She knew that, in natural energy, strength, and perseverance, she was far in advance of her companion, who had often confessed that strong motives were necessary to rouse her to exertion; but here she had been more than two years in Lowell, and who could say she had been benefited by her example or teachings?

"How in earnest she seems!" she said to herself, as her eyes continually wandered to her friend's class. She could not see the nine expectant faces turned so fixedly toward their teacher; but she could see Juliette, her whole soul radiating from her expressive eyes as she glanced from one to another of the youth before her.

She began most heartily to despise herself, and to wish she had commenced earlier to imitate the conduct of one so worthy, just as Mr. Monson had come to the conclusion that his new scholar would not be much of an addition to his class.

Recovering herself with a start as he addressed a question to her, and apologizing for her inattention with a frankness that won his regard, Agnes bent the whole force of her mind to the subject of the lesson, asking questions, and expressing her own opinion with a power and originality that woke up the class and delighted the teacher.

The tinkle of the small bell, reminding them that the hour was closed, occasioned a feeling of regret to Agnes that surprised herself. After the school dispersed, Mr. Monson, with a tone of great interest, urged her to become a regular member, assuring her it would do both him and the class good to have one associated with them so resolute in investigating truth. She confessed frankly that during the first part of the lesson she was so interested in watching the earnestness of one of the teachers, who seemed to forget there were other persons in the world except the little foreigners before her, that she gave no heed to his instructions; but that for months she had not enjoyed herself more than during the latter part, and readily agreed to come again.

"I saw you watching Miss Edwards," he replied, more and more pleased with his new scholar. "We consider her a model of a Sabbath-school teacher. Though looking so delicate in health, and evidently little accustomed to exposure, her place has never been vacant one Sabbath since she entered upon its duties, while her zeal and interest in her scholars never flag."

"I can bear testimony that she prays earnestly for them," exclaimed Agnes, tears gushing to her eyes. The next moment, ashamed of this exhibition of feeling, she turned, with almost a haughty air, away from him, and hastened to join her friend at the door.

As they hurried up the steps, Juliette only found time to say, hastily, "Are you sorry you came?" when, to her surprise and disappointment, Agnes replied, "I never was more vexed in all my life."

The glance of sorrowful reproach from her friend cut her to the heart; and even after they had stepped within the door, Agnes drew her back to add, "to think I never came before."

Juliette's large eyes glistened with pleasure as she waited upon Agnes to her own seat, intending, if the pew was full, to seek another herself; but Mr. McIntire, who always seemed to be at hand when she was in trouble, relieved her, by inviting a boy of ten years, who had also a seat in her pew, to occupy one with him.

During the service, Juliette was almost sure she saw

tears drop from Agnes' eyes; but she avoided appearing to watch her, and afterwards thought she must have been mistaken; for, on their leaving the church, Mr. McIntire joined them, and the young girl had never seemed in such high spirits.

She talked gayly of the congregation, the appearance of the minister, who was a stranger, and the choir, but not a word of what they hoped had impressed her in the sermon.

After dinner, she rose hastily from the table and retired to her room, leaving Juliette for a few moments below. The latter was much distressed at her levity after listening to so solemn an appeal, and sighed heavily as she slowly ascended the stairs.

Her coming seemed to be unexpected, for Agnes shut up the Bible, which she held in her hands, in great confusion, her color visibly heightened at being found reading it.

But when her friend invited her to accompany her again, she coolly declined, muttering almost inaudibly something about "a nap."

Retiring as usual to her closet a few moments for prayer, she was much grieved to hear Agnes singing a stanza of a song altogether unsuited to the day, — a rudeness and want of reverence she had never before been guilty of. She came forth from her retirement, her countenance, instead of wearing the look of elevation and peace her companion had often wondered at and envied, overshadowed with sorrow. Gently approaching her room-mate, who sat listlessly gazing from the window, she kissed her tenderly, her voice trembling with emotion as she said, softly, "I have prayed for you, dear Agnes, but it will be of no avail unless you pray for yourself."

The effect of this speech was electrical. The young girl sprang from her chair, and, throwing her arms closely around her friend, gave way to a paroxysm of grief.

"O Juliette!" she cried, "if you stop praying, I'm undone forever; I've tried to pray, but I can't. I hate myself. Oh, I'm afraid there is no mercy for me, I've been such a sinner! You don't know, Juliette, how wicked and stubborn my heart is. If you did, you'd think 'twas no use for me to pray."

The young disciple, in a tone of joyful exultation, cried, "Dear, *dear* Agnes! I will never stop praying. I feel that God has heard my earnest petitions for your soul. Oh, why will you not cry to the Saviour for mercy? He has never refused such a prayer."

The weeping girl shook her head. "I can't; I've tried; I've always been hearing from ministers, 'Go to the Saviour, — give your heart to the Saviour;' but I don't know how."

"If you were drowning, Agnes, and when you felt the water rushing over you, you suddenly realized that you were lost, and all the actions of your past life swept over you with the conviction that you were hastening to the bar of God, you suddenly saw a man standing near the shore with a boat, which you were sure could save you, would you not know how to cry

out, "O sir, take me into that boat, or I shall perish'?
Would you stop to say, 'I know I'm in dreadful
danger; I should like to be saved, but I don't know
how to ask you to save me; I'm really afraid I must
be drowned, for I can't see my way clear to cry for
help'? No; you would summon all your strength,
and, with your whole heart and soul, utter the cry,
'Save me, or I perish!'"

While Juliette was thus earnestly speaking, her
friend stood with clasped hands and protruded eyes,
gazing and listening as if for her life. Her color
came and went, while her heaving breast showed the
terrible conflict within.

"Now, dear Agnes," added the earnest disciple,
"you are just in the condition of a drowning person.
You are sunk in a sea of guilt, until there is no hope
for you unless you cry to the Saviour to take you into
his life-boat. He stands on the shore, waiting to rescue you; but he cannot do it until you call, — until you
perceive your danger, and feel that it is only by his
help that you can be brought safely to land. One
earnest, heartfelt cry, dear Agnes, one humble, peni-
tent prayer, 'God be merciful to me, a sinner!' and
you will be safe, — your soul will be at peace."

With a low, despairing cry, "Lord, save me!"
Agnes threw herself on her knees, and buried her
face in her hands.

Who can describe the workings of the spirit of
grace? Who can tell the fierce struggle between

indwelling sin and the mercy of God? It shook the bowed form, while groans of anguish filled the room.

Juliette stood gazing upon her, large tears rolling unconsciously down her cheeks; while, with her whole soul, she besought God to hear the agonized cry for mercy, and to send an answer of peace.

The first peal of the bell had scarcely vibrated on the ear, when Agnes started from her lowly position, exclaiming, in a tone of wonder mixed with awe, "Can it be that He has heard me? O Juliette, the burden which I have carried so many weeks has all gone! Can He have heard my cry?"

"Yes, dear friend," answered the other, scarcely able to control her voice. "Yes, his promise is sure, 'Him that cometh to me I will in no wise cast off.' 'Come unto me, all ye that are weary and heavy-laden, and I will give you rest!'"

"Precious Saviour!" exclaimed the new-born soul. "Oh, how precious he seems now! But I can't realize that it is indeed true. I am so wicked; I have so long abused his dying love; so scornfully turned from his offers of mercy. What if it is only an ecstatic dream?" and she turned upon her friend a glance so full of anguish that Juliette hastened to reassure her.

"No wonder, dear Agnes, you are at a loss to comprehend the wonders of divine grace. But it is in the power of the gracious, waiting Spirit in one moment of time to dispel all darkness from the hardest heart, to remove the proud, stubborn will, and implant within the humbled soul a spark of grace which will gradually

27*

kindle into a flame of love and praise durable as
eternity."

The young friends, overcome by the fervor of their
gratitude, closed their arms about each other in a long
embrace, such as the angels about the throne, ready to
spread their wings to shout through heaven the glad
news of a sinner purified in the Saviour's blood, might
well envy.

CHAPTER XXX.

"Life is real, life is earnest,
And the grave is not its goal;
Dust thou art, to dust returnest,
Was not spoken of the soul."

TWO days later Agnes wrote her parents, giving an account of the entire change in her feelings and sentiments; but before the letter had reached its destination, she received a note from Mr. Ashley containing the intelligence of her sister's death.

It was read with many tears, but not bitter ones, for Mr. Ashley remarked, "We can scarcely call it death, — only the beginning of an immortal, glorious life. For her the grim messenger had no terror. With a heavenly smile, and words of welcome, she greeted him as the long expected friend who was sent to summon her to the Paradise above."

"We longed to have you with us," added the young pastor, at the close, "and our earnest prayers ascended to heaven from the grave of our departed friend, that from her death spiritual life might commence in your soul."

"He will rejoice with me as he has sorrowed over

319

my wayward, guilty heart," faltered Agnes, giving the letter into the hands of her friend.

"I must now begin life in earnest," she exclaimed, returning from the factory one evening, having on her way home pressed one and another of her companions to embrace Christ as her Saviour. "It seems dreadful to me to pass so many hours in tending those senseless looms, when I ought to be praising God, and trying to persuade others to praise him."

Neither the family of Mrs. Palmer nor her fellow-boarders at the Corporation House, where she and Juliette took their dinner, were long left in doubt as to the cause of the brightly beaming eyes, the calm serenity of the brow, and the subdued, humble manners of the once haughty girl. She had formerly rejoiced at the position of superiority her talents and education had won for her; but she now rejoiced more than ever because it gave her influence with her friends, and enabled her more earnestly to work for her Saviour.

"Oh, how I wish I could be a missionary!" exclaimed the impetuous girl, as, after the second service on the Sabbath, they had accompanied Juliette to the home of one of her scholars, who was sick. "How delightful it must be to spend one's whole life in teaching the ignorant the name of Jesus!"

"Yes," replied her friend, with a smile; "but there is much we can do, situated as we are now. There is work for a score of missionaries in this one city."

The spring and summer months fled swiftly by, and

as yet Juliette had found no opportunity to visit
her friends in Stamford. Susan's letters represented
James as at home, at work upon the farm ; his manners
growing every week more grave and quiet. "If he is
still suffering from disappointment, how cruel," she
thought, "to renew it by visiting him." It was not,
however, without keen regret that she determined to
postpone her visit till another summer, and accept
Agnes' invitation to accompany her home.

In July they had joined an excursion, planned by
Mr. McIntire for their Sabbath school. Whether the
following proposal was a part of his programme at
that time is not known ; but it is certain that, having
waited as long as he thought was reasonable for the
appearance of Juliette's lover, he took this opportunity once more to urge his own affection.

Her answer was so decided that, feeling there was
no longer hope, and knowing it would increase his
suffering to be where he could see her, he accepted a
good offer, and removed his business to New York.

It was a glorious day in September that our heroine·
and her friend, having obtained from the overseer
leave of absence for a fortnight, left the cars at E——,
the nearest station to the Barnard homestead, packed
themselves and their baggage into the covered wagon
belonging to the farm, and started, in company with
Caleb, for home.

He was a reserved man, but on this occasion gave
himself up to the pleasure of meeting his sister, and

answered her numerous questions with playful frankness.

"Yes, father and mother are well; the children
more so, and Ishmael most of all. Old Duke has
been turned out to green pastures for the term of his
natural life; having won this inscription for his
memory : "Served well in his day and generation."
A pair of steers now follow in the steps his feet have
trod, and the family ride to church after Cæsar, Mr.
Ashley's horse.

"So he is still there," said Agnes, assuming an
indifferent tone, and hiding her blushes by looking
from the tiny window of the carriage.

"Of course he is. Why he's as much at home at
the farm as mother is, and takes almost as much
interest in the family."

With a sudden recollection of her cold hauteur
toward the pastor the last time she was at home, he
added, with more earnestness, —

"If you had been there, Agnes, when Clara was
sick, and seen him ministering to her with a brother's
tenderness, you would have got over your old prejudice; you couldn't have helped it."

Juliette caught the sound of a low, suppressed sob;
but she could not see her friend's face, as it was still
turned toward the window; but presently Agnes
spoke in a tremulous voice, —

"Tell me about Clara, Caleb."

For the remainder of the ride he did tell of her
sufferings and of her triumphs; of her peaceful ap-

proach to the dark valley; of her entreaties to her parents and brothers to follow her to heaven; of the holy teachings of their loved pastor, who gently led her on to the very gates of the New Jerusalem, and of her ecstatic visions of the joys in reserve for her.

The tears of Agnes flowed fast, and Juliette's eyes glistened with sympathizing drops.

"We missed you sadly," continued Caleb. "Mr. Ashley thought of sending for you; but her death was very sudden at the last, so there was no time."

They rode on in silence, and at last Agnes began to gaze eagerly about, as she recognized familiar objects.

"Whose horse is this, Caleb?" she inquired. "He is a splendid creature."

"Why, it's Cæsar. Didn't you know him? Mr. Ashley had a funeral to attend at the West District; but as-soon as he heard this was the day you were expected, he insisted I should take him. 'Three miles,' he urged, 'is not much of a walk.'"

"Three miles, why it's six there and back!" exclaimed Agnes, with some impatience. "I wish you had refused to take him. I had rather have rode after the oxen. I hate to be under an obligation."

"We're under too much to him now, to feel moved at a trifle more or less," remarked Caleb, gravely. "But I do hope, if you dislike him, as it seems to me to be entirely without cause, you'll keep it to yourself."

To Juliette's surprise, the sister made no reply;

and presently, in a gayer tone, Caleb asked, "Did we write you about the 'Squire?"

"No, I've heard nothing."

"Well, he's married."

"To whom?" cried Agnes, with a laugh.

"To a widow lady he found in Boston. But that isn't the worst of it; they've separated again."

"Just what she might have expected. I told you about my old beau, Juliette. He lives in this large house we're just passing. I might have lived there, too, if I had chosen, and had a Mrs. tackled on to my name."

Agnes' eyes danced with merriment, while her friend remarked, with a smile, "It is a fine place. Those grand old trees are worth a fortune."

Every house, tree, and shrub were now regarded with interest; and, in a few minutes, Agnes announced, with a glad shout, "There's home and father!"

How Juliette's heart vibrated to these words, "Home and father!" "Shall I ever be allowed to return to mine?"

The whole family quickly assembled at the door, in their own peculiar way making known their joy at receiving the daughter and sister. Nor was the friend forgotten; as one loved by Agnes, they welcomed her with all their hearts.

Mr. Ashley, whose seat was at the right hand of the matron, did not arrive until they were seated at the bountifully spread table.

Agnes recognized his step before he entered the

house, and was vexed at herself that she could not keep down the rising color.

With her eyes fixed intently on her plate, she said not a word until a lad with light, wavy hair, and earnest blue eyes, cried out, "There's Mr. Ashley! You haven't seen him yet, have you, Agnes?"

The gentleman entered, and with extended hand approached the table.

The young girl arose from her chair, and gave him hers with great cordiality. There was one searching glance into his face, a rushing of blood from the heart, and she recovered herself directly to introduce "Miss Edwards."

He started, and Juliette turned pale; emotion not unnoticed by Agnes; but he instantly gave her his hand, and added his welcome to W——.

His coming seemed to produce a constraint. Agnes, before so talkative, relapsed into silence, or only answered briefly as possible the questions put to her.

Mr. Ashley talked with Juliette, asking about factory life, the length of time she had resided in Lowell, etc., etc.; she answering with readiness, and appearing much pleased with his frank, cordial address.

Agnes, with a sharp pain at her heart, watched them closely, and noticed that whenever Juliette's eyes were fixed on her plate, he regarded her with a peculiar expression. Notwithstanding every effort to throw it off, her manner toward him grew every moment more reserved. This, however, instead of producing an unfavorable impression on the gentleman,

28

rather seemed to raise his spirits. He exerted himself to be agreeable, and soon, while enjoying his
bread and milk, the diet to which he confined himself
at night, set the whole table laughing at an account he
gave them of a scene he had witnessed.

After tea Agnes immediately left the room, Mr.
Ashley following, and detaining her a moment in the
entry. He spoke in a low voice; but Juliette heard
her answer firmly, "Certainly not, sir. It is not at all
necessary."

"Very well!" was his cool rejoinder, returning to
the sitting-room. He sat down for a moment and
knit his brows, as if something unpleasant had
occurred; but presently rallied, and carried on a
lively conversation with Juliette. "Have you ever
been in this part of the country before, Miss Juliette?"

"No, sir," she answered, rather surprised at his
familiar address.

"You are not a native of Lowell, I think?"

Again he regarded her with that peculiar expression.
She blushed as she answered, "Oh, no, sir! I was
born in New York."

"Ah, well, that is a stirring city. I used to visit
it frequently when I was a member of Yale College."

"Indeed!" responded Juliette, a rush of memories
sweeping over her, and in the midst of them a vague
recollection of having seen a gentleman strongly
resembling Mr. Ashley; but the name, certainly, was
not familiar.

What should she do if he remembered her, too?

In great confusion she attempted to turn the conversation, when he added, "What a wonderful faculty is memory! Your countenance is strangely familiar, and carries me back to college life and college days. Did you ever visit the colleges in New Haven?"

"No, sir, never; but I, too, have seen somewhere a person very like you; I noticed it when we first met."

Again that curious, expressive glance.

Poor Agnes, unperceived by them, had advanced to the door to call Juliette, stood there a moment, just long enough to see that look, and the confusion it caused, and quickly retired without speaking.

"Possibly you may hereafter be able to call it to mind," he remarked, with a pleasant smile.

He then began to talk of Agnes; of the change in her feelings; was glad to know her friend thought it genuine; should have supposed from the little he had seen of her at the table that she was much the same as before. Agnes had written often of her friend, and ascribed her conversion, under God, to her earnest prayer.

Juliette expatiated on the character of her roommate; described their first meeting in the factory, and the pains Agnes had taken to provide her a pleasant home. Growing warm with the subject, as she saw her hearer's keen eye flash with interest, she spoke of her friend's energy and enthusiasm; how eager she was for instruction, — how quick to acquire knowledge, — the perseverance with which she had learned to play the piano, while neglecting none of her daily duties, but above all, her untiring zeal in serving Christ,—her influence in the mills, having prevailed upon so many of the operatives to join the Sabbath school, that four new classes had been formed.

"And is she a teacher?" inquired the gentleman, rising and looking from the window.

"No, sir. It is a rule, I think, of the school, that none but professors should fill that office. Perhaps it is necessary in such a place."

"Then she is not a church member?"

Juliette wondered at the apparent indifference with which he asked this question; but replied, "No, sir. She says this is her home; and it is her wish to join here. I think she is a noble girl; and, though she may never become a missionary, as she desires, yet she will be useful anywhere.

This time Mr. Ashley walked deliberately to the outer door, stood there a moment, and then as coolly returned to his seat by her side. "Miss Agnes is very happy in having so warm a friend. I am glad to hear this account, nor am I surprised at it. She has the elements which would well fit her for the life of a missionary. I am not so fortunate as to enjoy her confidence, but — "

The lad the family sportively called Ishmael came in suddenly at this moment, and approaching the gentleman, leaned on his shoulder with the confidence and affection of a brother.

Mr. Ashley smiled as he patted the boy's cheek,

and asked, "How now, Willie, does Cæsar need my services?"

"I'll feed him, if you'll let me, sir," responded the boy, his bright eyes fixed on his friend.

"You shall help me, Willie. I suppose you're very glad to see your cousin again."

"Oh, yes, sir!" then speaking in a whisper, "She didn't call me Ishmael; and she kissed me, too."

"I'm very glad, dear," he responded in the same low tone; then, glancing archly at Juliette, —

"This is my young friend, Willie Porter," he added, bringing forward the boy; "an orphan child adopted by his uncle, Mr. Barnard."

"How do you do, Willie?" she asked, giving him her hand with a smile that quite won his heart.

The boy made a bow, a natural and not ungraceful one as he replied, "I thank you, I am well."

"Now Cæsar shall have his supper," said the gentleman, rising. "Run, Willie, I'll be there presently."

"Miss Juliette," he remarked, turning toward her, "It must be I have met you before; and yet the lady I saw was scarcely older than you are now, and that was four years ago. She must have been, let me see, as much as nineteen."

"Which is just my age," remarked Juliette, regretting her frankness, however, as soon as she had spoken..

"Ah! I should have supposed you much younger." And with a bow, he left her.

She went to the kitchen to find Agnes, wondering

28*

much she had been left so long with a stranger; but
the room was deserted; and, hearing voices upstairs,
she ventured to follow the sound, and presently, saw
the young girl weeping over a tress of soft, brown
hair; her mother sitting by her side, their faces bearing the marks of strong emotion.

They started up when they saw her, and Agnes said,
"This is dear Clara's hair. Mother has been telling
me about her last hours. But you are tired, and I
will show you our room. It is a small one, you see,"
she added. "Clara used to occupy it with me. I didn't
realize before how much I should miss her."

Their trunks had been brought up, and they proceeded to unpack them, and hang the dresses in the
closet.

"How glad you must be to get home!" remarked
Juliette, in a cheerful tone; "they are all so pleased
to see you."

To her surprise, her companion burst into tears;
but almost instantly controlling herself said, gravely,
"Yes; but it does not seem as I expected. I don't
think I shall stay as long as I mentioned to you at
first."

Juliette did not wonder at her emotion, supposing it
to refer to the decease of her sister.

"I ought to tell you, perhaps," said Agnes, in a constrained voice, "that Mr. Ashley offered to give up his
room to you, and take this; a civility not often exercised, I imagine. I took the liberty to refuse for
you."

"Certainly; I would not have taken his room for anything." She gazed earnestly in her friend's flushed face, and was about to say, "I think you do wrong to be so prejudiced against him," but checked herself, and presently the bell rung for family prayers.

"How strange it will seem!" murmured Agnes. "It was Mr. Ashley's plan a few months before Clara's death. Mother has been telling me about it. Come, let's go down."

CHAPTER XXXI

"Nor less was she in heart affected;
But that she masked it with haughtiness,
For fear she should of lightness be detected."

THE next afternoon, as Mrs. Barnard, her daughter, and Juliette were sitting together in the parlor, Mr. Ashley, who passed every morning in his study, opened the door, his riding-whip in his hand. "I am going to the South Parish," he said, turning to Agnes, "and it has just occurred to me that you might like to see your old friends there; if so, I should be most happy of your company."

The young girl was startled at this sudden proposal, blushed rosy-red, but with the least tinge of haughtiness declined.

"Miss Juliette, perhaps, will take your place," said he, no ways disconcerted. "I should like her first impressions of our town."

"Oh, no, I thank you," she commenced; but both Mrs. Barnard and Agnes urged her so strongly, — the gentleman reminding her that it was a fine day, and not to be wasted in the house, — that almost before she was aware, her bonnet and mantilla were donned, and she was flying along the road after black Cæsar, who seemed to be in fine spirits.

After a few moments, Mr. Ashley succeeded in calming him, and they rode on through the village in silence; when turning a little on his seat, where he could watch her countenance, he said, suddenly, "Were you ever in D——, Miss Juliette?"

"Yes, sir," she faltered, alarmed, she knew not why; "I attended school there many years."

"At Mrs. Osborn's, probably."

"Yes, sir."

A pause again.

"Miss Juliette, you may think me very abrupt; possibly I may excite your displeasure; but I am a frank man, and dislike mysteries. I recognized you at once as Miss Fearing. I went to D—— four years ago, in company with a half-brother of yours, and passed two or three hours in your society. You will not think it flattery when I say yours is not a countenance easily forgotten. Knowing well your brilliant position in society, you can easily imagine I was not a little surprised to meet you here in this obscure place, having been an operative in Lowell, known by the name of Edwards."

Surprise, joy, and grief, by turns, contended for mastery in Juliette's breast while he was speaking; but joy was uppermost at hearing the name of her cherished friend from one who knew and loved him.

"Oh, yes!" she exclaimed, her truthful eyes steadily meeting his; "I recollect it all, now; but your name was not Ashley then."

"My name is George Benson Ashley; probably you heard me addressed as Benson; your brother generally called me so, as there were two other Ashleys in college at the time."

"Mine is Juliette Edwards Fearing," rejoined the young girl. "I don't know whether it was wise to drop the last name. If you are willing to hear me, I should like to tell you some things about myself; but have you heard of late from my brother, — from Horace? I have heard nothing for eighteen months."

"He is abroad still. I suppose, of course, you knew of his marriage?"

With a convulsive sob she tried to say "No;" but from her white lips no sound could be distinguished. She gazed at her companion with such an expression of agony that he realized he had made a mistake in imparting the news too suddenly; though why she should be thus overcome in hearing of the marriage of her brother, he could not even conjecture. After an awkward pause, he added, —

"It may, after all, be only rumor. A college friend met him abroad, travelling with a party of our countrymen. I think he said that it was one of the latest on-dits in Paris that Mr. Everett was engaged to his cousin. Afterwards I heard the rumor of his marriage."

Poor Juliette! and this was to be the end of all her hopes. Vague and faint as they had been, in that one moment that they were rudely torn away she realized how much they had comforted and sustained her. A sickening faintness made her shudder. She reached out her hand to grasp something for support; a darkness obscured her vision. Her companion, hearing a low groan, turned quickly to see her fall back insensible.

It was but the work of a moment to stop the horse, and loosen the strings of her bonnet, which he did with a consciousness of having committed some terrible mistake. "What?" he asked himself again and again, "what can it be?"

With the poor girl, it was but a momentary suspension of consciousness. With a deep sigh she revived; but there rushed over her such an overwhelming tide of emotion, that she trembled like a reed shaken with the wind. In vain she endeavored to recover her composure; the dagger had sunk into her heart. "He never loved me," was the conviction she could neither resist nor shake off.

Mr. Ashley had never found himself in a more embarrassing position, and was delighted, when, at length a flow of tears gave vent to her too evident distress. For a time he allowed her to weep without striving to check her; but presently began to suggest such thoughts as might strengthen her faith in her heavenly Father; and before the ride was ended, she became sufficiently composed to relate many incidents in her eventful life, already known to the reader.

"I am afraid I have done you no good, though I

hoped to," said he, gazing with keen regret into her pallid face, on which an expression of patient suffering was already stamped. "Be assured you have my warmest sympathies. In regard to your brother, I shall take the earliest opportunity to learn the truth of the rumor which has so distressed you."

She shook her head sadly, but made no reply.

"May I ask, is your friend, Miss Agnes, acquainted with your real position in society?"

"No, sir."

"May I tell her?"

"If you think it best; but it will do no good."

This was said in such a heart-broken tone, that he was obliged to turn from her to conceal a sympathizing tear.

On reaching the farm, Mr. Ashley called Willie, and gave him permission to unharness the horse; then assisting Juliette from the carriage, he was obliged to put his arm around her to support her from falling.

Agnes and her mother ran to the door, — all the reserve of the haughty girl vanishing at sight of her friend's distress. "Are you ill? What has happened?" she inquired, darting a quick, indignant glance at the gentleman.

"I will explain presently. Mrs. Barnard, will you assist Miss Juliette to retire? The ride was too much for her, and probably she will wish time to compose herself. I will send up some quieting drops presently."

"No; I'll go, mother," urged Agnes. "I'd rather go with her."

"Your mother will do better now, Miss Agnes. If you will sit down a minute, till I procure the drops, I have some explanations to make to you." This was said gravely, and in a tone of authority, as if he expected his wishes to be complied with.

Agnes hesitated a moment, and then seated herself, while he procured a small vial from the closet, poured a teaspoon half full of drops, and brought a glass of fresh water from the kitchen.

"May I take them up ? " she asked humbly. "I will return immediately."

He gave them into her hand without speaking.

"Miss Agnes," he began on her return, drawing a chair near her side, but at once leaving it to pace the floor, "you noticed my surprise at meeting your friend, and probably inferred we had met before. This was true. I met her under widely different circumstances, and my astonishment, for a moment, was great. You noticed, too, that I did not address her as Miss Edwards. I did not choose to do so, until I knew why she had dropped her real name.

"The only daughter of a New York banker of immense wealth, highly accomplished, and thoroughly educated, — heiress in her own right to a large fortune, — idolized by those who knew her; is it strange I wondered at finding her here, knowing her life for months had been passed in a factory?

"You were surprised, no doubt, that I paid her the courtesy to offer her my room; but I did so, apprised

29

of her high social position, and recollecting the many favors I had received from her friends."

The quickly changing color of the young lady addressed proved her deep interest in this tale. And there were other feelings produced by it which caused her the keenest mortification. With a blush that mounted to her temples, she sprang forward, extending her hand, as she exclaimed, "Mr. Ashley, I have been suspicious and unjust to you. I am thoroughly ashamed of myself. I scarcely dare ask you to forgive me."

He took her offered hand, clasped it in both his, as he gazed earnestly into her blushing face. "Are you aware," he asked, with his peculiar smile, "that you have scarcely looked at me since your return? Have I not something to forgive there, too? I'm afraid you have not told the half of your offences against me, —the unkind thoughts, the proud determination to show me you could be as coolly indifferent as you deemed me. Foolish girl! how little you understand my heart."

"I did not consider it necessary or proper to confess my sins in detail," murmured Agnes, becoming painfully confused, and struggling to release her hand. "I am sufficiently conscious that, from some cause, I have forfeited your esteem, and only make the acknowledgment because it was due to myself. You have not yet said you would overlook it."

"No, because I have some acknowledgments to make myself; of affections and hopes cherished for three weary years; affections I for a long time strove to uproot, because the one I loved was, at best, an unbeliever in the doctrines of the cross; affections which, now that objection is overruled by the abounding grace of God, may never be reciprocated. Oh, yes, Agnes! There is much I have to confess. If I forgive you, will you promise to be merciful also?"

Her answer was so low it was unintelligible; but the gentleman argued well that she allowed her hand to rest passively in his; and when, at a call from the stairs, she said, softly, "I must go now," he felt so sure of a favorable verdict, that he ventured to raise the delicate member tenderly to his lips.

One quick glance into his earnest eyes, and she flew from the room to the bedside of her friend; trying to quell the tumult of joy in her heart, to minister to one so dearly loved. At any time, the story of Juliette's early history would have been deeply exciting, proving as it did, the truth of her own vague suspicions; but now, as she bent tenderly over her, watched the spasmodic movement of the closed eyelids, and listened to the deep, heavy sighs that almost convulsed the breast of the sufferer, she realized through what fearful trials the poor girl must have passed. Not yet aware that it was love to her Saviour which had prompted the sacrifice of all that was generally esteemed among men, she began to form conjectures as to what could have produced so unhappy a result.

The supper-bell found her still with her cool hand bathing the brow of her distressed friend, and, hearing her father's voice below, she said, softly, "I will bring you a cup of tea. No, dear, don't try to rise; lie quietly till I come. Oh, how your temples throb!"

Mr. Ashley was quite concerned that Miss Juliette remained so ill, and said very gravely, "I am heartily sorry I persuaded her to ride out."

With a crisp slice of toast, Agnes returned to her friend, while Caleb, who had been absent with his father, since dinner, requested an explanation of what had passed.

The next morning, Mr. Ashley, as usual, passed in his study; but when Juliette, having sought and found comparative tranquillity at the throne of grace, appeared at the dinner-table, she heard him giving directions at the door for letters of importance to be sent to the post.

Making a great effort to appear cheerful and interested in what was passing, she could but notice a change in the manners of Agnes toward her clerical friend. She talked no more than before, but there was a winning softness in her voice, a subdued timidity in the quick casting down of her eyes, that well became her.

Her brother Caleb, who had been indignant at her treatment the night before, watched and wondered too.

In the afternoon, Mr. Ashley brought an interesting biography and read aloud to the young ladies as they sat sewing; but toward night, while hearing his favorite

Willie recite a Latin lesson, he was summoned to a distant part of the town to visit a sick woman.

"If it were not for leaving Miss Juliette alone," he said (turning to Agnes), "I would solicit your company. It would do you good to review your Latin, and I could hear you on the way."

A peculiarly arch smile stole over his face as the young lady rose in great confusion, to conceal her blushes, declaring she could not think of leaving her sick friend.

Juliette, however, would not consent to detain her, and they finally drove away.

Agnes, who had always been pleased that she was able to retain her self-possession, was vexed that the color would rush into her face, and that she could scarcely control her voice to utter a sentence. She was afraid her companion would perceive the violent beating of her heart; and was immensely relieved when he began to talk upon the most indifferent subjects. When she had had time to compose herself, he referred to Juliette, and gave in detail the account he had received from her lips.

"Dear girl," exclaimed Agnes, "how nobly has she endured all these trials! I feel terribly condemned when I remember that I have sometimes thought her wanting in courage and resolution; but I see she has triumphed where I should have fallen in the way."

"We can seldom be assured how we should comport ourselves under prospective trials," remarked Mr. Ashley. "I have no doubt, however, that it would be

29*

more trying to you, constituted as you are, to wait
patiently the developments of God's providence, than
to her. You could scarcely feel, I fear, that, —

"‘ They also serve who only stand and wait.’

"But I have strong hope in her case. She tells me
her father and one brother went instantly abroad;
probably before his wrath had time to cool. The
other brother, whom I well knew, being his senior in
college, had left a month or two previous. I have
already written to a mutual friend, to obtain his
address, and shall write at once, detailing with perfect
frankness in what circumstances I have found his
sister. He is a noble fellow; and she assures me he
became an experimental Christian before he left the
country."

"Thank you!" responded Agnes, warmly, ."thank
you for this interest in my friend. She has been a
blessing indeed to me."

"And through you to me also," returned the young
pastor, deeply moved. "Can you think I have not
often blessed God for her prayers and labors for one
whose future character was to exert such an influence
on me and on my people? O Agnes, my faith has
sometimes wavered, as month after month fled by, and
still you remained careless and thoughtless of the concerns of your immortal soul! Yet I prayed and waited,
knowing God would answer in his own good time.
When Clara died, I felt that her loss must be the
means of arousing you; but we see he works accord-

ing to the counsel of his own will. The sad tidings had not reached you when the letter came announcing the glorious news of your hopeful conversion.

"I read that letter on my knees, thanking God that he had listened to my humble cry. With, perhaps, too great confidence, I looked forward to a return of my affection, now that I could implore the blessing of God on our union. Shall I go on, dear Agnes?" he added, catching a glimpse of her glistening eyes, "Shall I venture to interpret your conduct on the night of your return, after I had taken a hurried walk to meet you? Your first, blushing, friendly glance, expressed this, 'You have been a good friend to the family, and I am right glad to see you.' But before we arose from table, the conversation, carried on with I cannot tell you how great an effort on my part, received no aid from you, while your manners grew every moment more constrained. I was not wholly discouraged, however, because I perceived that you had noticed my start of surprise on meeting Miss Juliette, and I thought it augured well for me that —"

"Oh, don't; don't! Don't expose me any more," cried the blushing girl; "I'm mortified enough already. I will make any acknowledgment you wish, if you'll forget all my foolish conduct since I came home."

"Even to the present indicative of the verb *amo?*" urged the gentleman, archly glancing into her downcast eyes.

"Yes, sir, even that, if nothing else will satisfy you;"

and Agnes, after one quick, searching glance into his face, frankly put her hand in his.

"Now AND FOREVER," he said, in a solemn tone, and, clasping it to his heart, 'Now know I that I have obtained favor of the Lord, because he has heard my prayer.'"

CHAPTER XXXII.

" I cannot speak, tears so obstruct my words
And choke me with unutterable joy."

LEAVING our heroine slowly recovering from the effects of her ride with the clergyman, let us turn for a while to our Stamford friends.

On the same day that Juliette, in company with her room-mate left Lowell for W——, Mr. Allen, happening to be glancing over a late issue from the New York press, was a good deal excited by the following brief passage, —

"Among the arrivals by the last steamer, we are happy to announce that of Edward Fearing, Esq., his son, and Mr. Everett, a promising young member of the bar. We are sorry to learn, however, that Mr. Fearing, having left the country in search of health, has not obtained the benefit from his foreign travels which was to be desired."

An hour later the kind pastor knocked at the farm-house door. Having inquired how lately they had heard from Juliette, he proceeded, in the presence of the family, to relate the fact that she was the daughter of a New York banker, and then read to the astonished group the paragraph above named.

345

James sprang to his feet in open-mouthed wonder; while Susan laughed and cried, declared she was glad and she was sorry, all in a breath.

Mrs. Smith fully agreed with Mr. Allen that the young lady ought to be informed of this intelligence, and Susan gladly consented to write. Cutting the small but important item from the paper, she enfolded it in her letter, and directed it as usual to Lowell; but Mrs. Palmer, having received no orders to forward letters, laid it carefully away to await her boarder's return.

Early the next morning, Mrs. Smith was surprised to see James preparing for a journey. At last, attired in his Sunday suit, looking brighter and handsomer, as his sister said, than she had ever seen him, he announced his intention of going in the first train of cars to New York.

Susan accompanied him as far as the depot to drive back the horse, and, also, to communicate the intelligence to her sister, Mrs. Dudley Houghton, whose marriage had taken place in June.

It was a noble impulse which prompted the young farmer to visit Mr. Fearing and plead with him in his daughter's behalf. During the ride of two hours in the cars he had time to reflect upon the probable character of a man who would be guilty of turning a child from his door. Wholly unconscious of the frantic efforts of the father to find any trace of his lost Juliette, he supposed Mr. Fearing either aware of, or indifferent to, her present abode, and intended to base his plea upon the fact of her absorbing grief at the unnatural separation.

Having readily obtained the direction to the street and number, our friend James walked leisurely back and forth in front of the imposing mansion; a feeling of self-degradation stealing over him as he realized that he had tried to woo the heiress of all this grandeur; and, when at last he slowly ascended the steps, it was with the feeling of a man who was about to beard the lion in his den.

Let it not be supposed that fear for himself quickened one pulse of the warm-hearted yeoman. No, the fear of man was not in his category; it was the thought that he might, in his ignorance of the ways of the world, do something injurious to the interests of her he still loved.

In answer to his loud, and, it must be confessed, plebeian ring, our old friend Rufus instantly showed his smiling face at the door.

"Is Mr. Fearing at home?"

"Oh, yes, massa!"

"I should like to see him, on private business."

Rufus was puzzled, and scratched his woolly head to wake up his ideas. The fact was, Mr. Fearing, being an invalid, had denied himself to all visitors; but this, as he said afterwards, struck him "as a new kind of chap." He was sure there was something "oncommon," about him.

James quietly waited until the servant had scanned

him from head to foot, and then repeated his wish to see the gentleman.

"Massa Fearing is sick," said Rufus, at length, "and he isn't at home to anybody in these days."

"But you said just now he *was* at home."

"Oh, law, massa! I mean he don't see anybody. He stays in his chamber from morning till night."

Two gentlemen at this moment came to the door, talking earnestly, but stopped as they saw the young man.

"I have come some distance to see Mr. Fearing, on business," said James, addressing the elder one; "but his servant tells me he is too sick to see me."

"Walk in, sir; walk in!" exclaimed the younger man, whom we should scarcely recognize as Henry.

"Rufus, you old scoundrel, don't you know enough to ask a gentleman to walk in?"

This was aside; and the servant answered with a grin, —

"I was only waiting, massa."

James followed the older one, who was Mr. Everett, to the parlor, almost bewildered at the magnificence by which he was surrounded.

"Is your business important?" inquired the gentleman, politely.

"I'll have the horses round in a few minutes," exclaimed Henry, suddenly throwing open the door.

"Very well;" and Mr. Everett turned again to the stranger.

"I consider it of much importance; but it is of a private nature. I mean it is not pecuniary."

"Perhaps," returned Horace, with a smile, "you can transact it with me, as my father is ill."

"Oh, yes, sir, in that case," and James glanced with new interest at the stranger as the brother of Juliette.

"I came from Stamford," said he, frankly, "to plead with Mr. Fearing to be reconciled to his daughter."

"His daughter!—reconciled! Is Juliette living?"

Horace sprang forward, but immediately sank back in his chair, pale and trembling with agitation. By a powerful effort, recovering himself, he exclaimed, in a broken voice,—

"Mr. Fearing would give all he is worth in the world so have her restored to him."

It was now James's turn to be surprised.

"There must be some mistake," he urged, growing very red in the face. "I understood—"

"But where is she now?" cried Horace, impatiently interrupting him.

"She is in Lowell, where, for a year, she has been working in a factory."

"Gracious heaven!" exclaimed the gentleman, covering his face with his hands. "O Juliette! *Juliette!*"

"She was a member of my father's family for months," added the young man, seeing the other was too much agitated to speak. "We used every inducement to keep her there, for my sisters dearly loved

30

her; but she chose to be independent, and left soon
after she had recovered from a dangerous illness."

Horace groaned aloud; but suddenly starting from
his seat, said, —

"Remain here. I must go and prepare her father
to see you."

James cast his eyes around the spacious apartment,
and sighed as he said to himself, "And I asked her to
share my humble home." Presently he heard a loud
scream for help, hurried sounds in the hall, quick steps
up and down the stairs, then a servant ran in, breathless with terror, to say that Mr. Fearing was in a fit,
and that Mr. Horace begged he would not leave the
house.

Horace himself soon ran in, pale and agitated, to state
that the intelligence from his daughter had so affected
Mr. Fearing that he was in a most dangerous condition; but begged as a favor that the young man would
remain for the present.

"Perhaps," said James, "I can be of service. I
am somewhat used to sickness;" and, in the excitement of the occasion, he at once threw off all the restraint which intercourse with strangers had caused, and
showed himself, as he was, a warm-hearted, sympathizing, Christian man.

Following Horace to the chamber, he beheld an
elderly gentleman struggling convulsively in the arms
of a servant, his eyes rolling wildly and his face of a
ghastly pallor. Male and female attendants were

running around the room, or wringing their hands, or uttering shrill screams of terror.

Ordering these from the chamber, Horace inquired whether Peter, who had been sent for the doctor, had returned; while James advanced to the relief of Rufus, suggesting that, unless a physician soon arrived, Mr. Fearing ought to be placed in a warm bath.

Horace caught at the idea, and, without a moment's delay, by the efficient aid of the young farmer, the convulsed form was presently borne to an adjoining room, where a bath was prepared.

The happy results of this treatment became evident from the relaxing of the different limbs; so that when Dr. M—— reached his patient the worst symptoms had already abated.

Leaving James, at his own request, with the servant to envelop the cold limbs with warm flannels, Horace retired to Juliette's boudoir to state briefly to Dr. M——, the cause of this sudden attack.

In the midst of the confusion, Henry drove to the door with a span of noble grays, and rang loudly for Horace to join him.

He was much excited by the intelligence from Juliette, and proposed to start in the next train for Lowell; but his brother said, firmly, "That must be my privilege; and, in the mean time, father's state needs your constant attention."

In company with the physician, they re-entered Mr. Fearing's room, where James still lingered. The sick man was now restored to consciousness, but feeble and helpless as a babe. His eye wandered wistfully from one to another, as they stood around his bed, but ever turned to the frank, open countenance of the young farmer, as if in some way he connected him with his daughter.

He motioned feebly for Horace to come nearer, and said, in a low, shaking voice, "Leave the gentleman with me — while you go for — Juliette. Tell her —'"

The features of his face began to be convulsed again, and Horace, at a sign from the doctor, said, "Yes, father; I know all you wish to say. I'll tell her your arms and your heart are open to receive her."

"Tell her," gasped the poor man, with a look of agony, "to — for — give — all — "

At these humble words, forced from the lips of the once proud, haughty man, those standing around the bed were deeply moved. Horace withdrew with James to the further end of the apartment, followed by the anxious glance of the sufferer.

"You see how he is," he said, grasping the stranger by the hand. "For the sake of your sister's friend, will you remain with him till I return?"

"Yes," answered James, with a quivering lip, "for her sake I will do anything but violate my conscience."

Here was a new tie between them, and the young men clasped each other by the hand.

"As he is able to bear it, soothe him with an account of her love; I am sure she loves him," with a quick, inquiring glance into his companion's face.

"As if nothing had occurred."

"Tell him so," continued the other, much affected; "tell him of her life in the country; but don't, for the world, hint where she is now; it might kill him. He has sinned; but he has suffered. Let us hope God will deal with him in mercy."

Then making minute inquiries concerning her residence in Lowell, etc., etc., and saying he thou ht they might be back in three days at farthest, they returned to the bed.

"I am going now, father; but Mr. Smith has consented to remain till I return, which will be at the first moment I am able. He will tell you all you wish to know."

He turned to leave; but, with sudden strength, Mr. Fearing grasped his hand, and, pulling him down to the bed, whispered, "Tell her — I'm willing — now."

Not daring to trust his voice, the young lawyer bowed his assent, and hastily left the room.

Henry followed him to his chamber, where Horace made hurried preparations for his absence, receiving, at the same time, directions as to arrangements to be made for his sister. The boudoir must be restored to the state it was when she left; and, if possible, Eliza, her waiting-maid, must be found and reinstalled in her place. He also reminded Henry that great pains must be taken to soothe and quiet their father, especially if any unforeseen event should occur to delay his return.

"This young Smith is a real Godsend!" exclaimed

30 *

Henry. "I can see he will be the one to manage father."

"Yes; I could scarcely have gone yet without his aid. Did you see how father grasped his hand when I left?"

CHAPTER XXXIII.

" But while hope lives,
Let not the generous die. 'Tis late before
The brave despair."

MOST unfortunately, in the hurry and excitement of the sick-room, James forgot to mention that Juliette had always been known as Miss Edwards; so that when Mr. Everett, having lost not a moment in unnecessary delay, reached Lowell at an early hour the morning after he left home, hastened to inquire for Miss Fearing at Mrs. Palmer's, he was assured no such person resided there.

Disappointed more than he could express, he requested the servant to inform her mistress that a gentleman wished to see her on business.

"Mrs. Palmer is sick," she replied; " her daughter and the other boarders are in the factory."

"Ah!" he exclaimed, catching eagerly at the idea of finding her there; and, learning the name of the Corporation who employed them, he proceeded with a wildly beating heart to obtain the address of the agent, and get a permit to go in and begin his search.

Mr. Proctor readily granted him every help that was possible, but assured the gentleman that he had no recollection of any weaver by the name of Fearing. A ticket of admittance gave him access to every part of the buildings, and a written request to the overseer obtained for him the assistance of that gentleman.

"Fearing, — Fletcher, —" repeated the man, half-aloud. "You are sure it's not Fletcher?"

"No; I'm sure it's Fearing," replied Horace, trying to conceal his impatience.

"No such person employed in this factory," said the man, decidedly; "however, I will walk with you through the rooms, that you may see for yourself."

Mr. Everett readily agreed to this proposition, and leisurely walked back and forth through the aisles, casting a quick glance at each operative, his talkative guide little imagining the mingled feelings of disappointment and relief in not finding her he sought.

At length, with many thanks for the politeness of the overseer, he left the factory and turned his steps wearily back to the hotel.

While eating his hurried meal (he had not breakfasted before), the thought occurred to him, that as Mr. Smith had happened to mention that Juliette was a Sabbath-school teacher, he might here learn something of her. "But which church did she attend?" In the midst of such a city it would be an endless task to find a Sabbath-school teacher by a given name.

"O Juliette! my poor, persecuted Juliette!" he groaned, in agony; "shall I ever find you? and how?"

It had been his intention to give no publicity to his

search; but now he was glad to avail himself of the efficient aid of the police. With a full description of Juliette as he last saw her (alas! with what a heavy heart he realized that she might be sadly changed now!), and the exhibition of a tiny miniature he always wore next his heart, he employed them to visit every factory, clergyman, and Sabbath-school superintendent, reporting their progress to him at the hotel every two or three hours.

In this manner the weary, tedious moments crept by, until at a late hour Horace, with a heavy heart, retired to his chamber for the night. His first business was to write to Henry for more specific directions from Mr. Smith, directing them to be telegraphed to him at once, stating in cautious terms his entire want of success in the search.

Then he leaned his head on his hands and gave himself up to his grief. How differently he had hoped to pass this evening! How ardently he had longed to fold his sister to his heart, and tell her that amidst all the scenes he had passed through in foreign lands, he had ever been faithful to her memory, though he supposed her soul had ascended to God! Had she been constant also?

How keenly now he blamed himself that he had not insisted upon learning from Henry, as their father could not endure the mention of her name, their grounds for the supposition that she was not living; that he had not at once returned to his native land, to convince the homeless wanderer that though all others forsook her, he would be brother, father, husband!

How long he sat thus he did not know. The noise of hurried steps up and down the long flights, the echo of loud voices in the hall, did not rouse him from the dreadful grief into which he was plunged. But at last the sound of suppressed voices outside his door caused him to spring forward and open it.

"A telegram, sir," said the host, "just come to hand. We were debating whether to awaken you for it."

Horace eagerly tore it open, and read, "Mr. Smith forgot to tell you Juliette has called herself Miss Edwards. Inquire at Mrs. Palmer's, M—— Street."

He hastily consulted his watch, but found it was near twelve; and, having learned from the landlord the hour operatives were called to the factories, he requested that all further search might be postponed, and threw himself upon the bed, where, in the relief he had experienced, he soon lost himself in a heavy slumber.

Mrs. Palmer's family were seated at the breakfast-table when Hannah, the servant, entered, saying, "The gentleman who was here yesterday has called again, and is waiting in the parlor for Miss Edwards."

Miss Palmer arose from the table to inform him that she had left for the country.

As may well be supposed, this intelligence was not received with much calmness. Mr. Everett, having ascertained from the servant that Miss Edwards resided here, started forward, when the door opened, to receive her in his arms.

He sank back in his chair, and for a moment could scarcely attach any meaning to Miss Palmer's words, but, with an effort recovering himself, he received directions sufficiently explicit to enable him to find W—— and Mr. Barnard's house.

He had barely time to hasten back to the hotel, deposit money with the landlord to pay the expenses of the search, and drink a cup of coffee, before the carriage he had ordered drove to the door to convey him to the cars.

It was a delightful autumnal day, the air clear but soft, the sky serene. The excited young lawyer rushed on after the gigantic iron horse through one village after another, remembering that Juliette had passed over this road, perhaps occupied this very seat, only a few days earlier; and his thoughts flew forward to the moment of their meeting. As he approached nearer, he could scarcely restrain his impatience; and yet among his friends Mr. Everett was considered a calm, quiet, self-possessed man.

But now he was to meet one who was to him like a person raised from the dead. Indeed, he had so long been accustomed to think of her in the presence and enjoyment of her Saviour, that it seemed at times like a wild dream to be expecting to meet her again on earth.

At last the conductor opened the car door, and screamed W——, as if he were warning the passengers to escape for their lives. The depot was surrounded by a few houses; but this was evidently not the village.

On inquiring for Mr. Josiah Barnard, Mr. Everett found his house was several miles distant. There was no carriage to be hired, and the young man, fretting with impatience, started to walk, when the depot-master hailed a man who was going in the same direction, and asked him to take the gentleman along.

This was on Thursday, two days after Juliette's ride with Mr. Ashley. Though by no means restored to her usual spirits, yet she had almost succeeded in convincing herself that the report concerning Horace must be a mere rumor. At any rate, she found the very idea of his marriage so distressing, that she determined to regard it as untrue, until Mr. Ashley had received an answer from his college friend.

On Thursday afternoon, therefore, she had been enticed into a walk around the farm, Mr. Ashley and Agnes a little in advance, while Caleb and Willie were by her side. She wore the straw hat which James had given her the previous summer, and which, being trimmed with oak leaves, her companions pronounced very becoming.

Caleb had just remarked that the engagement between his sister and their pastor had taken him entirely by surprise, when Willie shouted, "Agnes, there's 'Squire Owen coming to see you, I guess;" and an open wagon was seen driving slowly toward them.

Agnes turned her face haughtily in the opposite direction; but Juliette, who was curious to see one who had been so much smitten with her friend's charms, glanced back in time to notice a gentleman spring from the wagon, and rapidly approach the house.

As he came nearer, the color suddenly left her cheeks. She stopped, clasped her hands to her heart, scarcely able to support herself; but Horace had recognized her, and, with a low cry, "My Juliette at last!" dashed forward, and caught her in his arms.

"Found at last, dear one!" he whispered; but she could not speak; her heart was too full. It was with difficulty she walked to the house. She seemed to herself to be flying through the air, and had not afterwards the most distant recollection of the meeting between Mr. Ashley and her brother, nor of the introduction to their friends.

Not until she found herself alone with him in the small parlor, and heard his voice of playful reproach, saying, "Have you no welcome for me, Juliette?" did the color return to her pale cheeks.

"I'm so afraid I'm not awake," said she, gazing at him with a bewildered air, and putting her hand to her head. "I've dreamed of you so many times;" she sighed, even now, at the recollection, "and then, after all, it was *only* a dream."

"Well," exclaimed Horace, trying to conceal how much her plaintive voice had affected him, "what shall I do to convince you I'm a true, living, loving man, and no vision of the night?"

"Tell me of my father."

31

And Horace did tell of his suffering and sorrow, his remorse at his treatment of his beloved daughter, and his message to her "to forgive all."

Juliette wept tears of gratitude, and was only restrained from starting at once to go to him, on hearing of his alarming sickness, by the assurance that the cars did not leave for Boston until the next day.

"We have never received a letter from you, — at least I have never heard of one," answered Horace, when she told him of her last address to her father from Stamford; "but we heard you were in Lowell from one of your Stamford friends."

"Dear James!" she murmured, after he had given her an account of what had passed. "He is a noble man. He has been a dear brother to me."

All this time Horace had not even intimated the existence of any new tie, such as Mr. Ashley had mentioned, and though his ardent manner was such as to render his marriage highly improbable, yet she longed to hear from his own lips the assurance of his continued attachment to herself.

"You have changed far less than I feared," he said, gazing tenderly in her face, and laying his hand fondly on her silky curls. "Perhaps this new style of wearing the hair makes you look younger." He took the small locket from his breast, and began to compare it with the living face before him.

"O Juliette!" he exclaimed, "how often I have wept over this, when no eye but that of God saw me! For almost two years I have mourned you as dead."

He drew her to him, and, with her head resting on his shoulder, they mingled their tears together.

At length, after he had soothed her with loving words, she lifted her face to his, and with an arch expression said, " Did you never think of me as married? "

"Married!" he repeated. "No. If I had supposed you living, I should have judged you by my own heart. You cannot imagine, though, what a continued subject of regret it was to me that I did not persuade you, young as you were, to accompany me abroad. Of course, you have not heard from us; you do not know that my cousin, Mr. William Everett, married in France, and, with his wife, joined us in our travels."

He misinterpreted the rich, warm glow which spread over her cheek as she thought she could trace in this marriage the origin of the rumor which had reached her, and said softly, "Would you like to travel, Juliette? I am willing to go anywhere with you, even to the ends of the earth. But you are such a slippery person, running away from home, and sojourning in the most unheard-of places, I shall scarcely venture you out of my sight."

The tea-bell and Mr. Ashley's entrance interrupted them.

"Will you forgive me now," asked the gentleman, coming forward frankly, "for my alarming rumor, concerning your brother, the other day?"

"What," inquired Mr. Everett, retaining Juliette's hand; "have you been telling tales of me?"

"Don't, oh, please, don't!" urged the young girl with a rosy blush.

"If it concerns me, I ought, in justice, to have an opportunity to answer for myself," said Horace, with mock gravity.

"I think so," answered the pastor. "I heard through Walker, who was in college with us, that you were married, and repeated the rumor to your sister, who — "

"Stop, oh, do stop!" cried Juliette, in distress.

Mr. Ashley was more and more mystified, still supposing Horace and Juliette to be children of one mother, when the young man said earnestly, "But you never believed it, Juliette. Even though I thought you dead, the memory of your love was more than all the world to me. You look surprised, Benson, and call Juliette my sister. Thank God, there is no blood relation between us, for I love her with far more than a brother's love."

"Ah," cried Mr. Ashley, with a quiet smile, "all is explained now. But let me wait upon you to the table."

CHAPTER XXXIV.

AFTER tea, Juliette and Agnes repaired to their chamber to make preparations for the departure of the former at an early hour the next morning.

"I am right glad," cried Agnes, "that I am not to return to Lowell. I should be so homesick without you. As you are going away," she said, turning her back, and proceeding vigorously with her packing, "I may as well tell you that Mr. Ashley considers it absolutely necessary to become a benedict as soon as possible; and so I have consented to be married in two months. It's absurd, I know, for I can't begin to get ready; but, as he considers that no good excuse, I —"

."That's a good girl!" responded Juliette, interrupting her. "I'm so pleased to have seen him; and then Horace knows him so well."

Agnes laughed merrily, "I've found out now, why poor Mr. McIntire succeeded no better. It seemed very strange to Mr. Ashley that you should be so much affected at hearing of the marriage of your brother.

He asked me what it could mean. And you've loved him all these years, my poor child?"

"Ever since I can remember," answered Juliette, with a heightened color, "and when I had given up all hope of ever seeing him again."

The packing was speedily completed; but still the young girls lingered in their room, realizing that it was the last evening they should pass together for a long time; until at length one of the children was sent by Mr. Ashley to summon them below.

"I have done my best to entertain my old friend," added the gentleman, as they appeared, "but Mr. Everett has found something so fascinating in that door, and has watched so eagerly for its opening, that I gave up in despair."

Horace smiled as he led Juliette to a seat next himself on the sofa, while the young girl, with a roguish expression, returned the pleasantry by saying, "Agnes has just told me some news about you, Mr. Ashley."

"Has she, indeed? You are more highly favored than I am. May I be allowed the benefit of it?"

"No, indeed!" cried Agnes, hastily approaching the group. "Don't tell him, Juliette," and, turning to Mr. Everett, she said, gayly, "It is but fair to warn you that you have a rival in New York."

"Ah, who is it?"

"A gentleman who was so much in earnest that he was not satisfied with one refusal."

A shadow rested upon the young lawyer's countenance. He glanced at Juliette, who looked much distressed.

"O Agnes!" she remonstrated, "that is not right. That was only your conjecture."

"But it was true. I saw enough of his devotion myself, and read his love long before you suspected it."

"By the way," remarked Mr Ashley, quietly, as he perceived that Horace was far from pleased, "we expect to take New York on our wedding tour, and may call upon you there."

"You must come directly to our house," cried Juliette, joyfully, while Agnes cast down her eyes in great confusion.

"We expect to be married in four weeks," he added, gravely, with a sly glance at his lady, "and shall take New York on our return."

Juliette's silvery laugh rang through the room, as she caught Agnes' start of astonishment at this stroke of policy on the part of her lover.

"October is a delightful month to travel," the gentleman went on, in a tone of smothered merriment, without taking the least notice of her decided shake of the head, "and, as we intend to go as far as Niagara Falls, the sooner we start the better."

Mr. Barnard and his son coming in at this moment, the conversation became general, though Juliette perceived pretty vigorous signs of disapproval from Agnes, only returned by roguish glances from the pastor.

At an early hour the family assembled for evening devotions. Mr. Ashley read a portion of Scripture;

they all united in singing a hymn of praise, and then Mr. Everett, at the request of his friend, offered a prayer for direction and support through all the trials and duties of life.

Juliette wept as he fervently thanked God for restoring to her friends one who had been so painfully separated from them, and earnestly implored mercy for him who lay weak and languishing upon a sick-bed.

Mr. Ashley soon followed the family from the room, and our young friend was about to impart to Mr. Everett her wish to present Agnes with some token of friendship, when she perceived that he was struggling to conceal some painful emotion.

"I don't know," he began, seriously, " but there is a terrible trial yet in store for me. It was so unexpected, so overwhelming, to learn that you were still living." He took her hand, but instantly dropped it, and, gazing in her upturned face as if he would read her very soul, said, in a quivering voice, "Tell me, Juliette, tell me frankly, — and may God give me strength to endure it, if, after having this cup of happiness at my lips, it is to be dashed to the ground, — tell me, what did you mean by asking whether I had never thought of you as married? What does your friend mean by her account of my New York rival? Have I taken too much for granted in supposing you returned my affection, or has some more recent attachment won you from me?

"You are agitated, — you look down. O Juliette! speak frankly; it will be best for both of us. I exonerate you from all blame. You knew I loved you; but I, I only have been in fault. I have left you two long weary years. I gave too easy credence to —"

"Horace! O Horace! why will you speak so bitterly! You frighten me. I have never loved but once, and that affection began when we used to sit together in our mother's room, and you told me stories from the Bible."

She placed her hand confidingly in his, and, with a fervent "Thank God!" he strained her to his heart.

"I can rest quietly now," he said, "and, as I have scarcely slept for two nights, I shall be much refreshed. But what could I have done if my dreadful suspicion had proved true?"

After arranging for their journey, he placed a well-filled purse in her hands; but she returned it, saying, "I should like to send Agnes a wedding present of a piano; please keep it for me till then."

It was not until a very late hour that the young girls, having retired to bed, could compose themselves sufficiently to sleep.

Agnes wished to talk of her friend the clergyman, and relate their plans. Her father, being now able to bear the expense, had proposed adding a dining-room and kitchen, with two chambers, to the farm-house, which, with the parlor and Mr. Ashley's study, would make a comfortable tenement for the newly-married pair. She could scarcely express her delight, when Juliette informed her of the intention to add a handsome piano to the furniture of the parlor.

"I see," she cried, half laughing, "that Mr. Ashley intends to be obeyed. Did you see how he went right on, settling our wedding-day as if I had not a word to add to the subject?"

Juliette then, taking advantage of her knowledge of her friend's independent character, proceeded to make some very wise remarks upon the duty of wives to yield both obedience and reverence to their husbands, assuring her this doctrine was explicitly taught in the Bible, which they had both taken for their guide.

Agnes quite broke down at this, and began, with tears, to lament her unfitness for the duties before her, and at last ended by declaring that, after all, if she did not love Mr. Ashley with her whole heart she never could and never would promise to obey him; but now Juliette should see, when they visited her in New York, what a pattern of submission and obedience she had become.

Then with a good-night kiss they went quietly to sleep, little imagining that the gentleman most interested was only separated from them by a thin partition which did not prevent his having the full benefit of their conversation.

Mr. Ashley, without mentioning his intention to any one, had shown his friend to his study, and gone in to share Willie's narrow bed, which, with a very demure look, he told Agnes the next morning, he did not regret, as it enabled him to hear her friend's most able exposition of Paul's directions to wives.

The young girl bit her lips with vexation; but, finally,

after a few low-spoken words from the young clergyman, endeavored to turn off the whole subject as a
joke.

The parting between the friends was much softened
by the anticipation of soon meeting again; and, in
truth, Juliette now began to be so impatient to commence her journey, and see her father, that she could
scarcely be pained by anything.

They reached Boston in season to take the evening
express train for New York, where they arrived at an
early hour the following morning.

Seeing that their own carriage was nowhere in sight,
Horace called a hack-driver to take them to Madison
Square, and, in a few minutes, with a wildly beating
heart and tear-dimmed eyes, Juliette ascended the
steps to her fondly remembered home.

Rufus, the porter, after a few moments' delay,
opened the door and gave a scream of joy, when he
recognized her; but she could only whisper, —

"How is my father?"

"Very sick, miss, I'm sorry to say; but your
coming home will cure him, and set everything right."

Horace, seeing with how much difficulty she con-
trolled herself, led her hastily to the parlor, and rang
the bell for a servant to bring a glass of wine.

It was still very early, but the glad news speedily
flew through the house that their young mistress had
returned; and Eliza, who was back in her old place,
hastily dressed, in order to meet and welcome her.
A burst of tears, however, prevented a word being

spoken until Juliette asked Horace to inform her father at once that she longed to see him.

"I am only waiting for a tinge of color in your cheeks and lips," he said gently. "Now I'll go, while you take off your bonnet and prepare to come to him."

"Will you go to your own room, miss?" asked Eliza, wiping her eyes. "It is in readiness for you."

An almost overwhelming tide of emotion swept over the poor girl as she stood at the entrance to the suite of elegant apartments from which she had so long been banished. She quickly covered her face as she murmured, —

"Oh, how little I ever expected to be here again! My dear, *dear* home!"

Eliza eagerly drew forward a large chair, and began to talk about her master.

To Juliette each moment seemed like an age as she sat impatiently listening to every step. "Is he changed? How will he receive me?" she asked herself. At length she could control her desire no longer; and, stealing gently through the hall, listened through the closed door for a sound of his well-remembered voice.

Presently it was opened from within, and Horace, smiling as he saw her, led her forward into the chamber.

There were several persons in the apartment, but the happy daughter saw only a pair of keen, expectant eyes gazing wistfully toward the entrance, and, with one bound, was by his side. An impressive silence reigned in the room, as, sinking on her knees, she cried out, —

"My father! O my father!"

She caught his extended hand and covered it with kisses, while the glad tears rained from her eyes.

The doctor was just about to interfere, as he saw what a terrible struggle was going on in the breast of his patient, when the convulsed features relaxed.

"Juliette," gasped the broken voice, "will you forgive all my cruel wrong? Can you forgive all this, my child?"

"Dear, *dear* father, all is forgiven; all is forgotten in this happy meeting;" and, with a gush of joyful tears, she imprinted kiss after kiss on his cheeks, brow, and lips.

"God is merciful!" murmured the sick man, sinking back wholly overcome.

Dr. M——, wiping his eyes, came quickly to the bed, and in a whisper suggested to Juliette that she had better leave the chamber until he were more composed; but Mr. Fearing, overhearing him, feebly shook his head, and caught his daughter's hand pressing it to his bosom.

"I will be calm, doctor; I will do anything you wish, only let me stay. I can soothe him to sleep. I used often to do it;" and she laid her hand caressingly on his burning temples.

The physician shook his head, but made no further objection. He administered a powder, after asking some one behind him how long since he had taken the last.

Juliette started and turned quickly around with a smile, as James's voice answered, "Half an hour, sir."

Henry then came across the room and kissed his sister with much affection; after which she bowed a recognition of the old servants who were present.

After a few moments the medicine began to take effect, and the patient, still grasping the hand of his daughter, sank into a doze.

Horace, who was at her side, softly suggested that now was her time to go below and take some breakfast; but she would not consent to leave the room, lest her father should awake and miss her.

She begged him to go, however, with James and Henry, promising to drink a cup of chocolate, if he would send it to her there.

She motioned to James to come nearer, and, in a low tone, said, —

"Thank you, my kind brother, for your tender care of my father."

How much reason she had to thank him she was not aware until afterwards.

When alone with her charge she had time to gaze at his emaciated countenance. Whether from sickness or sorrow, or both, he looked ten years older than when she had last seen him. His hair, which was then black as a raven's wing, was now thickly threaded with silver; while his cheeks were furrowed, and his brow lined with care. Still, there was a softened, subdued expression she had never seen there before. She bowed her head in gratitude as she remembered his last words to Horace, —

"Tell her I'm willing now!"

"Who can tell," she said to herself, as she gazed, "whether he may not have become a participant in the religion of Jesus? Perhaps God has answered my poor prayers for his conversion."

She started from her reverie as he smiled in his sleep and murmured, "Juliette."

"Yes, dear father," she whispered, "your Juliette is here, — your happy Juliette! — feeling that, if God has heard her prayers in your behalf, her cup of blessings is full to overflowing."

She pressed her lips softly on his hand, which she still held; but even this did not awaken him.

Eliza gently opened the door, bringing a silver tray with chocolate, fresh eggs, and toast, from the breakfast table.

These she placed on a small tea-poy by the bed, saying, in a low tone, —

"Mr. Horace broke the eggs and seasoned them for you, and he hoped you'd eat all he has sent."

She stood near, watching her young lady as she smilingly proceeded to the discussion of her tempting repast. Probably the night-ride had given her an appetite; or her heart was more at rest than usual, or both these causes combined; for her maid had never known her to eat with so keen a relish; and she had not yet finished when the young men returned to the chamber.

Beckoning her from the bed, Horace informed her that Mr. Smith proposed to leave New York, and he knew she would wish to speak with him before he did so.

"Indeed we can't spare you," she said, in a subdued tone. "Is the farm work so pressing that you cannot give one day to your old friend?"

"I have already written twice to postpone my return," said the young man; "and now that he and Mr. Everett are here, I think he will not need me."

"But I have had no time to inquire for your father and mother, and dear Susan and Maria. How are they all? I long so much to see them."

"They are well. I have promised your father that Susan shall come, if you wish it, and make you a long visit. I am afraid there is not much left to tell him about your residence in Stamford. It was the only way I could soothe him when hour after hour passed, and you did not return."

"Does he know of my being in Lowell?" she inquired.

"Yes; I could not deceive him. He saw there was something I kept back, and grew so much excited that I thought it best to tell him. He knows all about your joining Mr. Allen's church."

"And what did he say?" she inquired, with an eager glance toward the bed.

"He nodded, and said, 'Yes, I expected it.' He did not speak again for some time. I think he was praying.'

Juliette darted a quick, inquiring look at the young man.

"Yes, Juliette, I think your father is a Christian. I know he prays; and that he regards his cruel persecution of you, on account of your religion, as the most dreadful sin of his life.

"He knows, too, of your terrible illness. He wept like a child when I told him of your dream that you had a letter from him; and how afraid we were to tell you there was none. Yes," added James, speaking quickly, and growing very red in the face, "I confessed all, — even that I, a poor farmer, dependent upon my daily labor, had dared to love his child; and he did not despise me."

With an anxious glance at Horace, Juliette replied, —

"I know, dear James, you did not begin to tell the generous, brotherly care you exercised over me; nor the thousand acts of tender affection from all your dear family."

A slight movement from the bed caused the watchful daughter to spring to his side just as the sick man opened his eyes.

He gazed wildly about for a moment; but a warm smile played about his mouth as he saw his daughter bending over him.

"I feel better and stronger," said he, in a more cheerful voice than they had heard from him for

32*

a long time. "The sight of you, Juliette, will do me
more good than all Dr. M——'s prescriptions."

James drew nearer to bid Mr. Fearing "good-by;"
but the sick man urged him to remain one day longer.
"You will not regret it," said he, impressively.

"If I can really be of service, I am quite willing
and glad to remain," replied James, cordially.

The reason for this urgency was not apparent until
the evening, when Mr. Fearing, being really more like
himself than since their return from abroad, requested
Horace to invite Mr. Smith and Henry to his room.

Holding his daughter's hand, he turned his eye
slowly from one to another of the group before him,
and then, in a quivering voice, began, —

"I wish, before you all, to make acknowledgment
of my harsh persecution of my daughter on account
of her religion, even to driving her from her home;
and I wish to exonerate her here from all suspicion of
blame. God has dealt mercifully with me in restoring
her to my arms before I die; and also in allowing me
to hope that the blood of his Son can wash away guilt
even as great as mine. Yes, Mr. Smith," he added
fervently, as he extended his hand to the young man,
"I do believe in him. I do cast myself at the foot of
his cross; and I do and will forever plead his promise
of pardon to such as, repenting of their sins, and turning from them with self-abhorrence and loathing, come
to him for mercy."

James covered his face and shook with agitation,
while Juliette sobbed aloud, as after a few moments'

pause for strength, he went on. "I shall never forget your faithfulness, though at the time it was like a dagger piercing to my very heart. To my daughter's consistent, self-denying devotion to her Saviour I owe the doubts and fears which filled my soul respecting my own acceptance, and the determination to live a new life. Your prayers and labors, under God, have been the means of opening my eyes to his astonishing grace, so that I can see in his glorious Son a being who acts as mediator between me and my offended Judge."

The hand which held his daughter's slightly relaxed its grasp, and Juliette saw a pallor settling around his mouth. Alarmed beyond measure, she motioned to Horace to observe the change, when James calmly took from the table some drops, and gave them to him.

In the midst of her terror, Juliette's heart beat more warmly as she noticed that Henry seemed much affected at his father's words. All stood silently watching the sufferer, who lay with his eyes closed, until at length he spoke, feebly. "I am relieved. Mr. Smith, will you pray with me?"

Even after James had taken the position of prayer, Mr. Fearing touched his hand and added, "Pray that I may not deceive myself, but may be ready to appear before Him when my summons comes."

This remark, showing that he thought himself near his end, so affected his daughter, that she was obliged to put a great constraint upon her feelings to keep from weeping aloud ; but, after a moment, the fervor of the petitions soothed her, and her heart echoed the words as James implored grace and strength for the duties of life, triumph in death, and immortal blessedness for the life to come.

CHAPTER XXXV.

" When love's well-timed, 'tis not a fault to love;
The strong, the weak, the virtuous, and the wise
Sink in the soft captivity together."

ONE week later the same party were assembled in
Mr. Fearing's room, except that, instead of
James Smith, Susan occupied a seat near the bed.

Mr. Fearing was now so far recovered as to be able
to sit up several hours at a time ; but, except for necessary exercise in the open air, he could not bear his daughter out of his sight. She read to him, combed his hair,
and chatted by the hour together. Indeed, at no time
in her life had she ever been so truly happy. In the
confidence and affection now subsisting between her
and her father; in the ardent love of Horace; in the
tender sympathy of her reformed brother; in the en-
dearing friendship of the lively Susan, day after day
passed, and she often asked herself, " What could I
wish for more? "

Mr. Fearing had conceived a great fondness for the
warm-hearted girl who had been such a firm friend to
his daughter; and this feeling was shared by Henry;
so much so, that hour after hour he passed in his father's room, listening to her ever-ready sallies of wit.

In contrast to the silly belles, there was something so
fresh, so piquant, so charming in this child of nature,
that he could not tear himself from her society. Then
she talked so unreservedly to him, — told him so frankly
what she deemed his faults, — recommended so earnestly
that he would come out to Stamford and put himself
under James's tuition, with the hope, that in time, he
might exchange his life of listless indolence for that of
an energetic farmer, — that, although he received her
suggestions with bursts of laughter, yet he remembered
and determined to profit by them.

Mr. Fearing one day glanced at his daughter with
a quiet smile, as Henry and Susan, too intent upon
their own conversation to notice that others were listening to them, were eagerly discussing the comparative advantages of country and of city life.

"Oh!" exclaimed the impulsive girl; "I should die
to be shut up from one year's end to the other between
stone walls, where I never could see the green fields,
and the waving, golden grain. There is nothing in
this city you boast so much of, that can compare with
father's ten-acre lot, when the barley is just beginning
to shoot forth its bearded head. I don't believe you
ever saw anything so beautiful."

"But think of whole streets of magnificent houses,"
returned Henry. "Think of continuous blocks of
stores, such as Stewart's, their windows filled with rich
goods. You have nothing like these in Stamford, or
in the country anywhere."

"Houses and stores do not constitute my happiness,"

she exclaimed, with a disdainful toss of her head. "Nature is better than art, any time. I know I can't reason well," she added, as he smiled; "but nothing can convince me that the people who have lived in the country are not better, more natural, and happier than those who live in the city. Now, for instance, the city gentlemen think of nothing but making money, from one year's end to the other; or, if they have enough, as you have, they either grow dissipated and vicious for want of some active employment, or, if fortunately, principle restrains them from such excesses, their lives are passed in watching the growth of their mustaches " (she had been laughing at him for his habit of curling his with his fingers), "giving orders for new suits of clothes, driving fast horses, lolling in saloons, or in similar expedients for killing time."

"Or in discussing questions of importance with young ladies from the country," added Henry, demurely. "But let us hear how a young man who had some money at his command would do in the country."

Susan was wide-awake now, and, with her head very erect, began: "Oh, he would first select some beautiful spot where there were trees, and a lake, and sloping green lawns, and build a fine house; not a high, stone building like the city houses, but a lovely cottage, with bay-windows, and porticoes, and verandas, and all sorts of cosey places; and then plant woodbine and honeysuckle to run over them. It would be splendid; and then he would marry a beautiful girl like Juliette."

"A city belle, after all."

"No, she was brought up in the country; but you put me out. I was just having him bring home his wife, and then he really begins to live; for now everybody respects him. He carries on his place, and this gives employment to a great many poor people who look up to him, and whom, of course, he can benefit if he chooses. Then his wife is so happy! She goes singing about the house, or walking over the pleasant grounds, planning improvements with her husband, or visiting the cottages of their laborers, and encouraging them to do their best.

"Then, as years go by, this man is beloved and respected in the whole town. He is an example to his neighbors of moral integrity, sanctified by religious principle. When he passes, the children point to him and say, 'There goes our good Mr.——. He's a friend to the poor, and Heaven's blessings will rest upon him.' Sometimes, to be sure, he will have trials. Everybody does; but when they come, God will give him strength to bear them. At any rate," she added, drawing her description to a sudden close as she met his earnest eye, "his time will be so usefully and happily employed that he will never suffer from ennui, so that he will yawn, and exclaim a dozen times in an hour, 'What shall I do with myself till dinner? How terribly tedious these long days are!'"

Henry laughed heartily. "You'd make a capital preacher, Susan; you never end without a personal application; but you've convinced me. I'll never say a word about the pleasures of city life again; and if I only knew some fair damsel who would consent to plan improvements about my grounds, I should be tempted to begin the life of a country gentleman at once."

"There are a plenty of them," she replied, frankly; "but whether they would dare venture their happiness with so thoroughly a city gentleman is a question." And, with an arch glance into his grave face, she suddenly left the room.

It was true, as James had said, that Mr. Fearing had delighted to hear of the manner in which his daughter had passed her time in Stamford; how quickly she won both the love and respect of all who knew her; nor was Juliette soon tired of relating to him instances of the watchful care of Mr. and Mrs. Smith for her comfort, the hearty generosity of James, and the sisterly affection of the young girls.

They consulted earnestly together as to some method of returning these obligations, especially to the young farmer whose faithfulness had been so much blessed to the soul of the sick man.

Mr. Fearing, a thorough business man, proposed to give him a place in his own store, with capital enough to ensure his success; but Juliette was positive he would prefer a farm in the country, with money enough to stock it.

To anticipate a few months, this was happily accomplished, and the young girl had the pleasure of beholding her friends, James and Josey, comfortably settled in their own pretty cottage, surrounded by well-tilled fields connected with their farm, about three miles from his father's residence.

As Mr. Fearing's health became established, Horace claimed Juliette's promise to name an early day for their wedding. Their father's glad consent had been given soon after her return to her home; and as he insisted that they should still constitute one family, there seemed no reason for delay.

In the intimacy of their new relation, the young lawyer often acknowledged the truth of the trite adage, —

"Sweet are the uses of adversity."

The trials and persecutions through which she had passed had given to our heroine far more strength and firmness of character. Indeed, in speaking of the past, she said with tears, "I shudder when I think how near I was to the fearful vortex of worldliness which has engulfed so many, even professing Christians." In her case, certainly, Mr. Everett could realize the truth of the inspired words, "No chastening for the present seemeth to be joyous, but grievous; nevertheless, afterward it yieldeth the peaceable fruits of righteousness unto them which are exercised thereby."

In accordance with the will of their mother, Henry and Juliette shared alike the inheritance they received from her, and of which they came into possession on reaching their majority. The portion of our heroine, which amounted to a handsome fortune, remained untouched. Unfortunately, her brother acquired the

right to spend his before his father's dangerous illness
and his sister's departure from home led him to reflect
upon his mad career, and determine to begin a refor-
mation. Before this time his father had absolutely
refused to squander any more money in paying debts
of honor, as Henry falsely called the demands of the
vilest gamblers of the city; so that, when he reached
his twenty-first year, one-third of his entire fortune
was sacrificed to blacklegs.

Before his daughter's marriage, it was Mr. Fearing's
determination to make his will, bequeathing to his son,
at his decease, the elegant mansion in which they then
resided, and such a proportion of his interest in their
firm as would make him independent for life. It had
for many years been a subject of keen regret that the
young man did not devote himself, as he had done, to
mercantile pursuits, which, from the first, Henry had
declared distasteful to him.

Now the animated conversations of Susan regarding
the pleasures of country life recalled his own long-
cherished plan of passing his last days remote from
the turmoil and confusion of the busy world in which
he dwelt.

His father, enfeebled more by sorrow than by age,
had long wished to give up the care attendant upon so
large an estate, and would, he was sure, be delighted
to have his only grandson settled upon it.

Several long and earnest conversations took place
between the father and son, Henry being roused to a
new energy by the thought of commencing life afresh

in the character of a country gentleman. Whatever visions of a bright-eyed, laughing, and withal somewhat saucy, lass had to do with his determination, he did not say; but declared and reiterated his resolve to live in the country.

At length he went out to consult his grandfather and Dr. Morrison, and returned two days later with the joyful announcement that he was no longer a loafer about town, as Susan had laughingly called him, but the true and veritable owner of a country-seat, upon which he was determined to live henceforth and forever.

He was rather vexed that this news did not in the least alter the young lady's manner toward him, except to make her laugh the more at the idea of the New York exquisite, with his embossed slippers, his gorgeous dressing-gown, and his perfumed cigar, loitering about the farm, hindering the workmen with his unmeaning questions; or volunteering orders one day, to be countermanded the next.

"I think you are too bad, Susan," urged Juliette, one day, as in more lively, caustic terms than usual, she had been setting his sins in order before him, until the young man left the room in great displeasure. "Henry is really trying to reform, and I think a little encouragement would do him good."

For a moment the young girl was silent, and remained with her eyes fixed intently on her work; but presently said, frankly, "If you think I have really said more than I ought, I will tell him so."

Juliette smiled her approval, and Susan left the room in search of the gentleman, whom she found at last, lying at full length upon the sofa, his face concealed by the rich cushion.

He sprang up when he recognized her step, but only to meet an arch glance at the listless attitude in which she had discovered him.

"Mr. Fearing," she began, in a voice which she vainly tried to render serious, "you have lived such a life of self-indulgence, and been so excessively flattered for traits which you did or did not possess, that I fear you have lost the power of recognizing who are your true friends, and who seek your best good. You, who have only to exhibit yourself and your beautifully curled mustaches in society, in order to be caressed and cajoled by manœuvring mammas, and lisping, listless daughters, surely cannot take offence at any joking remark a poor, ignorant country girl may make. Nevertheless, I may, and probably have been disrespectful and too familiar toward one so much my superior in rank, wealth, and wisdom; and, if so, justice to myself requires me to ask you to excuse it."

Then, with a low courtesy of mock humility, before he could catch his breath to reply, she had resumed her seat and her work near Juliette, unmindful of his earnest call, "Susan! Stop, Susan!"

At the dinner-table, both Horace and Juliette found it almost impossible to conceal their merriment at the suddenly changed manners of the once lively girl.

33*

With her eyes fixed immovably upon her plate, she did not speak except when addressed; and then, when in answer to a question from Henry, in a tone of humility and deference so unlike herself, that the young man was wholly disconcerted, while Mr. Fearing glanced inquiringly from one to another, entirely unable to account for the silence of his favorite guest.

"Juliette," cried the young girl, after they had returned to the parlor, suddenly throwing off her forced reserve, "New York air doesn't agree with me. I'm going home to morrow."

"Then I shall accompany you," exclaimed Henry. "I have important business in Stamford."

He returned, however, thoroughly disheartened, ready to renounce his plan of living in the country, and to fall back into his old pursuits; for Susan had virtually declined to be his companion in his new home. From some source she had learned of his former dissipation; and, though he frankly confessed the vicious courses which he now deeply lamented, she could not venture to give the happiness of her whole life to the keeping of a man who, as yet, had scarcely commenced the work of reform.

In a letter, however, which she wrote to Juliette, she accepted the invitation to act as bridesmaid at the rapidly approaching nuptials, and confessed, in her usual frank manner, that if Henry persevered in rousing himself, and in proving that he was a man of energy and worth, she should love him with all her heart.

This epistle, which the young lady lost no time in

showing to her brother, so revived his drooping spirits, that he provided himself with treatises on the management of lands, orchards, and stocks, and went to work in earnest to fit himself for the onerous duties he was about to assume.

CHAPTER XXXVI.

"A. guardian angel o'er his life presiding,
Doubling his pleasure, and his cares dividing."

ONE of the first calls made by our heroine after her return to New York was upon her former pastor, Dr. A——. To her great delight, her father accompanied her, and made known to the good man the entire change which had taken place in his views and feelings on the subject of religion. After a protracted interview, he requested to be considered as a candidate for admission to the church, and it was agreed that Juliette should remove her church relation from Stamford on the same Sabbath.

During the conversation between her father and Dr. A——, the young girl was exceedingly affected by the humility and deep sense of sin expressed by the former, and the ardor with which he looked forward to serving Christ. As soon as they were seated in the carriage, she clasped his hand in hers, as she exclaimed, " How safe it is to trust ourselves and those dear to us in the hands of a gracious God ! I prayed month after month, and year after year, until I began almost to despond ; but in his own good time he has granted me the desire of my heart."

A most interesting conversation followed, in which Mr. Fearing related many incidents in the life of his beloved Juliette, the mother of Horace, — events which, now that he loved prayer and the services of religion, had caused him bitter tears, lest, in denying her the consolations of Christian friendship, he had caused her many hours of sorrow.

From Mrs. Ward Folsom, lately returned from Scotland, where she had relatives, Juliette also received a most cordial welcome. From this lady she learned with deep emotion, for the first time, of the inconsolable grief of her father on finding she had abandoned her home; and the extensive search that had been made for her all along the route of the Harlem cars.

Almost as soon as she reached New York, Juliette had written to her dear teacher, Mrs. Osborn, and was now daily expecting a visit from her, to continue until after her marriage, the preparations for which were going rapidly forward.

It was neither her desire nor that of Mr. Everett to have a public wedding, even if Mr. Fearing's health would have allowed him to be present in scenes of excitement. Since their return from abroad they had not re-entered society; nor did she ever wish to be involved in such an extensive circle as during her first winter in the city; a more select company of friends being far more congenial to her feelings.

The determination of Henry to establish himself permanently at H——, as soon as the spring opened, had caused an entire change in the disposition of Mr. Fearing's estate. As Mr. Everett's business would detain him in town during the greater part of the year, the house in Madison Square was, at his decease, to become the property of his daughter, together with a considerable fortune in bank stocks. To his son he bequeathed an equal portion, in addition to the estate made over to him by his grandfather. The remainder of his fortune was distributed among different benevolent societies and objects of charity in the city.

With the zeal and energy which had always characterized him, Mr. Fearing gave himself no rest until his affairs were definitely arranged.

"Now," said he, when Horace, having spent some hours with him in looking over and signing papers, announced the business completed, "in case of my sudden decease, my executors will find no difficulty in settling my estate."

It had been the intention of the young people to start immediately after their marriage for New Orleans, spending a few days in each of the principal cities on the route; but at the last this journey was indefinitely postponed on account of the repugnance Mr. Fearing expressed at his daughter's continued absence from home.

This was the more singular as never since his mother's death, nearly two years earlier, had he appeared in such firm health as at present. But Juliette delighted to yield her own wishes to his, and was more than repaid for any self-denial it might have cost her by the delight he manifested when told she would not leave him.

It was a beautiful morning in the early part of November when the nuptials were to be celebrated. The bridal dress consisted of a robe of white satin, covered with the most exquisitely rich lace, and decorated with orange blossoms and lilies of the valley. The chaplet was formed of similar flowers with pendants of jessamine.

Attached to the back of the head was a veil of costly Brussels lace, which had been worn by her step-mother, and which was of such a length that it swept the floor.

Susan wore a rich white silk, a present from Mr. Fearing, covered with gossamer lace and tastefully ornamented with flowers.

Our heroine, in company with her father and grandfather, Henry and Susan, rode to Dr. A——'s church; Horace, with Dr. and Mrs. Morrison and Mrs. Osborn having preceded them in another carriage.

The moment the steps were let down a crowd pressed near to catch a glimpse of the beautiful bride; and, though it was intended that the wedding should be private, yet on their entrance they found every part of the house filled with eager spectators.

Susan taking Henry's arm preceded the bridal pair through the crowded aisle. A mist before Juliette's eyes prevented her noticing or being embarrassed by the admiration her beauty called forth. She saw nothing but the venerable pastor, heard nothing but

the solemn words which united her to her chosen
friend until they were separated by death ; and then,
clinging to her husband's arm for support from the
emotions which almost overwhelmed her, was led once
more through the excited crowd of spectators, and
lifted faint and trembling into the carriage.

Mr. Fearing found it difficult to retain his composure as Horace leaned forward, and, imprinting a kiss
upon her pale cheek, whispered, "*My own dear one,
NOW AND FOREVER !*"

It was considered a relief by all when Susan exclaimed, in an animated tone, "Oh, dear, how glad I
am it's over ! I shook with fear just as if I myself was
being married. I never noticed before what solemn
words one has to say."

On their return to the house the bridal party had
scarcely time to collect their thoughts before carriage
after carriage of invited guests drove to the door.

From eleven until one, ladies with their respective
gentlemen closely followed one another into the large
parlors, were led up and introduced to the bride and
groom, to whom they offered their salutations and
congratulations.

The wedding repast was laid out in the spacious
dining-hall in the rear, elegantly decorated with long
garlands of flowers twined into the ornamental trellis-
work of the apartment, while the doors and windows
were hung with wreaths of orange blossoms and other
flowers emblematic of the happy occasion. These dec-

orations, combined with the subdued roseate hue from the damask curtains, produced a most beautiful effect.

In the centre of the table an immense salver of solid silver supported the loaf of wedding cake which was a perfect marvel of sugar architecture. The rest of the board was covered with rich cakes, jellies, sugared fruit in every variety, interspersed with massive silver tankards, elegantly chased and chastely flowered vases, Sevres, Dresden, and Worcester china.

At two the newly married pair took the cars for Boston, from which place they proposed to go to Lowell, and pass one day in bidding adieu to friends from whom she had so suddenly taken her departure.

Mrs. Palmer was quite surprised when her young servant announced that Miss Edwards, with a gentleman, had called upon her.

She went cordially forward to meet her former boarder, who, with a blush, introduced her companion as, " My husband, Mr. Everett."

"Indeed!" cried the lady, gazing at the gentleman's fine, open countenance with new interest.

The young bride then proceeded in her own artless, unaffected manner to inquire for Miss Palmer, and her other fellow-boarders.

" We missed you and Agnes, sadly," said the lady, after answering her questions. "It scarcely seemed like home to us, without your lively conversation and music."

"Does Annie play much now?" asked Mrs. Everett. "I have taken the liberty to bring her a few pieces of

34

new music. If Hannah will go out to the carriage, the
driver will give her the bundle containing them, and
also a small present for herself.

"You were always ready to oblige me, Hannah," she
added, meeting the girl at the door, "and here is a new
dress I bought in New York, on purpose to please
you."

"Indeed, miss!" exclaimed Hannah, ignorant of the
new title of the young lady, "you are very kind; but
I declare to my heart, miss, I'd rather have yourself
back again than six new dresses; and that's true for
you, miss."

Her husband and Mrs. Palmer overheard the brief
conversation.

"If you'll excuse the liberty, sir, in saying so," re-
-marked the lady, "I think you have been very fortunate in your choice of a wife. Mrs. Everett was in
my family nearly a year, and rendered herself beloved
by all the members. Hannah speaks the feelings of
all of us when she expresses her regret. She had a
hearty cry when we received the word from Agnes that
neither of them were to return."

Juliette found them smiling when she entered. She
informed the lady of Agnes' marriage, which had probably taken place the last of October.

She rose to go, and Mr. Everett took the opportunity to thank the lady for her kindness to his wife, expressing his cordial assent to her views as to the lovely
character of the lady.

"Oh!" exclaimed the widow, "how sorry Annie

will be to have missed your call! This music will be a great source of pleasure to her. I cannot bear the thought that I shall never hear you play again."

Without a word, the bride pulled off her gloves, and, seating herself at the instrument, played and sung a piece she remembered to have been a favorite with her hostess, and then, with kind messages to the absent ones, hastened to the carriage.

"I am afraid," she said, as they drove away, "that I have detained you too long; but I knew it would please her to hear me play and sing once more. She was very kind when I was with her."

What the young husband thought as he gazed in her glowing, expressive face I cannot tell; but he said, softly, "You did exactly right, Juliette, as you always do. I am constantly taking lessons of you."

They had ordered the driver to take them next to Mr. B——'s, and, on their way, they passed the Corporation boarding-house where poor Juliette spent her first days in Lowell. She was looking from the window, and sighed at the recollection.

Horace quickly demanded an explanation.

"I am almost afraid to tell you what I suffered in that house," she answered, seriously. "Even now I cannot recall those long days and weary nights without a shudder." In a few words, she gave him a sketch of the character of the landlady and her fellow-boarders.

"Do you wonder," she asked, "that I love Agnes, who helped me to remove so quickly? I think

I should have died if I had remained there much longer."

"Dear wife," murmured Mr. Everett, drawing her nearer to his side, as if he would shield her from even the recollection of such trials; "you endured all this for the love of Him who had bought you with his own blood, and he has given you a rich reward."

"Oh, yes!" exclaimed Juliette, her face brightening at once. "Think of dear father; I can scarcely realize it, even now, that he has taken the very step he refused to allow me to take. How anxious he was that I should go forward publicly, with him, to profess his faith in the merits of his Saviour, before I was married, as if he wished to show that it was by his sanction I did it!"

"Yes," rejoined her husband, "I could hardly account for his haste in confessing Christ, though I have no doubt the change in his feelings is a genuine one, except from the knowledge of his general character. I have heard my mother say that whatever he undertook, he carried into it all the zeal and energy of his nature. She ascribed his wonderful success in business to this cause."

"This is Mr. B——'s," murmured Juliette, as the carriage stopped.

The interview was a delightful one. The good pastor thanked her for her former interest in his church and the Sabbath school; told her he missed her as a hearer, and wished that the zeal she had manifested for her young scholars might be exhibited for others in her native city.

It was now past noon; and Juliette hastened to give the driver directions for the part of the town where many of the foreign population lived, in the hope of seeing her scholars while they were out of school for dinner.

It had been one of her most pleasant employments, a few. days before she left New York, to purchase a handsome Bible for each of the young girls she had taught; and nothing could exceed their delight, as, entering the crowded rooms, she sought out one and another, and presented the precious volume as a token of her interest in their welfare.

Scarcely one of the nine received the announcement that she could not continue their teacher, without a burst of tears, until poor Juliette was quite overcome.

"What is there," she exclaimed, as they drove rapidly toward the hotel, "in the gayeties of fashionable life that can compensate for pleasures like these? I am indebted to those nine girls for some of the happiest hours I ever passed."

"I am glad, indeed, to have seen them," answered her husband, with much feeling. "Agnes told me of your indefatigable labors for their good."

. Early evening found them back in their rooms at the Tremont, from which place they returned the next day to New York, to be in season for the visit of Agnes and Mr. Ashley early the following week.

They were disappointed, on reaching home, to find

34*

that Mr. Fearing, the morning after they left, had had a slight return of his illness, occasioned, as the physician supposed, by the excitement of the previous day. His father, who had never seen him suffering under an attack of convulsions was greatly alarmed, and supposed him dying, and was urgent with Henry to telegraph at once for his daughter.

Dr. M—— did not consider this necessary; but Susan was determined, unless he were speedily relieved, to send to Stamford for James.

Juliette was quite unnerved at the delight of her father on seeing her enter his chamber. Though now able to sit up, and looking nearly as well as when she left home, she was startled at the impressive tone in which he said, "I can't let you leave me again; for his mother's sake, Horace must allow you to be with me the short time I shall remain."

Through the whole of the next day, which was the Sabbath, Juliette scarcely left him a moment, though, as he seemed nearly as well as usual, her husband somewhat urged her to accompany him to church in the morning, and even Mr. Fearing added, " Perhaps you had better go, dear; Susan will read to me till you return."

But a feeling, which she could not explain to herself, prompted her to remain by his side, and a most profitable Sabbath it proved.

Mr. Fearing related to his daughter, more fully than he had ever done before, an account of the various exercises of his mind, beginning from the hour of his

mother's decease, when he resolved to search the
Bible for those truths so precious to her in her last moments. Then the anguish he endured in finding his
idolized child had acted upon the words he had uttered
in his hot anger, and, dreading to be forced to give up
her Saviour, had fled from temptation and from the
endearments of home. After every effort at finding
her had failed, a constantly increasing conviction of her
death had fastened itself upon his mind, and from that
moment he knew no rest. He shut up his house and
fled to foreign lands, to drown the ever-recurring cry
of conscience, "You have killed her. Your cruelty
has murdered your daughter." When they met Horace, it was with such a torrent of emotion that he communicated the probability of her decease, that the
young man, wholly misunderstanding the statement,
had never ventured to advert to the subject again in
his presence.

"I travelled with the gay party from one place to
another," he went on, "finding no solace except in the
society of my sorrowing son, who mourned the loss of
one so dearly loved, until, one day in my room, I took
up a small Bible with these words written in a school-
girl's hand, on the fly-leaf, "To my very dear brother,
Horace Everett, from his affectionate little sister, Juliette." It bore the marks of constant use, and I began
to wonder whether he, too, loved the Bible. Clinging
to it because it had been yours, I hid it in my breast-
pocket; and when Horace entered and looked anx-

iously around the room, I said nothing of having it in my possession.

"I kept it for months and read in it daily; and only returned it on hearing the owner one day deploring its loss. I never shall forget his joy at recovering his lost treasure, nor the haste with which he gave me in its place the one he had purchased for himself. Though I well knew he loved you, I had no idea, until then, of the ardor of his attachment, nor of the depth of his suffering at your supposed decease.

"Under the subduing influence of this discovery, I ventured to hint at the state of my own heart; but he was reserved. I suppose his knowing my bitter prejudices against the doctrines of grace, together with the feeling that he owed me the respect of a son, prevented his addressing me with the frank unreserve and faithfulness which, in the case of your friend, Mr. Smith, have been so blessed to my soul.

"Tired at last of this constant struggle with conscience, I announced my intention of returning home. 'It can't be worse there,' I said to myself, 'and I shall have the comfort of being under my own roof.'

"But once here, the thought of you, my daughter, returned with tenfold anguish. I shut myself up from all society, and found no peace but in perusing again, and for the hundredth time, the parable of the prodigal son returning to his father. 'I have sinned, I have sinned,' was the agonizing cry of my heart; but how could I, a murderer, dare add, 'God be merciful to me a sinner'? 'God have mercy upon me'?

"In this state I was, when Horace entered one morning, gasping with some ill-concealed emotion. He tried to prepare me ; but the joyful words, 'Juliette is alive ! Juliette is well and will soon return to us !' sounded in my ears. The next moment, reason and consciousness were lost in the wild excess of my joy.

"Can you wonder, my dear, that I was carried to the gates of death? But I struggled for life ; for one precious glimpse of you ; and hope began to whisper, 'God is merciful. It may be he is willing to save you, even you, the chief of sinners.'

"You came at last, and know how rich his grace, how abounding his love has proved to me."

Juliette, who had wept tears of mingled joy and pain, began to fear lest this excitement would prove a serious injury to his health. She put her arm around him, seating herself on a taboret at his feet, as she had done on her first return from school.

He kissed her affectionately, as he said, taking a soiled, worn envelope from his pocket, "The day after you were married, a bundle of letters and papers were sent to me from the store, and among them this," pressing his lips upon it, "written by you in Stamford, and which has followed us from place to place, in Europe, until, at length, I received it here.

"O Juliette, I hope you will never experience such agony as I felt when I perused that heart-rending appeal ! My emotion was too much for my feeble frame, and I had a slight convulsion. I determined then, that if I lived to see you again, I would lay my heart bare before you, and then once more implore your forgiveness."

Folding the letter carefully he placed it in another envelope prepared for the purpose, with the words written upon it, "To be placed unopened in my coffin and buried with me," saying, in a broken voice, "No eye must see this; it is too sacred."

CHAPTER XXXVII.

"Full of repentance,
Continual meditation, tears, and sorrows,
He gave his riches to the world again;
His humbled soul to God, and slept in peace."

AFTER the second service, Mrs. Everett rang for Eliza to bring a cup of tea to her father's room, as she intended to excuse herself from the table.

When he saw the preparations for his evening meal, Mr. Fearing smiled as he pointed to the dainty little tête-à-tête set, and said, "Well, I have no doubt I shall eat with a better relish."

At last Eliza announced that all was ready, and Juliette playfully waited upon her father to a seat at one end of the small table, while she took her place opposite him. The tea was served in small china cups of an antique pattern, and the bride was just about to pour his, when he put up his hand, "Stop a minute, my dear."

He then in a few fervent words implored the blessing of their heavenly Father upon the food now set before them, ending thus: "That in living and dying we may glorify thy name."

There was a solemnity in his manner, and an impressiveness in his tone, as he pronounced the last words, which sent a thrill of pain through his daughter's heart. She tried to shake it off and appear composed, but was sure he noticed the trembling of her hand as she passed him the cup.

He conversed cheerfully during the repast which, he assured her, owing to her presence, he enjoyed much; spoke of his hope regarding his son, and of his interest in Susan. "I am glad," he said, "to have had my father meet her here, and still more so to see that her artless, unaffected warmth of manner has quite won his heart."

Horace excused himself from the table after the first course, to join the party above stairs; and here, at an early hour in the evening, the others were summoned for family devotion.

Horace, as usual, read a short portion of Scripture, and was about to lead in prayer, when, with a slight motion, Mr. Fearing interrupted him, and, rising slowly from his seat, began the exercise himself.

The old gentleman was greatly affected, and hurried from the room the moment the prayer was concluded. Juliette noticed, too, that Henry's eyes glistened with interest.

"Now," said Mr. Fearing, "Johnson may come to me. I wish to retire to rest."

This man, who had accompanied him in all his travels, was a most faithful servant, and had slept in his room ever since his first attack of sickness. When he came, in answer to the bell, Juliette kissed her father and bade him good-night.

He patted her cheek affectionately, saying, "You have been a good girl, to-day;" and then added, "run away now, dear, and get all the sleep you can."

She repeated this remark to her husband, and wondered what he meant.

Toward noon, on Monday, Mr. and Mrs. Ashley arrived, but only to remain for a few hours, as the pastor had been summoned home in consequence of the severe illness of one of his parishioners.

The two brides met most cordially, and began to chat at once on subjects interesting to both.

"I am disappointed," said Agnes, "not to return home through Lowell, as we intended, but must defer my visit there until another time."

Juliette then gave a brief account of her calls upon their former friends.

"I find Mr. Ashley is a perfect tyrant!" exclaimed the young bride, in a tone intended to reach his ears. "I had no idea he was so set in his way. Why, after we received the letter from home, he seemed so grave and anxious, that I urged him to go direct from Albany; but he was as firm as a rock, and I had to submit with the best grace I could."

Juliette glanced at the gentleman, but he appeared wholly unmoved at this serious charge against his character, while her friend added in a lower tone, "He knew how terribly disappointed I should be to go home without seeing you, and thought, by taking the express train to-night, we could reach W—— almost as soon."

Juliette presently invited Mrs. Ashley to her suite

35

of apartments upstairs, which had been handsomely
decorated on the occasion of her marriage.

"And though you had been accustomed to all this
luxury, you could content yourself in our small room
at Mrs. Palmer's," cried Agnes, raising her hands in
astonishment. "O Juliette! how few there are who
would not have compromised between their two masters!"

"I brought you here to whisper one little word of
advice, dear friend," said Mrs. Everett, affectionately
taking Agnes' hand. "If you wish to have your
people respect their pastor you must show them that
you do so. It grieved me to hear you call so good a
man and so kind a husband a *tyrant*, even in joke."

"I'm likely to learn all my faults between you and
Mr. Ashley," returned the other, half laughing.
"But," she added, more earnestly, "I do love you,
Juliette, and wish I were more like you, and really I
thank you for your advice."

Mr. Fearing well remembered his son's friend, who
had passed one of their college vacations at his house,
and sent down word to his daughter that he should
like to see them in his room.

Mrs. Ashley, who had heard from her husband of
his cruelty to her dear friend, had conceived a strong
prejudice against him, and was rather reluctant to
obey the summons; but a single glance into his face,
glowing as it was with interest for one who had be-
friended his daughter, and all resentment against him
vanished.   •

He extended his hand with great cordiality, tenderness even; apologized for being obliged to receive them in his chamber, and then went on to thank the young lady for her attention to his Juliette, every now and then casting upon the latter a glance brimful of affection.

With Mr. Ashley he conversed about his parish, and subjects in general, for an hour, until the servant summoned them to the early dinner, which Mrs. Everett had ordered for her guests.

"Mr. Everett," cried Agnes, as they stood together while the carriage was waiting to take them to the cars, "Juliette and I have been talking about our husbands; and we each are satisfied that our own is the best in the world. Mr. Ashley has promised if I'm good and dutiful and so forth, that I may come to New York for a longer visit next year; so by that time you'll scarcely know me, I'm going to try so hard to imitate your wife."

"No, no," rejoined Juliette, playfully, "try to be and act yourself. I should be sorry to lose my friend Agnes."

"I am so glad to have seen your father," said her companion. "I do think he has a most heavenly expression."

Mrs. Everett sighed; she had thought the same, but a nameless fear crept over her at hearing it expressed.

"She is a noble-hearted woman," she exclaimed to her husband, as they were ascending the stairs to her father's chamber after their friends had left. "Mrs.

Ashley has been telling me about her brother Caleb whom she has supported all the time she has worked in the factory, that he might acquire an education.

"He is now ready to be licensed to preach, but is intending to take a school for the winter in order to pay his expenses at a theological seminary for a few months next year."

Mr. Fearing seemed much interested in the conversation, but at an earlier hour then usual requested Horace to read and pray. He then called Juliette to his side and asked whether she expected Henry would return to-night from Stamford (he had gone early in the morning to accompany Susan home).

His father came in while they were talking to bid his son good-night; and he held the old gentleman's hand in his for a moment, as if he had something more he desired to say to him; but at last only repeated the wish that he might enjoy a refreshing sleep.

When her grandfather had left the room Juliette said, "You are tired, father; and I ought to go, too;" but instead of that, she slid down on a taboret at his feet, and in her fond way laid her head on his knee.

He placed his hand on her cheek, and she could feel that it trembled as he said to Horace, "Be gentle with her, my son. She has a loving heart. You must make up to her, by your affection, for all the harsh treatment she has received from me."

"Father! father!" she cried, catching his hand, "oh, why will you refer to that which I have so long forgotten? Never had child so tender, so loving a father."

With a sudden gasp, Mr. Fearing pressed his hand to his heart, but when his companions, alarmed at his pallor, quickly asked, "Are you ill?" he answered with a smile, "It has passed now."

His daughter, however, could not shake off the idea that he was suffering, and even after she had reluctantly bid him good-night when Johnson came to assist him to bed, she made an excuse to go back to ask whether she could do nothing more for his comfort?

He held her before him and gazed earnestly in her face a moment, saying, "I never noticed how much you resemble your mother, my dear." Then requesting her to hold a miniature of his deceased Juliette, which he wore on his neck, where he could see it, he regarded it tenderly, and added, "Don't let this be removed from my breast."

Johnson stood waiting, and at last suggested a fear that his master would become too much excited to sleep, when his daughter reluctantly left the room.

It was but little past midnight, when a loud cry for help started her from her slumber. Throwing hastily over her shoulders a large shawl, she rushed to the door exclaiming, "O Horace! quick! quick! it is father! let us go to him!"

They met Johnson at the door coming to rouse them, his cheeks blanched with terror. "He's going fast, miss," he said, in a shaking voice.

35*

But Juliette had rushed past them both, and was already on her knees beside the dying man. Yes, one glance into his face, and the fatal truth fastened itself with irresistible force upon her mind.

With one heart-rending cry, she hid her face in the bedclothes, but his voice, calm and clear, roused her. " Stand up, Juliette, where I can see you. My summons has come. It is not unwelcome, nor unexpected. I have a blessed assurance that I am going into the presence of my Saviour to spend an eternity in singing his matchless love."

He raised his eyes, while a seraphic smile illuminated his whole countenance.

At this moment his father, whom Horace had hastily summoned, came forward, weeping and trembling, to the side of the bed.

After a short spasm of pain, the dying son took his father's hand and said, "I am going home. I shall see mother there. Shall I tell her you love her Saviour, and will soon follow us?"

A terrible groan was the only reply. " Dear father, listen to the words of a dying man; you will never have peace till you find it at the foot of the cross."

By this time all the servants in the house were collected in the room, and stood weeping around the bed.

Mr. Fearing alone seemed calm and undismayed. " Tell Henry," he said, turning to Horace, " not to waste his youth and manhood as I have done; but to devote his best strength to the service of his heavenly

Master. On you, my dear son, I have bestowed the most precious gift in my possession. I am sure you will aid each other in every Christian virtue."

Turning to his daughter, he added, " I want to hear you sing once more."

She tried in vain to suppress her sobs, and at last shook her head to intimate that she could not command her voice.

"For his sake, try to compose yourself, dear Juliette," whispered her husband.

One minute more of almost convulsive effort, and her sweet voice, feeble and trembling, commenced the precious words, —

" Now and forever!
This promise our trust,
Though ashes to ashes,
And dust unto dust,
Now and forever
Our union shall be
Made perfect our glorious
Redeemer in thee.

" When the sins and the sorrows
Of time shall be o'er,
Its pangs and its partings
Remembered no more,
When life cannot fail,
And when death cannot sever,
Christians with Christ shall be
Now and forever."

Juliette bent over him, her tears falling unconsciously upon his head.

" Thank you, my daughter," he said, feebly drawing her toward him and kissing her cheek. " Now I must bid you farewell."

He closed his eyes, and his lips moved as if he were praying; but presently spoke in a loud voice, —

"I wish to bear my testimony to the truth as it is in Jesus."

These were his last words, though for nearly an hour he appeared to breathe.

At the end of that time Horace led the weeping daughter from the room, exclaiming, as he pointed to the bright smile which lingered upon the countenance of the departed, "It may be he is hearing even now his Saviour's voice, 'This day thou shalt be with me in Paradise.'"